THE TIME MACHINE

THE TIME MACHINE:

AN INVENTION

H. G. Wells

edited by Nicholas Ruddick

broadview literary texts

Canadian Cataloguing in Publication Data

Wells, H.G. (Herbert George), 1866–1946
    The Time Machine: an invention

(Broadview literary texts)
Includes bibliographical references.
ISBN 1-55111-305-8

I. Ruddick, Nicholas. II. Title. III. Series.

PR5774.T5 2001   823'.912   C00-932935-8

Broadview Press Ltd., is an independent, international publishing house, incorporated in 1985.

North America:
P.O. Box 1243, Peterborough, Ontario, Canada K9J 7H5
3576 California Road, Orchard Park, NY 14127
TEL: (705) 743-8990; FAX: (705) 743-8353;
E-MAIL: customerservice@broadviewpress.com

United Kingdom:
Turpin Distribution Services Ltd.,
Blackhorse Rd., Letchworth, Hertfordshire SG6 1HN
TEL: (1462) 672555; FAX (1462) 480947; E-MAIL: turpin@rsc.org

Australia:
St. Clair Press, P.O. Box 287, Rozelle, NSW 2039
TEL: (02) 818-1942; FAX: (02) 418-1923

www.broadviewpress.com

Broadview Press gratefully acknowledges the financial support of the Book
Publishing Industry Development Program, Ministry of Canadian Heritage,
Government of Canada.

Broadview Press is grateful to Professor Eugene Benson for advice on
editorial matters for the Broadview Literary Texts series.

Text design and composition by George Kirkpatrick

PRINTED IN CANADA

FSC Recycled
Supporting responsible use
of forest resources
www.fsc.org Cert no. SGS-COC-003153
© 1996 Forest Stewardship Council

Contents

In Loving Memory of Alice Bradley ("Peg")

Acknowledgements

I'd like to thank Don LePan for the enthusiasm with which he embraced my proposal to edit *The Time Machine*, and Julia Gaunce for her guidance in putting together a prospectus. I am very grateful to the staff at the Dr. John Archer Library at the University of Regina for their assistance. I'd particularly like to thank Marion Lake, Susan Robertson-Krezel and the rest of the staff at Interlibrary Loan/Document Delivery for their patience, kindness, and efficiency. Linda M. Winkler (Humanities Librarian), Larry McDonald (Reference Librarian, Social Sciences/Humanities), Doris Hein (micromaterials), and Gordon Priest (circulation) all made my job easier in different ways. Thanks to the Mills Library, McMaster University, for providing a photocopy of the Heinemann first edition. I am grateful to Dr. Amit Chakma, Vice-President (Research), Janet Campbell, Research Adminstrator, and the Office of the Vice-President (Research) at the University of Regina for financial assistance with the permission fees associated with this volume. Thanks also to Don Morse for his useful suggestions, and to all previous editors of *The Time Machine*, without whose pioneering work this project would have been very much more difficult.

Formal acknowledgements are due to the following:

A.P. Watt Ltd. on behalf of The Literary Executors of the Estate of H.G. Wells for permission to reprint extracts from Wells's correspondence in Appendix F and extracts from the writings on *The Time Machine* by Wells reprinted in Appendices G2, G3, G4, G5, and G6.

The Hackett Publishing Company, Inc. for permission to reprint the extract from *The Writings of the Young Marx on Philosophy and Society* in Appendix B2.

Lawrence and Wishart 1956 (& Foreign Languages Publishing House, Moscow) for permission to reprint two extracts from letters included in the *Selected Correspondence* of Karl Marx in Appendix B2.

International Publishers Co. for permission to reprint the

extracts from Marx's *Economic and Philosophical Manuscripts of 1844* and "Inaugural Address of the Working Men's International Association" in Appendix B2.

Imperial College Archives for providing a photocopy of the article from *Science Schools Journal* excerpted in Appendix D4.

Introduction

The Time Machine: An Invention (1895) launched the literary career of H.G. Wells, and it remains his masterpiece. This short novel confronts some of the major issues of the late nineteenth century, a period when the modern world was coming into being. Consequently, many themes explored in *The Time Machine* retain their interest for the reader today. They include the complex nature of time; the uncertain relation between biological evolution and social progress; and the ultimate meaning of human life in the context of the universe as understood by science.

Wells did not invent a time machine because he believed in the feasibility of time travel. The idea for the device first came to him at college from undergraduate speculations about a mysterious fourth dimension. He elaborated upon this idea slowly until his time machine became a metaphorical vehicle for exploring the future of the human race. This exploration would become part of a lifelong project for Wells, but *The Time Machine*, its first fruit, remains the tastiest—highly original, partly satirical, sometimes poetic, always absorbing. The novel synthesizes many diverse strands of nineteenth-century thought and dramatizes the result in an unforgettable way. It is one of the seminal works of that fascinating period at the end of the nineteenth century during which Victorian optimism became clouded by modern anxieties, and it is perhaps *the* seminal work of that genre of fantastic literature that would later come to be known as science fiction.

The Time Machine is, as its subtitle tells us, an invention. Indeed, if authors were allowed to patent fictional devices, then Wells could have claimed full credit as the inventor of a vehicle for travelling through time in a direction and at a speed determined by the will of its operator. But Wells knew that the invention of the machine was inconsequential, until he had decided where—or rather *when*—in time to go with it. He came early to the realization that if he could rise to the challenge of using the machine effectively, his literary career would be launched. Nevertheless, it took him many years and several false starts to respond satisfactorily. (That no other writer pre-empted him as he struggled to bring *The Time Machine* into being was more than good luck, for Wells was perhaps unique-ly qualified to exploit his invention.) By the end of 1894 he had got the story right, and by the middle of the next year the world had begun to beat a path to his door.

But as 1895 dawned, H.G. Wells was unknown, approaching thirty, and in failing health. As an exceptionally gifted youth, he had struggled hard to rise above the unpromising circumstances of his birth, had deservedly earned the chance to better himself by a scientific education—and had thrown that chance away. He had had to struggle once again to become a teacher, but no sooner had he belatedly begun to fulfil his early promise, than he had risked his new pedagogical career by a scandalous elopement, then been forced to abandon teaching for health reasons. He had long wanted to write serious works about the destiny of the human race, but was reduced to making ends meet by hack journalism. His fate rested with what he referred to as his "trump card," adding that "if it does not come off very much I shall know my place for the rest of my career" (Smith 1:226; see Appendix F6). This "trump card" was *The Time Machine*, a synopsis of which might have seemed presumptuous given that it was a first novel by a nonentity. For in a mere 32,400 words it described a journey across thirty million years, and concluded by practically dismissing the significance of the whole of human history, past, present, and future.

The Inventor of *The Time Machine*

Herbert George Wells, born on 21 September 1866, was of the generation that grew up in the immediate aftermath of the rev-olution in human thought—a "new Reformation" (qtd. in Desmond 253)—ignited by the publication of Darwin's *The Origin of Species* in 1859. Wells, the first major literary figure to receive a modern scientific education, was a generation younger than such late Victorians as Samuel Butler (born 1835) and Thomas Hardy (born 1840), who were confronted with

Darwinism early in their writing careers and in whose work is a nostalgia for a pre-Darwinian era. He was almost a generation older than such modernists as James Joyce and Virginia Woolf (both born 1882), for whom the Darwinian revolution was a *fait accompli* and whose chief concerns lay elsewhere.

Wells was born in a small bedroom above his father's shop, Atlas House, 47 High Street, Bromley, Kent, about ten miles south-east of central London. Bromley at this time was a town of more than 5,000 people—large enough to have its own cultural institute and lending library—on the metropolitan fringe. As a result of having been connected to the railway network in 1861, Bromley, though still partly rural during Wells's childhood, was undergoing a process of rapid suburbanization. Wells's native ground was thus the Home Counties, the rapidly-developing outer London commuter zone. But the reduced economic circumstances of his family did not allow him to share in the Home Counties' ethos of smug affluence. In *The Time Machine* and in many subsequent works of fiction, Wells would revisit this area south of the Thames, furiously determined to shake it from its bourgeois complacency.

"Bertie," as Wells was called as a child, was the third and youngest son of Joseph Wells (1827–1910), shopkeeper and cricketer, and Sarah Wells (née Neal) (1822–1905), formerly a lady's maid to a wealthy family. In the fairly rigid social hierarchy of the time, the Wells family were in the lowest rank of the middle class. Though Joseph Wells owned the shop where the family lived, economically the Wellses were much closer to the Victorian propertyless labouring classes than to the professional bourgeoisie. The family's very modest living derived from the struggling business—a scanty stock of china and glassware, with a sideline in cricket equipment—and from Joseph's cricketing prowess. For Wells senior was a fast bowler good enough to have represented the county of Kent, and whose services as player or coach were for hire. While Joe Wells was athletic, sociable, and liked reading, he was irreligious and unambitious, with a feckless streak and a susceptibility to alcohol—it was not just a chronic lack of capital that stopped Atlas House from prospering as Bromley's population soared.

Sarah Wells was no better suited than her husband to run a successful business. She was a low-church evangelical Anglican, accustomed to a life in service, intensely class-conscious, and long-suffering. It was she who set the moral tone and expressed the aspirations of the Wells family toward Respectability, the great idol of the Victorian middle classes. Joe and Sarah were very different, and their resentment of one another was magnified by their poverty. It might seem that Wells's parents, about both of whom clung the odour of failure, offered their youngest son only negative role models. However, from his father Wells inherited a sceptical, restless energy; from his mother, self-discipline and a strong will. Moreover, Wells's parents were both "unusually literate and articulate for their station" (Mackenzie 8n), and in their different ways enjoyed an enduring relationship of mutual affection with their remarkable son.[1]

In 1871, little Bertie, aged 5, started attending a "dame school" in Bromley (a dame school was a school in which a woman taught youngsters in her own home). In the summer of 1874, laid up in bed for some weeks with a broken leg, he began a lifetime's habit of prodigious reading, discovering from books his father borrowed for him from the Bromley library a particular liking for natural history. Later in the year he began to attend Thomas Morley's Commercial Academy for Young Gentlemen, a one-room private school. Its pretentious name indicated that, unlike the free National School for the lower orders, it was intended for boys whose parents could afford to pay for the privilege of acquiring a genteel education.

In October 1877, Joe Wells also broke his leg, but this was not as fortunate an injury as his son's three years earlier. For it ended his sporting career, and now, deprived of its cricketing income, the Wells family was plunged into serious financial

---

1 On 2 February 1895, just as his literary career was beginning to take off, Wells wrote to his parents: "Whatever success I have, you are responsible for the beginnings of it. However hard up you were when I was a youngster you let me have paper and pencils, books from the [Bromley] Institute and so forth and if I haven't my mother to thank for my imagination and my father for skill, where did I get these qualities?" (Smith 1:232).

hardship. As soon as he was old enough, Bertie must be placed in employment where he would not need the family's support, so in July 1880 the 13-year-old, at his mother's urging, became apprenticed to a draper in Windsor, Berkshire. His older brothers had met a similar fate: the drapery business to Sarah Wells represented a constant of respectability in a world of diminishing expectations. Shortly thereafter, Sarah took a job as housekeeper at Up Park (now usually spelled Uppark), the country house in West Sussex where she had been in service before her marriage. This involved a *de facto* separation from her husband, who would remain in Bromley until the collapse of the family shop in 1887.

As can be seen from his early letters and from the illustrated children's novel, *The Desert Daisy* (1957), which he completed before he turned 14, the young Wells was precociously well read and bursting with creative energy. Then, as later in life, he would become quickly bored and frustrated by routine tasks. His job as a draper's assistant involved sitting for most of the twelve-hour working day on a tall stool manning a cash desk, interrupted only by occasional dusting and window cleaning. Unsurprisingly, he soon demonstrated his temperamental unsuitability for the draper's trade, and was dismissed. His mother then sent him as a pupil-teacher to a village school run by one of her distant relations in Wookey, Somerset. But a few weeks later irregularities were discovered in the teaching credentials of this relation, who lost his job, and Wells, adrift again, went to stay with his mother at Up Park. Here he read widely in the well-equipped library, which included Plato's *Republic* and works by Thomas Paine, Swift, and Voltaire, and peered at the stars through an old telescope. At Christmas he undertook his first exercise in journalism—producing several issues of a handwritten newsletter, the *Up Park Alarmist*, for the residents.

In January 1881, Wells, 14, was briefly apprenticed to a dispensing chemist (i.e., pharmacist) in Midhurst, a small town near Up Park. Familiarity with Latin was necessary in the druggist's trade, and Wells was tutored in this subject by Horace Byatt, the headmaster of the local Grammar School, who quickly recognised his pupil's academic potential and consequently his monetary value to the school. For at that time government grants were awarded to schools according to the number of exams passed by their pupils. In February Wells briefly became a full-time "grant-earning" pupil at Midhurst Grammar School. However, at his mother's insistence he was in May again apprenticed as an assistant draper, this time at Hyde's Drapery Emporium, Southsea, Hampshire, where he remained for two years. During this difficult period he rejected religion, which he associated with his mother's values, and possibly contemplated suicide as the only way out of the economic predicament that was frustrating his energy and talent.

In July 1883, after suffering a mental crisis, Wells, now 16, quit Southsea and walked seventeen miles to Up Park to plead with his mother to allow him to leave the drapery business and try teaching. Sarah, who had scraped together from her own earnings the premium for a four-year apprenticeship, stood to lose her investment, but she was partially appeased when Byatt accepted her son as a pupil teacher at Midhurst. By now Wells was writing fiction, had read Henry George's *Progress and Poverty* (1879) (see Appendix B8), and, like many young people of that time who had abandoned conventional religious beliefs but sought an ethical system, was turning to socialism. He was also studying hard, ostensibly for Byatt's benefit, to pass national examinations in scientific subjects. But the real benefit was his own: as a result of his academic successes, he was invited the next year to sit for a scholarship to the Normal School of Science, South Kensington, London, an institution recently founded for the purpose of professionalizing scientific education.[1] He won a scholarship that included free tuition and minimal maintenance, and by September 1884 had moved to London to train as a science teacher.

In his first year at the Normal School Wells attended lectures on zoology by Thomas Henry Huxley (1825-95), the most distinguished living biologist. An agnostic who had been Charles

---

1 Founded in 1881 and located on Exhibition Road, the Normal School was renamed the Royal College of Science in 1890, and was later subsumed into the institution now known as Imperial College of Science, Technology and Medicine, a constituent college of the University of London.

Darwin's most prominent public advocate, Huxley was in the last year of his teaching career (Darwin had died in 1882). Huxley's relationship with Wells was never anything more than that between an eminent professor and an anonymous student in a crowded lecture theatre.[1] But simply to be in the master's proximity was an inspiration for Wells, and Huxley the man would serve him as an enduring paradigm: a fearless promoter of Scientific Truth who considered it his duty to change the way people thought and behaved.

Wells gained first-class honours in the summer examinations at the end of his first year. But in his second year, after Huxley's retirement, he was taught by less inspiring professors, and started to perform much worse academically. There were too many extracurricular distractions: student journalism, the debating society, college politics, socialism, and the possibility of romantic entanglements. He found it irresistible to vent some of his superabundant intellectual energy in debate with his fellow-students, and already he had adopted as a major interest no less a topic than the future of humanity in the light of Darwinian—and Huxleyan—ideas. In this year at South Kensington, for example, he gave a paper to the debating society on "The Past and Present of the Human Race." But his extracurricular activities led to a neglect of his studies, and in the summer of 1886, Wells, 19, did only just well enough in his exams to have his scholarship renewed for another year.

By his third year Wells had already been to hear William Morris and George Bernard Shaw promote their differing socialist prospectuses, and on 15 October 1886 he read a paper on democratic socialism to the debating society. That December Wells founded with some fellow-students a college magazine, the *Science Schools Journal*, and served as its editor until April 1887. He also met at this time the cousin who would become his first wife, Isabel Mary Wells, his father's brother's daughter, a photographic retoucher living in London. Isabel

---

1 "[T]hey spoke to each other only once, when Wells snatched open the door of the lecture theatre for Huxley, and the latter gravely bade him 'Good morning'" (West 49). It seems that the course of lectures by Huxley that Wells attended lasted no more than a few weeks in the spring of 1885 (see Desmond 540).

was a pretty but otherwise unexceptional young woman who liked to listen to her cousin's brilliant talk even if she did not understand it. Wells, sexually very naïve, projected onto her all his fervid desires relating to ideal womanhood. Meanwhile, his immersion in extracurricular activities, uncertainty about his proposed destiny as a science teacher, and lack of interest in geology caused him to fail his final exam in that subject in June 1887 and lose his scholarship.

Now he had to leave the Normal School and earn his living, but without the degree that would have eased his path into a professional career in science education. He simply had to take whatever position he could get, and in the summer of 1887 he was hired as a science teacher at a dismal private school, Holt Academy, near Wrexham, North Wales. On 30 August at Holt he was injured in the kidneys during a school football match. Probably because poverty had undermined his general health, this accident precipitated a serious lung condition—it was wrongly diagnosed as tuberculosis—that would cause him, on and off for the next twelve years, to cough up blood and fear the worst. By November he had left Holt and was once again staying with his mother at Up Park. Certain now that he wanted to be a writer, he was reading romances by Hawthorne and Stevenson and experimenting with fiction. But for several months he was forced to live the life of an invalid, which he found almost intolerably boring.

By March 1888, Wells, 21, felt well enough to go to stay with a former South Kensington fellow-student, William Burton, who was employed as an industrial chemist at the famous Wedgwood potteries near Stoke-on-Trent, Staffordshire. It was there that Wells wrote "The Chronic Argonauts," the earliest version of what eventually became *The Time Machine*. But by July he had overstayed his welcome and when his mother sent him £5 he returned to London, took cheap lodgings on Primrose Hill, and earned a pittance by drawing biological diagrams and answering questions on science for popular penny weeklies. The next half-year would be the most economically precarious of his life.

In January 1889, Wells found a relatively congenial position at £2 per week as a science teacher at the private Henley House School in Kilburn, London. Having painfully learnt that the world did not owe him a living, Wells used his free time to prepare for the examinations that would gain him an external University of London science degree. That July, he took the intermediate exam for the B.Sc., passing with second-class honours in zoology. The following January, he passed with honours the exams for a Licentiate in the College of Preceptors,[1] gaining three prizes. At last in October, Wells, now 24, got his B.Sc. with first class honours in zoology, and was elected a Fellow of the Zoological Society. Even before this, he had left schoolteaching to take a job with the University Tutorial College. This was a private "crammer" run by William Briggs, a pioneer in the development of university-level correspondence courses. His job involved undergraduate-level teaching, marking papers on biology, and editing Briggs's newsletter, the *University Correspondent*. His income was now sufficient to enable him to start saving enough to support a wife.

In February 1891, "The Rediscovery of the Unique," Wells's first important speculative article (see Appendix C3), was accepted by Frank Harris, the editor of the *Fortnightly Review*. Wells then offered the *Fortnightly* a follow-up article on the fourth dimension, "The Universe Rigid," but Harris rejected this as incomprehensible: the literary breakthrough was postponed. On 31 October that year, Wells, 25, married Isabel Wells, the couple having already settled in Wandsworth, in south-west London. But on 17 May 1893, Wells suffered another serious haemorrhage of the lungs. He took this to be a sign that his classroom career was over and, convinced that his days were numbered, he decided to make a living by his pen or die in the attempt. He was already working hard on a money-making project — the composition of textbooks geared to help science undergraduates pass exams — but it was now a matter of urgency to procure an immediate source of income.

Recuperating at Eastbourne on the Sussex coast, Wells read a novel by J. M. Barrie that inspired him to try his hand at pop-

---

1   I.e., he gained a formal teaching certificate.

ular journalism, using for subject-matter whatever lay to hand. Almost immediately, he began to sell articles to the *Pall Mall Gazette*, a London evening newspaper. The first, "On the Art of Staying at the Seaside," was published on 25 June, and about fifteen more appeared before the end of the year. Not all were on frivolous topics: "The Man of the Year Million" (see Appendix A8) appeared on 6 November. Meanwhile the textbook *Honours Physiography*, co-authored by Wells and Richard A. Gregory (a former fellow-student at the Normal School), and the two-volume *Text-Book of Biology* (see Appendix A5), by Wells alone, were published — the latter would prove to be very successful and run through many editions. Wells, 27, proudly recorded his yearly income for the first time: £380.13s.7d in 1893 from teaching and writing. He had suffered from poverty for too long ever again to underestimate the benefits of financial security.

In late 1892 Wells had met Amy Catherine Robbins (whom he called "Jane"), a student studying to be a science teacher through the University Tutorial College. Jane was much more intellectually responsive than Isabel, and she would also prove more willing to forgo cosy domesticity and more able to subordinate her powers to the furtherance of Wells's career. Early in 1894, having concluded that his marriage had been a mistake, Wells eloped with Jane to lodgings in Euston, London. The turbulence of his private life spurred him to a new level of literary production: he sold more than 140 articles, stories, and other pieces this year, the majority to the *Pall Mall Gazette*. Moreover, seven connected episodes of a preliminary version of *The Time Machine* appeared between 17 March and 23 June in the weekly *National Observer*, edited by W. E. Henley, while on 21 June "The Stolen Bacillus," the first science-fiction story to be signed "H. G. Wells," appeared in the *Pall Mall Budget*, a short-lived *Pall Mall Gazette* spin-off edited by Lewis Hind.

That summer, Wells and Jane (who was showing consumptive symptoms of her own) moved for the sake of their lungs out of London to Tusculum Villa, 23 Eardley Rd., Sevenoaks, Kent, where *The Time Machine* in an almost definitive form was finished, probably in a concerted spell of about two or three weeks' work from late July to early August. In October, Wells and Jane returned to London. On 10 November appeared the essay "The 'Cyclic' Delusion" (see Appendix E7), the first of Wells's over 130 contributions to the weekly *Saturday Review*, a periodical undergoing a vigorous revival under Frank Harris, who had moved there from the *Fortnightly*. Harris now proved far more amenable to a young man who had demonstrated his journalistic versatility. In 1894 Wells recorded earnings of £583.17s.7d for the year; it was a very decent income, and he had made it entirely by his pen.

In January 1895 Wells was divorced from Isabel, though he would maintain a cordial relationship with her till her death in 1931. From January to May, "The Time Machine" appeared as a serial under that title in the monthly *New Review*, a new venture by W.E. Henley. During the same period, Wells reviewed plays for the *Pall Mall Gazette*, beginning with Oscar Wilde's *An Ideal Husband*. In March, Wells began book-reviewing for the *Saturday Review*. On or about 7 May *The Time Machine* was published in book form by Holt in the U.S. A more authoritative text — a revision of the *New Review* version — was published in book form by Heinemann in London on 29 May in a first edition of 10,000 copies, for which Wells received an advance of £50 and a generous royalty of 15 per cent. Its very favourable critical reception alone would have been sufficient to launch his literary career, but Wells was not finished. In June *Select Conversations with an Uncle*, a volume of material chiefly reprinted from the *Pall Mall Gazette* and including two short stories, was published by John Lane. Then *The Wonderful Visit*, a comic romance, was published by Dent on 5 September. Wells and Jane moved to Woking, Surrey, in October, and it was there that they married on 27 October. To round out an extraordinarily productive year, *The Stolen Bacillus, and Other Incidents*, a collection of short stories, was published by Methuen in November. Wells earned the considerable sum of £792.2s.5d. (about U.S. $4,000, very roughly equivalent to $60,000 or more today) from his writing this year.

Wells, 29, had vaulted in the course of a single year from obscurity into renown as one of the rising stars of the literary firmament. Twenty years later, he would have become one of the dominant cultural forces of his age. Speaking of his own generation, George Orwell (1903-50) noted that "Thinking people who were born about the beginning of this century are in some sense Wells's own creation.... The minds of all of us, and therefore the physical world, would be perceptively different if Wells had never existed" (198). Yet though Wells would publish before his death in 1946 many distinguished works of fiction among his more than one hundred published books, none of them ever surpassed *The Time Machine* as a literary achievement. Like a well-constructed time machine, the work ensures its creator's survival into futurity.

The Evolution of *The Time Machine*

Bernard Bergonzi, in a pioneering textual study of *The Time Machine*, noted that the work was "remarkable not only for its literary merits, but for its complex bibliographical history, which must be unparalleled among works of modern fiction" ("Publication" 204). If this is hyperbole, it is forgivable. *The Time Machine* certainly did not spring into being as a fully-formed career-launching masterwork, even though Wells would sometimes suggest that he had dashed it off in two or three weeks (see p. 27, n. 1; see also Appendix F16). It evolved like an organism, fitfully, though always in the direction of greater complexity, over a period of more than seven years.

The Time Machine had its conceptual origin in speculations about the fourth dimension that had been circulating in the scientific community for some time and which were starting to come to more general attention in the mid-1880s. Towards the end of his life, Wells noted that he "was started by A. Square & 'Flatland'" (Smith 4:135; see Appendix F17), from which we may infer that the mathematician Edwin A. Abbott's *Flatland: A Romance of Many Dimensions* (published under the pseudonym "A Square" in 1884, the same year that Wells started at the Normal School) was an important source. *Flatland* (see Appendix D1) is indeed the kind of work that would have stimulated discussion among Wells's fellow-students at South Kensington.

It concerns Square, a being from a two-dimensional world who discovers our three-dimensional universe but cannot make his fellow Flatlanders believe in its existence. Square's experience is offered as an amusing but thought-provoking analogue of our blindness to the possibility of what may lie beyond our own three-dimensional plane of vision. Abbott's satire on intellectual narrow-mindedness is most clearly echoed in Chapter XVI of *The Time Machine* in the incredulous reaction of the dinner-guests to the Time Traveller's sombre tale of the future. The young Wells was constantly irritated by the confidence of the late Victorian bourgeoisie in its ascendancy over the material universe, and it is almost certainly the case that *The Time Machine* was at an early stage conceived by its author as an "assault on human self-satisfaction" ("Preface" [1934] ix; see Appendix G4).

Another important source of the ideas behind *The Time Machine* is C. H. Hinton's "What Is the Fourth Dimension?" (see Appendix D2). This ponderously-written piece is an attempt to account for the immateriality of ghosts by positing a fourth dimension of space, at right angles to the other three, which spectral beings might inhabit. Hinton, like Abbott, does not broach the idea of time as the fourth dimension. Hinton's theme was echoed by one of Wells's fellow-students at South Kensington, E. A. Hamilton Gordon, who published an paper entitled "The Fourth Dimension" (see Appendix D4) in the fifth issue of *Science Schools Journal* in April 1887. There is in this paper a single dismissive reference to the idea proposed by some people that Time was a candidate for the fourth dimension. Wells himself later noted that the idea of time as the fourth dimension "was begotten in the writer's mind by students' discussions in the laboratories and debating society of the Royal College of Science in the eighties" ("Preface" [1931] viii; see Appendix G3).[1] From Hinton or Hamilton Gordon, Wells borrowed the idea that a being in the fourth dimension would seem immaterial to us in the third, and be able (like both the Time Traveller's model and full-sized time machines)

---

1   For pre-Wellsian origins of the idea of duration as the fourth dimension see Raknem 391, Nahin 96.

to dematerialize like a ghost. This idea was already well enough known outside the scientific community to be used by Oscar Wilde in his short story "The Canterville Ghost" (1887) (see Appendix D4).

The idea of *time* as the fourth dimension was mooted in a letter to the weekly general scientific periodical *Nature* of 16 March 1885, entitled "Four-Dimensional Space" and signed with the pseudonym "S" (see Appendix D3). Wells almost certainly read *Nature* regularly once he had started at the Normal School — it was founded by, and then still closely associated with, T. H. Huxley. "S"'s letter, written in response to a review in *Nature* four days earlier of Hinton's "What Is the Fourth Dimension?" pamphlet, raises the idea of "a new kind of space ... which we may call time-space" (481). This is a remarkable anticipation of the concept of space-time that was formulated by Minkowski in 1907, and provided an important basis for Einsteinian relativity theory. A relation has been conjectured between "S" and "the debating group H.G. Wells attended" (Bork 330), though "S"'s letter precedes Hamilton Gordon's paper by two years. There remains the possibility that "S" was Wells himself, as there are several traces of the ideas in the letter in the early part of *The Time Machine*.

Wells's most definite original contribution to the set of ideas above was that of a vehicle which could take its rider quickly through time-as-the-fourth-dimension just as a bicycle carries one rapidly through the three dimensions of space.[1] He first put this idea into words in the unfinished story he wrote in Staffordshire called "The Chronic Argonauts," which is the earliest textual ancestor of *The Time Machine* and which was serialized in three issues of *Science Schools Journal* in 1888 (after he had left the Normal School).[2] Two closely-connected elements in "The Chronic Argonauts" — the time machine itself, and the short explanation by its inventor of how time might be viewed

---

1   Martin Gardner (1) notes that a "mediocre yarn" by Edward Page Mitchell, "The Clock That Went Backward," was actually the first story about a time machine, though this story, which appeared anonymously in the New York *Sun* on 18 September 1881, was quickly forgotten and remained so till 1973.
2   "The Chronic Argonauts" is reproduced in Bergonzi, *Early* 187-214, Geduld 135-52, and Stover 176-96.

as another dimension of space—form the embryo of what would become *The Time Machine*. These elements long ante-date the description of a journey into the far future that consti-tutes the bulk of the work as we know it.

"The Chronic Argonauts" shows very little literary promise. In *Experiment in Autobiography* (1934), Wells himself noted, "If a young man of twenty-one were to bring me a story like the *Chronic Argonauts* for my advice to-day I do not think I should encourage him to go on writing" (254; see Appendix G5). Relying heavily on the Gothic tradition of the half-mad scien-tist as developed in such works as Mary Shelley's *Frankenstein* (1818) and Nathaniel Hawthorne's "The Birth-Mark" (1843), "The Chronic Argonauts" concerns mystifying events in a remote Welsh village centring on Dr. Nebogipfel, inventor of a device for time travelling. The narrative trails off, however, before we are allowed to follow Nebogipfel into time. We have the later testimony of one of Wells's friends to the effect that after Wells had returned to London from Staffordshire he pro-duced two different revisions of the "Chronic Argonauts" material, the first of which described a visit to a future when mankind is divided into an upper and lower world, while in the second, future men are controlled by hypnotists (see West 262-64). We find, then, that by 1888, the young Wells, eager to explore the future of mankind in the light of the ideas about man's place in nature that he had absorbed at the Normal School, has come up with the idea of a time machine—but has not yet worked out where or when in the future to go with it.

"The Chronic Argonauts" project was an early result of Wells's discovery that he wanted to write speculative works about the human future, but during the subsequent years of financial hardship exacerbated by his failure to graduate from the Normal School, he would be unable to apply himself to this task with any consistency. It was not until he had got his career back on track and was earning a living wage at the Uni-versity Tutorial College that he was able to return to writing. "The Rediscovery of the Unique," the article accepted by the *Fortnightly* in 1891, was the first important fruit. It strikingly delineated the limits of then-current knowledge through the metaphor of modern science as a single match, got alight with difficulty, barely illuminating a vast surrounding darkness. (This metaphor would take on an epic dimension in the Morlock episodes of *The Time Machine*.) But Wells found it difficult to get to grips with the nagging question of how time-as-the-fourth-dimension might be used as a key to the secret of the future of humanity. His problem describing a four-dimensional universe with concepts drawn from pre-Einsteinian physics undoubtedly manifested itself in the incomprehensibility of his article "The Universe Rigid." However, this article, rejected by Frank Harris and subsequently lost, did not vanish without trace, for Wells simply could not let go of the thread of the ideas. Three and a half years later a paraphrase of "The Universe Rigid" would be placed in the mouth of a fictional Time Traveller in the *New Review*.

The next crucial phase of development in Wells's career was marked by his abandonment of teaching as a result of worsening health, and his resolution to make his living by his pen. This was the emotionally agitated time between his elopement with Jane and his divorce from Isabel. He resolved the precariousness of his economic position by a rapid and successful assault on the market for popular journalism, making a small name for himself in the *Pall Mall Gazette*, and then fostering a readership in the *Pall Mall Budget* for short stories in a speculative mode. But before the publication of "The Stolen Bacillus," there was a period in which he was experimenting with a form that was somewhere between the serious speculative article and the speculative short story. It was then that he returned to the subject of time travel, and produced between 17 March and 23 June 1894 seven loosely connected episodes of a story about time travel for W. E. Henley's weekly *National Observer*.[1]

Most of the important motifs associated with the main themes of the finished *Time Machine* are evident in the *National*

---

[1] Each of the seven episodes has its own title. They are, in order, "Time Travelling: Possibility or Paradox" (17 March); "The Time Machine" (24 March); "A.D. 12,203: A Glimpse of the Future" (31 March); "The Refinement of Humanity: A.D. 12,203" (21 April); "The Sunset of Mankind" (28 April); "In the Underworld" (19 May); and "The Time-Traveller Returns" (23 June). All are reproduced in Philmus and Hughes 57-90, in Geduld 154-74, and in Stover 196-220.

Observer sketches. The protagonist discourses to his dinner guests on duration as the fourth dimension before introducing his newly-invented time machine. There follows his account of a voyage to A.D. 12,203, when humanity has split into two species, one of which (unnamed) is frail, beautiful, and surface-dwelling, while the other (the Morlocks) is ape-like and sub-terranean. Then the protagonist offers theories to explain, against the objections of his progress-fixated guests, why such human divergence and degeneration might have occurred. However, the narrative is frequently interrupted by the guests; there is no Weena, so the plot that subsequently centres on her is totally undeveloped; the Morlock diet is not touched upon; and there is no voyage thirty million years thence.

W. E. Henley was known for his ability as editor to foster the talent of young writers. There is no doubt that his encouragement was important to Wells in the next major step in the evolution of the work: the transformation of the sketchy *National Observer* pieces into a short novel entitled *The Time Machine* that would first appear as a serial, beginning in January 1895 in the *New Review*, a new monthly magazine that Henley took on after losing his editorship of the failing *National Observer* at the end of 1894. But the actual impetus for the composition of *The Time Machine* during a period of about two or three weeks[1] from late July to early August 1894, was, as Wells put it "a sudden fall in my income" (*Experiment* 435; see Appendix G5) caused by a temporary lull in demand for articles in the *Pall Mall Gazette*. Wells and Jane, who were "living in sin" and therefore vulnerable to the moral qualms of landladies, had moved out of London to Sevenoaks. In this semi-rural retreat, encouraged at first only by a vague suggestion from Henley,

---

[1] On his American tour in 1906, Wells was interviewed by the *New York Herald* about his working methods. The result offers an interesting insight into the composition of *The Time Machine* in Sevenoaks: "Almost all his early works were fairly spontaneous.... It was his custom then to get up in the morning and talk with Mrs. Wells about any ideas that he had in his head, and after breakfast he would sit down to work them out.... 'The Time Machine' he wrote under an impulse in the same way. The material for it came wonderfully fast, and the final work of writing it was all done in a fortnight. Under those conditions he wrote steadily from nine in the morning until eleven at night, only stopping for the necessary intermissions of meals" ("Bouts" 3:5).

Wells set to rewriting his *National Observer* articles into a long story suitable for serialization. Soon the *Pall Mall Gazette*'s demand for articles resumed, but Henley, having moved to the *New Review*, had read a draft of the long story and, liking what he saw, responded with enthusiasm, offering Wells the generous sum of £100 for the serial rights.

The version serialized between January and May 1895 in the *New Review* reveals a giant step in the evolution of *The Time Machine* at the aesthetic level, just as the *National Observer* version had revealed a huge leap forward at the thematic level. In Sevenoaks Wells discovered the form in which a number of ambitious themes, all deriving from his long concern with human destiny in the light of evolutionary ideas, could best be articulated. The discovery was at least as important as the invention of the time machine itself. Wells greatly expanded the Time Traveller's narrative of his sojourn among the Eloi and Morlocks, which as a major speculation on the future of humanity forms the thematic focus of the novel, and now offered it as an uninterrupted central narrative. Through the creation of Weena, he mobilized a suspenseful adventure-mystery-romance plot that held readers' attention as they, in tandem with the Time Traveller, attempted to deduce from the very limited available evidence the course of human development between the late nineteenth century and A.D. 802,701.[1] He "discovered" the symbiotic link between the Eloi and Morlocks, and offered it as a culminating revelation that at the same time enforced the theme of degeneration. The fate of the earth itself—the grand eschatological question that naturally arises from the description of the fate of mankind—Wells dealt with in "The Further Vision" chapter, which is proportionally short and where interest is sustained no longer through plot but by means of a marvellously-sustained flight of poetic prose. The important satiric element—the way that the Time Traveller's tale is so to speak brought back home as an assault on Victorian complacency—was neatly provided by the framing device of

---

1   One may speculate that Wells advanced this date from the *National Observer*'s A.D. 12,203 to suggest a more biologically credible time scale for evolutionary divergence in the human species.

the scenes at the Time Traveller's house in the London suburb of Richmond.

The *New Review* serial differs little from the subsequent Heinemann book version. The former contains a lengthier opening scene at the Time Traveller's house that includes an abstract of the main idea in the lost "Universe Rigid" essay; and toward the end of the serial there is a scene in which the Time Traveller, escaping the world of the Eloi and Morlocks for the very far future, encounters the degenerate descendants of humanity in the form of rabbit-like creatures that are hunted by giant centipedes.[1] Both scenes were probably added at Henley's prompting simply to fill some available space in the *New Review*, as they are not in the Holt edition (see below); both were dropped for the Heinemann edition without any aesthetic damage, and Wells never subsequently tried to restore them. Aside from other minor details the *New Review* version of *The Time Machine* is close to the finished book as we know it today, and it began to attract favourable critical notices even as a serial (see Appendix H1).

The Time Machine: An Invention first appeared in book form in the U.S., in an edition published by Henry Holt & Co. of New York on about 7 May 1895. However, textual research has established that the text of this first American edition actually precedes that of the *New Review* serial. It seems to be based on a draft sent to the United States in February 1895, for it does not contain Wells's changes to the work as the *New Review* serial progressed through May. Moreover, as we have seen, the completed *New Review* serial was again revised for the Heinemann edition that appeared on 27 May 1895. Though this last revision was to a certain extent a reversion to the structure of the Holt text (by dropping of the material added as a result of the demands of serialization), the Heinemann text, by virtue of its posteriority and the evident care with which it has been prepared, is certainly the definitive one, and it is the one that made Wells's reputation.

---

1   The opening and closing chapters of the *New Review Time Machine* are reproduced entire in Philmus and Hughes 91-104, and are excerpted in Geduld 175-80 and Stover 221-28.

From "The Chronic Argonauts" to Heinemann, therefore, *The Time Machine* evolved through a period of seven and a half years, during which there were five printed versions, several more drafts, some complete, some partial, some surviving, some not. *The Time Machine* may have been Wells's first novel, but by the time it appeared in the form published by Heinemann at the end of May 1895, it was the product of a long and difficult refining process with few parallels in literary history. Wells's first biographer Geoffrey West, summarizing the evolution of *The Time Machine*, noted that "This struggle to embody satisfactorily the brilliantly original idea of time-travelling might in itself be said almost to constitute [Wells's] literary apprenticeship" (261).

The Influences Shaping *The Time Machine*

The Time Machine was produced by a young man who had received a thorough professional training as a scientist in the modern sense of the word. The originality of the work, which struck several commentators in 1895, is chiefly a result of this training, though the work is a literary, not a scientific masterpiece.

As we have seen, undergraduate speculations about the possibility of a fourth dimension played an important role in the genesis of *The Time Machine*. But more important still for Wells was the example of T. H. Huxley, struggling to find a human meaning in the daunting sweep of time opened up by Darwinian evolutionary theory. Huxley had played the leading role in the public debate that led to the intellectual triumph of evolutionary over scriptural accounts of origin, of Doubt over Faith. Huxley had also played a large role in the formation of the discipline of biology, and in the practical fulfilment of the idea that modern science is best carried out by a professional salaried body of scientists chosen on merit, rather than by gentlemen of independent means. One of Huxley's many concrete achievements was the foundation of the Normal School of Science, where young men born above a butcher's shop, as Huxley himself had been, or above a crockery shop, like Wells — young men of ability but with no social advantages or means—could make their way in the brave new world of the Scientific Age.

After 1859, there had been a rapid and largely successful attempt to reconcile evolutionary theory with Victorian ideas of progress. Darwin had encouraged this, concluding the *Origin* optimistically with the idea that evolution would inevitably lead to human perfection (see Appendix A1). Taking Darwin's lead, Herbert Spencer had articulated a natural "law" whereby organisms inevitably developed from homogeneity to heterogeneity, climbing steadily through stages of increasing complexity toward perfection, with man, of course, leading the way (see Appendix B6). Huxley had taken a less optimistic view, seeing the cosmos as essentially indifferent to humanity, but had gradually moved towards the idea that man had the capacity, even the duty, to humanize nature by applying to it his own ethical concerns (see Appendix A6).

Wells was almost two generations younger than Huxley, and his vision of the world as he began his writing career was darkened even more than his master's by specifically fin-de-siècle anxieties. By the time Wells came to maturity, ideas of degeneration had started to proliferate (see Appendix A2). Simply put, it was becoming common knowledge that there was a counter-principle in nature to elaboration (progressive evolutionary development), for some organisms degenerated or devolved (slid back down the evolutionary scale) even in the course of their own life-cycles. It was feared that humanity in the 1880s might actually have reached its peak, and down the darkling road ahead lurked devolution and extinction. Apprehensions about what Wells termed "Zoological Retrogression" (see Appendix A4) arising from new knowledge about the life-cycle of sea squirts and the fate of the dinosaurs began to mingle with fears associated with the economic slump of the 1880s, and with the impending end of Queen Victoria's long and prosperous reign. Who could ignore on the one hand the glaring inequality between the Haves and Have-nots that was visible everywhere in the streets of London, the greatest and richest city in the world, or on the other the triumphalist imperialism that seemed a form of hubris courting nemesis?

Wells in the early 1890s would scathingly dismiss optimistic associations between evolution and progress as "Excelsior biology" (see Appendix A4).

Darwin, with the support of geologists, had assumed that life on earth had evolved over hundreds of millions of years, for such a length of time was needed if his model of gradual evolution through natural selection was to be credible. In the later nineteenth century, however, this time-scale came under serious question, not by religious fundamentalists but by physicists. Lord Kelvin's interpretation of the second law of thermodynamics reinforced what Helmholtz and Clausius had foreseen as an ultimate heat-death for the universe, as stars' energy became dissipated and the entropy of the macrocosm inevitably increased. It had long been recognised that life on earth was entirely dependent on our local star, and Kelvin's calculations in 1862 on the age of the sun (see Appendix E2) concluded that it would burn itself out, not in hundreds of millions, but in a few tens of millions of years at the very latest. (Nuclear fusion was not yet understood, and the sun was supposed to be exhausting its radiant energy in roughly the same manner as a candle burns itself up.) In other words, the grim vision of global extinction thirty million years hence at the end of *The Time Machine* derives from theories of a cosmic time-scale that had just *shrunk* in an alarming manner.

Moreover, the end of the earth would not come suddenly in the far future but slowly in a process that had already begun. For extrapolations from the theories of orbital retardation by tidal (i.e., gravitationally-induced) drag proposed by G. H. Darwin (see Appendices E5, E6) suggested that the earth would eventually come always to offer the same face toward the sun, just as the moon now does to the earth, and that the moon, gradually losing orbital velocity, would fall into the earth, which would subsequently and for the same reason fall into the sun. From the perspective of those relatively few observers who, like Wells, were fully in touch with fin-de-siècle science, then, the future of human life on earth came to seem very precarious indeed. It is also not hard to understand why Wells felt so exercised about the complacency of the vast majority of educated people who blithely professed their ignorance of science or indifference to the amazing but terrifying vistas that scientists had opened up.

Wells's scientific background is visible everywhere in *The Time Machine*. The Time Traveller is a scientist (his specialty is physical optics), and he refers to real contemporary scientists and their recent theories. He mentions Simon Newcomb on the fourth dimension (see Appendix D7) and G. H. Darwin on tidal drag as a more conventional hero might allude to Wordsworth on mutability or Keats on melancholy. He is familiar with the names of dinosaurs and geological periods, with the properties of camphor, with the precession of the equinoxes, and with deep-sea fishes. He is trained in the scientific method, and offers his experiences in the far future as a set of theories which must be altered when a new fact that cannot be assimilated comes along, which cannot be verified without repeatable experimental results, and which are always provisional. Of his guests, only those who have some scientific knowledge — the Medical Man, the Psychologist, and the primary narrator[1] — are rendered with any sympathy; the rest seem fatuous and smug. Indeed, the chief purpose of the frame narrative in *The Time Machine* seems to be satirical: the "common sense" of the dinner-guests — a cross-section of the supposedly well-educated professional men who constitute the backbone of late-Victorian society — that causes the Editor in Chapter XVI to mock and reject the Time Traveller's tale as a "gaudy lie" is really a kind of stupidity, a symptom of cultural blindness that is the result of insufficient scientific training and imagination. The spirit of Swift allied to the vision of *Flatland* informs Wells's attitude to the dinner-guests at Richmond.

The world of A.D. 802,701, that of the Eloi and Morlocks, dominates the novel (22,000 out of 32,400 words, or about 68 per cent), and here, as elsewhere, it is science, and in particular biology, that informs the vision. The length of time that elapses between 1894 and 802,701 is to allow biology to predominate over culture. That is to say, it is long enough to ensure that

---

1   That the narrator has such knowledge is evident from the third and fourth sentences of the "Epilogue." See also p. 40, n. 1.

Darwinian natural and sexual selection will have worked upon that complacent species, late Victorian *homo sapiens*, until it is no longer one species at all.

The focus now shifts from biological to social evolution. There is little doubt that Wells's socialist leanings informed his grim vision of A.D. 802,701. The effete, helpless Eloi are presumed to be descended from the Victorian moneyed upper classes, who used to *metaphorically* prey upon (i.e., exploit) the lower classes, but in an ironic reversal of fortune are now *literally* preyed upon by the descendants of their victims.[1] It is a vision that can hardly have avoided being influenced by the analysis of class conflict carried out by Marx and Engels (see Appendices B2, B3) with particular reference to the grim forms of capitalist exploitation in industrial Britain in the 1840s. But the 1890s were not the 1840s, and Wells was very far from being a Marxist. There is no class conflict between the Eloi and Morlocks, any more than there can be a class war between livestock and farmers. Indeed, *lack* of conflict lies at the root of the Eloi-Morlock problem. What seems to have happened is that the total subjection of the natural environment to mankind has put an end to the struggle for existence, and this, as Huxley and Lankester prophesied, has led to degeneration. Moreover, through a process described by J. T. Gulick in 1891 as divergent evolution through cumulative segregation, which revised the accepted Darwinian view that two species occupying the same territory must necessarily struggle, the Eloi and Morlocks have arrived at a state of symbiosis — one which is both perfect and horrible.[2]

This idea of horrible perfection gives us a clue about the

---

1   This is actually a theme developed late in the evolution of *The Time Machine*. In the *National Observer* version, the Time Traveller suggests that the split is not between rich and poor, for there is enough social mobility to guard against divergence from economic circumstances, but between distinct personality types, "the sombre, mechanically industrious, arithmetical, inartistic type, the type of the Puritan and the American millionaire and the pleasure-loving, witty, and graceful type that gives us our clever artists, our actors and writers, some of our gentry, and many an elegant rogue" (Philmus and Hughes 86).

2   Gulick is specifically mentioned in the *National Observer* version of *The Time Machine*: see Philmus and Hughes 85-86.

relation of *The Time Machine* to the literary tradition. Oriented toward the human future, Wells gravitated toward utopian writing, which ever since Plato's *Republic* has concerned itself with how the deficiencies of society might be remedied. *The Time Machine*, with its strong basis in evolutionary biology, suggests that the utopian dream of a conflict-free, perfected social life is a dangerous illusion, and that those works which have promoted this ideal have failed to understand the exigences of biology. *The Time Machine* is thus strictly an *anti-utopian* work (rather than a *dystopian* one like Orwell's *Nineteen Eighty-Four* (1949), in which all is subordinated to the horrific vision). Indeed, Wells's novel specifically engages two contemporary and highly influential utopias, Edward Bellamy's *Looking Backward* (1888; see Appendix B9) and William Morris's *News from Nowhere* (1891; see Appendix B11). Both posit futures in which social conflict has been resolved, in Bellamy through socialism and technology, in Morris through pure communism and pastoralism. Wells also borrowed from or alluded to other utopian works, sometimes ironically. From Lord Lytton's *The Coming Race* (1871) he derived the idea of a subterranean-dwelling species that would inherit the future — but made it subhuman, not superhuman. From Samuel Butler's *Erewhon* (1871) he took the idea of a post-industrial world and the motif of a museum of broken machines. In *The Inner House* (1888) by Walter Besant he found a future utopia created by science that has led to the end of the human struggle for existence, to the disappearance of obvious differences between the sexes, and to an Eloi-like degeneration. And from W. H. Hudson's *A Crystal Age* (1887) he appropriated the narrative strategy of having the visitor from the past deduce from clues the nature of the future society, so avoiding the clumsy device of the utopian tour guide.

A Note on Genre

Although the term "science fiction" has been traced as far back as 1851, its application to a body of literature including *The Time Machine* did not become common until the 1930s. It is therefore slightly misleading to apply this term to a work published in 1895 when that work is being viewed in its fin-de-siècle context. So what kind of work did Wells think that he had written? And if *The Time Machine* was not a science-fiction novel in 1895, why do we view it as one today?

The short answer to the first question is that Wells in 1895 was not quite sure what kind of work he had written: that is why he chose *An Invention* for its subtitle. He had produced a substantial prose work of the imagination, but not a *novel*, which in 1895 signified a lengthy work of fiction in the realistic mode. Moreover, *The Time Machine* was not merely a *satire* nor strictly a *utopian work*, even if it was conceived partly as a satirical corrective to pre-existing utopias. Finally, Wells knew that *The Time Machine*'s unprecedented qualities had much to do with his own scientific education, though he did not feel that the work would only be accessible to science specialists. Indeed, he felt that he had already established a constituency of potential readers (see Appendices F8, F13) by means of a number of signed speculative essays and short stories with a scientific background.

Had Wells been pressed on the question of genre in 1895, he would have used either the term "scientific fantasy" (see Appendix G4) or, more likely, "scientific romance" (see Appendix F14), the phrase that would in 1933 be used in the title of the omnibus volume including *The Time Machine* and generically related works such as *The Island of Doctor Moreau* (1896), *The Invisible Man* (1897), *The War of the Worlds* (1898), and *The First Men in the Moon* (1901). There is evidence that what ended as *An Invention* began as a romance. For "The Chronic Argonauts" was written under the influence of Hawthorne, who had drawn a famous distinction between the Romance and the Novel.[1] C. H. Hinton, the first to use the phrase "scientific romance" (see Appendix D2), had meant by it chiefly the speculative essay, not fiction. However, Brian Stableford, who traced the development of the genre in Britain, has noted, "there has always been a close relationship between

---

1   In his Preface to *The House of the Seven Gables: A Romance* (1851).

British scientific romance and a typically British species of speculative essays" (5). As we have seen, during the years of the evolution of *The Time Machine*, this closeness was nowhere more evident than in Wells's own literary practice.

As a result of the development of the American "pulp" science-fiction magazines, initially under the aegis of Hugo Gernsback (1884-1967), and the subsequent evolution of "fandom," the genre of science fiction would crystallize slowly beginning in the late 1920s. Wells never revealed much interest in these transatlantic developments in popular culture, even though they began to percolate into Britain in the 1930s and Wells lived till 1946. From its earliest days, on the other hand, the originators of science fiction showed more than a passing interest in Wells. Every issue of Gernsback's pioneering monthly *Amazing Stories* from April 1926 to August 1928 reprinted fiction by Wells: *The Time Machine*, for example, appeared in the May 1927 issue. Thus the entire body of Wells's best scientific romances played a vital role in the constitution of the newly forming popular genre, and Wells's influence on subsequent science fiction would be enormous. Because of the high literary quality of his scientific romances, Wells would come to be referred to as the "Shakespeare of science fiction" (Aldiss 133), and his masterpiece *The Time Machine* would often be viewed as the seminal work in the genre.

The Reception of *The Time Machine* in 1895

In 1895, this first novel by an almost unknown author struck the reviewers as fresh, original, powerfully conceived, exciting to read, and pessimistic (though its effect was perhaps more bracing than depressing). In the fine phrase of the *Daily Chronicle*, the plot was "distressingly interesting" (see Appendix H8). The episodes describing the sensations of time travel and the end of life on earth were already being picked out as extraordinarily striking, even magnificent. There was in the critical response, to be sure, a certain measure of what the 1890s referred to as "log-rolling"—literary mutual admiration—that was not unusual at that time (or any other). Wells might have expected positive notices from *Nature*, with its South Kensington bias, and from Frank Harris's *Saturday Review*, to which he was a regular contributor and reviewer. In the main, though, independent reviewers seemed able to rise above their prejudices to affirm almost unanimously that *The Time Machine* had remarkable qualities.

As early as March 1895, when the serial in the *New Review* was in only its first instalment, *The Time Machine* was already attracting attention. A reviewer in the *Review of Reviews* began his brief notice, "H. G. Wells, who is writing the serial in the *New Review*, is a man of genius," adding that this author's imagination as evidenced in its description of the Eloi and Morlocks is "as gruesome as that of Poe" (see Appendix H1). A longer review in the June issue of the same periodical (see Appendix H2) affirmed that this "powerful imaginative romance" concluded without disappointing, alluding this time to its affinity with Richard Jefferies's post-catastrophic fantasy *After London* (1885).

The groping of the reviewers for comparisons with other works reveals their consciousness that *The Time Machine* was important enough to raise questions of generic redefinition. So, for example, the *Saturday Review* compared *The Time Machine* favourably with the ambiguous utopian works *The Coming Race* and *Erewhon* (see Appendix H7) while the *Daily Chronicle* noted that not since "Stevenson's creepy romance" *Dr Jekyll and Mr Hyde* had there been anything "in the domain of pure fantasy so bizarre as this 'invention' by Mr. H. G. Wells" (see Appendix H8). The only signed review, by the Anglo-Jewish novelist Israel Zangwill, who had a regular column called "Without Prejudice" in *Pall Mall Magazine* (see Appendix H10), mentions Besant's now largely forgotten *The Inner House*. Interestingly, Zangwill, whose review is generally very positive, raises problems of the plausibility of time travel—in particular the paradoxes that undermine cause and effect—that did not seem to trouble the more scientifically-oriented *Nature*, but which certainly troubled science fiction writers in later years. For example, how could a traveller into the future survive his own death?

A lengthy review in the conservative *Spectator* (Appendix H4) reveals that even those reviewers predisposed against Wells on ideological grounds found it difficult to resist the attractions of *The Time Machine*. The *Spectator* sneers at the idea of visiting the future where an author is "at liberty to imagine what he pleases," scoffs at the "hocus-pocus" of the device used to explore it, and bridles at the purely secular nature of Wells's vision. While suspicious of Darwinism, the *Spectator* at the same time disagrees with Wells's elaboration of the Huxleyan idea that a race that found ease would necessarily become degenerate. Is it not the rich, rather than the poor, who are the most aggressive in the struggle for existence? Yet the *Spectator*'s conclusion—"Mr. Wells's fanciful and lively dream is well worth reading, if only because it will draw attention to the great moral and religious factors in human nature which he appears to ignore"—sounds more like a reluctant tribute than a castigation.

It was in *Nature* more than ten years earlier that Wells, in his first year at South Kensington, had almost certainly read "S"'s letter proposing that time could be considered as a fourth dimension. *Nature* noted that *The Time Machine* "is well worth the attention of the scientific reader, for the reason that it is based so far as possible on scientific data" (See Appendix H6). *Nature* did not often review fiction, so its characterization of the author as someone well acquainted with the mathematics of cosmic evolution would have been viewed by Wells as a stamp of approval by the scientists whose work made the temporal perspective of *The Time Machine* possible. One thinks not only of Simon Newcomb and G. H. Darwin, whom Wells mentions by name in the text, but also and above all of T. H. Huxley, whose presence is everywhere in *The Time Machine* even if his name nowhere appears. Huxley died on 29 June 1895 without, as far as is known, ever reading the copy of *The Time Machine* that Wells had sent to him with a modest note some time the previous month (see Appendix F12).

The Time Machine: **Structure and Theme**

Jules Verne's fiction (see Appendix B7), familiar enough to the reader in 1895, often exploited the romance of nineteenth-century science and technology. Given sufficient know-how, will, funding, and raw material, Verne suggested that it was possible, for example, to engineer a heavier-than-air flying machine, a submarine, or a pneumatically-powered transatlantic subway train. Verne's extraordinary voyages were intended to stimulate people to make his fantasies realities—to a certain extent they did. But Wellsian scientific romance is typically driven by a different intention and is quite different at the thematic level. *The Time Machine* is not about the practicalities of constructing a time machine nor even about the inspiring theoretical possibility of time travel. Its major themes are more abstract, but also more universal and seem less superannuated than Verne's now often quaint technological fantasies.

The Time Machine is, in the most general way, about the post-Darwinian relationship between mankind and time. Astronomers, geologists, and biologists had radically revised man's temporal place in nature, yet as late as 1895 the implications of this revision had not fully registered with the reading public. The time was ripe for a work on the grand theme of man's place in time that would capture the popular imagination. Victorian novelists in the dominant realist tradition, ignorant of science or unused to dealing in timeframes measured in millennia, had largely ignored this theme.

The unusual structure of *The Time Machine* offers the chief clue to understanding Wells's approach to his grand temporal theme. The narrative has two main components of very unequal length. The shorter is the external or frame narrative with which the work begins and ends. As the novel opens, the primary narrator, who as a frequent visitor at the Time Traveller's house is almost certainly a professional man like the other guests,[1] is recalling in first person a sequence of events from his

---

1 His knowledge of science (see p. 33, n. 1) and allusions to the Linnaean Club (Chapter III), and his publisher (Chapter XVI), suggest that he is, like Wells, a science writer. As for his name, see p. 149, n. 1.

own past. He describes how he was present when the Time Traveller one Thursday evening in early 1894[1] introduced the idea of time travel through the fourth dimension and then demonstrated a model time machine to his six sceptical dinner-guests. The following Thursday, the narrator continues, he was one of a slightly different combination of guests who were assembled around the dinner-table awaiting the arrival of their host. The Time Traveller arrived hungry, dishevelled, and late, wolfed down some mutton, then told his tale of his experiences in the future. (The Time Traveller's tale, recounted verbatim by the narrator, then follows. It constitutes an internal or framed narrative.) Once the tale was over, only the narrator, who was affected by it enough to have a sleepless night, seemed prepared to believe it, and went the next day alone to see the Time Traveller, presumably to glean further proof that would allay his doubts about its credibility. The inventor was just about to leave on the time machine with a camera and supplies, precisely to gather harder evidence of his ability to travel in time, and asked the narrator to wait for half an hour. The narrator then caught a glimpse of his ghostly dematerialization on the machine. But the Time Traveller did not return—has not returned for three years. This establishes the narrative present —the location in time from which the narrator is addressing us —as 1897, three years after the disappearance of the Time Traveller.

The longer component of *The Time Machine* is the Time Traveller's story as reported by the primary narrator. This is an uninterrupted chronological narrative of just-experienced events by a first-person narrator who is also the protagonist of those events. It too is divided into two unequal sections. The longer first section of the Time Traveller's narrative is set in the degenerate world of the Eloi and Morlocks in A.D. 802,701. The shorter second section, comprising the chapter "The Further Vision," is set thirty million years thence, as the Time Traveller observes firsthand what seems likely to be the moment of total extinction of life on earth.

---

1   This date may be established from the reference to Simon Newcomb's actual address to the New York Mathematical Society. See Appendix D7.

Three different time-scales operate in *The Time Machine*. All coexist simultaneously, as they do in the real world, but two of them are not at first evident to the narratees (the Time Traveller's dinner-guests, the novel's readers). In the external narrative or frame, *historical time* dominates. The historical time-span of the frame is from 1894 to 1897, three years in the lives of the narrator and the other dinner-guests. The dinner-guests imagine that historical time is the only kind of time in the universe, or at least the only one that affects their lives; that is why they dismiss the Time Traveller's tale of the future as incredible. Historical time also serves as an apparently firm baseline for readers: it seems continuous with their own present — with their reading situation in real time. When the internal narrative ceases towards the end of the novel, historical time, which has been suspended, reasserts itself, but by then the reader, like the narrator, no longer has the same confidence in locating and grounding the self in time.

As the Time Traveller's story begins, historical time rapidly dissolves (this vertiginous idea is expressed through the famous description of the sensations of time travelling), and an underlying time scale, *evolutionary* or *geological time*, supersedes it. The existence of the concept of historical time depends upon the existence of an advanced, literate human culture that can measure and record time's passage. But the Eloi and Morlocks are in their different ways living in the ruins of culture, and there is no evidence that either species is numerate or literate enough to be measuring time or recording its passage as history. The Eloi indeed are not literate, while the Morlocks live in darkness, where reading and writing could hardly be expected to flourish, and avoid the sun, chief index of the passage of time on earth. The *A.D.* in A.D. 802,701 is consequently ironic, and not just because of the total disappearance of the Christian religion. It makes the date sound historical, and derives from the Time Traveller's initial assumption that after a very great leap in time into the future he will meet a race that has made a very great advance on humanity as it was in A.D. 1894. What has happened instead is that during this intervening period evolutionary elaboration has ceased and degeneration toward homogeneity, not progress toward heterogeneity, has become the dominant tendency in the biosphere. Incidentally, the meaningful units of evolutionary time are not years but Huxleyan *Great Years* (see p. 123, n. 3; also Appendix A6), suitable for measuring biological and geological change (the human species has subdivided, the course of the Thames has moved a mile).

The shift from historical time to evolutionary or geological time gives rise to a vision of the future that has serious repercussions for the late-Victorian dominant ideology in which evolution was associated with inevitable social and cultural progress — "Excelsior biology." As it was Wells's chief intention in *The Time Machine* to assail this ideology, the greater part of the internal narrative, amounting to a majority of the whole text, concerns itself with the world of the Eloi and Morlocks.

As the Time Traveller, escaping from the Morlocks' clutches, moves into the realm of "The Further Vision," we find that evolutionary time has itself been superseded by yet another time scale, that of *astronomical time*, which cannot be meaningfully measured by terrestrial yardsticks at all. The section set in the world thirty million years in the future is short, because once the effects upon the earth of astronomical change have been described (in the most highly charged passage in the novel) there is nothing more to say: the human plot is over. Wells offers a vision of global extinction, taking us to a point beyond which narrative cannot go. At the same time, it should be remembered that one of the less obvious but still striking elements of *The Time Machine* is its strict unity of place. That is to say, the area around the White Sphinx is the "same place" as the beach where the last creature is hopping about, and both are in the same physical location as the comfortable Richmond of 1894, for the time machine has the miraculous ability to travel in time without moving in space. This uncanny unity of place greatly strengthens the complex temporal theme and adds to the horror of the Time Traveller's narrative.

The Time Machine is an apocalypse for the scientific age, rather as the Book of Revelation served as an apocalypse for the age of faith that preceded it. Wells's romance is set on a planet that has been radically reshaped and recontextualized by the temporal revisions of astronomers, geologists, and evolutionary biologists, even though the consequences have not been properly understood, let alone accepted, by most ordinary educated people. *The Time Machine* dramatizes these consequences. Of course, this scientific apocalypse ends, not with the hope of human transcendence (a seat by God's side in the New Jerusalem), but with a vision of universal extinction.

Yet the vision of the far future in *The Time Machine* is not, I think, entirely pessimistic. The satirical thrust of the novel suggests that corrective behaviour is possible, that self and society can be actively transformed within historical time, so that, for example, the division between Haves and Have-nots may be remedied before historical change becomes evolutionary. Indeed, to the extent that the Eloi-Morlock episodes are an implied plea for the application of humane ethics to social evolution, *The Time Machine* is very much in the Huxleyan vein. As for "The Further Vision," universal extinction, though inevitable, is still very far off. Even thirty million years (and these days we have billions more, at least potentially) is an inconceivably long time, far longer than that promised mankind by most religions. In the meantime, the primary narrator's realism about extinction may serve as a guide. We might live, he suggests in the "Epilogue," "as though it were not so," cherishing the persistence of love under what are often the most unpromising circumstances.

Darwin's *The Origin of Species* was a revision of Genesis, the myth of origin that opens the scriptural cycle. *The Time Machine* is a revision of the Book of Revelation, the myth of the endtime that concludes that cycle. Darwin's works are non-fictional, for they are based on scientific observation of organic growth and fossil records. *The Time Machine*, beholden to Darwin, is set in the future, a temporal realm that can have left no record in the rocks, so from the point of view of a scientific age it is speculative, provisional—a fiction. Its ultimate function, however, is the same as that of scriptural apocalypses that compel belief: to reconcile mankind to death. Since the development of consciousness, human beings have known that personal extinction is inevitable, and that life on any terms is almost always preferable to death. How then to accept mortality? For most pre-scientific cultures, the answer involved the construction of an elaborate mythology of afterlife. Science finds no verifiable trace of an immortal soul nor of life after death, but that is no reason for nihilism, escapism, or despair. *The Time Machine* offers poetic consolation in its grand final vision of universal extinction: death, finality, is in the nature of things, and a star and a planet will come to an end in good astronomical time just as species become extinct in evolutionary time and individuals die in historical time. *The Time Machine* helps us confront, understand, and accept this grave and grand truth.

H.G. Wells: A Brief Chronology

[Dates refer to the first British edition of Wells's works, unless otherwise indicated. n = novel; nf = non-fiction work; r = romance; ss = short story collection.]

1866   Herbert George Wells born 21 September in Bromley, Kent, third and youngest son of Joseph and Sarah Wells.

1871   Attends dame school; learns to read.

1874   Breaks leg; while laid up, reads voraciously; starts to attend Thomas Morley's Commercial Academy.

1877   Father breaks leg in accident; Wells family plunged into financial hardship.

1878-80   Writes and illustrates *The Desert Daisy*, a children's story.

1880   Apprenticed to drapery in Windsor; is sent as pupil-teacher to village school in Somerset.

1881   Apprenticed to pharmacist in Midhurst; becomes full-time pupil at Midhurst Grammar School; apprenticed at drapery in Southsea.

1883   Accepted as pupil-teacher at Midhurst Grammar School; reads Plato and Henry George; becomes interested in socialism; studies for national exams in science education.

1884   Gains scholarship to Normal School of Science; moves to London.

1885   Attends lectures on zoology by T.H. Huxley; gains first-class honours in summer exams.

1886   Reads paper on democratic socialism to college debating society; launches *Science Schools Journal*, editing it until April 1887; meets first cousin Isabel Mary Wells.

1887   Publishes "A Tale of the Twentieth Century" (r) in *Science Schools Journal*; fails geology final exam, losing scholarship; hired by Holt Academy as science teacher; injured during football game, ruining health.

1888 Stays with William Burton in Staffordshire; "The Chronic Argonauts" (r) serialized in *Science Schools Journal* (April-June).

1889 Begins teaching science at Henley House School, London; passes intermediate exam for B.Sc.; makes two revisions (now lost) of "The Chronic Argonauts" between now and 1892.

1890 Passes exams for Licentiate in College of Preceptors; gains B.Sc. with first class honours in zoology; elected Fellow of the Zoological Society; hired by University Tutorial College.

1891 "The Rediscovery of the Unique" (nf) published in *Fortnightly Review*; meets *Fortnightly* editor Frank Harris, who rejects follow-up article, "The Universe Rigid"; marries Isabel Wells on 31 October.

1892 Meets Amy Catherine Robbins ("Jane").

1893 Suffers serious lung haemorrhage, ending teaching career; begins to sell popular journalism to *Pall Mall Gazette*; *Honours Physiography* (nf); *Text-Book of Biology* (nf); "The Man of the Year Million" (nf).

1894 Elopes with Jane; seven episodes of version of *The Time Machine* appear in *National Observer* (17 March-23 June); "The Stolen Bacillus," first signed short story, appears in *Pall Mall Budget*; moves to Sevenoaks, where *The Time Machine* is finished; "The Extinction of Man" (nf); sells more than 140 articles and stories this year.

1895 Divorces Isabel; *The Time Machine* serialized in *New Review* (January-May); reviews plays for *Pall Mall Gazette*; begins book-reviewing for *Saturday Review*; *The Time Machine* (r) published by Holt in New York (c. 7 May); *The Time Machine* published on 29 May by Heinemann in London; *Select Conversations with an Uncle* (ss); moves to Woking; *The Wonderful Visit* (r); marries Jane on 27 October; *The Stolen Bacillus, and Other Incidents* (ss).

1896 Moves to Worcester Park; meets George Gissing; *The Island of Dr Moreau* (r); *The Wheels of Chance* (n).

1897 Begins correspondence with Arnold Bennett; *The Plattner Story, and Others* (ss); *The Invisible Man* (r); *Certain Personal Matters* (nf); *Thirty Strange Stories* (U.S., ss).

1898 Meets Henry James, Joseph Conrad, Ford Madox Ford; *The War of the Worlds* (r).

1899 Meets Stephen Crane; *When the Sleeper Wakes* (r; revised as *The Sleeper Wakes* 1910); *Tales of Space and Time* (ss).

1900 Builds Spade House, Sandgate, Kent; *Love and Mr Lewisham* (n).

1901 First son George Philip Wells born to Jane; lives at Reform Club, London, during week; *The First Men in the Moon* (r); *Anticipations* (nf).

1902 *The Discovery of the Future* (nf); *The Sea Lady* (r).

1903 Second son Frank Wells born to Jane; joins Fabian Society; *Mankind in the Making* (nf); *Twelve Stories and a Dream* (ss).

1904 *The Food of the Gods* (r).

1905 Death of mother; *A Modern Utopia* (n); *Kipps* (n).

1906 Lecture tour in the U.S.; meets President Theodore Roosevelt, Booker T. Washington, Maxim Gorky; affair with Dorothy Richardson; begins affair with Amber Reeves; *In the Days of the Comet* (r); *The Future in America* (nf); *Socialism and the Family* (nf).

1907 *This Misery of Boots* (nf).

1908 Resigns from Fabian Society; *New Worlds for Old* (nf); *The War in the Air* (r); *First and Last Things* (nf, revised 1929).

1909 Daughter Anna Jane Blanco-White born to Amber Reeves; moves to Hampstead, London; *Tono-Bungay* (n); *Ann Veronica* (n).

1910 Death of father; begins affair with Elizabeth von Arnim; *The History of Mr Polly* (n).

1911 *The New Machiavelli* (n); *The Country of the Blind, and Other Stories* (ss); *The Door in the Wall, and Other Stories* (ss); *Floor Games* (nf).

1912 Moves to Dunmow, Essex; *Marriage* (n).

1913 Begins affair with Rebecca West; *Little Wars* (nf);
The Passionate Friends (n).

1914 Makes first visit to Russia; third son Anthony West
born to Rebecca West; *An Englishman Looks at the
World* (nf, U.S. *Social Forces in England and America*);
The World Set Free (r); *The Wife of Sir Isaac Harman*
(n); *The War That Will End War* (nf).

1915 Breaks with Henry James; *Boon* (n, under the pseudonym 'Reginald Bliss'); *Bealby* (n); *The Research
Magnificent* (n); *The Peace of the World* (nf).

1916 Tours battlefields in France and Italy; *What Is Coming?* (nf); *Mr Britling Sees It Through* (n); *The Elements
of Reconstruction* (nf).

1917 Meets Enid Bagnold; *War and the Future* (nf); *God
The Invisible King* (nf); *The Soul of a Bishop* (n).

1918 *In the Fourth Year: Anticipations of World Peace* (nf);
Joan and Peter (n); *British Nationalism and the League of
Nations* (nf).

1919 *The Undying Fire* (n); *The Idea of a League of Nations*
(nf, part-author); *History Is One* (nf, U.S.).

1920 Makes second visit to Russia; meets Lenin, Trotsky,
Moura Budberg; meets Margaret Sanger; *The Outline
of History* (nf); *Russia in the Shadows* (nf).

1921 Visits U.S.; *The Salvaging of Civilisation* (nf); *The New
Teaching of History* (nf).

1922 Joins Labour Party; stands unsuccessfully for Parliament as candidate for University of London; *Washington and the Hope of Peace* (nf); *The Secret Places of
the Heart* (n); *A Short History of the World* (nf); *The
World, Its Debts, and the Rich Men* (nf).

1923 Again stands unsuccessfully for Parliament; begins to
winter near Grasse in Provence; meets Odette Keun;
Men Like Gods (r); *The Story of a Great Schoolmaster*
(nf); *The Dream* (n); *The Labour Ideal of Education*
(nf); *Socialism and the Scientific Motive* (nf).

1924 The Atlantic Edition of *The Works of H. G. Wells*

published in a limited edition of 1,670 sets with new prefaces by Wells (1924-27); *A Year of Prophesying* (nf).

1925   *Christina Alberta's Father* (n); *A Forecast of the World's Affairs* (nf).

1926   *The World of William Clissold* (n); *Mr Belloc Objects to The Outline of History* (nf).

1927   Death of Jane; builds house in Grasse; *Meanwhile* (n); *The Short Stories of H. G. Wells* (ss, rep. as *The Complete Short Stories of H. G. Wells*, 1966); *Democracy Under Revision* (nf).

1928   *The Way the World Is Going* (nf); *The Open Conspiracy* (nf, rev. as *What Are We To Do with Our Lives?* 1931); *The Book of Catherine Wells* (nf); *Mr. Blettsworthy on Rampole Island* (n).

1929   *The King Who was a King* (screenplay); *The Adventures of Tommy* (n for children); *The Common-Sense of World Peace* (nf).

1929-30   *The Science of Life* (nf, 3 vols, with Julian Huxley and G. P. Wells).

1930   *The Autocracy of Mr Parham* (r); *The Way to World Peace* (nf).

1931   Diagnosed as diabetic; death of first wife Isabel.

1932   *After Democracy* (nf); *The Work, Wealth and Happiness of Mankind* (nf, 2 vols.); *The Bulpington of Blup* (n).

1933   *The Shape of Things to Come* (r); *The Scientific Romances* (collection of romances, with preface by Wells).

1934   Third visit to Russia; meets Stalin; visits U.S.; meets President F. D. Roosevelt; *Experiment in Autobiography* (nf); *Seven Famous Novels by H. G. Wells* (U.S., with preface by Wells).

1935   Moves to 13 Hanover Terrace, Regent's Park; *The New America* (nf); *Things To Come* (screenplay).

1936   Public dinner for 70th birthday given by PEN; *The Anatomy of Frustration* (nf); *The Croquet Player* (r); *The Man Who Could Work Miracles* (screenplay); *The Idea of a World Encyclopaedia* (nf); *The Favorite Short Stories of H. G. Wells* (ss, U.S.).

1937   *Star-Begotten* (r); *Brynhild* (n); *The Camford Visitation* (r).

1938   Lecture tour in Australia; Orson Welles's radio broadcast of *The War of the Worlds* causes panic in U.S.; *The Brothers* (n); *Apropos of Dolores* (n); *World Brain* (nf).

1939   *The Holy Terror* (n); *Travels of a Republican Radical in Search of Hot Water* (nf); *The Fate of Homo Sapiens* (nf, U.S. *The Fate of Man*); *The New World Order* (nf, revised as *The Outlook for Homo Sapiens*, 1942).

1940   Lecture tour in U.S.; in London during Blitz; *The Rights of Man* (nf); *Babes in the Darkling Wood* (n); *The Common Sense of War and Peace* (nf); *All Aboard for Ararat* (r); *Two Hemispheres or One World?* (nf).

1941   *You Can't Be Too Careful* (n); *Guide to the New World* (nf).

1942   *Science and the World-Mind* (nf); *The Conquest of Time* (nf); *Phoenix* (nf); D.Sc. thesis in zoology, *On the Quality of Illusion in the Continuity of the Individual Life in the Higher Metazoa, with Particular Reference to the Species Homo Sapiens* (nf).

1943   *Crux Ansata* (nf).

1944   *'42 to '44* (nf).

1945   *The Happy Turning* (n); *Mind at the End of Its Tether* (nf).

1946   Dies 13 August at age of 79 at 13 Hanover Terrace; cremated on 16 August at Golders Green; ashes scattered over English Channel.

A Note on the Text

The text of *The Time Machine* that follows is that of the first British book edition, published by Heinemann in London in 1895. The first American edition published by Holt in New York preceded it by about three weeks. In spite of their almost simultaneous appearance, the British and American first editions differ, and scholarship has established that the Heinemann text is more authoritative. Essentially, the Heinemann is the result of the polishing of the *New Review* serial version of the text that appeared in 1895, while the Holt text precedes that of the serial.

Many modern editions of *The Time Machine* are reprints of the text in Volume I of the Atlantic edition of *The Works of H.G. Wells* (1924), or of subsequent editions based on the Atlantic text. It is true that for the Atlantic edition Wells made some further revisions to the Heinemann text, the chief of which are the deletion of chapter titles and the reduction of the number of chapters from sixteen to twelve. (These and other changes were apparently first proposed by Wells in 1898 or 1899, but did not see print till 1924; see Appendix G2.) But none of these later changes has any significant effect on *The Time Machine* at the thematic or stylistic level.

As this Broadview edition attempts to place the novel in the context of the era in which it first appeared, it seems appropriate to provide its readers today with the best edition available to the reader in 1895 — the Heinemann. Moreover, it was the Heinemann *Time Machine*, quickly recognized by the critics as a major achievement (see Appendix H), that launched Wells's literary career.

I have made the following three emendations to the 1895 Heinemann text in order to correct typographical errors:

	Heinemann	*Emendation*
Chapter IV, p. 81	the hawk wins above	the hawk wings above

Chapter V, p. 83	I begun the conversation	I began the conversation
Chapter X', p. 119	Like the Carlovignan kings	like the Carlovingian kings

The
Time Machine

An Invention

By
H. G. Wells

London
William Heinemann
MDCCCXCV

CONTENTS

NOTE. — The substance of the first chapter of this story and of several paragraphs from the context appeared in the 'National Observer' in 1894. The "Time Traveller's Story" appeared, almost as it stands here, in the pages of the 'New Review.' The Author desires to make the customary acknowledgments. [Wells's note.]

THE TIME MACHINE[1]

I

INTRODUCTION

THE Time Traveller (for so it will be convenient to speak of him) was expounding a recondite matter to us. His grey eyes shone and twinkled, and his usually pale face was flushed and animated. The fire burnt brightly, and the soft radiance of the incandescent lights in the lilies of silver caught the bubbles that flashed and passed in our glasses. Our chairs, being his patents, embraced and caressed us rather than submitted to be sat upon, and there was that luxurious after-dinner atmosphere, when thought runs gracefully free of the trammels[2] of precision. And he put it to us in this way — marking the points with a lean forefinger — as we sat and lazily admired his earnestness over this new paradox (as we thought it) and his fecundity.

"You must follow me carefully. I shall have to controvert one or two ideas that are almost universally accepted. The geometry, for instance, they taught you at school is founded on a misconception."

"Is not that rather a large thing to expect us to begin upon?" said Filby, an argumentative person with red hair.

"I do not mean to ask you to accept anything without reasonable ground for it. You will soon admit as much as I need from you. You know of course that a mathematical line, a line of thickness *nil*, has no real existence. They taught you that?

---

1   The Heinemann text is preceded by a dedication "To William Ernest Henley." Henley, poet and man of letters (1849-1903), was the editor of the weekly *National Observer* from 1891-94 and then the monthly *New Review* from 1894-98, in both of which earlier versions of *The Time Machine* had appeared. He had encouraged Wells to turn the *National Observer* sketches into a long story suitable for *New Review* serialization.
2   Shackles, restraints.

Neither has a mathematical plane. These things are mere abstractions."

"That is all right," said the Psychologist.

"Nor, having only length, breadth, and thickness, can a cube have a real existence."

"There I object," said Filby. "Of course a solid body may exist. All real things—"

"So most people think. But wait a moment. Can an *instantaneous* cube exist?"

"Don't follow you," said Filby.

"Can a cube that does not last for any time at all, have a real existence?"

Filby became pensive. "Clearly," the Time Traveller proceeded, "any real body must have extension in *four* directions: it must have Length, Breadth, Thickness, and—Duration. But through a natural infirmity of the flesh, which I will explain to you in a moment, we incline to overlook this fact. There are really four dimensions, three which we call the three planes of Space, and a fourth, Time. There is, however, a tendency to draw an unreal distinction between the former three dimensions and the latter, because it happens that our consciousness moves intermittently in one direction along the latter from the beginning to the end of our lives."

"That," said a very young man, making spasmodic efforts to relight his cigar over the lamp; "that ... very clear indeed."

"Now, it is very remarkable that this is so extensively overlooked," continued the Time Traveller, with a slight accession of cheerfulness. "Really this is what is meant by the Fourth Dimension, though some people who talk about the Fourth Dimension do not know they mean it. It is only another way of looking at Time. *There is no difference between Time and any of the three dimensions of Space except that our consciousness moves along it.* But some foolish people have got hold of the wrong side of that idea. You have all heard what they have to say about this Fourth Dimension?"

"*I* have not," said the Provincial Mayor.

"It is simply this. That Space, as our mathematicians have it, is spoken of as having three dimensions, which one may call

Length, Breadth, and Thickness, and is always definable by reference to three planes, each at right angles to the others. But some philosophical people have been asking why *three* dimensions particularly — why not another direction at right angles to the other three? — and have even tried to construct a Four-Dimensional geometry. Professor Simon Newcomb[1] was expounding this to the New York Mathematical Society only a month or so ago. You know how on a flat surface, which has only two dimensions, we can represent a figure of a three-dimensional solid, and similarly they think that by models of three dimensions they could represent one of four — if they could master the perspective of the thing. See?"

"I think so," murmured the Provincial Mayor; and, knitting his brows, he lapsed into an introspective state, his lips moving as one who repeats mystic words. "Yes, I think I see it now," he said after some time, brightening in a quite transitory manner.

"Well, I do not mind telling you I have been at work upon this geometry of Four Dimensions for some time. Some of my results are curious. For instance, here is a portrait of a man at eight years old, another at fifteen, another at seventeen, another at twenty-three, and so on. All these are evidently sections, as it were, Three-Dimensional representations of his Four-Dimensioned being, which is a fixed and unalterable thing."

"Scientific people," proceeded the Time Traveller, after the pause required for the proper assimilation of this, "know very well that Time is only a kind of Space. Here is a popular scientific diagram, a weather record. This line I trace with my finger shows the movement of the barometer. Yesterday it was so high, yesterday night it fell, then this morning it rose again, and so gently upward to here. Surely the mercury did not trace this line in any of the dimensions of Space generally recognized? But certainly it traced such a line, and that line, therefore, we must conclude was along the Time-Dimension."

"But," said the Medical Man, staring hard at a coal in the fire, "if Time is really only a fourth dimension of Space, why is it, and why has it always been, regarded as something different?

---

1   American mathematician, astronomer, and naval officer (1835-1909). See Appendix D7.

And why cannot we move about in Time as we move about in the other dimensions of Space?"

The Time Traveller smiled. "Are you so sure we can move freely in Space? Right and left we can go, backward and forward freely enough, and men always have done so. I admit we move freely in two dimensions. But how about up and down? Gravitation limits us there."

"Not exactly," said the Medical Man. "There are balloons."

"But before the balloons, save for spasmodic jumping and the inequalities of the surface, man had no freedom of vertical movement."

"Still they could move a little up and down," said the Medical Man.

"Easier, far easier down than up."

"And you cannot move at all in Time, you cannot get away from the present moment."

"My dear sir, that is just where you are wrong. That is just where the whole world has gone wrong. We are always getting away from the present moment. Our mental existences, which are immaterial and have no dimensions, are passing along the Time-Dimension with a uniform velocity from the cradle to the grave. Just as we should travel *down* if we began our existence fifty miles above the earth's surface."

"But the great difficulty is this," interrupted the Psychologist. "You *can* move about in all directions of Space, but you cannot move about in Time."

"That is the germ of my great discovery. But you are wrong to say that we cannot move about in Time. For instance, if I am recalling an incident very vividly I go back to the instant of its occurrence: I become absent-minded, as you say. I jump back for a moment. Of course we have no means of staying back for any length of Time, any more than a savage or an animal has of staying six feet above the ground. But a civilized man is better off than the savage in this respect. He can go up against gravitation in a balloon, and why should he not hope that ultimately he may be able to stop or accelerate his drift along the Time-Dimension, or even turn about and travel the other way?"

"Oh, *this*," began Filby, "is all—"

"Why not?" said the Time Traveller.

"It's against reason," said Filby.

"What reason?" said the Time Traveller.

"You can show black is white by argument," said Filby, "but you will never convince me."

"Possibly not," said the Time Traveller. "But now you begin to see the object of my investigations into the geometry of Four Dimensions. Long ago I had a vague inkling of a machine—"

"To travel through Time!" exclaimed the Very Young Man.

"That shall travel indifferently in any direction of Space and Time, as the driver determines."

Filby contented himself with laughter.

"But I have experimental verification," said the Time Traveller.

"It would be remarkably convenient for the historian," the Psychologist suggested. "One might travel back and verify the accepted account of the Battle of Hastings,[1] for instance!"

"Don't you think you would attract attention?" said the Medical Man. "Our ancestors had no great tolerance for anachronisms."

"One might get one's Greek from the very lips of Homer and Plato," the Very Young Man thought.

"In which case they would certainly plough you for the Little-go. The German scholars have improved Greek so much."[2]

"Then there is the future," said the Very Young Man. "Just think! One might invest all one's money, leave it to accumulate at interest, and hurry on ahead!"

"To discover a society," said I, "erected on a strictly communistic basis."[3]

---

1   The victory of the Normans under William the Conqueror over the Saxons of King Harold in A.D. 1066 heralded the last successful conquest of England and is often considered the most important event in English history.

2   "The Little-go" was a slang term for the first exam towards the B.A. degree at Cambridge University; "to plough" was to fail or flunk. In the nineteenth century, German scholars dominated classical studies, including the arguments about the correct pronunciation of Ancient Greek.

3   Such as the moneyless society described in William Morris's utopian romance *News from Nowhere* (1890). See Appendix B11.

"Of all the wild extravagant theories!" began the Psychologist.

"Yes, so it seemed to me, and so I never talked of it until—"

"Experimental verification!" cried I. "You are going to verify *that*?"

"The experiment!" cried Filby, who was getting brain-weary.

"Let's see your experiment anyhow," said the Psychologist, "though it's all humbug, you know."

The Time Traveller smiled round at us. Then, still smiling faintly, and with his hands deep in his trousers pockets, he walked slowly out of the room, and we heard his slippers shuffling down the long passage to his laboratory.

The Psychologist looked at us. "I wonder what he's got?"

"Some sleight-of-hand trick or other," said the Medical Man, and Filby tried to tell us about a conjuror he had seen at Burslem,[1] but before he had finished his preface the Time Traveller came back, and Filby's anecdote collapsed.

---

1   Town in the pottery-producing area of Staffordshire, England, near where Wells had stayed in 1888 when working on the earliest version of *The Time Machine*.

II

THE MACHINE

THE thing the Time Traveller held in his hand was a glittering metallic framework, scarcely larger than a small clock, and very delicately made. There was ivory in it, and some transparent crystalline substance. And now I must be explicit, for this that follows—unless his explanation is to be accepted—is an absolutely unaccountable thing. He took one of the small octagonal tables that were scattered about the room, and set it in front of the fire, with two legs on the hearthrug. On this table he placed the mechanism. Then he drew up a chair, and sat down. The only other object on the table was a small shaded lamp, the bright light of which fell full upon the model. There were also perhaps a dozen candles about, two in brass candlesticks upon the mantel and several in sconces, so that the room was brilliantly illuminated. I sat in a low arm-chair nearest the fire, and I drew this forward so as to be almost between the Time Traveller and the fireplace. Filby sat behind him, looking over his shoulder. The Medical Man and the Provincial Mayor watched him in profile from the right, the Psychologist from the left. The Very Young Man stood behind the Psychologist. We were all on the alert. It appears incredible to me that any kind of trick, however subtly conceived and however adroitly done, could have been played upon us under these conditions.

The Time Traveller looked at us, and then at the mechanism. "Well?" said the Psychologist.

"This little affair," said the Time Traveller, resting his elbows upon the table and pressing his hands together above the apparatus, "is only a model. It is my plan for a machine to travel through time. You will notice that it looks singularly askew, and that there is an odd twinkling appearance about this bar, as though it was in some way unreal." He pointed to the part with his finger. "Also, here is one little white lever, and here is another."

The Medical Man got up out of his chair and peered into the thing. "It's beautifully made," he said.

"It took two years to make," retorted the Time Traveller. Then, when we had all imitated the action of the Medical Man, he said: "Now I want you clearly to understand that this lever, being pressed over, sends the machine gliding into the future, and this other reverses the motion. This saddle represents the seat of a time traveller. Presently I am going to press the lever, and off the machine will go. It will vanish, pass into future time, and disappear. Have a good look at the thing. Look at the table too, and satisfy yourselves there is no trickery. I don't want to waste this model, and then be told I'm a quack."

There was a minute's pause perhaps. The Psychologist seemed about to speak to me, but changed his mind. Then the Time Traveller put forth his finger towards the lever. "No," he said suddenly. "Lend me your hand." And turning to the Psychologist, he took that individual's hand in his own and told him to put out his forefinger. So that it was the Psychologist himself who sent forth the model Time Machine on its interminable voyage. We all saw the lever turn. I am absolutely certain there was no trickery. There was a breath of wind, and the lamp flame jumped. One of the candles on the mantel was blown out, and the little machine suddenly swung round, became indistinct, was seen as a ghost for a second perhaps, as an eddy of faintly glittering brass and ivory; and it was gone — vanished! Save for the lamp the table was bare.

Every one was silent for a minute. Then Filby said he was damned.

The Psychologist recovered from his stupor, and suddenly looked under the table. At that the Time Traveller laughed cheerfully. "Well?" he said, with a reminiscence of the Psychologist. Then, getting up, he went to the tobacco jar on the mantel, and with his back to us began to fill his pipe.

We stared at each other. "Look here," said the Medical Man, "are you in earnest about this? Do you seriously believe that that machine has travelled into time?"

"Certainly," said the Time Traveller, stooping to light a spill[1] at the fire. Then he turned, lighting his pipe, to look at the Psychologist's face. (The Psychologist, to show that he was not unhinged, helped himself to a cigar and tried to light it uncut.) "What is more, I have a big machine nearly finished in there"—he indicated the laboratory—"and when that is put together I mean to have a journey on my own account."

"You mean to say that that machine has travelled into the future?" said Filby.

"Into the future or the past—I don't, for certain, know which."

After an interval the Psychologist had an inspiration. "It must have gone into the past if it has gone anywhere," he said.

"Why?" said the Time Traveller.

"Because I presume that it has not moved in space, and if it travelled into the future it would still be here all this time, since it must have travelled through this time."

"But," said I, "if it travelled into the past it would have been visible when we came first into this room; and last Thursday when we were here; and the Thursday before that; and so forth!"

"Serious objections," remarked the Provincial Mayor, with an air of impartiality, turning towards the Time Traveller.

"Not a bit," said the Time Traveller, and, to the Psychologist: "You think. *You* can explain that. It's presentation below the threshold,[2] you know, diluted presentation."

"Of course," said the Psychologist, and reassured us. "That's a simple point in psychology. I should have thought of it. It's plain enough, and helps the paradox delightfully. We cannot see it, nor can we appreciate this machine, any more than we can the spoke of a wheel spinning, or a bullet flying through the air. If it is travelling through time fifty times or a hundred times faster than we are, if it gets through a minute while we get through a second, the impression it creates will of course be only one-fiftieth or one-hundredth of what it would make if it were not travelling in time. That's plain enough." He passed his

---

1   A slip of wood or twisted paper used to transfer flame, e.g., from a fire to a pipe.
2   I.e., below the threshold of consciousness, subliminal.

hand through the space in which the machine had been. "You see?" he said, laughing.

We sat and stared at the vacant table for a minute or so. Then the Time Traveller asked us what we thought of it all.

"It sounds plausible enough to-night," said the Medical Man; "but wait until to-morrow. Wait for the common-sense of the morning."

"Would you like to see the Time Machine itself?" asked the Time Traveller. And therewith, taking the lamp in his hand, he led the way down the long, draughty corridor to his laboratory. I remember vividly the flickering light, his queer, broad head in silhouette, the dance of the shadows, how we all followed him, puzzled but incredulous, and how there in the laboratory we beheld a larger edition of the little mechanism which we had seen vanish from before our eyes. Parts were of nickel, parts of ivory, parts had certainly been filed or sawn out of rock crystal. The thing was generally complete, but the twisted crystalline bars lay unfinished upon the bench beside some sheets of drawings, and I took one up for a better look at it. Quartz it seemed to be.

"Look here," said the Medical Man, "are you perfectly serious? Or is this a trick—like that ghost you showed us last Christmas?"

"Upon that machine," said the Time Traveller, holding the lamp aloft, "I intend to explore time. Is that plain? I was never more serious in my life."

None of us quite knew how to take it.

I caught Filby's eye over the shoulder of the Medical Man, and he winked at me solemnly.

III

THE TIME TRAVELLER RETURNS

I THINK that at that time none of us quite believed in the Time Machine. The fact is, the Time Traveller was one of those men who are too clever to be believed: you never felt that you saw all round him; you always suspected some subtle reserve, some ingenuity in ambush, behind his lucid frankness. Had Filby shown the model and explained the matter in the Time Traveller's words, we should have shown *him* far less scepticism. For we should have perceived his motives: a pork-butcher could understand Filby. But the Time Traveller had more than a touch of whim among his elements, and we distrusted him. Things that would have made the fame of a less clever man seemed tricks in his hands. It is a mistake to do things too easily. The serious people who took him seriously never felt quite sure of his deportment: they were somehow aware that trusting his reputations for judgment with him was like furnishing a nursery with eggshell china. So I don't think any of us said very much about time travelling in the interval between that Thursday and the next, though its odd potentialities ran, no doubt, in most of our minds: its plausibility, that is, its practical incredibleness, the curious possibilities of anachronism and of utter confusion it suggested. For my own part, I was particularly preoccupied with the trick of the model. That I remember discussing with the Medical Man, whom I met on Friday at the Linnæan.[1] He said he had seen a similar thing at Tübingen,[2] and laid considerable stress on the blowing-out of the candle. But how the trick was done he could not explain.

---

1 I.e., The Linnaean Society, a distinguished scientific society founded in London in 1788, named for the great Swedish botanic taxonomist Carolus Linnaeus (Carl von Linné, 1707-78), and famous as the forum at which Charles Darwin in July 1858 first presented his theory of evolution.
2 University city in south-west Germany.

The next Thursday I went again to Richmond[1] — I suppose I was one of the Time Traveller's most constant guests — and, arriving late, found four or five men already assembled in his drawing-room. The Medical Man was standing before the fire with a sheet of paper in one hand and his watch in the other. I looked round for the Time Traveller, and — "It's half-past seven now," said the Medical Man. "I suppose we'd better have dinner?"

"Where's ——?" said I, naming our host.

"You've just come? It's rather odd. He's unavoidably detained. He asks me in this note to lead off with dinner at seven if he's not back. Says he'll explain when he comes."

"It seems a pity to let the dinner spoil," said the Editor of a well-known daily paper; and thereupon the Doctor rang the bell.

The Psychologist was the only person besides the Doctor and myself who had attended the previous dinner. The other men were Blank, the Editor afore-mentioned, a certain journalist, and another — a quiet, shy man with a beard — whom I didn't know, and who, as far as my observation went, never opened his mouth all the evening. There was some speculation at the dinner-table about the Time Traveller's absence, and I suggested time travelling, in a half jocular spirit. The Editor wanted that explained to him, and the Psychologist volunteered a wooden account of the "ingenious paradox and trick" we had witnessed that day week. He was in the midst of his exposition when the door from the corridor opened slowly and without noise. I was facing the door, and saw it first. "Hallo!" I said. "At last!" And the door opened wider, and the Time Traveller stood before us. I gave a cry of surprise. "Good heavens! man, what's the matter?" cried the Medical Man, who saw him next. And the whole tableful turned towards the door.

He was in an amazing plight. His coat was dusty and dirty, and smeared with green down the sleeves; his hair disordered, and as it seemed to me greyer — either with dust and dirt or

---

1   The Time Traveller's house is located in this attractive Thames-side suburb of south-west London, surrounded by parkland and offering views to the south and west.

because its colour had actually faded. His face was ghastly pale; his chin had a brown cut on it—a cut half-healed; his expression was haggard and drawn, as by intense suffering. For a moment he hesitated in the doorway, as if he had been dazzled by the light. Then he came into the room. He walked with just such a limp as I have seen in footsore tramps. We stared at him in silence, expecting him to speak.

He said not a word, but came painfully to the table, and made a motion towards the wine. The Editor filled a glass of champagne, and pushed it towards him. He drained it, and it seemed to do him good: for he looked round the table, and the ghost of his old smile flickered across his face. "What on earth have you been up to, man?" said the Doctor. The Time Traveller did not seem to hear. "Don't let me disturb you," he said, with a certain faltering articulation. "I'm all right." He stopped, held out his glass for more, and took it off at a draught. "That's good," he said. His eyes grew brighter, and a faint colour came into his cheeks. His glance flickered over our faces with a certain dull approval, and then went round the warm and comfortable room. Then he spoke again, still as it were feeling his way among his words. "I'm going to wash and dress, and then I'll come down and explain things…. Save me some of that mutton. I'm starving for a bit of meat."

He looked across at the Editor, who was a rare visitor, and hoped he was all right. The Editor began a question. "Tell you presently," said the Time Traveller. "I'm—funny! Be all right in a minute."

He put down his glass, and walked towards the staircase door. Again I remarked his lameness and the soft padding sound of his footfall, and standing up in my place, I saw his feet as he went out. He had nothing on them but a pair of tattered, blood-stained socks. Then the door closed upon him. I had half a mind to follow, till I remembered how he detested any fuss about himself. For a minute, perhaps, my mind was wool gathering. Then, "Remarkable Behaviour of an Eminent Scientist," I heard the Editor say, thinking (after his wont) in headlines. And this brought my attention back to the bright dinner-table.

"What's the game?" said the Journalist. "Has he been doing the Amateur Cadger?[1] I don't follow." I met the eye of the Psychologist, and read my own interpretation in his face. I thought of the Time Traveller limping painfully up-stairs. I don't think any one else had noticed his lameness.

The first to recover completely from this surprise was the Medical Man, who rang the bell—the Time Traveller hated to have servants waiting at dinner—for a hot plate. At that the Editor turned to his knife and fork with a grunt, and the silent man followed suit. The dinner was resumed. Conversation was exclamatory for a little while, with gaps of wonderment; and then the Editor got fervent in his curiosity. "Does our friend eke out his modest income with a crossing? or has he his Nebuchadnezzar phases?"[2] he inquired. "I feel assured it's this business of the Time Machine," I said, and took up the Psychologist's account of our previous meeting. The new guests were frankly incredulous. The Editor raised objections. "What *was* this time travelling? A man couldn't cover himself with dust by rolling in a paradox, could he?" And then, as the idea came home to him, he resorted to caricature. Hadn't they any clothes-brushes in the Future? The Journalist, too, would not believe at any price, and joined the Editor in the easy work of heaping ridicule on the whole thing. They were both the new kind of journalist—very joyous, irreverent young men. "Our Special Correspondent in the Day after To-morrow reports," the Journalist was saying—or rather shouting—when the Time Traveller came back.. He was dressed in ordinary evening clothes, and nothing save his haggard look remained of the change that had startled me.

"I say," said the Editor, hilariously, "these chaps here say you have been travelling into the middle of next week! Tell us all

---

1   The Journalist's question is based on his suspicion that respectable people some-
    times disguise themselves as beggars in order to supplement their income.
2   The Editor wants to know if the Time Traveller leads a Jekyll-and-Hyde existence.
    "A crossing" is obscure, but "to cross" is slang for to cheat, and suggests devious
    practices, perhaps those of a part-time confidence trickster or criminal who
    ambushes his victims. King Nebuchadnezzar of Babylon was abased by God and
    led the life of a beast for seven years (see Daniel 4:33).

about little Rosebery,[1] will you? What will you take for the lot?"

The Time Traveller came to the place reserved for him without a word. He smiled quietly, in his old way. "Where's my mutton?" he said. "What a treat it is to stick a fork into meat again!"

"Story!" cried the Editor.

"Story be damned!" said the Time Traveller. "I want something to eat. I won't say a word until I get some peptone[2] into my arteries. Thanks. And the salt."

"One word," said I. "Have you been time travelling?"

"Yes," said the Time Traveller, with his mouth full, nodding his head.

"I'd give a shilling a line for a verbatim note,"[3] said the Editor. The Time Traveller pushed his glass towards the Silent Man and rang it with his finger nail; at which the Silent Man, who had been staring at his face, started convulsively, and poured him wine. The rest of the dinner was uncomfortable. For my own part, sudden questions kept on rising to my lips, and I dare say it was the same with the others. The Journalist tried to relieve the tension by telling anecdotes of Hettie Potter.[4] The Time Traveller devoted his attention to his dinner, and displayed the appetite of a tramp. The Medical Man

---

1   A topical allusion. This dinner-party takes place in early 1894, and the Editor wants political information or racing tips based on the Time Traveller's inside knowledge of the very near future as it might affect the fate of the politician and turf enthusiast Lord Rosebery (1847-1929). Rosebery would briefly be Liberal Prime Minister of England from March 1894 to June 1895. Moreover, in the 1894 season, Rosebery's horse, Ladas, would perform the remarkable feat of winning three major races: the 2,000 Guineas, the Newmarket Stakes, and the Derby. The epithet "little" derives from Rosebery's boyish appearance, especially in contrast to his patriarchal predecessor, Gladstone.

2   Protein as it has been partly processed by the digestive system, thus suggesting a restoration of energy to the system.

3   The offer of a shilling per line for the Time Traveller's firsthand account was twelve times the common fee of one penny per line. A shilling was a coin that was equivalent to twelve pence, and there were twenty shillings in a pound; one shilling was worth about $ 0.25 U.S. at that time.

4   This name is almost certainly fictitious, and is intended to suggest a music-hall artiste, actress, spiritualist, or other well-known "lady of dubious virtue," comic anecdotes about whom might relieve the suspense around the table.

smoked a cigarette, and watched the Time Traveller through his eyelashes. The Silent Man seemed even more clumsy than usual, and drank champagne with regularity and determination out of sheer nervousness. At last the Time Traveller pushed his plate away, and looked round us. "I suppose I must apologize," he said. "I was simply starving. I've had a most amazing time." He reached out his hand for a cigar, and cut the end. "But come into the smoking-room. It's too long a story to tell over greasy plates." And ringing the bell in passing, he led the way into the adjoining room.

"You have told Blank, and Dash, and Chose[1] about the machine?" he said to me, leaning back in his easy-chair and naming the three new guests.

"But the thing's a mere paradox," said the Editor.

"I can't argue to-night. I don't mind telling you the story, but I can't argue. I will," he went on, "tell you the story of what has happened to me, if you like, but you must refrain from interruptions. I want to tell it. Badly. Most of it will sound like lying. So be it! It's true — every word of it, all the same. I was in my laboratory at four o'clock, and since then ... I've lived eight days ... such days as no human being ever lived before! I'm nearly worn out, but I sha'n't sleep till I've told this thing over to you. Then I shall go to bed. But no interruptions! Is it agreed?"

"Agreed," said the Editor, and the rest of us echoed "Agreed." And with that the Time Traveller began his story as I have set it forth. He sat back in his chair at first, and spoke like a weary man. Afterwards he got more animated. In writing it down I feel with only too much keenness the inadequacy of pen and ink — and, above all, my own inadequacy — to express its quality. You read, I will suppose, attentively enough; but you cannot see the speaker's white, sincere face in the bright circle of the little lamp, nor hear the intonation of his voice. You cannot know how his expression followed the turns of his story! Most of us hearers were in shadow, for the candles in the

---

1 Names suggesting that the narrator is preserving the anonymity of the Time Traveller's guests (*chose* means "thing" in French).

smoking-room had not been lighted, and only the face of the Journalist and the legs of the Silent Man from the knees downward were illuminated. At first we glanced now and again at each other. After a time we ceased to do that, and looked only at the Time Traveller's face.

IV

TIME TRAVELLING

"I TOLD some of you last Thursday of the principles of the Time Machine, and showed you the actual thing itself, incomplete in the workshop. There it is now, a little travel-worn, truly; and one of the ivory bars is cracked, and a brass rail bent; but the rest of it's sound enough. I expected to finish it on Friday; but on Friday, when the putting together was nearly done, I found that one of the nickel bars was exactly one inch too short, and this I had to get re-made; so that the thing was not complete until this morning. It was at ten o'clock today that the first of all Time Machines began its career. I gave it a last tap, tried all the screws again, put one more drop of oil on the quartz rod, and sat myself in the saddle.[1] I suppose a suicide who holds a pistol to his skull feels much the same wonder at what will come next as I felt then. I took the starting lever in one hand and the stopping one in the other, pressed the first, and almost immediately the second. I seemed to reel; I felt a nightmare sensation of falling; and, looking round, I saw the laboratory exactly as before. Had anything happened? For a moment I suspected that my intellect had tricked me. Then I noted the clock. A moment before, as it seemed, it had stood at a minute or so past ten; now it was nearly half-past three!

"I drew a breath, set my teeth, gripped the starting lever with both hands, and went off with a thud. The laboratory got hazy and went dark. Mrs. Watchett[2] came in, and walked, apparently without seeing me, towards the garden door. I suppose it took her a minute or so to traverse the place, but to me she seemed to shoot across the room like a rocket. I pressed the lever over to its extreme position. The night came like the turning out of a lamp, and in another moment came to-mor-

---

1 From this description, it is clear that Wells had a bicycle in mind as the model for the time machine.
2 The Time Traveller's housekeeper.

row. The laboratory grew faint and hazy, then fainter and ever fainter. To-morrow night came black, then day again, night again, day again, faster and faster still. An eddying murmur filled my ears, and a strange, dumb confusedness descended on my mind.

"I am afraid I cannot convey the peculiar sensations of time travelling. They are excessively unpleasant. There is a feeling exactly like that one has upon a switchback[1]—of a helpless headlong motion! I felt the same horrible anticipation, too, of an imminent smash. As I put on pace, night followed day like the flapping of a black wing. The dim suggestion of the laboratory seemed presently to fall away from me, and I saw the sun hopping swiftly across the sky, leaping it every minute, and every minute marking a day. I supposed the laboratory had been destroyed and I had come into the open air. I had a dim impression of scaffolding, but I was already going too fast to be conscious of any moving things. The slowest snail that ever crawled dashed by too fast for me. The twinkling succession of darkness and light was excessively painful to the eye. Then, in the intermittent darknesses, I saw the moon spinning swiftly through her quarters from new to full, and had a faint glimpse of the circling stars. Presently, as I went on, still gaining velocity, the palpitation of night and day merged into one continuous greyness; the sky took on a wonderful deepness of blue, a splendid luminous colour like that of early twilight; the jerking sun became a streak of fire, a brilliant arch, in space, the moon a fainter, fluctuating band; and I could see nothing of the stars, save now and then a brighter circle flickering in the blue.

"The landscape was misty and vague. I was still on the hill-side upon which this house now stands, and the shoulder rose above me grey and dim. I saw trees growing and changing like puffs of vapour, now brown, now green: they grew, spread, shivered, and passed away. I saw huge buildings rise up faint and fair, and pass like dreams. The whole surface of the earth seemed changed—melting and flowing under my eyes. The

---

1   A roller-coaster.

little hands upon the dials that registered my speed raced round faster and faster. Presently I noted that the sun-belt swayed up and down, from solstice to solstice,[1] in a minute or less, and that, consequently, my pace was over a year a minute; and minute by minute the white snow flashed across the world, and vanished, and was followed by the bright, brief green of spring.

"The unpleasant sensations of the start were less poignant now. They merged at last into a kind of hysterical exhilaration. I remarked, indeed, a clumsy swaying of the machine, for which I was unable to account. But my mind was too confused to attend to it, so with a kind of madness growing upon me, I flung myself into futurity. At first I scarce thought of stopping, scarce thought of anything but these new sensations. But presently a fresh series of impressions grew up in my mind—a certain curiosity and therewith a certain dread—until at last they took complete possession of me. What strange developments of humanity, what wonderful advances upon our rudimentary civilization, I thought, might not appear when I came to look nearly into the dim elusive world that raced and fluctuated before my eyes! I saw great and splendid architecture rising about me, more massive than any buildings of our own time, and yet, as it seemed, built of glimmer and mist. I saw a richer green flow up the hill-side, and remain there without any wintry intermission. Even through the veil of my confusion the earth seemed very fair. And so my mind came round to the business of stopping.

"The peculiar risk lay in the possibility of my finding some substance in the space which I, or the machine, occupied. So long as I travelled at a high velocity through time, this scarcely mattered: I was, so to speak, attenuated—was slipping like a vapour through the interstices of intervening substances! But to come to a stop involved the jamming of myself, molecule by

---

1 From an earthly perspective, the summer and winter solstices (in late June and late December respectively in the northern hemisphere) are the times when the sun in its yearly cycle reaches its highest and lowest points in the sky at noon. As the Time Traveller is moving fast through time while staying in the same place, he sees the sun's path (the ecliptic) as an oscillating bright belt in the sky. Each movement of this belt up and down lasts less than a minute, but represents the passage of more than a year of real time.

molecule, into whatever lay in my way: meant bringing my atoms into such intimate contact with those of the obstacle that a profound chemical reaction—possibly a far-reaching explosion—would result, and blow myself and my apparatus out of all possible dimensions—into the Unknown. This possibility had occurred to me again and again while I was making the machine; but then I had cheerfully accepted it as an unavoidable risk—one of the risks a man has got to take! Now the risk was inevitable, I no longer saw it in the same cheerful light. The fact is that, insensibly, the absolute strangeness of everything, the sickly jarring and swaying of the machine, above all, the feeling of prolonged falling, had absolutely upset my nerve. I told myself that I could never stop, and with a gust of petulance I resolved to stop forthwith. Like an impatient fool, I lugged over the lever, and incontinently the thing went reeling over, and I was flung headlong through the air.

"There was the sound of a clap of thunder in my ears. I may have been stunned for a moment. A pitiless hail was hissing round me, and I was sitting on soft turf in front of the overset machine. Everything still seemed grey, but presently I remarked that the confusion in my ears was gone. I looked round me. I was on what seemed to be a little lawn in a garden, surrounded by rhododendron bushes, and I noticed that their mauve and purple blossoms were dropping in a shower under the beating of the hailstones. The rebounding, dancing hail hung in a little cloud over the machine, and drove along the ground like smoke. In a moment I was wet to the skin. 'Fine hospitality,' said I, 'to a man who has travelled innumerable years to see you.'

"Presently I thought what a fool I was to get wet. I stood up and looked round me. A colossal figure, carved apparently in some white stone, loomed indistinctly beyond the rhododendrons through the hazy downpour. But all else of the world was invisible.

"My sensations would be hard to describe. As the columns of hail grew thinner, I saw the white figure more distinctly. It was very large, for a silver birch tree touched its shoulder. It was of white marble, in shape something like a winged sphinx,[1] but the wings, instead of being carried vertically at the sides, were spread so that it seemed to hover. The pedestal, it appeared to me, was of bronze, and was thick with verdigris.[2] It chanced that the face was towards me; the sightless eyes seemed to watch me; there was the faint shadow of a smile on the lips. It was greatly weather-worn, and that imparted an unpleasant suggestion of disease. I stood looking at it for a little space — half-a-minute, perhaps, or half-an-hour. It seemed to advance and to recede as the hail drove before it denser or thinner. At last I tore my eyes from it for a moment, and saw that the hail curtain had worn threadbare, and that the sky was lightening with the promise of the sun.

"I looked up again at the crouching white shape, and the full temerity of my voyage came suddenly upon me. What might appear when that hazy curtain was altogether withdrawn? What might not have happened to men? What if cruelty had grown into a common passion? What if in this interval the race had lost its manliness, and had developed into something inhuman, unsympathetic, and overwhelmingly powerful? I might seem some old-world savage animal, only the more dreadful and disgusting for our common likeness — a foul creature to be incontinently[3] slain.

"Already I saw other vast shapes — huge buildings with intricate parapets and tall columns, with a wooded hill-side dimly creeping in upon me through the lessening storm. I was seized with a panic fear. I turned frantically to the Time Machine, and strove hard to readjust it. As I did so the shafts of the sun smote through the thunder-storm. The grey downpour was swept aside and vanished like the trailing garments of a ghost. Above me, in the intense blue of the summer sky, some faint brown shreds of cloud whirled into nothingness. The great buildings about me stood out clear and distinct, shining with the wet of the thunderstorm, and picked out in white by

---

1   A fabulous creature with the head of a woman and the body of a winged lion. A picture of a recumbent winged sphinx adorned the front cover of the 1895 Heinemann edition of *The Time Machine*. For possible sources of the Sphinx motif, see Appendices B1, B9, C1, D1.

2   The green rust forming on copper, brass, or bronze.

3   Immediately; without hesitation.

the unmelted hailstones piled along their courses. I felt naked in a strange world. I felt as perhaps a bird may feel in the clear air, knowing the hawk wings above and will swoop. My fear grew to frenzy. I took a breathing space, set my teeth, and again grappled fiercely, wrist and knee, with the machine. It gave under my desperate onset and turned over. It struck my chin violently. One hand on the saddle, the other on the lever, I stood panting heavily in attitude to mount again.

"But with this recovery of a prompt retreat my courage recovered. I looked more curiously and less fearfully at this world of the remote future. In a circular opening, high up in the wall of the nearer house, I saw a group of figures clad in rich soft robes. They had seen me, and their faces were directed towards me.

"Then I heard voices approaching me. Coming through the bushes by the White Sphinx were the heads and shoulders of men running. One of these emerged in a pathway leading straight to the little lawn upon which I stood with my machine. He was a slight creature—perhaps four feet high— clad in a purple tunic, girdled at the waist with a leather belt. Sandals or buskins[1]—I could not clearly distinguish which— were on his feet; his legs were bare to the knees, and his head was bare. Noticing that, I noticed for the first time how warm the air was.

"He struck me as being a very beautiful and graceful creature, but indescribably frail. His flushed face reminded me of the more beautiful kind of consumptive—that hectic[2] beauty of which we used to hear so much. At the sight of him I suddenly regained confidence. I took my hands from the machine.

---

1 Sandals laced up the leg.
2 Someone suffering from consumption (tuberculosis of the lungs) will have a hectic complexion (feverish, fluctuating between redness and pallor).

V

IN THE GOLDEN AGE

"IN another moment we were standing face to face, I and this fragile thing out of futurity. He came straight up to me and laughed into my eyes. The absence from his bearing of any sign of fear struck me at once. Then he turned to the two others who were following him and spoke to them in a strange and very sweet and liquid tongue.

"There were others coming, and presently a little group of perhaps eight or ten of these exquisite creatures were about me. One of them addressed me. It came into my head, oddly enough, that my voice was too harsh and deep for them. So I shook my head, and pointing to my ears, shook it again. He came a step forward, hesitated, and then touched my hand. Then I felt other soft little tentacles upon my back and shoulders. They wanted to make sure I was real. There was nothing in this at all alarming. Indeed, there was something in these pretty little people that inspired confidence — a graceful gentleness, a certain childlike ease. And besides, they looked so frail that I could fancy myself flinging the whole dozen of them about like nine-pins. But I made a sudden motion to warn them when I saw their little pink hands feeling at the Time Machine. Happily then, when it was not too late, I thought of a danger I had hitherto forgotten, and reaching over the bars of the machine, I unscrewed the little levers that would set it in motion, and put these in my pocket. Then I turned again to see what I could do in the way of communication.

"And then, looking more nearly into their features, I saw some further peculiarities in their Dresden china[1] type of prettiness. Their hair, which was uniformly curly, came to a sharp end at the neck and cheek; there was not the faintest suggestion

---

1   Fine porcelain from Meissen, near Dresden in Germany; typical Dresden ware in the later nineteenth century were statuettes of coy Arcadian shepherdesses in rococo style.

of it on the face, and their ears were singularly minute. The mouths were small, with bright red, rather thin lips, and the little chins ran to a point. The eyes were large and mild; and—this may seem egotism on my part—I fancied even then that there was a certain lack of the interest I might have expected in them.

"As they made no effort to communicate with me, but simply stood round me smiling and speaking in soft cooing notes to each other, I began the conversation. I pointed to the Time Machine and to myself. Then, hesitating for a moment how to express Time, I pointed to the sun. At once a quaintly pretty little figure in chequered purple and white followed my gesture, and then astonished me by imitating the sound of thunder.

"For a moment I was staggered, though the import of his gesture was plain enough. The question had come into my mind abruptly: were these creatures fools? You may hardly understand how it took me. You see I had always anticipated that the people of the year Eight Hundred and Two Thousand odd[1] would be incredibly in front of us in knowledge, art, everything. Then one of them suddenly asked me a question that showed him to be on the intellectual level of one of our five-year-old children—asked me, in fact, if I had come from the sun in a thunderstorm! It let loose the judgment I had suspended upon their clothes, their frail light limbs and fragile features. A flow of disappointment rushed across my mind. For a moment I felt that I had built the Time Machine in vain.

"I nodded, pointed to the sun, and gave them such a vivid rendering of a thunderclap as startled them. They all withdrew a pace or so and bowed. Then came one laughing towards me, carrying a chain of beautiful flowers altogether new to me, and put it about my neck. The idea was received with melodious applause; and presently they were all running to and fro for flowers, and laughingly flinging them upon me until I was almost smothered with blossom. You who have never seen the like can scarcely imagine what delicate and wonderful flowers

---

1   See p. 87, n. 2.

countless years of culture had created. Then some one suggested that their plaything should be exhibited in the nearest building, and so I was led past the sphinx of white marble, which had seemed to watch me all the while with a smile at my astonishment, towards a vast grey edifice of fretted[1] stone. As I went with them the memory of my confident anticipations of a profoundly grave and intellectual posterity came, with irresistible merriment, to my mind.

"The building had a huge entry, and was altogether of colossal dimensions. I was naturally most occupied with the growing crowd of little people, and with the big open portals that yawned before me shadowy and mysterious. My general impression of the world I saw over their heads was of a tangled waste of beautiful bushes and flowers, a long-neglected and yet weedless garden. I saw a number of tall spikes of strange white flowers, measuring a foot perhaps across the spread of the waxen petals. They grew scattered, as if wild, among the variegated shrubs, but, as I say, I did not examine them closely at this time. The Time Machine was left deserted on the turf among the rhododendrons.

"The arch of the doorway was richly carved, but naturally I did not observe the carving very narrowly, though I fancied I saw suggestions of old Phœnician[2] decorations as I passed through, and it struck me that they were very badly broken and weather-worn. Several more brightly-clad people met me in the doorway, and so we entered, I, dressed in dingy nineteenth-century garments, looking grotesque enough, garlanded with flowers, and surrounded by an eddying mass of bright, soft-coloured robes and shining white limbs, in a melodious whirl of laughter and laughing speech.

"The big doorway opened into a proportionately great hall hung with brown. The roof was in shadow, and the windows, partially glazed with coloured glass and partially unglazed,

---

1   Either "decorated with carved patterns," or "worn into holes." The ambiguity may deliberately convey the Time Traveller's uncertainty about the status of the civilization he has arrived at.

2   Ancient Semitic people of the Middle East, known in particular for their invention of the alphabet. The Time Traveller, expecting cultural advancement, is instead everywhere reminded of the long-gone glories of the past.

admitted a tempered light. The floor was made up of huge blocks of some very hard white metal, not plates nor slabs — blocks, and it was so much worn, as I judged by the going to and fro of past generations, as to be deeply channelled along the more frequented ways. Transverse to the length were innumerable tables made of slabs of polished stone, raised, perhaps, a foot from the floor, and upon these were heaps of fruits. Some I recognized as a kind of hypertrophied[1] raspberry and orange, but for the most part they were strange.

"Between the tables was scattered a great number of cushions. Upon these my conductors seated themselves, signing for me to do likewise. With a pretty absence of ceremony they began to eat the fruit with their hands, flinging peel and stalks, and so forth, into the round openings in the sides of the tables. I was not loth to follow their example, for I felt thirsty and hungry. As I did so I surveyed the hall at my leisure.

"And perhaps the thing that struck me most was its dilapidated look. The stained-glass windows, which displayed only a geometrical pattern, were broken in many places, and the curtains that hung across the lower end were thick with dust. And it caught my eye that the corner of the marble table near me was fractured. Nevertheless, the general effect was extremely rich and picturesque. There were, perhaps, a couple of hundred people dining in the hall, and most of them, seated as near to me as they could come, were watching me with interest, their little eyes shining over the fruit they were eating. All were clad in the same soft, and yet strong, silky material.

"Fruit, by the bye, was all their diet. These people of the remote future were strict vegetarians, and while I was with them, in spite of some carnal cravings, I had to be frugivorous[2] also. Indeed, I found afterwards that horses, cattle, sheep, dogs, had followed the Ichthyosaurus[3] into extinction. But the fruits were very delightful; one, in particular, that seemed to be in

---

1   Overgrown as a result of excessive nutrition (or in this case long cultivation).
2   Feeding (usually exclusively) on fruit.
3   An extinct porpoise-like marine reptile of the Mesozoic era (approx. 245-66.4 million years ago). The discovery of an ichthyosaurus fossil by a 12-year-old English girl in 1811 gave an important impetus to evolutionary theory.

season all the time I was there—a floury thing in a three-sided husk—was especially good, and I made it my staple. At first I was puzzled by all these strange fruits, and by the strange flowers I saw, but later I began to perceive their import.

"However, I am telling you of my fruit dinner in the distant future now. So soon as my appetite was a little checked, I determined to make a resolute attempt to learn the speech of these new men of mine. Clearly that was the next thing to do. The fruits seemed a convenient thing to begin upon, and holding one of these up I began a series of interrogative sounds and gestures. I had some considerable difficulty in conveying my meaning. At first my efforts met with a stare of surprise or inextinguishable laughter, but presently a fair-haired little creature seemed to grasp my intention and repeated a name. They had to chatter and explain their business at great length to each other, and my first attempts to make their exquisite little sounds of the language caused an immense amount of genuine, if uncivil, amusement. However, I felt like a school-master amidst children, and persisted, and presently I had a score of noun substantives at least at my command; and then I got to demonstrative pronouns, and even the verb 'to eat.' But it was slow work, and the little people soon tired and wanted to get away from my interrogations, so I determined, rather of necessity, to let them give their lessons in little doses when they felt inclined. And very little doses I found they were before long, for I never met people more indolent or more easily fatigued.

VI

THE SUNSET OF MANKIND

"A QUEER thing I soon discovered about my little hosts, and that was their lack of interest. They would come to me with eager cries of astonishment, like children, but, like children, they would soon stop examining me, and wander away after some other toy. The dinner and my conversational beginnings ended, I noted for the first time that almost all those who had surrounded me at first were gone. It is odd, too, how speedily I came to disregard these little people. I went out through the portal into the sunlit world again so soon as my hunger was satisfied. I was continually meeting more of these men of the future, who would follow me a little distance, chatter and laugh about me, and, having smiled and gesticulated in a friendly way, leave me again to my own devices.

"The calm of evening was upon the world as I emerged from the great hall, and the scene was lit by the warm glow of the setting sun. At first things were very confusing. Everything was so entirely different from the world I had known—even the flowers. The big building I had left was situate on the slope of a broad river valley, but the Thames had shifted, perhaps, a mile from its present position.[1] I resolved to mount to the summit of a crest, perhaps a mile and a half away, from which I could get a wider view of this our planet in the year Eight Hundred and Two Thousand Seven Hundred and One, A.D.[2] For that, I should explain, was the date the little dials of my machine recorded.

"As I walked I was watchful for every impression that could possibly help to explain the condition of ruinous splendour in which I found the world—for ruinous it was. A little way up the hill, for instance, was a great heap of granite, bound to–

---

1 I.e., a mile distant from where Richmond used to be.
2 Several commentators have noted that the date, when presented as two sequences—802 and 701—forms a descending numerical series that suggests a kind of temporal running-down. See also p. 123, n. 3.

gether by masses of aluminium, a vast labyrinth of precipitous walls and crumbled heaps, amidst which were thick heaps of very beautiful pagoda-like plants—nettles possibly—but wonderfully tinted with brown about the leaves, and incapable of stinging. It was evidently the derelict remains of some vast structure, to what end built I could not determine. It was here that I was destined, at a later date, to have a very strange experience—the first intimation of a still stranger discovery—but of that I will speak in its proper place.

"Looking round, with a sudden thought, from a terrace on which I rested for awhile, I realized that there were no small houses to be seen. Apparently, the single house, and possibly even the household, had vanished. Here and there among the greenery were palace-like buildings, but the house and the cottage, which form such characteristic features of our own English landscape, had disappeared.

"'Communism,'[1] said I to myself.

"And on the heels of that came another thought. I looked at the half-dozen little figures that were following me. Then, in a flash, I perceived that all had the same form of costume, the same soft hairless visage, and the same girlish rotundity of limb. It may seem strange, perhaps, that I had not noticed this before. But everything was so strange. Now, I saw the fact plainly enough. In costume, and in all the differences of texture and bearing that now mark off the sexes from each other, these people of the future were alike. And the children seemed to my eyes to be but the miniatures of their parents. I judged then that the children of that time were extremely precocious, physically at least, and I found afterwards abundant verification of my opinion.

"Seeing the ease and security in which these people were living, I felt that this close resemblance of the sexes was after all what one would expect; for the strength of a man and the softness of a woman, the institution of the family, and the differentiation of occupations are mere militant necessities of an age of

---

1   The Time Traveller's preconceptions are almost certainly being governed by the description of the deindustrialized London under pure communism of William Morris's *News from Nowhere*. See Appendix B11.

physical force. Where population is balanced and abundant, much child-bearing becomes an evil rather than a blessing to the State: where violence comes but rarely and offspring are secure, there is less necessity—indeed there is no necessity—of an efficient family, and the specialization of the sexes with reference to their children's needs disappears. We see some beginnings of this even in our own time, and in this future age it was complete.[1] This, I must remind you, was my speculation at the time. Later, I was to appreciate how far it fell short of the reality.

"While I was musing upon these things, my attention was attracted by a pretty little structure, like a well under a cupola. I thought in a transitory way of the oddness of wells[2] still existing, and then resumed the thread of my speculations. There were no large buildings towards the top of the hill, and as my walking powers were evidently miraculous, I was presently left alone for the first time. With a strange sense of freedom and adventure I pushed on up to the crest.

"There I found a seat of some yellow metal that I did not recognize, corroded in places with a kind of pinkish rust and half-smothered in soft moss, the arm-rests cast and filed into the resemblance of griffins'[3] heads. I sat down on it, and I surveyed the broad view of our old world under the sunset of that long day. It was as sweet and fair a view as I have ever seen. The sun had already gone below the horizon and the west was flaming gold, touched with some horizontal bars of purple and crimson. Below was the valley of the Thames, in which the river lay like a band of burnished steel. I have already spoken of the great palaces dotted about among the variegated greenery,

---

1 An extrapolation from Darwin's ideas in Part III, Chapter XX of *The Descent of Man* (1871, 1874) on how natural and sexual selection have combined to produce sexual dimorphism in the human species. The Time Traveller suggests that once the population pressures intensifying selection have been removed, the human species will start to approach homomorphism. Both W. H. Hudson and Walter Besant in their respective utopian romances *A Crystal Age* (1887) and *The Inner House* (1888) had made similar extrapolations.

2 As this is the first of eight occurrences of this word in the text of *The Time Machine*, one suspects that Wells was deliberately punning on his own name.

3 Fabulous animals with the heads and wings of eagles, the bodies of lions. Cf. p. 80, n. 1.

some in ruins and some still occupied. Here and there rose a white or silvery figure in the waste garden of the earth, here and there came the sharp vertical line of some cupola or obelisk. There were no hedges, no signs of proprietary rights, no evidences of agriculture; the whole earth had become a garden.

"So watching, I began to put my interpretation upon the things I had seen, and as it shaped itself to me that evening, my interpretation was something in this way. (Afterwards I found I had got only a half truth—or only a glimpse of one facet of the truth):

"It seemed to me that I had happened upon humanity upon the wane. The ruddy sunset set me thinking of the sunset of mankind. For the first time I began to realize an odd consequence of the social effort in which we are at present engaged. And yet, come to think, it is a logical consequence enough. Strength is the outcome of need: security sets a premium on feebleness. The work of ameliorating the conditions of life— the true civilizing process that makes life more and more secure—had gone steadily on to a climax. One triumph of a united humanity over Nature had followed another. Things that are now mere dreams had become projects deliberately put in hand and carried forward. And the harvest was what I saw!

"After all, the sanitation and the agriculture of to-day are still in the rudimentary stage. The science of our time has attacked but a little department of the field of human disease, but, even so, it spreads its operations very steadily and persistently. Our agriculture and horticulture destroy a weed just here and there and cultivate perhaps a score or so of wholesome plants, leaving the greater number to fight out a balance as they can. We improve our favourite plants and animals—and how few they are—gradually by selective breeding; now a new and better peach, now a seedless grape, now a sweeter and larger flower, now a more convenient breed of cattle. We improve them gradually, because our ideals are vague and tentative, and our knowledge is very limited; because Nature, too, is shy and slow in our clumsy hands. Some day all this will be better organized, and still better. That is the drift of the current in spite of the eddies. The whole world will be intelligent, educated, and co-operating; things will move faster and faster towards the subjugation of Nature. In the end, wisely and carefully we shall readjust the balance of animal and vegetable life to suit our human needs.

"This adjustment, I say, must have been done, and done well: done indeed for all time, in the space of Time across which my machine had leapt. The air was free from gnats, the earth from weeds or fungi; everywhere were fruits and sweet and delightful flowers; brilliant butterflies flew hither and thither. The ideal of preventive medicine was attained. Diseases had been stamped out. I saw no evidence of any contagious diseases during all my stay. And I shall have to tell you later that even the processes of putrefaction and decay had been profoundly affected by these changes.[1]

"Social triumphs, too, had been effected. I saw mankind housed in splendid shelters, gloriously clothed, and as yet I had found them engaged in no toil. There were no signs of struggle, neither social nor economical struggle. The shop, the advertisement, traffic, all that commerce which constitutes the body of our world, was gone. It was natural on that golden evening that I should jump at the idea of a social paradise. The difficulty of increasing population had been met, I guessed, and population had ceased to increase.

"But with this change in condition comes inevitably adaptations to the change. What, unless biological science is a mass of errors, is the cause of human intelligence and vigour? Hardship and freedom: conditions under which the active, strong, and subtle survive and the weaker go to the wall; conditions that put a premium upon the loyal alliance of capable men, upon self-restraint, patience, and decision. And the institution of the family, and the emotions that arise therein, the fierce jealousy, the tenderness for offspring, parental self-devotion, all found their justification and support in the imminent dangers of the young. *Now*, where are these imminent dangers? There is a sentiment arising, and it will grow, against connubial jealousy,

1 See Chapter XI, p. 128.

against fierce maternity, against passion of all sorts; unnecessary things now, and things that make us uncomfortable, savage survivals, discords in a refined and pleasant life.

"I thought of the physical slightness of the people, their lack of intelligence, and those big abundant ruins, and it strengthened my belief in a perfect conquest of Nature. For after the battle comes Quiet. Humanity had been strong, energetic, and intelligent, and had used all its abundant vitality to alter the conditions under which it lived. And now came the reaction of the altered conditions.

"Under the new conditions of perfect comfort and security, that restless energy, that with us is strength, would become weakness. Even in our own time certain tendencies and desires, once necessary to survival, are a constant source of failure. Physical courage and the love of battle, for instance, are no great help—may even be hindrances—to a civilized man. And in a state of physical balance and security, power, intellectual as well as physical, would be out of place. For countless years I judged there had been no danger of war or solitary violence, no danger from wild beasts, no wasting disease to require strength of constitution, no need of toil. For such a life, what we should call the weak are as well equipped as the strong, are indeed no longer weak.[1] Better equipped indeed they are, for the strong would be fretted by an energy for which there was no outlet. No doubt the exquisite beauty of the buildings I saw was the outcome of the last surgings of the now purposeless energy of mankind before it settled down into perfect harmony with the conditions under which it lived—the flourish of that triumph which began the last great peace. This has ever been the fate of energy in security; it takes to art and to eroticism, and then come languor and decay.[2]

"Even this artistic impetus would at last die away—had almost died in the Time I saw. To adorn themselves with flowers, to dance, to sing in the sunlight; so much was left of the artistic spirit, and no more. Even that would fade in the end into a contented inactivity. We are kept keen on the grindstone

---

1   See Appendix A6.
2   See Appendix C4.

of pain and necessity, and, it seemed to me, that here was that hateful grindstone broken at last!

"As I stood there in the gathering dark I thought that in this simple explanation I had mastered the problem of the world— mastered the whole secret of these delicious people. Possibly the checks they had devised for the increase of population had succeeded too well, and their numbers had rather diminished than kept stationary. That would account for the abandoned ruins. Very simple was my explanation, and plausible enough— as most wrong theories are!

VII

A SUDDEN SHOCK

"As I stood there musing over this too perfect triumph of man, the full moon, yellow and gibbous,[1] came up out of an overflow of silver light in the north-east. The bright little figures ceased to move about below, a noiseless owl flitted by, and I shivered with the chill of the night. I determined to descend and find where I could sleep.

"I looked for the building I knew. Then my eye travelled along to the figure of the White Sphinx upon the pedestal of bronze, growing distinct as the light of the rising moon grew brighter. I could see the silver birch against it. There was the tangle of rhododendron bushes, black in the pale light, and there was the little lawn. I looked at the lawn again. A queer doubt chilled my complacency. 'No,' said I stoutly to myself, 'that was not the lawn.'

"But it *was* the lawn. For the white leprous[2] face of the sphinx was towards it. Can you imagine what I felt as this conviction came home to me? But you cannot. The Time Machine was gone!

"At once, like a lash across the face, came the possibility of losing my own age, of being left helpless in this strange new world. The bare thought of it was an actual physical sensation. I could feel it grip me at the throat and stop my breathing. In another moment I was in a passion of fear, and running with great leaping strides down the slope. Once I fell headlong and cut my face; I lost no time in stanching the blood, but jumped up and ran on, with a warm trickle down my cheek and chin. All the time I ran I was saying to myself, 'They have moved it a little, pushed it under the bushes out of the way.' Nevertheless, I ran with all my might. All the time, with the certainty that

---

1   Rounded, humped; when used of the moon, it usually means that phase between a
    half-moon and a full moon.
2   Covered with white scales as though afflicted with leprosy.

sometimes comes with excessive dread, I knew that such assurance was folly, knew instinctively that the machine was removed out of my reach. My breath came with pain. I suppose I covered the whole distance from the hill crest to the little lawn, two miles, perhaps, in ten minutes. And I am not a young man. I cursed aloud, as I ran, at my confident folly in leaving the machine, wasting good breath thereby. I cried aloud, and none answered. Not a creature seemed to be stirring in that moonlit world.

"When I reached the lawn my worst fears were realized. Not a trace of the thing was to be seen. I felt faint and cold when I faced the empty space, among the black tangle of bushes. I ran round it furiously, as if the thing might be hidden in a corner, and then stopped abruptly, with my hands clutching my hair. Above me towered the sphinx, upon the bronze pedestal, white, shining, leprous, in the light of the rising moon. It seemed to smile in mockery of my dismay.

"I might have consoled myself by imagining the little people had put the mechanism in some shelter for me, had I not felt assured of their physical and intellectual inadequacy. That is what dismayed me: the sense of some hitherto unsuspected power, through whose intervention my invention had vanished. Yet, of one thing I felt assured: unless some other age had produced its exact duplicate, the machine could not have moved in time. The attachment of the levers—I will show you the method later—prevented any one from tampering with it in that way when they were removed. It had moved, and was hid, only in space. But then, where could it be?

"I think I must have had a kind of frenzy. I remember running violently in and out among the moonlit bushes all round the sphinx, and startling some white animal that, in the dim light, I took for a small deer. I remember, too, late that night, beating the bushes with my clenched fists until my knuckles were gashed and bleeding from the broken twigs. Then, sobbing and raving in my anguish of mind, I went down to the great building of stone. The big hall was dark, silent, and deserted. I slipped on the uneven floor, and fell over one of the malachite[1] tables, almost breaking my shin. I lit a match and went on past the dusty curtains, of which I have told you.

"There I found a second great hall covered with cushions, upon which, perhaps, a score or so of the little people were sleeping. I have no doubt they found my second appearance strange enough, coming suddenly out of the quiet darkness with inarticulate noises and the splutter and flare of a match. For they had forgotten about matches. 'Where is my Time Machine?' I began, bawling like an angry child, laying hands upon them and shaking them up together. It must have been very queer to them. Some laughed, most of them looked sorely frightened. When I saw them standing round me, it came into my head that I was doing as foolish a thing as it was possible for me to do under the circumstances, in trying to revive the sensation of fear. For, reasoning from their daylight behaviour, I thought that fear must be forgotten.

"Abruptly, I dashed down the match, and knocking one of the people over in my course, went blundering across the big dining-hall again, out under the moonlight. I heard cries of terror and their little feet running and stumbling this way and that. I do not remember all I did as the moon crept up the sky. I suppose it was the unexpected nature of my loss that maddened me. I felt hopelessly cut off from my own kind—a strange animal in an unknown world. I must have raved to and fro, screaming and crying upon God and Fate. I have a memory of horrible fatigue, as the long night of despair wore away; of looking in this impossible place and that; of groping among moonlit ruins and touching strange creatures in the black shadows; at last, of lying on the ground near the sphinx, and weeping with absolute wretchedness, even anger at the folly of leaving the machine having leaked away with my strength. I had nothing left but misery. Then I slept, and when I woke again it was full day, and a couple of sparrows were hopping round me on the turf within reach of my arm.

"I sat up in the freshness of the morning, trying to remember how I had got there, and why I had such a profound sense

---

1   Copper carbonate, a green mineral capable of being highly polished.

of desertion and despair. Then things came clear in my mind. With the plain, reasonable daylight, I could look my circumstances fairly in the face. I saw the wild folly of my frenzy overnight, and I could reason with myself. Suppose the worst? I said. Suppose the machine altogether lost—perhaps destroyed? It behoves me to be calm and patient, to learn the way of the people, to get a clear idea of the method of my loss, and the means of getting materials and tools; so that in the end, perhaps, I may make another. That would be my only hope, a poor hope, perhaps, but better than despair. And, after all, it was a beautiful and curious world.

"But probably the machine had only been taken away. Still, I must be calm and patient, find its hiding-place, and recover it by force or cunning. And with that I scrambled to my feet and looked about me, wondering where I could bathe. I felt weary, stiff, and travel-soiled. The freshness of the morning made me desire an equal freshness. I had exhausted my emotion. Indeed, as I went about my business, I found myself wondering at my intense excitement overnight. I made a careful examination of the ground about the little lawn. I wasted some time in futile questionings, conveyed, as well as I was able, to such of the little people as came by. They all failed to understand my gestures: some were simply stolid; some thought it was a jest, and laughed at me. I had the hardest task in the world to keep my hands off their pretty laughing faces. It was a foolish impulse, but the devil begotten of fear and blind anger was ill curbed, and still eager to take advantage of my perplexity. The turf gave better counsel. I found a groove ripped in it, about midway between the pedestal of the sphinx and the marks of my feet where, on arrival, I had struggled with the overturned machine. There were other signs of removal about, with queer narrow footprints like those I could imagine made by a sloth. This directed my closer attention to the pedestal. It was, as I think I have said, of bronze. It was not a mere block, but highly decorated with deep framed panels on either side. I went and rapped at these. The pedestal was hollow. Examining the panels with care I found them discontinuous with the frames. There were no handles or keyholes, but possibly the panels, if they were doors as I supposed, opened from within. One thing was clear enough to my mind. It took no very great mental effort to infer that my Time Machine was inside that pedestal. But how it got there was a different problem.

"I saw the heads of two orange-clad people coming through the bushes and under some blossom-covered apple-trees towards me. I turned smiling to them, and beckoned them to me. They came, and then, pointing to the bronze pedestal, I tried to intimate my wish to open it. But at my first gesture towards this they behaved very oddly. I don't know how to convey their expression to you. Suppose you were to use a grossly improper gesture to a delicate-minded woman — it is how she would look. They went off as if they had received the last possible insult. I tried a sweet-looking little chap in white next, with exactly the same result. Somehow, his manner made me feel ashamed of myself. But, as you know, I wanted the Time Machine, and I tried him once more. As he turned off, like the others, my temper got the better of me. In three strides I was after him, had him by the loose part of his robe round the neck, and began dragging him towards the sphinx. Then I saw the horror and repugnance of his face, and all of a sudden I let him go.

"But I was not beaten yet. I banged with my fist at the bronze panels. I thought I heard something stir inside — to be explicit, I thought I heard a sound like a chuckle — but I must have been mistaken. Then I got a big pebble from the river, and came and hammered till I had flattened a coil in the decorations, and the verdigris came off in powdery flakes. The delicate little people must have heard me hammering in gusty outbreaks a mile away on either hand, but nothing came of it. I saw a crowd of them upon the slopes, looking furtively at me. At last, hot and tired, I sat down to watch the place. But I was too restless to watch long; I am too Occidental[1] for a long vigil. I could work at a problem for years, but to wait inactive for twenty-four hours — that is another matter.

"I got up after a time, and began walking aimlessly through

---

1 Too much the product of Western culture.

the bushes towards the hill again. 'Patience,' said I to myself. 'If you want your machine again you must leave that sphinx alone. If they mean to take your machine away, it's little good your wrecking their bronze panels, and if they don't, you will get it back as soon as you can ask for it. To sit among all those unknown things before a puzzle like that is hopeless. That way lies monomania.[1] Face this world. Learn its ways, watch it, be careful of too hasty guesses at its meaning. In the end you will find clues to it all.' Then suddenly the humour of the situation came into my mind: the thought of the years I had spent in study and toil to get into the future age, and now my passion of anxiety to get out of it. I had made myself the most complicated and the most hopeless trap that ever a man devised. Although it was at my own expense, I could not help myself. I laughed aloud.

"Going through the big palace, it seemed to me that the little people avoided me. It may have been my fancy, or it may have had something to do with my hammering at the gates of bronze. Yet I felt tolerably sure of the avoidance. I was careful, however, to show no concern, and to abstain from any pursuit of them, and in the course of a day or two things got back to the old footing. I made what progress I could in the language, and, in addition, I pushed my explorations here and there. Either I missed some subtle point, or their language was excessively simple—almost exclusively composed of concrete substantives[2] and verbs. There seemed to be few, if any, abstract terms, or little use of figurative language. Their sentences were usually simple and of two words, and I failed to convey or understand any but the simplest propositions. I determined to put the thought of my Time Machine, and the mystery of the bronze doors under the sphinx, as much as possible in a corner of memory, until my growing knowledge would lead me back to them in a natural way. Yet a certain feeling, you may understand, tethered me in a circle of a few miles round the point of my arrival.

---

1   Insanity deriving from an obsession with one idea.
2   Nouns.

VIII

EXPLANATION

"So far as I could see, all the world displayed the same exuberant richness as the Thames valley. From every hill I climbed I saw the same abundance of splendid buildings, endlessly varied in material and style; the same clustering thickets of evergreens, the same blossom-laden trees and tree ferns. Here and there water shone like silver, and beyond, the land rose into blue undulating hills, and so faded into the serenity of the sky. A peculiar feature, which presently attracted my attention, was the presence of certain circular wells, several, as it seemed to me, of a very great depth. One lay by the path up the hill, which I had followed during my first walk. Like the others, it was rimmed with bronze, curiously wrought, and protected by a little cupola from the rain. Sitting by the side of these wells, and peering down into the shafted darkness, I could see no gleam of water, nor could I start any reflection with a lighted match. But in all of them I heard a certain sound: a thud — thud — thud, like the beating of some big engine; and I discovered, from the flaring of my matches, that a steady current of air set down the shafts. Further, I threw a scrap of paper into the throat of one; and, instead of fluttering slowly down, it was at once sucked swiftly out of sight.

"After a time, too, I came to connect these wells with tall towers standing here and there upon the slopes; for above them there was often just such a flicker in the air as one sees on a hot day above a sun-scorched beach. Putting things together, I reached a strong suggestion of an extensive system of subterranean ventilation, whose true import it was difficult to imagine. I was at first inclined to associate it with the sanitary apparatus[1] of these people. It was an obvious conclusion, but it was absolutely wrong.

---

1   Euphemism for the sewage system.

"And here I must admit that I learned very little of drains and bells and modes of conveyance, and the like conveniences, during my time in this real future. In some of these visions of Utopias and coming times which I have read, there is a vast amount of detail about building, and social arrangements, and so forth.[1] But while such details are easy enough to obtain when the whole world is contained in one's imagination, they are altogether inaccessible to a real traveller amid such realities as I found here. Conceive the tale of London which a negro, fresh from Central Africa,[2] would take back to his tribe! What would he know of railway companies, of social movements, of telephone and telegraph wires, of the Parcels Delivery Company, and postal orders and the like? Yet we, at least, should be willing enough to explain these things to him! And even of what he knew, how much could he make his untravelled friend either apprehend or believe? Then, think how narrow the gap between a negro and a white man of our own times, and how wide the interval between myself and these of the Golden Age![3] I was sensible of much which was unseen, and which contributed to my comfort; but, save for a general impression of automatic organization, I fear I can convey very little of the difference to your mind.

"In the matter of sepulture,[4] for instance, I could see no signs of crematoria nor anything suggestive of tombs. But it occurred to me that, possibly, there might be cemeteries (or crematoria) somewhere beyond the range of my explorings. This, again, was a question I deliberately put to myself, and my

---

1   Utopias are descriptions of imaginary ideal societies in the tradition of the *Republic* (c. 380 B.C.) of Plato and Sir Thomas More's *Utopia* (1516). For influential utopian visions set in the future that the Time Traveller (and Wells) might particularly have had in mind, see Appendices B9, B11.

2   The inhabitants of the upper Congo basin in central Africa were among the last peoples to come into contact with Western explorers and colonizers, thus in the mid-1890s likely to be very unfamiliar with Western technology. "Negro" was a standard term during this period for black African; the Time Traveller's ethnocentrism in this paragraph was mild for his time.

3   "The Golden Age" is a phrase used to refer to a (usually imaginary) time when life was or will be idyllic compared to the present. The Time Traveller's use of this phrase will reveal itself to be ironic.

4   Burial, from an anthropological perspective.

curiosity was at first entirely defeated upon the point. The thing puzzled me, and I was led to make a further remark, which puzzled me still more: that aged and infirm among this people there were none.

"I must confess that my satisfaction with my first theories of an automatic civilization and a decadent[1] humanity did not long endure. Yet I could think of no other. Let me put my difficulties. The several big palaces I had explored were mere living places, great dining-halls and sleeping apartments. I could find no machinery, no appliances of any kind. Yet these people were clothed in pleasant fabrics that must at times need renewal, and their sandals, though undecorated, were fairly complex specimens of metal-work. Somehow such things must be made. And the little people displayed no vestige of a creative tendency. There were no shops, no workshops, no sign of importations[2] among them. They spent all their time in playing gently, in bathing in the river, in making love in a half-playful fashion, in eating fruit and sleeping. I could not see how things were kept going.

"Then, again, about the Time Machine: something, I knew not what, had taken it into the hollow pedestal of the White Sphinx. *Why?* For the life of me I could not imagine. Those waterless wells, too, those flickering pillars. I felt I lacked a clue. I felt—how shall I put it? Suppose you found an inscription, with sentences here and there in excellent plain English, and, interpolated therewith, others made up of words, of letters even, absolutely unknown to you? Well, on the third day of my visit, that was how the world of Eight Hundred and Two Thousand Seven Hundred and One presented itself to me!

"That day, too, I made a friend—of a sort. It happened that, as I was watching some of the little people bathing in a shallow, one of them was seized with cramp, and began drifting down stream. The main current ran rather swiftly, but not too strongly for even a moderate swimmer. It will give you an idea, therefore, of the strange deficiency in these creatures, when I tell you

---

1   In a state of cultural decline from former strength.
2   I.e., there is no sign of trading in imported goods that might explain the origin of their clothing.

that none made the slightest attempt to rescue the weakly-crying little thing which was drowning before their eyes. When I realized this, I hurriedly slipped off my clothes, and, wading in at a point lower down, I caught the poor mite, and drew her safe to land. A little rubbing of the limbs soon brought her round, and I had the satisfaction of seeing she was all right before I left her. I had got to such a low estimate of her kind that I did not expect any gratitude from her. In that, however, I was wrong.

"This happened in the morning. In the afternoon I met my little woman, as I believe it was, as I was returning towards my centre from an exploration: and she received me with cries of delight, and presented me with a big garland of flowers— evidently made for me and me alone. The thing took my imagination. Very possibly I had been feeling desolate. At any rate I did my best to display my appreciation of the gift. We were soon seated together in a little stone arbour, engaged in conversation, chiefly of smiles. The creature's friendliness affected me exactly as a child's might have done. We passed each other flowers, and she kissed my hands. I did the same to hers. Then I tried talk, and found that her name was Weena,[1] which, though I don't know what it meant, somehow seemed appropriate enough. That was the beginning of a queer friendship which lasted a week, and ended—as I will tell you!

"She was exactly like a child. She wanted to be with me always. She tried to follow me everywhere, and on my next journey out and about it went to my heart to tire her down, and leave her at last, exhausted and calling after me rather plaintively. But the problems of the world had to be mastered. I had not, I said to myself, come into the future to carry on a miniature flirtation. Yet her distress when I left her was very great, her expostulations at the parting were sometimes frantic, and I think, altogether, I had as much trouble as comfort from her devotion. Nevertheless she was, somehow, a very great

---

1   A name suggesting smallness, childishness (in British children's slang "teeny-weeny" means tiny), and weakness, possibly influenced by the name of the character Arowhena, the narrator's love-interest in Samuel Butler's satirical utopian romance *Erewhon* (1872).

comfort. I thought it was mere childish affection that made her cling to me. Until it was too late, I did not clearly know what I had inflicted upon her when I left her. Nor until it was too late did I clearly understand what she was to me. For, by merely seeming fond of me, and showing in her weak futile way that she cared for me, the little doll of a creature presently gave my return to the neighbourhood of the White Sphinx almost the feeling of coming home; and I would watch for her tiny figure of white and gold so soon as I came over the hill.

"It was from her, too, that I learnt that fear had not yet left the world. She was fearless enough in the daylight, and she had the oddest confidence in me; for once, in a foolish moment, I made threatening grimaces at her, and she simply laughed at them. But she dreaded the dark, dreaded shadows, dreaded black things. Darkness to her was the one thing dreadful. It was a singularly passionate emotion, and it set me thinking and observing. I discovered then, among other things, that these little people gathered into the great houses after dark, and slept in droves.[1] To enter upon them without a light was to put them into a tumult of apprehension. I never found one out of doors, or one sleeping alone within doors, after dark. Yet I was still such a blockhead that I missed the lesson of that fear, and, in spite of Weena's distress, I insisted upon sleeping away from these slumbering multitudes.

"It troubled her greatly, but in the end her odd affection for me triumphed, and for five of the nights of our acquaintance, including the last night of all, she slept with her head pillowed on my arm. But my story slips away from me as I speak of her. It must have been the night before her rescue that I was awakened about dawn. I had been restless, dreaming most disagreeably that I was drowned, and that sea-anemones were feeling over my face with their soft palps.[2] I woke with a start, and with an odd fancy that some greyish animal had just rushed out of the chamber. I tried to get to sleep again, but I felt restless and uncomfortable. It was that dim grey hour when things are

---

1   The literal meaning, "as a large group of cattle," has an ominous meaning in this context.
2   Feelers.

just creeping out of darkness, when everything is colourless and clear cut, and yet unreal. I got up, and went down into the great hall, and so out upon the flagstones in front of the palace. I thought I would make a virtue of necessity, and see the sunrise.

"The moon was setting, and the dying moonlight and the first pallor of dawn were mingled in a ghastly half-light. The bushes were inky black, the ground a sombre grey, the sky colourless and cheerless. And up the hill I thought I could see ghosts. Three several times, as I scanned the slope, I saw white figures. Twice I fancied I saw a solitary white, ape-like creature running rather quickly up the hill, and once near the ruins I saw a leash[1] of them carrying some dark body. They moved hastily. I did not see what became of them. It seemed that they vanished among the bushes. The dawn was still indistinct, you must understand. I was feeling that chill, uncertain, early-morning feeling you may have known. I doubted my eyes.

"As the eastern sky grew brighter, and the light of the day came on and its vivid colouring returned upon the world once more, I scanned the view keenly. But I saw no vestige of my white figures. They were mere creatures of the half-light. 'They must have been ghosts,' I said; 'I wonder whence they dated.' For a queer notion of Grant Allen's[2] came into my head, and amused me. If each generation die and leave ghosts, he argued, the world at last will get overcrowded with them. On that theory they would have grown innumerable some Eight Hundred Thousand Years hence, and it was no great wonder to see four at once. But the jest was unsatisfying, and I was thinking of these figures all the morning, until Weena's rescue drove

1   A group of three animals (usually hounds).
2   Canadian-born English naturalist and man of letters (1848-99) noted especially for his works popularizing the implications of Darwinian biology, as well as for his fiction, some of which anticipates the Wellsian scientific romance. The specific allusion by the Time Traveller is to Allen's story, "Pallinghurst Barrow" (1892), collected in *Ivan Greet's Masterpiece, etc* (1893), in which one of the characters, a materialist, notes that "millions of ghosts of remote antiquity must swarm about the world." This story, in which a writer, under the influence of cannabis, hallucinates that he travels back in time to remote antiquity and is attacked by subterranean cannibalistic savages, has several echoes in the Morlock episodes of *The Time Machine*.

them out of my head. I associated them in some indefinite way with the white animal I had startled in my first passionate search for the Time Machine. But Weena was a pleasant substitute. Yet all the same, they were soon destined to take far deadlier possession of my mind.

"I think I have said how much hotter than our own was the weather of this Golden Age. I cannot account for it. It may be that the sun was hotter, or the earth nearer the sun. It is usual to assume that the sun will go on cooling steadily in the future. But people, unfamiliar with such speculations as those of the younger Darwin,[1] forget that the planets must ultimately fall back one by one into the parent body. As these catastrophes occur, the sun will blaze with renewed energy; and it may be that some inner planet had suffered this fate. Whatever the reason, the fact remains that the sun was very much hotter than we know it.

"Well, one very hot morning—my fourth, I think—as I was seeking shelter from the heat and glare in a colossal ruin near the great house where I slept and fed, there happened this strange thing. Clambering among these heaps of masonry, I found a narrow gallery, whose end and side windows were blocked by fallen masses of stone. By contrast with the brilliancy outside, it seemed at first impenetrably dark to me. I entered it groping, for the change from light to blackness made spots of colour swim before me. Suddenly I halted spellbound. A pair of eyes, luminous by reflection against the daylight without, was watching me out of the darkness.

"The old instinctive dread of wild beasts came upon me. I clenched my hands and steadfastly looked into the glaring eyeballs. I was afraid to turn. Then the thought of the absolute security in which humanity appeared to be living came to my mind. And then I remembered that strange terror of the dark. Overcoming my fear to some extent, I advanced a step and spoke. I will admit that my voice was harsh and ill-controlled. I put out my hand and touched something soft. At once the eyes darted sideways, and something white ran past

---

1   Sir George Howard Darwin (1845-1912), mathematician and astronomer, second son of Charles Darwin and authority on tidal effects. See Appendices E5, E6.

me. I turned with my heart in my mouth, and saw a queer little ape-like figure, its head held down in a peculiar manner, running across the sunlit space behind me. It blundered against a block of granite, staggered aside, and in a moment was hidden in a black shadow beneath another pile of ruined masonry.

"My impression of it is, of course, imperfect; but I know it was a dull white, and had strange large greyish-red eyes; also that there was flaxen hair on its head and down its back. But, as I say, it went too fast for me to see distinctly. I cannot even say whether it ran on all fours, or only with its forearms held very low. After an instant's pause I followed it into the second heap of ruins. I could not find it at first; but, after a time in the profound obscurity, I came upon one of those round well-like openings of which I have told you, half closed by a fallen pillar. A sudden thought came to me. Could this Thing have vanished down the shaft? I lit a match, and, looking down, I saw a small, white moving creature, with large bright eyes which regarded me steadfastly as it retreated. It made me shudder. It was so like a human spider! It was clambering down the wall, and now I saw for the first time a number of metal foot- and hand-rests forming a kind of ladder down the shaft. Then the light burned my fingers and fell out of my hand, going out as it dropped, and when I had lit another the little monster had disappeared.

"I do not know how long I sat peering down that well. It was not for some time that I could succeed in persuading myself that the thing I had seen was human. But, gradually, the truth dawned on me: that Man had not remained one species, but had differentiated into two distinct animals: that my graceful children of the Upper World were not the sole descendants of our generation, but that this bleached, obscene, nocturnal Thing, which had flashed before me, was also heir to all the ages.[1]

"I thought of the flickering pillars and of my theory of an underground ventilation. I began to suspect their true import.

---

[1] An allusion to Tennyson's "Locksley Hall" (1835), line 178, from a passage in which the speaker counterposes progress and reversion to bestiality.

And what, I wondered, was this Lemur[1] doing in my scheme of a perfectly balanced organization? How was it related to the indolent serenity of the beautiful Overworlders? And what was hidden down there, at the foot of that shaft? I sat upon the edge of the well telling myself that, at any rate, there was nothing to fear, and that there I must descend for the solution of my difficulties. And withal[2] I was absolutely afraid to go! As I hesitated, two of the beautiful upperworld people came running in their amorous sport across the daylight into the shadow. The male pursued the female, flinging flowers at her as he ran.

"They seemed distressed to find me, my arm against the overturned pillar, peering down the well. Apparently it was considered bad form to remark these apertures; for when I pointed to this one, and tried to frame a question about it in their tongue, they were still more visibly distressed and turned away. But they were interested by my matches, and I struck some to amuse them. I tried them again about the well, and again I failed. So presently I left them, meaning to go back to Weena, and see what I could get from her. But my mind was already in revolution; my guesses and impressions were slipping and sliding to a new adjustment. I had now a clue to the import of these wells, to the ventilating towers, to the mystery of the ghosts: to say nothing of a hint at the meaning of the bronze gates and the fate of the Time Machine! And very vaguely there came a suggestion towards the solution of the economic problem that had puzzled me.

"Here was the new view. Plainly, this second species of Man was subterranean. There were three circumstances in particular which made me think that its rare emergence above ground was the outcome of a long-continued underground habit. In the first place, there was the bleached look common in most animals that live largely in the dark—the white fish of the Kentucky caves,[3] for instance. Then, those large eyes, with that

---

1   Appropriately, a Lemur is both a spirit of the dead in Roman mythology, and (with a lower-case l) a nocturnal mammal that Darwin, in *The Descent of Man* (Part I Chapter VI) identified as representing the lowest order of man's primate relatives.

2   Yet, nevertheless.

3   The blindness (rather than the whiteness) of these fish in what is now known as Mammoth Cave National Park was used by Darwin in *The Origin of Species* (Chap-

capacity for reflecting light, are common features of nocturnal things—witness the owl and the cat. And last of all, that evident confusion in the sunshine, that hasty yet fumbling and awkward flight towards dark shadow, and that peculiar carriage of the head while in the light—all reinforced the theory of an extreme sensitiveness of the retina.

"Beneath my feet then the earth must be tunnelled enormously, and these tunnellings were the habitat of the New Race. The presence of ventilating-shafts and wells along the hill slopes—everywhere, in fact, except along the river valley—showed how universal were its ramifications. What so natural, then, as to assume that it was in this artificial Underworld that such work as was necessary to the comfort of the daylight race was done? The notion was so plausible that I at once accepted it, and went on to assume the *how* of this splitting of the human species. I dare say you will anticipate the shape of my theory, though, for myself, I very soon felt that it fell far short of the truth.

"At first, proceeding from the problems of our own age, it seemed clear as daylight to me that the gradual widening of the present merely temporary and social difference between the Capitalist and the Labourer, was the key to the whole position. No doubt it will seem grotesque enough to you—and wildly incredible!—and yet even now there are existing circumstances to point that way. There is a tendency to utilize underground space for the less ornamental purposes of civilization; there is the Metropolitan Railway in London, for instance, there are new electric railways, there are subways,[1] there are underground workrooms and restaurants, and they increase and multiply. Evidently, I thought, this tendency had increased till Industry had gradually lost its birthright in the sky. I mean that

ter V) as evidence of the adaptation of species to their environment. See also Appendix B7.

1 The Metropolitan Railway, using steam trains, was the world's first underground railway, opening in London in January 1863. The first stretch of underground electric "tube" railway was opened in London in 1890. (Both have long been incorporated into the modern Underground system.) A subway in British usage is not a railway but an underground passage for pedestrians, such as the tunnel (1843) under the Thames at Greenwich.

it had gone deeper and deeper into larger and ever larger underground factories, spending a still-increasing amount of its time therein, till, in the end—! Even now, does not an East-end[1] worker live in such artificial conditions as practically to be cut off from the natural surface of the earth?

"Again, the exclusive tendency of richer people—due, no doubt, to the increasing refinement of their education, and the widening gulf between them and the rude violence of the poor—is already leading to the closing, in their interest, of considerable portions of the surface of the land. About London, for instance, perhaps half the prettier country is shut in against intrusion. And this same widening gulf—which is due to the length and expense of the higher educational process and the increased facilities for and temptations towards refined habits on the part of the rich—will make that exchange between class and class, that promotion by intermarriage which at present retards the splitting of our species along lines of social stratification, less and less frequent. So, in the end, above ground you must have the Haves, pursuing pleasure and comfort and beauty, and below ground the Have-nots; the Workers getting continually adapted to the conditions of their labour. Once they were there, they would, no doubt, have to pay rent, and not a little of it, for the ventilation of their caverns; and if they refused, they would starve or be suffocated for arrears. Such of them as were so constituted as to be miserable and rebellious would die; and, in the end, the balance being permanent, the survivors would become as well adapted to the conditions of underground life, and as happy in their way, as the Overworld people were to theirs. As it seemed to me, the refined beauty and the etiolated pallor[2] followed naturally enough.

"The great triumph of Humanity I had dreamed of took a different shape in my mind. It had been no such triumph of moral education and general co-operation as I had imagined. Instead, I saw a real aristocracy, armed with a perfected science

---

1   The East End of London (in contrast to the affluent West End) was proverbial for the overcrowded poverty and squalor in which its working-class population lived.
2   As a green plant whitened by lack of sunlight.

and working to a logical conclusion the industrial system of to-day. Its triumph had not been simply a triumph over nature, but a triumph over nature and the fellow-man. This, I must warn you, was my theory at the time. I had no convenient cicerone in the pattern of the Utopian books.[1] My explanation may be absolutely wrong. I still think it is the most plausible one. But even on this supposition the balanced civilization that was at last attained must have long since passed its zenith, and was now far fallen into decay. The too-perfect security of the Overworlders had led them to a slow movement of degenera-tion,[2] to a general dwindling in size, strength, and intelligence. That I could see clearly enough already. What had happened to the Undergrounders I did not yet suspect; but, from what I had seen of the Morlocks[3]—that, by the bye, was the name by which these creatures were called—I could imagine that the modification of the human type was even far more profound than among the 'Eloi,'[4] the beautiful race that I already knew.

"Then came troublesome doubts. Why had the Morlocks taken my Time Machine? For I felt sure it was they who had taken it. Why, too, if the Eloi were masters, could they not restore the machine to me? And why were they so terribly afraid of the dark? I proceeded, as I have said, to question

1 A cicerone is a tour guide; typically in utopian fiction the visitor to utopia is con-ducted around by someone who is able to answer all the visitor's questions.
2 Primarily a biological term signifying organic reversion to a less complex state, but with many social, psychological, and cultural overtones. See Appendices A2, A4, C4.
3 A Wellsian coinage, aptly combining allusions to "mullock" (garbage, low-class human trash), "warlock" (evil spirit, male witch), "Moloch" (god of Ammonites to whom children were sacrificed, viewed as a devil by Christianity; see Appendix B2), "Mohock" (an eighteenth-century London ruffian), "more" or "*mort*" (means "death" in French) and "locks" (suggesting both imprisonment and hairiness).
4 Another coinage. If pronounced "ee-loy," as is standard among most Wellsians today, the word vaguely suggests "elite," "elect," or "elfin," and may allude to St. Eloi, the patron saint of metal-workers (perhaps an ironic reference to the Mor-locks), who was known for his personal beauty and courtesy. If pronounced "ell-o-ee," the word (uttered twice by Christ on the cross in Mark 15:34) is Aramaic for God, so perhaps ironically suggests the Eloi's former elevated social status. The smooth, liquid, foreign (French-Greek-Aramaic) tonal quality of the word contrasts with the harsher, quasi-Anglo-Saxon "Morlock," enforcing at the linguistic level the idea of distinct evolution based on social class.

Weena about this Underworld, but here again I was disappointed. At first she would not understand my questions, and presently she refused to answer them. She shivered as though the topic was unendurable. And when I pressed her, perhaps a little harshly, she burst into tears. They were the only tears, except my own, I ever saw in that Golden Age. When I saw them I ceased abruptly to trouble about the Morlocks, and was only concerned in banishing these signs of her human inheritance from Weena's eyes. And very soon she was smiling and clapping her hands, while I solemnly burnt a match.

IX

THE MORLOCKS

"It may seem odd to you, but it was two days before I could follow up the new-found clue in what was manifestly the proper way. I felt a peculiar shrinking from those pallid bodies. They were just the half-bleached colour of the worms and things one sees preserved in spirit in a zoological museum. And they were filthily cold to the touch. Probably my shrinking was largely due to the sympathetic influence of the Eloi, whose disgust of the Morlocks I now began to appreciate.

"The next night I did not sleep well. Probably my health was a little disordered. I was oppressed with perplexity and doubt. Once or twice I had a feeling of intense fear for which I could perceive no definite reason. I remember creeping noiselessly into the great hall where the little people were sleeping in the moonlight—that night Weena was among them—and feeling reassured by their presence. It occurred to me, even then, that in the course of a few days the moon must pass through its last quarter, and the nights grow dark, when the appearances of these unpleasant creatures from below, these whitened Lemurs, this new vermin that had replaced the old, might be more abundant. And on both these days I had the restless feeling of one who shirks an inevitable duty. I felt assured that the Time Machine was only to be recovered by boldly penetrating these mysteries of underground. Yet I could not face the mystery. If only I had had a companion it would have been different. But I was so horribly alone, and even to clamber down into the darkness of the well appalled me. I don't know if you will understand my feeling, but I never felt quite safe at my back.

"It was this restlessness, this insecurity, perhaps, that drove me further and further afield in my exploring expeditions. Going to the south-westward towards the rising country that is now called Combe Wood,[1] I observed far off, in the direction of nineteenth-century Banstead,[2] a vast green structure, different in character from any I had hitherto seen. It was larger than the largest of the palaces or ruins I knew, and the façade had an Oriental look: the face of it having the lustre, as well as the pale-green tint, a kind of bluish-green, of a certain type of Chinese porcelain. This difference in aspect suggested a difference in use, and I was minded to push on and explore. But the day was growing late, and I had come upon the sight of the place after a long and tiring circuit; so I resolved to hold over the adventure for the following day, and I returned to the welcome and the caresses of little Weena. But next morning I perceived clearly enough that my curiosity regarding the Palace of Green Porcelain was a piece of self-deception, to enable me to shirk, by another day, an experience I dreaded. I resolved I would make the descent without further waste of time, and started out in the early morning towards a well near the ruins of granite and aluminium.

"Little Weena ran with me. She danced beside me to the well, but when she saw me lean over the mouth and look downward, she seemed strangely disconcerted. 'Good-bye, little Weena,' I said, kissing her; and then, putting her down, I began to feel over the parapet for the climbing hooks. Rather hastily, I may as well confess, for I feared my courage might leak away! At first she watched me in amazement. Then she gave a most piteous cry, and, running to me, began to pull at me with her little hands. I think her opposition nerved me rather to proceed. I shook her off, perhaps a little roughly, and in another moment I was in the throat of the well. I saw her agonized face over the parapet, and smiled to reassure her. Then I had to look down at the unstable hooks to which I clung.

"I had to clamber down a shaft of perhaps two hundred yards. The descent was effected by means of metallic bars projecting from the sides of the well, and these being adapted to the needs of a creature much smaller and lighter than myself, I

---

1   I.e., Coombe Wood, an area now in the Greater London Borough of Kingston 3.5 miles south-east of Richmond.
2   Town in Surrey occupying high ground about 8 miles south-east of Richmond.

was speedily cramped and fatigued by the descent. And not simply fatigued! One of the bars bent suddenly under my weight, and almost swung me off into the blackness beneath. For a moment I hung by one hand, and after that experience I did not dare to rest again. Though my arms and back were presently acutely painful, I went on clambering down the sheer descent with as quick a motion as possible. Glancing upward, I saw the aperture, a small blue disk, in which a star was visible, while little Weena's head showed as a round black projection. The thudding sound of a machine below grew louder and more oppressive. Everything save that little disk above was profoundly dark, and when I looked up again Weena had disappeared.

"I was in an agony of discomfort. I had some thought of trying to go up the shaft again, and leave the Underworld alone. But even while I turned this over in my mind I continued to descend. At last, with intense relief, I saw dimly coming up, a foot to the right of me, a slender loophole in the wall. Swinging myself in, I found it was the aperture of a narrow horizontal tunnel in which I could lie down and rest. It was not too soon. My arms ached, my back was cramped, and I was trembling with the prolonged terror of a fall. Besides this, the unbroken darkness had had a distressing effect upon my eyes. The air was full of the throb-and-hum of machinery pumping air down the shaft.

"I do not know how long I lay. I was roused by a soft hand touching my face. Starting up in the darkness I snatched at my matches and, hastily striking one, I saw three stooping white creatures similar to the one I had seen above ground in the ruin, hastily retreating before the light. Living, as they did, in what appeared to me impenetrable darkness, their eyes were abnormally large and sensitive, just as are the pupils of the abysmal[1] fishes, and they reflected the light in the same way. I have no doubt they could see me in that rayless obscurity, and they did not seem to have any fear of me apart from the light. But, so soon as I struck a match in order to see them, they fled

---

1 I.e., from the ocean depths.

incontinently, vanishing into dark gutters and tunnels, from which their eyes glared at me in the strangest fashion.

"I tried to call to them, but the language they had was apparently different from that of the overworld people; so that I was needs left to my own unaided efforts, and the thought of flight before exploration was even then in my mind. But I said to myself, 'You are in for it now,' and, feeling my way along the tunnel, I found the noise of machinery grow louder. Presently the walls fell away from me, and I came to a large open space, and, striking another match, saw that I had entered a vast arched cavern, which stretched into utter darkness beyond the range of my light. The view I had of it was as much as one could see in the burning of a match.

"Necessarily my memory is vague. Great shapes like big machines rose out of the dimness, and cast grotesque black shadows, in which dim spectral Morlocks sheltered from the glare. The place, by the bye, was very stuffy and oppressive, and the faint halitus[1] of freshly-shed blood was in the air. Some way down the central vista was a little table of white metal, laid with what seemed a meal. The Morlocks at any rate were carnivorous! Even at the time, I remember wondering what large animal could have survived to furnish the red joint I saw. It was all very indistinct: the heavy smell, the big unmeaning shapes, the obscene figures lurking in the shadows, and only waiting for the darkness to come at me again! Then the match burnt down, and stung my fingers, and fell, a wriggling red spot in the blackness.

"I have thought since how particularly ill-equipped I was for such an experience. When I had started with the Time Machine, I had started with the absurd assumption that the men of the Future would certainly be infinitely ahead of ourselves in all their appliances. I had come without arms, without medicine, without anything to smoke—at times I missed tobacco frightfully!—even without enough matches. If only I had thought of a Kodak![2] I could have flashed that glimpse of

---

1   Strictly "vapour," but here signifying "odour."
2   Patented name of a hand camera using roll film invented by George Eastman in 1888 that greatly simplified, cheapened, and popularized the art of photography.

the Underworld in a second, and examined it at leisure. But, as it was, I stood there with only the weapons and the powers that Nature had endowed me with—hands, feet, and teeth; these, and four safety matches that still remained to me.

"I was afraid to push my way in among all this machinery in the dark, and it was only with my last glimpse of light I discovered that my store of matches had run low. It had never occurred to me until that moment that there was any need to economize them, and I had wasted almost half the box in astonishing the Overworlders, to whom fire was a novelty. Now, as I say, I had four left, and while I stood in the dark, a hand touched mine, lank fingers came feeling over my face, and I was sensible of a peculiar unpleasant odour. I fancied I heard the breathing of a crowd of those dreadful little beings about me. I felt the box of matches in my hand being gently disengaged, and other hands behind me plucking at my clothing. The sense of these unseen creatures examining me was indescribably unpleasant. The sudden realization of my ignorance of their ways of thinking and doing came home to me very vividly in the darkness. I shouted at them as loudly as I could. They started away, and then I could feel them approaching me again. They clutched at me more boldly, whispering odd sounds to each other. I shivered violently, and shouted again— rather discordantly. This time they were not so seriously alarmed, and they made a queer laughing noise as they came back at me. I will confess I was horribly frightened. I determined to strike another match and escape under the protection of its glare. I did so, and eking out the flicker with a scrap of paper from my pocket, I made good my retreat to the narrow tunnel. But I had scarce entered this when my light was blown out, and in the blackness I could hear the Morlocks rustling like wind among leaves, and pattering like the rain, as they hurried after me.

"In a moment I was clutched by several hands, and there was no mistaking that they were trying to haul me back. I struck another light, and waved it in their dazzled faces. You can scarce imagine how nauseatingly inhuman they looked—those pale, chinless faces and great, lidless, pinkish-grey eyes!—as they stared in their blindness and bewilderment. But I did not stay to look, I promise you: I retreated again, and when my second match had ended, I struck my third. It had almost burnt through when I reached the opening into the shaft. I lay down on the edge, for the throb of the great pump below made me giddy. Then I felt sideways for the projecting hooks, and, as I did so, my feet were grasped from behind, and I was violently tugged backward. I lit my last match … and it incontinently went out. But I had my hand on the climbing bars now, and, kicking violently, I disengaged myself from the clutches of the Morlocks, and was speedily clambering up the shaft, while they stayed peering and blinking up at me: all but one little wretch who followed me for some way, and well-nigh secured my boot as a trophy.

"That climb seemed interminable to me. With the last twenty or thirty feet of it a deadly nausea came upon me. I had the greatest difficulty in keeping my hold. The last few yards was a frightful struggle against this faintness. Several times my head swam, and I felt all the sensations of falling. At last, however, I got over the well-mouth somehow, and staggered out of the ruin into the blinding sunlight. I fell upon my face. Even the soil smelt sweet and clean. Then I remember Weena kissing my hands and ears, and the voices of others among the Eloi. Then, for a time, I was insensible.

X

WHEN THE NIGHT CAME

"Now, indeed, I seemed in a worse case than before. Hitherto, except during my night's anguish at the loss of the Time Machine, I had felt a sustaining hope of ultimate escape, but that hope was staggered by these new discoveries. Hitherto I had merely thought myself impeded by the childish simplicity of the little people, and by some unknown forces which I had only to understand to overcome; but there was an altogether new element in the sickening quality of the Morlocks—a something inhuman and malign. Instinctively I loathed them. Before, I had felt as a man might feel who had fallen into a pit: my concern was with the pit and how to get out of it. Now I felt like a beast in a trap, whose enemy would come upon him soon.

"The enemy I dreaded may surprise you. It was the darkness of the new moon. Weena had put this into my head by some at first incomprehensible remarks about the Dark Nights. It was not now such a very difficult problem to guess what the coming Dark Nights might mean. The moon was on the wane: each night there was a longer interval of darkness. And I now understood to some slight degree at least the reason of the fear of the little upper-world people for the dark. I wondered vaguely what foul villainy it might be that the Morlocks did under the new moon. I felt pretty sure now that my second hypothesis was all wrong. The upper-world people might once have been the favoured aristocracy, and the Morlocks their mechanical servants; but that had long since passed away. The two species that had resulted from the evolution of man were sliding down towards, or had already arrived at, an altogether new relationship. The Eloi, like the Carlovingian kings,[1] had decayed to a mere beautiful futility. They still possessed the

---

1   Carlovingian (French *carlovingien*) or Carolingian refers to the weak descendants of the Emperor Charlemagne (A.D. 742-814).

earth on sufferance: since the Morlocks, subterranean for innumerable generations, had come at last to find the daylit surface intolerable. And the Morlocks made their garments, I inferred, and maintained them in their habitual needs, perhaps through the survival of an old habit of service. They did it as a standing horse paws with his foot, or as a man enjoys killing animals in sport: because ancient and departed necessities had impressed it on the organism. But, clearly, the old order was already in part reversed. The Nemesis[1] of the delicate ones was creeping on apace. Ages ago, thousands of generations ago, man had thrust his brother man out of the ease and the sunshine. And now that brother was coming back—changed! Already the Eloi had begun to learn one old lesson anew. They were becoming reacquainted with Fear. And suddenly there came into my head the memory of the meat I had seen in the under-world. It seemed odd how it floated into my mind: not stirred up as it were by the current of my meditations, but coming in almost like a question from outside. I tried to recall the form of it. I had a vague sense of something familiar, but I could not tell what it was at the time.

"Still, however helpless the little people in the presence of their mysterious Fear, I was differently constituted. I came out of this age of ours, this ripe prime of the human race, when Fear does not paralyze and mystery has lost its terrors. I at least would defend myself. Without further delay I determined to make myself arms and a fastness where I might sleep. With that refuge as a base, I could face this strange world with some of that confidence I had lost in realizing to what creatures night by night I lay exposed. I felt I could never sleep again until my bed was secure from them. I shuddered with horror to think how they must already have examined me.

"I wandered during the afternoon along the valley of the Thames, but found nothing that commended itself to my mind as inaccessible. All the buildings and trees seemed easily practicable to such dexterous climbers as the Morlocks, to judge by their wells, must be. Then the tall pinnacles of the Palace of

---

1   Victorious rival, named for the Greek goddess of retribution.

Green Porcelain and the polished gleam of its walls came back to my memory; and in the evening, taking Weena like a child upon my shoulder, I went up the hills towards the south-west. The distance, I had reckoned, was seven or eight miles, but it must have been nearer eighteen. I had first seen the place on a moist afternoon when distances are deceptively diminished. In addition, the heel of one of my shoes was loose, and a nail was working through the sole—they were comfortable old shoes I wore about indoors—so that I was lame. And it was already long past sunset when I came in sight of the palace, silhouetted black against the pale yellow of the sky.

"Weena had been hugely delighted when I began to carry her, but after a time she desired me to let her down, and ran along by the side of me, occasionally darting off on either hand to pick flowers to stick in my pockets. My pockets had always puzzled Weena, but at the last she had concluded that they were an eccentric kind of vases for floral decoration. At least she utilized them for that purpose. And that reminds me! In changing my jacket I found ..."

The Time Traveller paused, put his hand into his pocket, and silently placed two withered flowers, not unlike very large white mallows,[1] upon the little table. Then he resumed his narrative.[2]

"As the hush of evening crept over the world and we proceeded over the hill crest towards Wimbledon,[3] Weena grew tired and wanted to return to the house of grey stone. But I pointed out the distant pinnacles of the Palace of Green Porcelain to her, and contrived to make her understand that we were seeking a refuge there from her fear. You know that great pause that comes upon things before the dusk? Even the breeze stops in the trees. To me there is always an air of expectation about that evening stillness. The sky was clear, remote, and empty save for a few horizontal bars far down in the sunset. Well, that night the expectation took the colour of my fears. In that dark-

---

1 One of a large family of plants often with five-part flowers widely distributed over the globe, including marsh mallow, hibiscus, okra, hollyhock, and the cotton plant.
2 The italics are in the original, signifying the only break in the continuity of the Time Traveller's narrative.
3 Suburb of south London about 5 miles south-east of Richmond.

ling calm my senses seemed preternaturally[1] sharpened. I fancied I could even feel the hollowness of the ground beneath my feet: could, indeed, almost see through it the Morlocks on their ant-hill going hither and thither and waiting for the dark. In my excitement I fancied that they would receive my invasion of their burrows as a declaration of war. And why had they taken my Time Machine?

"So we went on in the quiet, and the twilight deepened into night. The clear blue of the distance faded, and one star after another came out. The ground grew dim and the trees black. Weena's fears and her fatigue grew upon her. I took her in my arms and talked to her and caressed her. Then, as the darkness grew deeper, she put her arms round my neck, and, closing her eyes, tightly pressed her face against my shoulder. So we went down a long slope into a valley, and there in the dimness I almost walked into a little river. This I waded, and went up the opposite side of the valley, past a number of sleeping-houses, and by a statue—a Faun,[2] or some such figure, *minus* the head. Here, too, were acacias. So far I had seen nothing of the Morlocks, but it was yet early in the night, and the darker hours before the old moon rose were still to come.

"From the brow of the next hill I saw a thick wood spreading wide and black before me. I hesitated at this. I could see no end to it, either to the right or the left. Feeling tired—my feet in particular, were very sore—I carefully lowered Weena from my shoulder as I halted, and sat down upon the turf. I could no longer see the Palace of Green Porcelain, and I was in doubt of my direction. I looked into the thickness of the wood and thought of what it might hide. Under that dense tangle of branches one would be out of sight of the stars. Even were there no other lurking danger—a danger I did not care to let my imagination loose upon—there would still be all the roots to stumble over and the tree boles to strike against. I was very tired, too, after the excitements of the day; so I decided that I would not face it, but would pass the night upon the open hill.

---

1 Abnormally, exceptionally.
2 Woodland creature from Roman mythology, half man, half goat.

"Weena, I was glad to find, was fast asleep. I carefully wrapped her in my jacket, and sat down beside her to wait for the moonrise. The hill-side was quiet and deserted, but from the black of the wood there came now and then a stir of living things. Above me shone the stars, for the night was very clear. I felt a certain sense of friendly comfort in their twinkling. All the old constellations had gone from the sky, however: that slow movement which is imperceptible in a hundred human lifetimes, had long since re-arranged them in unfamiliar groupings. But the Milky Way, it seemed to me, was still the same tattered streamer of star-dust as of yore. Southward (as I judged it) was a very bright red star that was new to me: it was even more splendid than our own green Sirius.[1] And amid all these scintillating points of light one bright planet shone kindly and steadily like the face of an old friend.[2]

"Looking at these stars suddenly dwarfed my own troubles and all the gravities of terrestrial life. I thought of their unfathomable distance, and the slow inevitable drift of their movements out of the unknown past into the unknown future. I thought of the great precessional cycle that the pole of the earth describes. Only forty times[3] had that silent revolution occurred during all the years that I had traversed. And during these few revolutions all the activity, all the traditions, the complex organizations, the nations, languages, literatures, aspirations, even the mere memory of Man as I knew him, had been swept out of existence. Instead were these frail creatures who

1   The Dog Star in *Canis Major*, the brightest true star visible in the night sky.
2   Probably the planet Venus, which after the moon is the brightest and most recognisable object in the night sky.
3   The precession of the equinoxes refers to their slightly earlier occurrence every year, a phenomenon reflected in the gradually shifting position of the "fixed" stars and observed but not understood by the ancients. It is a result of the slight retrograde motion of the circle described by the earth's axis, itself caused by the combined gravitational drag of the sun and moon. This circle or cycle is completed once roughly every 25,800 years, which the ancients called a Great Year, imagining that after that time all the heavenly bodies would occupy the same place as they did at the creation. As for the *forty* Great Years that the Time Traveller refers to, either his math is incorrect, or he is assuming that a Great Year is 20,000 years long. An explanation for the just over 800,000 years elapsed derives from this error: Wells perhaps liked the biblical resonances of the number forty when attached to what Huxley had memorably used as the unit of evolutionary time. See Appendix A6.

had forgotten their high ancestry, and the white Things of which I went in terror. Then I thought of the Great Fear that was between the two species, and for the first time, with a sudden shiver, came the clear knowledge of what the meat I had seen might be. Yet it was too horrible! I looked at little Weena sleeping beside me, her face white and starlike under the stars, and forthwith dismissed the thought.

"Through that long night I held my mind off the Morlocks as well as I could, and whiled away the time by trying to fancy I could find signs of the old constellations in the new confusion. The sky kept very clear, except for a hazy cloud or so. No doubt I dozed at times. Then, as my vigil wore on, came a faintness in the eastward sky, like the reflection of some colourless fire, and the old moon rose, thin and peaked[1] and white. And close behind, and overtaking it, and overflowing it, the dawn came, pale at first, and then growing pink and warm. No Morlocks had approached us. Indeed, I had seen none upon the hill that night. And in the confidence of renewed day it almost seemed to me that my fear had been unreasonable. I stood up and found my foot with the loose heel swollen at the ankle and painful under the heel; so I sat down again, took off my shoes, and flung them away.

"I awakened Weena, and we went down into the wood, now green and pleasant[2] instead of black and forbidding. We found some fruit wherewith to break our fast. We soon met others of the dainty ones, laughing and dancing in the sunlight as though there was no such thing in nature as the night. And then I thought once more of the meat that I had seen. I felt assured now of what it was, and from the bottom of my heart I pitied this last feeble rill[3] from the great flood of humanity. Clearly, at some time in the Long-Ago of human decay the Morlocks' food had run short. Possibly they had lived on rats and suchlike vermin. Even now man is far less discriminating and exclusive

---

1   Sharp-featured, sickly-looking.
2   An ironic allusion to the famous lyric usually known as "Jerusalem" (c. 1804–10) by William Blake; this far-future deindustrialized England, while "green & pleasant," is far from being a New Jerusalem.
3   Narrow stream.

in his food than he was—far less than any monkey. His prejudice against human flesh is no deep-seated instinct. And so these inhuman sons of men—! I tried to look at the thing in a scientific spirit. After all, they were less human and more remote than our cannibal ancestors of three or four thousand years ago. And the intelligence that would have made this state of things a torment had gone. Why should I trouble myself? These Eloi were mere fatted[1] cattle, which the ant-like Morlocks preserved and preyed upon—probably saw to the breeding of. And there was Weena dancing at my side!

"Then I tried to preserve myself from the horror that was coming upon me, by regarding it as a rigorous punishment of human selfishness. Man had been content to live in ease and delight upon the labours of his fellow-man, had taken Necessity as his watchword and excuse, and in the fulness of time Necessity had come home to him. I even tried a Carlyle-like scorn of this wretched aristocracy-in-decay.[2] But this attitude of mind was impossible. However great their intellectual degradation, the Eloi had kept too much of the human form not to claim my sympathy, and to make me perforce a sharer in their degradation and their Fear.

"I had at that time very vague ideas as to the course I should pursue. My first was to secure some safe place of refuge, and to make myself such arms of metal or stone as I could contrive. That necessity was immediate. In the next place, I hoped to procure some means of fire, so that I should have the weapon of a torch at hand, for nothing, I knew, would be more efficient against these Morlocks. Then I wanted to arrange some contrivance to break open the doors of bronze under the White Sphinx. I had in mind a battering-ram. I had a persuasion that if I could enter these doors and carry a blaze of light before me I should discover the Time Machine and escape. I

---

1   I.e., fattened-up: a biblical allusion (Luke 15:30).
2   The allusion may be to a number of passages from the work of the Scottish-born historian and cultural critic Thomas Carlyle (1795-1881; see Appendix B1). Wells may have had in mind a description of the *ancien régime* in Carlyle's *The French Revolution* (1837), as he cited it at length when later recounting that event in *The Outline of History* (Chapter XXV para. 9).

could not imagine the Morlocks were strong enough to move it far away. Weena I had resolved to bring with me to our own time. And turning such schemes over in my mind I pursued our way towards the building which my fancy had chosen as our dwelling.

XI

THE PALACE OF GREEN PORCELAIN

"I FOUND the Palace of Green Porcelain, when we approached it about noon, deserted and falling into ruin. Only ragged vestiges of glass remained in its windows, and great sheets of the green facing had fallen away from the corroded metallic framework. It lay very high upon a turfy down, and looking north-eastward before I entered it, I was surprised to see a large estuary, or even creek, where I judged Wandsworth and Battersea[1] must once have been. I thought then — though I never followed up the thought — of what might have happened, or might be happening, to the living things in the sea.

"The material of the Palace proved on examination to be indeed porcelain, and along the face of it I saw an inscription in some unknown character. I thought, rather foolishly, that Weena might help me to interpret this, but I only learnt that the bare idea of writing had never entered her head. She always seemed to me, I fancy, more human than she was, perhaps because her affection was so human.

"Within the big valves[2] of the door — which were open and broken — we found, instead of the customary hall, a long gallery lit by many side windows. At the first glance I was reminded of a museum. The tiled floor was thick with dust, and a remarkable array of miscellaneous objects was shrouded in the same grey covering. Then I perceived, standing strange and gaunt in the centre of the hall, what was clearly the lower part of a huge skeleton. I recognized by the oblique feet that it was some extinct creature after the fashion of the Megatherium.[3] The skull and the upper bones lay beside it in the thick dust, and in one place, where rainwater had dropped through a

---

1   Suburbs of south-west London on the Thames five to seven miles downstream from Richmond.
2   I.e., the two hinged halves of a double door.
3   An extinct giant ground sloth, about the size of a modern elephant.

leak in the roof, the thing itself had been worn away. Further in the gallery was the huge skeleton barrel of a Brontosaurus.[1] My museum hypothesis was confirmed. Going towards the side I found what appeared to be sloping shelves, and, clearing away the thick dust, I found the old familiar glass cases of our own time. But they must have been air-tight, to judge from the fair preservation of some of their contents.

"Clearly we stood among the ruins of some latter-day South Kensington![2] Here, apparently, was the Palæontological[3] Section, and a very splendid array of fossils it must have been, though the inevitable process of decay that had been staved off for a time, and had, through the extinction of bacteria and fungi, lost ninety-nine hundredths of its force, was, nevertheless, with extreme sureness if with extreme slowness at work again upon all its treasures. Here and there I found traces of the little people in the shape of rare fossils broken to pieces or threaded in strings upon reeds. And the cases had in some instances been bodily removed—by the Morlocks as I judged. The place was very silent. The thick dust deadened our footsteps. Weena, who had been rolling a sea-urchin[4] down the sloping glass of a case, presently came, as I stared about me, and very quietly took my hand and stood beside me.

"And at first I was so much surprised by this ancient monument of an intellectual age, that I gave no thought to the possibilities it presented. Even my pre-occupation about the Time Machine receded a little from my mind.

"To judge from the size of the place, this Palace of Green Porcelain had a great deal more in it than a Gallery of Palæontology; possibly historical galleries; it might be, even a library! To me, at least in my present circumstances, these would be vastly more interesting than this spectacle of old-time geology in decay. Exploring, I found another short gallery running

---

1   Now called apatosaurus, a huge plant-eating quadripedal dinosaur.
2   South Kensington is the area of west London known for its great Victorian museums. In 1895 these were the South Kensington Museum (1852; now the Victoria and Albert Museum), and the Natural History Museum (1881).
3   Of the study of extinct animals.
4   A sea-creature often resembling a ball covered with brittle spines.

transversely to the first. This appeared to be devoted to minerals, and the sight of a block of sulphur set my mind running on gunpowder. But I could find no saltpetre;[1] indeed, no nitrates of any kind. Doubtless they had deliquesced[2] ages ago. Yet the sulphur hung in my mind, and set up a train of thinking. As for the rest of the contents of that gallery, though, on the whole, they were the best preserved of all I saw, I had little interest. I am no specialist in mineralogy, and I went on down a very ruinous aisle running parallel to the first hall I had entered. Apparently this section had been devoted to natural history, but everything had long since passed out of recognition. A few shrivelled and blackened vestiges of what had once been stuffed animals, desiccated mummies in jars that had once held spirit, a brown dust of departed plants: that was all! I was sorry for that, because I should have been glad to trace the patient re-adjustments by which the conquest of animated nature had been attained. Then we came to a gallery of simply colossal proportions, but singularly ill-lit, the floor of it running downward at a slight angle from the end at which I entered. At intervals white globes hung from the ceiling—many of them cracked and smashed—which suggested that originally the place had been artificially lit. Here I was more in my element, for rising on either side of me were the huge bulks of big machines, all greatly corroded and many broken down, but some still fairly complete. You know I have a certain weakness for mechanism, and I was inclined to linger among these: the more so as for the most part they had the interest of puzzles, and I could make only the vaguest guesses at what they were for. I fancied that if I could solve their puzzles I should find myself in possession of powers that might be of use against the Morlocks.

"Suddenly Weena came very close to my side. So suddenly that she startled me. Had it not been for her I do not think I should have noticed that the floor of the gallery sloped at all.[3] The end I had come in at was quite above ground, and was lit

---

1   Potassium nitrate, the chief constituent of gunpowder.

2   Melted away over time as a result of absorbing moisture from the air.

3   It may be, of course, that the floor did not slope, but that the museum was built into the side of a hill.—ED. [This footnote was part of the 1895 text.]

by rare slit-like windows. As you went down the length, the ground came up against these windows, until at last there was a pit like the 'area' of a London house before each, and only a narrow line of daylight at the top. I went slowly along, puzzling about the machines, and had been too intent upon them to notice the gradual diminution of the light, until Weena's increasing apprehensions drew my attention. Then I saw that the gallery ran down at last into a thick darkness. I hesitated, and then, as I looked round me, I saw that the dust was less abundant and its surface less even. Further away towards the dimness, it appeared to be broken by a number of small narrow footprints. My sense of the immediate presence of the Morlocks revived at that. I felt that I was wasting my time in this academic examination of machinery. I called to mind that it was already far advanced in the afternoon, and that I still had no weapon, no refuge, and no means of making a fire. And then down in the remote blackness of the gallery I heard a peculiar pattering, and the same odd noises I had heard down the well.

"I took Weena's hand. Then, struck with a sudden idea, I left her and turned to a machine from which projected a lever not unlike those in a signal-box. Clambering upon the stand, and grasping this lever in my hands, I put all my weight upon it sideways. Suddenly Weena, deserted in the central aisle, began to whimper. I had judged the strength of the lever pretty correctly, for it snapped after a minute's strain, and I rejoined her with a mace in my hand more than sufficient, I judged, for any Morlock skull I might encounter. And I longed very much to kill a Morlock or so. Very inhuman, you may think, to want to go killing one's own descendants! But it was impossible, somehow, to feel any humanity in the things. Only my disinclination to leave Weena, and a persuasion that if I began to slake my thirst for murder my Time Machine might suffer, restrained me from going straight down the gallery and killing the brutes I heard.

"Well, mace in one hand and Weena in the other, I went out of that gallery and into another and still larger one, which at the first glance reminded me of a military chapel hung with tattered flags. The brown and charred rags that hung from the sides of it, I presently recognized as the decaying vestiges of books. They had long since dropped to pieces, and every semblance of print had left them. But here and there were warped boards and cracked metallic clasps that told the tale well enough. Had I been a literary man I might, perhaps, have moralized upon the futility of all ambition. But as it was, the thing that struck me with keenest force was the enormous waste of labour to which this sombre wilderness of rotting paper testified. At the time I will confess that I thought chiefly of the *Philosophical Transactions*[1] and my own seventeen papers upon physical optics.

"Then, going up a broad staircase, we came to what may once have been a gallery of technical chemistry. And here I had not a little hope of useful discoveries. Except at one end where the roof had collapsed, this gallery was well preserved. I went eagerly to every unbroken case. And at last, in one of the really air-tight cases, I found a box of matches. Very eagerly I tried them. They were perfectly good. They were not even damp. I turned to Weena. 'Dance,' I cried to her in her own tongue. For now I had a weapon indeed against the horrible creatures we feared. And so, in that derelict museum, upon the thick soft carpeting of dust, to Weena's huge delight, I solemnly performed a kind of composite dance, whistling *The Land of the Leal*[2] as cheerfully as I could. In part it was a modest *cancan*, in part a step dance, in part a skirt dance (so far as my tail-coat permitted), and in part original. For I am naturally inventive, as you know.

"Now, I still think that for this box of matches to have escaped the wear of time for immemorial years was a most strange, as for me it was a most fortunate, thing. Yet, oddly enough, I found a far unlikelier substance, and that was camphor.[3] I found it in a sealed jar, that by chance, I suppose, had

---

1   The scholarly journal of the Royal Society, Britain's most distinguished scientific society.

2   A popular ballad by Carolina, Baroness Nairne (1766-1845). "Land o' the Leal" (Land of the Loyal) is a Scottish phrase meaning Heaven.

3   A white, volatile, crystalline substance with a bitter taste and characteristic smell, used in the 1890s as an inhalant against catarrh.

been really hermetically sealed. I fancied at first that it was paraffin wax, and smashed the glass accordingly. But the odour of camphor was unmistakable. In the universal decay this volatile substance had chanced to survive, perhaps through many thousands of centuries. It reminded me of a sepia painting I had once seen done from the ink of a fossil Belemnite[1] that must have perished and become fossilized millions of years ago. I was about to throw it away, but I remembered that it was inflammable and burnt with a good bright flame — was, in fact, an excellent candle — and I put it in my pocket. I found no explosives, however, nor any means of breaking down the bronze doors. As yet my iron crowbar was the most helpful thing I had chanced upon. Nevertheless I left that gallery greatly elated.

"I cannot tell you all the story of that long afternoon. It would require a great effort of memory to recall my explorations in at all the proper order. I remember a long gallery of rusting stands of arms, and how I hesitated between my crowbar and a hatchet or a sword. I could not carry both, however, and my bar of iron promised best against the bronze gates. There were numbers of guns, pistols, and rifles. The most were masses of rust, but many were of some new metal, and still fairly sound. But any cartridges or powder there may once have been had rotted into dust. One corner I saw was charred and shattered: perhaps, I thought, by an explosion among the specimens. In another place was a vast array of idols — Polynesian, Mexican, Grecian, Phœnician, every country on earth I should think. And here, yielding to an irresistible impulse, I wrote my name upon the nose of a steatite[2] monster from South America that particularly took my fancy.

"As the evening drew on, my interest waned. I went through gallery after gallery, dusty, silent, often ruinous, the exhibits sometimes mere heaps of rust and lignite,[3] sometimes fresher. In one place I suddenly found myself near the model of a tin

---

1   A convex, tapered species of extinct cuttlefish; sepia is a brown pigment obtained from cuttlefish.
2   I.e., carved from soapstone.
3   Carbonized wood.

mine, and then by the nearest accident I discovered, in an airtight case, two dynamite cartridges! I shouted 'Eureka,' and smashed the case with joy. Then came a doubt. I hesitated. Then, selecting a little side gallery, I made my essay.[1] I never felt such a disappointment as I did in waiting five, ten, fifteen minutes for an explosion that never came. Of course the things were dummies, as I might have guessed from their presence. I really believe that, had they not been so, I should have rushed off incontinently and blown Sphinx, bronze doors, and (as it proved) my chances of finding the Time Machine, all together into non-existence.

"It was after that, I think, that we came to a little open court within the palace. It was turfed, and had three fruit-trees. So we rested and refreshed ourselves. Towards sunset I began to consider our position. Night was creeping upon us, and my inaccessible hiding-place had still to be found. But that troubled me very little now. I had in my possession a thing that was, perhaps, the best of all defences against the Morlocks—I had matches! I had the camphor in my pocket, too, if a blaze were needed. It seemed to me that the best thing we could do would be to pass the night in the open, protected by a fire. In the morning there was the getting of the Time Machine. Towards that, as yet, I had only my iron mace. But now, with my growing knowledge, I felt very differently towards those bronze doors. Up to this, I had refrained from forcing them, largely because of the mystery on the other side. They had never impressed me as being very strong, and I hoped to find my bar of iron not altogether inadequate for the work.

---

1 Attempt.

XII

IN THE DARKNESS

"WE emerged from the Palace while the sun was still in part above the horizon. I was determined to reach the White Sphinx early the next morning, and ere the dusk I purposed pushing through the woods that had stopped me on the previous journey. My plan was to go as far as possible that night, and then, building a fire, to sleep in the protection of its glare. Accordingly, as we went along I gathered any sticks or dried grass I saw, and presently had my arms full of such litter. Thus loaded, our progress was slower than I had anticipated, and besides Weena was tired. And I, also, began to suffer from sleepiness too; so that it was full night before we reached the wood. Upon the shrubby hill of its edge Weena would have stopped, fearing the darkness before us; but a singular sense of impending calamity, that should indeed have served me as a warning, drove me onward. I had been without sleep for a night and two days, and I was feverish and irritable. I felt sleep coming upon me, and the Morlocks with it.

"While we hesitated, among the black bushes behind us, and dim against their blackness, I saw three crouching figures. There was scrub and long grass all about us, and I did not feel safe from their insidious approach. The forest, I calculated, was rather less than a mile across. If we could get through it to the bare hill-side, there, as it seemed to me, was an altogether safer resting-place: I thought that with my matches and my camphor I could contrive to keep my path illuminated through the woods. Yet it was evident that if I was to flourish matches with my hands I should have to abandon my firewood: so, rather reluctantly, I put it down. And then it came into my head that I would amaze our friends behind by lighting it. I was to discover the atrocious folly of this proceeding, but it came to my mind as an ingenious move for covering our retreat.

"I don't know if you have ever thought what a rare thing

flame must be in the absence of man and in a temperate climate. The sun's heat is rarely strong enough to burn, even when it is focussed by dewdrops, as is sometimes the case in more tropical districts. Lightning may blast and blacken, but it rarely gives rise to wide-spread fire. Decaying vegetation may occasionally smoulder with the heat of its fermentation, but this rarely results in flame. In this decadence, too, the art of fire-making had been forgotten on the earth. The red tongues that went licking up my heap of wood were an altogether new and strange thing to Weena.

"She wanted to run to it and play with it. I believe she would have cast herself into it had I not restrained her. But I caught her up, and, in spite of her struggles, plunged boldly before me into the wood. For a little way the glare of my fire lit the path. Looking back presently, I could see, through the crowded stems, that from my heap of sticks the blaze had spread to some bushes adjacent, and a curved line of fire was creeping up the grass of the hill. I laughed at that, and turned again to the dark trees before me. It was very black, and Weena clung to me convulsively, but there was still, as my eyes grew accustomed to the darkness, sufficient light for me to avoid the stems. Overhead it was simply black, except where a gap of remote blue sky shone down upon us here and there. I lit none of my matches because I had no hands free. Upon my left arm I carried my little one, in my right hand I had my iron bar.

"For some way I heard nothing but the crackling twigs under my feet, the faint rustle of the breeze above, and my own breathing and the throb of the blood-vessels in my ears. Then I seemed to know of a pattering about me. I pushed on grimly. The pattering grew more distinct, and then I caught the same queer sounds and voices I had heard in the under-world. There were evidently several of the Morlocks, and they were closing in upon me. Indeed, in another minute I felt a tug at my coat, then something at my arm. And Weena shivered violently, and became quite still.

"It was time for a match. But to get one I must put her down. I did so, and, as I fumbled with my pocket, a struggle began in the darkness about my knees, perfectly silent on her part and with the same peculiar cooing sounds from the Mor-locks. Soft little hands, too, were creeping over my coat and back, touching even my neck. Then the match scratched and fizzed. I held it flaring, and saw the white backs of the Mor-locks in flight amid the trees. I hastily took a lump of camphor from my pocket, and prepared to light it as soon as the match should wane. Then I looked at Weena. She was lying clutching my feet and quite motionless, with her face to the ground. With a sudden fright I stooped to her. She seemed scarcely to breathe. I lit the block of camphor and flung it to the ground, and as it split and flared up and drove back the Morlocks and the shadows, I knelt down and lifted her. The wood behind seemed full of the stir and murmur of a great company!

"She seemed to have fainted. I put her carefully upon my shoulder and rose to push on, and then there came a horrible realization. In manœuvring with my matches and Weena, I had turned myself about several times, and now I had not the faintest idea in what direction lay my path. For all I knew, I might be facing back towards the Palace of Green Porcelain. I found myself in a cold sweat. I had to think rapidly what to do. I determined to build a fire and encamp where we were. I put Weena, still motionless, down upon a turfy bole, and very hasti-ly, as my first lump of camphor waned, I began collecting sticks and leaves. Here and there out of the darkness round me the Morlocks' eyes shone like carbuncles.[1]

"The camphor flickered and went out. I lit a match, and as I did so, two white forms that had been approaching Weena dashed hastily away. One was so blinded by the light that he came straight for me and I felt his bones grind under the blow of my fist. He gave a whoop of dismay, staggered a little way, and fell down. I lit another piece of camphor, and went on gathering my bonfire. Presently I noticed how dry was some of the foliage above me, for since my arrival on the Time Machine, a matter of a week, no rain had fallen. So, instead of casting about among the trees for fallen twigs, I began leaping up and dragging down branches. Very soon I had a choking

---

1   Precious stones of a fiery red colour.

smoky fire of green wood and dry sticks, and could economize my camphor. Then I turned to where Weena lay beside my iron mace. I tried what I could to revive her, but she lay like one dead. I could not even satisfy myself whether or not she breathed.

"Now, the smoke of the fire beat over towards me, and it must have made me heavy of a sudden. Moreover, the vapour of camphor was in the air. My fire would not need replenishing for an hour or so. I felt very weary after my exertion, and sat down. The wood, too, was full of a slumbrous murmur that I did not understand. I seemed just to nod and open my eyes. But all was dark, and the Morlocks had their hands upon me. Flinging off their clinging fingers I hastily felt in my pocket for the match-box, and—it had gone! Then they gripped and closed with me again. In a moment I knew what had happened. I had slept, and my fire had gone out, and the bitterness of death came over my soul. The forest seemed full of the smell of burning wood. I was caught by the neck, by the hair, by the arms, and pulled down. It was indescribably horrible in the darkness to feel all these soft creatures heaped upon me. I felt as if I was in a monstrous spider's web. I was overpowered, and went down. I felt little teeth nipping at my neck. I rolled over, and as I did so my hand came against my iron lever. It gave me strength. I struggled up, shaking the human rats from me, and, holding the bar short, I thrust where I judged their faces might be. I could feel the succulent giving of flesh and bone under my blows, and for a moment I was free.

"The strange exultation that so often seems to accompany hard fighting came upon me. I knew that both I and Weena were lost, but I determined to make the Morlocks pay for their meat. I stood with my back to a tree, swinging the iron bar before me. The whole wood was full of the stir and cries of them. A minute passed. Their voices seemed to rise to a higher pitch of excitement, and their movements grew faster. Yet none came within reach. I stood glaring at the blackness. Then suddenly came hope. What if the Morlocks were afraid? And close on the heels of that came a strange thing. The darkness seemed to grow luminous. Very dimly I began to see the Morlocks about me — three battered at my feet — and then I recognized, with incredulous surprise, that the others were running, in an incessant stream, as it seemed, from behind me, and away through the wood in front. And their backs seemed no longer white, but reddish. As I stood agape, I saw a little red spark go drifting across a gap of starlight between the branches, and vanish. And at that I understood the smell of burning wood, the slumbrous murmur that was growing now into a gusty roar, the red glow, and the Morlocks' flight.

"Stepping out from behind my tree and looking back, I saw, through the black pillars of the nearer trees, the flames of the burning forest. It was my first fire coming after me. With that I looked for Weena, but she was gone. The hissing and crackling behind me, the explosive thud as each fresh tree burst into flame, left little time for reflection. My iron bar still gripped, I followed in the Morlocks' path. It was a close race. Once the flames crept forward so swiftly on my right as I ran, that I was outflanked, and had to strike off to the left. But at last I emerged upon a small open space, and as I did so, a Morlock came blundering towards me, and past me, and went on straight into the fire!

"And now I was to see the most weird and horrible thing, I think, of all that I beheld in that future age. This whole space was as bright as day with the reflection of the fire. In the centre was a hillock or tumulus,[1] surmounted by a scorched hawthorn. Beyond this was another arm of the burning forest, with yellow tongues already writhing from it, completely encircling the space with a fence of fire. Upon the hill-side were some thirty or forty Morlocks, dazzled by the light and heat, and blundering hither and thither against each other in their bewilderment. At first I did not realize their blindness, and struck furiously at them with my bar, in a frenzy of fear, as they approached me, killing one and crippling several more. But when I had watched the gestures of one of them groping under the hawthorn against the red sky, and heard their moans, I was

---

1   Ancient burial mound.

assured of their absolute helplessness and misery in the glare, and I struck no more of them.

"Yet every now and then one would come straight towards me, setting loose a quivering horror that made me quick to elude him. At one time the flames died down somewhat, and I feared the foul creatures would presently be able to see me. I was even thinking of beginning the fight by killing some of them before this should happen; but the fire burst out again brightly, and I stayed my hand. I walked about the hill among them and avoided them, looking for some trace of Weena. But Weena was gone.

"At last I sat down on the summit of the hillock, and watched this strange incredible company of blind things groping to and fro, and making uncanny noises to each one, as the glare of the fire beat on them. The coiling uprush of smoke streamed across the sky, and through the rare tatters of that red canopy, remote as though they belonged to another universe, shone the little stars. Two or three Morlocks came blundering into me, and I drove them off with blows of my fists, trembling as I did so.

"For the most part of that night I was persuaded it was a nightmare. I bit myself and screamed in a passionate desire to awake. I beat the ground with my hands, and got up and sat down again, and wandered here and there, and again sat down. Then I would fall to rubbing my eyes and calling upon God to let me awake. Thrice I saw Morlocks put their heads down in a kind of agony and rush into the flames. But, at last, above the subsiding red of the fire, above the streaming masses of black smoke and the whitening and blackening tree stumps, and the diminishing numbers of these dim creatures, came the white light of the day.

"I searched again for traces of Weena, but there were none. It was plain that they had left her poor little body in the forest. I cannot describe how it relieved me to think that it had escaped the awful fate to which it seemed destined. As I thought of that, I was almost moved to begin a massacre of the helpless abominations about me, but I contained myself. The hillock, as I have said, was a kind of island in the forest. From its summit I could now make out through a haze of smoke the Palace of Green Porcelain, and from that I could get my bearings for the White Sphinx. And so, leaving the remnant of these damned souls still going hither and thither and moaning, as the day grew clearer, I tied some grass about my feet and limped on across smoking ashes and among black stems that still pulsated internally with fire, towards the hiding-place of the Time Machine. I walked slowly, for I was almost exhausted, as well as lame, and I felt the intensest wretchedness for the horrible death of little Weena. It seemed an overwhelming calamity. Now, in this old familiar room, it is more like the sorrow of a dream than an actual loss. But that morning it left me absolutely lonely again — terribly alone. I began to think of this house of mine, of this fireside, of some of you, and with such thoughts came a longing that was pain.

"But, as I walked over the smoking ashes under the bright morning sky, I made a discovery. In my trouser pocket were still some loose matches. The box must have leaked before it was lost.

XIII

THE TRAP OF THE WHITE SPHINX

"ABOUT eight or nine in the morning I came to the same seat of yellow metal from which I had viewed the world upon the evening of my arrival. I thought of my hasty conclusions upon that evening, and could not refrain from laughing bitterly at my confidence. Here was the same beautiful scene, the same abundant foliage, the same splendid palaces and magnificent ruins, the same silver river running between its fertile banks. The gay robes of the beautiful people moved hither and thither among the trees. Some were bathing in exactly the place where I had saved Weena, and that suddenly gave me a keen stab of pain. And like blots upon the landscape rose the cupolas above the ways to the under-world. I understood now what all the beauty of the over-world people covered. Very pleasant was their day, as pleasant as the day of the cattle in the field. Like the cattle, they knew of no enemies, and provided against no needs. And their end was the same.

"I grieved to think how brief the dream of the human intellect had been. It had committed suicide. It had set itself steadfastly towards comfort and ease, a balanced society with security and permanency as its watchword, it had attained its hopes—to come to this at last. Once, life and property must have reached almost absolute safety. The rich had been assured of his wealth and comfort, the toiler assured of his life and work. No doubt in that perfect world there had been no unemployed problem, no social question left unsolved. And a great quiet had followed.

"It is a law of nature we overlook, that intellectual versatility is the compensation for change, danger, and trouble. An animal perfectly in harmony with its environment is a perfect mechanism. Nature never appeals to intelligence until habit and instinct are useless. There is no intelligence where there is no change and no need of change. Only those animals partake of intelligence that have to meet a huge variety of needs and dangers.

"So, as I see it, the upper-world man had drifted towards his feeble prettiness, and the under-world to mere mechanical industry. But that perfect state had lacked one thing even for mechanical perfection—absolute permanency. Apparently as time went on, the feeding of the under-world, however it was effected, had become disjointed. Mother Necessity,[1] who had been staved off for a few thousand years, came back again, and she began below. The under-world being in contact with machinery, which, however perfect, still needs some little thought outside habit, had probably retained perforce rather more initiative, if less of every other human character, than the upper. And when other meat failed them, they turned to what old habit had hitherto forbidden. So I say I saw it in my last view of the world of Eight Hundred and Two Thousand Seven Hundred and One. It may be as wrong an explanation as mortal wit could invent. It is how the thing shaped itself to me, and as that I give it to you.

"After the fatigues, excitements, and terrors of the past days, and in spite of my grief, this seat and the tranquil view and the warm sunlight were very pleasant. I was very tired and sleepy, and soon my theorizing passed into dozing. Catching myself at that, I took my own hint, and spreading myself out upon the turf I had a long and refreshing sleep.

"I awoke a little before sunsetting. I now felt safe against being caught napping by the Morlocks, and, stretching myself, I came on down the hill towards the White Sphinx. I had my crowbar in one hand, and the other hand played with the matches in my pocket.

"And now came a most unexpected thing. As I approached the pedestal of the sphinx I found the bronze valves were open. They had slid down into grooves.

"At that I stopped short before them, hesitating to enter.

"Within was a small apartment, and in a raised place in the corner of this was the Time Machine. I had the small levers in

---

1   An allusion to the proverb "Necessity is the mother of invention."

my pocket. So here, after all my elaborate preparations for the siege of the White Sphinx, was a meek surrender. I threw my iron bar away, almost sorry not to use it.

"A sudden thought came into my head as I stooped towards the portal. For once, at least, I grasped the mental operations of the Morlocks. Suppressing a strong inclination to laugh, I stepped through the bronze frame and up to the Time Machine. I was surprised to find it had been carefully oiled and cleaned. I have suspected since that the Morlocks had even partially taken it to pieces while trying in their dim way to grasp its purpose.

"Now as I stood and examined it, finding a pleasure in the mere touch of the contrivance, the thing I had expected happened. The bronze panels suddenly slid up and struck the frame with a clang. I was in the dark—trapped. So the Morlocks thought. At that I chuckled gleefully.

"I could already hear their murmuring laughter as they came towards me. Very calmly I tried to strike the match. I had only to fix on the levers and depart then like a ghost. But I had overlooked one little thing. The matches were of that abominable kind that light only on the box.

"You may imagine how all my calm vanished. The little brutes were close upon me. One touched me. I made a sweeping blow in the dark at them with the levers, and began to scramble into the saddle of the machine. Then came one hand upon me and then another. Then I had simply to fight against their persistent fingers for my levers, and at the same time feel for the studs over which these fitted. One, indeed, they almost got away from me. As it slipped from my hand, I had to butt in the dark with my head—I could hear the Morlock's skull ring—to recover it. It was a nearer thing than the fight in the forest, I think, this last scramble.

"But at last the lever was fixed and pulled over. The clinging hands slipped from me. The darkness presently fell from my eyes. I found myself in the same grey light and tumult I have already described.

XIV

THE FURTHER VISION

"I HAVE already told you of the sickness and confusion that comes with time travelling. And this time I was not seated properly in the saddle, but sideways and in an unstable fashion. For an indefinite time I clung to the machine as it swayed and vibrated, quite unheeding how I went, and when I brought myself to look at the dials again I was amazed to find where I had arrived. One dial records days, another thousands of days, another millions of days, and another thousands of millions. Now, instead of reversing the levers I had pulled them over so as to go forward with them, and when I came to look at these indicators I found that the thousands hand was sweeping round as fast as the seconds hand of a watch—into futurity.

"As I drove on, a peculiar change crept over the appearance of things. The palpitating greyness grew darker; then—though I was still travelling with prodigious velocity—the blinking succession of day and night, which was usually indicative of a slower pace, returned, and grew more and more marked. This puzzled me very much at first. The alternations of night and day grew slower and slower, and so did the passage of the sun across the sky, until they seemed to stretch through centuries. At last a steady twilight brooded over the earth, a twilight only broken now and then when a comet glared across the darkling sky. The band of light that had indicated the sun had long since disappeared; for the sun had ceased to set—it simply rose and fell in the west, and grew ever broader and more red. All trace of the moon had vanished. The circling of the stars, growing slower and slower, had given place to creeping points of light. At last, some time before I stopped, the sun, red and very large, halted motionless upon the horizon, a vast dome glowing with a dull heat, and now and then suffering a momentary extinction. At one time it had for a little while glowed more brilliantly again, but it speedily reverted to its sullen red-heat. I perceived by this slowing down of its rising and setting that the work of the tidal drag was done. The earth had come to rest with one face to the sun, even as in our own time the moon faces the earth. Very cautiously, for I remembered my former headlong fall, I began to reverse my motion. Slower and slower went the circling hands until the thousands one seemed motionless, and the daily one was no longer a mere mist upon its scale. Still slower, until the dim outlines of a desolate beach grew visible.

"I stopped very gently and sat upon the Time Machine, looking round. The sky was no longer blue. North-eastward it was inky black, and out of the blackness shone brightly and steadily the pale white stars. Overhead it was a deep Indian red[1] and starless, and south-eastward it grew brighter to a glowing scarlet where, cut by the horizon, lay the huge hull of the sun, red and motionless. The rocks about me were of a harsh reddish colour, and all the trace of life that I could see at first was the intensely green vegetation that covered every projecting point on their south-eastern face. It was the same rich green that one sees on forest moss or on the lichen in caves: plants which like these grow in a perpetual twilight.

"The machine was standing on a sloping beach. The sea stretched away to the south-west, to rise into a sharp bright horizon against the wan sky. There were no breakers and no waves, for not a breath of wind was stirring. Only a slight oily swell rose and fell like a gentle breathing, and showed that the eternal sea was still moving and living. And along the margin where the water sometimes broke was a thick incrustation of salt—pink under the lurid sky. There was a sense of oppression in my head, and I noticed that I was breathing very fast. The sensation reminded me of my only experience of mountaineering, and from that I judged the air to be more rarefied than it is now.

"Far away up the desolate slope I heard a harsh scream, and saw a thing like a huge white butterfly go slanting and fluttering up into the sky and, circling, disappear over some low

---

1   I.e., like a deep red pigment of the kind originally obtained from the East Indies.

hillocks beyond. The sound of its voice was so dismal that I shivered and seated myself more firmly upon the machine. Looking round me again, I saw that, quite near, what I had taken to be a reddish mass of rock was moving slowly towards me. Then I saw the thing was really a monstrous crab-like creature. Can you imagine a crab as large as yonder table, with its many legs moving slowly and uncertainly, its big claws swaying, its long antennæ, like carters' whips,[1] waving and feeling, and its stalked eyes gleaming at you on either side of its metallic front? Its back was corrugated and ornamented with ungainly bosses,[2] and a greenish incrustation blotched it here and there. I could see the many palps of its complicated mouth flickering and feeling as it moved.

"As I stared at this sinister apparition crawling towards me, I felt a tickling on my cheek as though a fly had lighted there. I tried to brush it away with my hand, but in a moment it returned, and almost immediately came another by my ear. I struck at this, and caught something threadlike. It was drawn swiftly out of my hand. With a frightful qualm, I turned, and saw that I had grasped the antenna of another monster crab that stood just behind me. Its evil eyes were wriggling on their stalks, its mouth was all alive with appetite, and its vast ungainly claws, smeared with an algal slime,[3] were descending upon me. In a moment my hand was on the lever, and I had placed a month between myself and these monsters. But I was still on the same beach, and I saw them distinctly now as soon as I stopped. Dozens of them seemed to be crawling here and there, in the sombre light, among the foliated[4] sheets of intense green.

"I cannot convey the sense of abominable desolation that hung over the world. The red eastern sky, the northward blackness, the salt Dead Sea,[5] the stony beach crawling with these

---

1 I.e., whips used by those who drive horse-drawn carts. For the source of these crabs, see Appendix A9.
2 Round projections.
3 I.e., a slime from a kind of algae or scummy seaweed.
4 Composed of small leaves.
5 An allusion to the lake in the Holy Land known for its extreme saltiness and almost complete sterility.

foul, slow-stirring monsters, the uniform poisonous-looking green of the lichenous plants, the thin air that hurts one's lungs: all contributed to an appalling effect. I moved on a hundred years, and there was the same red sun—a little larger, a little duller—the same dying sea, the same chill air, and the same crowd of earthy crustacea creeping in and out among the green weed and the red rocks. And in the westward sky I saw a curved pale line like a vast new moon.

"So I travelled, stopping ever and again, in great strides of a thousand years or more, drawn on by the mystery of the earth's fate, watching with a strange fascination the sun grow larger and duller in the westward sky, and the life of the old earth ebb away. At last, more than thirty million years hence, the huge red-hot dome of the sun had come to obscure nearly a tenth part of the darkling heavens. Then I stopped once more, for the crawling multitude of crabs had disappeared, and the red beach, save for its livid green liverworts and lichens, seemed lifeless. And now it was flecked with white. A bitter cold assailed me. Rare white flakes ever and again came eddying down. To the north-eastward, the glare of snow lay under the starlight of the sable sky, and I could see an undulating crest of hillocks pinkish-white. There were fringes of ice along the sea margin, with drifting masses further out; but the main expanse of that salt ocean, all bloody under the eternal sunset, was still unfrozen.

"I looked about me to see if any traces of animal-life remained. A certain indefinable apprehension still kept me in the saddle of the machine. But I saw nothing moving, in earth or sky or sea. The green slime on the rocks alone testified that life was not extinct. A shallow sandbank had appeared in the sea and the water had receded from the beach. I fancied I saw some black object flopping about upon this bank, but it became motionless as I looked at it, and I judged that my eye had been deceived, and that the black object was merely a rock. The stars in the sky were intensely bright and seemed to me to twinkle very little.

"Suddenly I noticed that the circular westward outline of the sun had changed; that a concavity, a bay, had appeared in the curve. I saw this grow larger. For a minute perhaps I stared aghast at this blackness that was creeping over the day, and then I realized that an eclipse was beginning. Either the moon or the planet Mercury was passing across the sun's disk. Naturally, at first I took it to be the moon, but there is much to incline me to believe that what I really saw was the transit of an inner planet passing very near to the earth.

"The darkness grew apace; a cold wind began to grow in freshening gusts from the east, and the showering white flakes in the air increased in number. From the edge of the sea came a ripple and whisper. Beyond these lifeless sounds the world was silent. Silent? It would be hard to convey the stillness of it. All the sounds of man, the bleating of sheep, the cries of birds, the hum of insects, the stir that makes the background of our lives—all that was over. As the darkness thickened, the eddying flakes grew more abundant, dancing before my eyes; and the cold of the air more intense. At last, one by one, swiftly, one after the other, the white peaks of the distant hills vanished into blackness. The breeze rose to a moaning wind. I saw the black central shadow of the eclipse sweeping towards me. In another moment the pale stars alone were visible. All else was rayless obscurity. The sky was absolutely black.

"A horror of this great darkness came on me. The cold, that smote to my marrow, and the pain I felt in breathing overcame me. I shivered, and a deadly nausea seized me. Then like a red-hot bow in the sky appeared the edge of the sun. I got off the machine to recover myself. I felt giddy and incapable of facing the return journey. As I stood sick and confused I saw again the moving thing upon the shoal[1]—there was no mistake now that it was a moving thing—against the red water of the sea. It was a round thing, the size of a football[2] perhaps, or, it may be, bigger, and tentacles trailed down from it; it seemed black against the weltering blood-red water, and it was hopping fitfully about. Then I felt I was fainting. But a terrible dread of lying helpless in that remote and awful twilight sustained me while I clambered upon the saddle.

---

1 Sandbank.
3 I.e., a soccer ball, about 27-28 inches in circumference.

XV

THE TIME TRAVELLER'S RETURN

"So I came back. For a long time I must have been insensible upon the machine. The blinking succession of the days and nights was resumed, the sun got golden again, the sky blue. I breathed with greater freedom. The fluctuating contours of the land ebbed and flowed. The hands spun backward upon the dials. At last I saw again the dim shadows of houses, the evidences of decadent humanity. These, too, changed and passed, and others came. Presently, when the million dial was at zero, I slackened speed. I began to recognize our own petty and familiar architecture, the thousands hand ran back to the starting-point, the night and day flapped slower and slower. Then the old walls of the laboratory came round me. Very gently, now, I slowed the mechanism down.

"I saw one little thing that seemed odd to me. I think I have told you that when I set out, before my velocity became very high, Mrs. Watchett had walked across the room, travelling, as it seemed to me, like a rocket. As I returned, I passed again across that minute when she traversed the laboratory. But now her every motion appeared to be the exact inversion of her previous ones. The door at the lower end opened, and she glided quietly up the laboratory, back foremost, and disappeared behind the door by which she had previously entered. Just before that I seemed to see Hillyer[1] for a moment; but he passed like a flash.

"Then I stopped the machine, and saw about me again the old familiar laboratory, my tools, my appliances just as I had left them. I got off the thing very shakily, and sat down upon my

---

1 Hillyer is sometimes taken to be the narrator of the external or frame narrative of *The Time Machine*, here entering the laboratory the day after the Time Traveller has told his tale, just in time to see the Time Traveller disappear on his machine for good (see Chapter XVI). But he may simply be the man-servant referred to at the end of Chapter XVI.

bench. For several minutes I trembled violently. Then I became calmer. Around me was my old workshop again, exactly as it had been. I might have slept there, and the whole thing have been a dream.

"And yet, not exactly! The thing had started from the south-east corner of the laboratory. It had come to rest again in the north-west, against the wall where you saw it. That gives you the exact distance from my little lawn to the pedestal of the White Sphinx, into which the Morlocks had carried my machine.

"For a time my brain went stagnant. Presently I got up and came through the passage here, limping, because my heel was still painful, and feeling sorely begrimed. I saw the *Pall Mall Gazette*[1] on the table by the door. I found the date was indeed to-day, and looking at the timepiece, saw the hour was almost eight o'clock. I heard your voices and the clatter of plates. I hesitated—I felt so sick and weak. Then I sniffed good wholesome meat, and opened the door on you. You know the rest. I washed, and dined, and now I am telling you the story."

---

1   A London evening newspaper, to which Wells contributed many articles in the period 1893-95.

XVI

AFTER THE STORY

"I KNOW," he said after a pause, "that all this will be absolutely incredible to you, but to me the one incredible thing is that I am here to-night in this old familiar room, looking into your friendly faces, and telling you all these strange adventures." He looked at the Medical Man. "No. I cannot expect you to believe it. Take it as a lie — or a prophecy. Say I dreamed it in the workshop. Consider I have been speculating upon the destinies of our race, until I have hatched this fiction. Treat my assertion of its truth as a mere stroke of art to enhance its interest. And taking it as a story, what do you think of it?"

He took up his pipe, and began, in his old accustomed manner, to tap with it nervously upon the bars of the grate. There was a momentary stillness. Then chairs began to creak and shoes to scrape upon the carpet. I took my eyes off the Time Traveller's face, and looked round at his audience. They were in the dark, and little spots of colour swam before them. The Medical Man seemed absorbed in the contemplation of our host. The Editor was looking hard at the end of his cigar — the sixth. The Journalist fumbled for his watch. The others, as far as I remember, were motionless.

The Editor stood up with a sigh. "What a pity it is you're not a writer of stories!" he said, putting his hand on the Time Traveller's shoulder.

"You don't believe it?"

"Well — "

"I thought not."

The Time Traveller turned to us. "Where are the matches?" he said. He lit one and spoke over his pipe, puffing. "To tell you the truth ... I hardly believe it myself.... And yet ..."

His eye fell with a mute inquiry upon the withered white flowers upon the little table. Then he turned over the hand holding his pipe, and I saw he was looking at some half-healed scars on his knuckles.

The Medical Man rose, came to the lamp, and examined the flowers. "The gynæceum's[1] odd," he said. The Psychologist leant forward to see, holding out his hand for a specimen.

"I'm hanged if it isn't a quarter to one," said the Journalist. "How shall we get home?"

"Plenty of cabs at the station," said the Psychologist.

"It's a curious thing," said the Medical Man; "but I certainly don't know the natural order[2] of these flowers. May I have them?"

The Time Traveller hesitated. Then suddenly, "Certainly not."

"Where did you really get them?" said the Medical Man.

The Time Traveller put his hand to his head. He spoke like one who was trying to keep hold of an idea that eluded him. "They were put into my pocket by Weena, when I travelled into Time." He stared round the room. "I'm damned if it isn't all going. This room and you and the atmosphere of every day is too much for my memory. Did I ever make a Time Machine, or a model of a Time Machine? Or is it all only a dream? They say life is a dream, a precious poor dream at times — but I can't stand another that won't fit. It's madness. And where did the dream come from?... I must look at that machine. If there *is* one!"

He caught up the lamp swiftly, and carried it, flaring red, through the door into the corridor. We followed him. There in the flickering light of the lamp was the machine sure enough, squat, ugly, and askew, a thing of brass, ebony, ivory, and translucent glimmering quartz. Solid to the touch — for I put out my hand and felt the rail of it — and with brown spots and smears upon the ivory, and bits of grass and moss upon the lower parts, and one rail bent awry.

The Time Traveller put the lamp down on the bench, and ran his hand along the damaged rail. "It's all right now," he said. "The story I told you was true. I'm sorry to have brought you

---

1   The female reproductive organ (the pistils) of a flower.
2   I.e., their botanical classification.

out here in the cold." He took up the lamp, and, in an absolute silence, we returned to the smoking-room.

He came into the hall with us, and helped the Editor on with his coat. The Medical Man looked into his face and, with a certain hesitation, told him he was suffering from overwork, at which he laughed hugely. I remember him standing in the open doorway, bawling good-night.

I shared a cab with the Editor. He thought the tale a "gaudy lie." For my own part I was unable to come to a conclusion. The story was so fantastic and incredible, the telling so credible and sober. I lay awake most of the night thinking about it. I determined to go next day, and see the Time Traveller again. I was told he was in the laboratory, and being on easy terms in the house, I went up to him. The laboratory, however, was empty. I stared for a minute at the Time Machine and put out my hand and touched the lever. At that the squat substantial-looking mass swayed like a bough shaken by the wind. Its instability startled me extremely, and I had a queer reminiscence of the childish days when I used to be forbidden to meddle. I came back through the corridor. The Time Traveller met me in the smoking-room. He was coming from the house. He had a small camera under one arm and a knapsack under the other. He laughed when he saw me, and gave me an elbow to shake. "I'm frightfully busy," said he, "with that thing in there."

"But is it not some hoax?" I said. "Do you really travel through time?"

"Really and truly I do." And he looked frankly into my eyes. He hesitated. His eye wandered about the room. "I only want half an hour," he said. "I know why you came, and it's awfully good of you. There's some magazines here. If you'll stop to lunch I'll prove you this time travelling up to the hilt, specimens and all. If you'll forgive my leaving you now?"

I consented, hardly comprehending then the full import of his words, and he nodded and went on down the corridor. I heard the door of the laboratory slam, seated myself in a chair, and took up a daily paper. What was he going to do before lunch-time? Then suddenly I was reminded by an advertisement that I had promised to meet Richardson, the publisher, at two. I looked at my watch, and saw that I could barely save that engagement. I got up and went down the passage to tell the Time Traveller.

As I took hold of the handle of the door I heard an exclamation, oddly truncated at the end, and a click and a thud. A gust of air whirled round me as I opened the door, and from within came the sound of broken glass falling on the floor. The Time Traveller was not there. I seemed to see a ghostly, indistinct figure sitting in a whirling mass of black and brass for a moment—a figure so transparent that the bench behind with its sheets of drawings was absolutely distinct; but this phantasm vanished as I rubbed my eyes. The Time Machine had gone. Save for a subsiding stir of dust, the further end of the laboratory was empty. A pane of the skylight had, apparently, just been blown in.

I felt an unreasonable amazement. I knew that something strange had happened, and for the moment could not distinguish what the strange thing might be. As I stood staring, the door into the garden opened, and the man-servant appeared.

We looked at each other. Then ideas began to come. "Has Mr.—— gone out that way?" said I.

"No, sir. No one has come out this way. I was expecting to find him here."

At that I understood. At the risk of disappointing Richardson I stayed on, waiting for the Time Traveller: waiting for the second, perhaps still stranger story, and the specimens and photographs he would bring with him. But I am beginning now to fear that I must wait a lifetime. The Time Traveller vanished three years ago. And, as everybody knows now, he has never returned.

EPILOGUE

ONE cannot choose but wonder. Will he ever return? It may be that he swept back into the past, and fell among the blood-drinking, hairy savages of the Age of Unpolished Stone; into the abysses of the Cretaceous Sea; or among the grotesque saurians, the huge reptilian brutes of the Jurassic times.[1] He may even now—if I may use the phrase—be wandering on some plesiosaurus-haunted Oolitic coral reef,[2] or beside the lonely saline seas of the Triassic Age.[3] Or did he go forward, into one of the nearer ages, in which men are still men, but with the riddles of our own time answered and its wearisome problems solved? Into the manhood of the race: for I, for my own part, cannot think that these latter days of weak experiment, fragmentary theory, and mutual discord are indeed man's culminating time! I say, for my own part. He, I know—for the question had been discussed among us long before the Time Machine was made—thought but cheerlessly of the Advancement of Mankind,[4] and saw in the growing pile of civilization only a foolish heaping that must inevitably fall back upon and destroy its makers in the end. If that is so, it remains for us to live as though it were not so. But to me the future is still black and blank—is a vast ignorance, lit at a few casual places by the

---

1   The Age of Unpolished Stone, more usually called the Old Stone Age or Palae-olithic period, was the earliest phase of human development and is characterised by the production of crude stone tools. It lasted from about 2.5 million years ago to as recently as 10,000 years ago. The Cretaceous geological period, most recent of the Mesozoic era and marked by extensive submergence of the continents, lasted from about 144 to 66.4 million years ago. The Jurassic period, characterized by the emergence of many now extinct reptiles of the saurian order, lasted from about 208 to 144 million years ago.

2   Oolite is a fossil-bearing limestone that was laid down in the Jurassic period, when plesiosaurus, an extinct long-necked predatory marine reptile, haunted the shallow seas.

3   The Triassic period, the earliest phase of the Mesozoic era, lasted from about 245 to 208 million years ago.

4   A catch-phrase expressing the confidence of the Victorian period in inevitable progress.

memory of his story. And I have by me, for my comfort, two strange white flowers—shrivelled now, and brown and flat and brittle—to witness that even when mind and strength had gone, gratitude and a mutual tenderness still lived on in the heart of man.

Appendix A: The Evolutionary Context: Biology

1. Charles Darwin. From _The Origin of Species_. 1859. 6th ed. 2 vols. New York and London: D. Appleton, 1872.

[Darwin's great work had both a positive and negative influence on Wells. The first extract is taken from the summary concluding Chapter IV, "Natural Selection; or The Survival of the Fittest," of the sixth edition, the one Wells is likely to have known best. In it, Darwin (1809-82) connects the ideas of natural selection, diversification, and extinction, together so crucial in determining Wells's vision in _The Time Machine_ of the fate of humanity in the far future.]

If under changing conditions of life organic beings present individual differences in almost every part of their structure, and this cannot be disputed; if there be, owing to their geometrical rate of increase, a severe struggle for life at some age, season, or year, and this certainly cannot be disputed; then, considering the infinite complexity of the relations of all organic beings to each other and to their conditions of life, causing an infinite diversity in structure, constitution, and habits, to be advantageous to them, it would be a most extraordinary fact if no variations had ever occurred useful to each being's own welfare, in the same manner as so many variations have occurred useful to man. But if variations useful to any organic being ever do occur, assuredly individuals thus characterised will have the best chance of being preserved in the struggle for life; and from the strong principle of inheritance, these will tend to produce offspring similarly characterised. This principle of preservation, or the survival of the fittest, I have called Natural Selection.

... we have already seen how [Natural Selection] entails extinction; and how largely extinction has acted in the world's history, geology plainly declares. Natural Selection, also, leads to divergence of character; for the more organic beings diverge in structure, habits, and constitution, by so much the more can a large number be supported on the area, — of which we see proof by looking to the inhabitants of any small spot, and to the productions naturalised in foreign lands. Therefore, during the modification of the descendants of any one species, and during the incessant struggle of all species to increase in numbers, the more diversified the descendants become, the better will be their chance of success in the battle for life. Thus the small differences distinguishing varieties of the same species, steadily tend to increase, till they equal the greater differences between species of the same genus, or even of distinct genera. (I:159-61)

[In this second extract, from Chapter XV: "Recapitulation and Conclusion," Darwin encourages the optimistic attitude to the future of humanity that Wells, following Huxley's cue, would refer to scathingly as "Excelsior biology" (see Appendix A4) and attacked in *The Time Machine*.]

As all the living forms of life are the lineal descendants of those which lived long before the Cambrian epoch, we may feel certain that the ordinary succession by generation has never once been broken, and that no cataclysm has desolated the whole world. Hence we may look with some confidence to a secure future of great length. And as natural selection works solely by and for the good of each being, all corporeal and mental endowments will tend to progress towards perfection. (II:305)

2. E. Ray Lankester. From *Degeneration: A Chapter in Darwinism*. London: Macmillan, 1880.

[Sir Edwin Ray Lankester (1847-1929) had a distinguished career as a marine biologist, and became a close friend of Wells. In this short early work Lankester provided evidence of biological degeneration from his research on the life-cycle of molluscs, especially ascidians (sea squirts). His pessimistic analogies between biological degeneration and cultural processes (the fall of ancient Rome, linguistic decay, moral decadence) were characteristic of that body of late-nineteenth-century Darwinian thought out of which also emerged the world of the Eloi and Morlocks.]

Degeneration may be defined as a gradual change of the structure in which the organism becomes adapted to *less* varied and *less* complex conditions of life; whilst Elaboration is a gradual change of structure in which the organism becomes adapted to more and more varied and complex conditions of existence. In Elaboration there is a new *expression* of form, corresponding to new perfection of work in the animal machine. In Degeneration there is *suppression* of form, corresponding to the cessation of work. Elaboration of some one organ *may* be a necessary accompaniment of Degeneration in all the others; in fact, this is very generally the case; and it is only when the total result of the Elaboration of some organs, and the Degeneration of others, is such as to leave the whole animal in a *lower* condition, that is, fitted to less complex action and reaction in regard to its surroundings, than was the ancestral form with which we are comparing it (either actually or in imagination) that we speak of that animal as an instance of Degeneration.

Any new set of conditions occurring to an animal which render its food and safety very easily attained, seem to lead as a rule to Degeneration; just as an active healthy man sometimes degenerates when he becomes suddenly possessed of a fortune; or as Rome degenerated when possessed of the riches of the ancient world. The habit of parasitism clearly acts upon animal organisation in this way. Let the parasitic life once be secured, and away go legs, jaws, eyes, and ears; the active, highly-gifted crab, insect, or annelid[1] may become a mere sac, absorbing nourishment and laying eggs. (32-33)

... wherever in fact the great principle of evolution has been recognised, degeneration plays an important part. In tracing the development of languages, philologists have long made use of the hypothesis of degeneration. Under certain conditions, in the mouths and minds of this or that branch of a race, a highly elaborate language has sometimes degenerated and become no longer fit to express complex or subtle conceptions, but only such as are simpler and more obvious.

The traditional history of mankind furnishes us with notable

---

1 A class of worms.

examples of degeneration. High states of civilisation have decayed and given place to low and degenerate states. At one time it was a favourite doctrine that the savage races of mankind were degenerate descendants of the higher and civilised races. This general and sweeping application of the doctrine of degeneration has been proved to be erroneous by careful study of the habits, arts, and beliefs of savages; at the same time there is no doubt that many savage races as we at present see them are actually degenerate and are descended from ancestors possessed of a relatively elaborate civilisation. As such we may cite some of the Indians of Central America, the modern Egyptians, and even the heirs of the great oriental monarchies of præ-Christian times....

With regard to ourselves, the white races of Europe, the possibility of degeneration seems to be worth some consideration. In accordance with a tacit assumption of universal progress — an unreasoning optimism — we are accustomed to regard ourselves as necessarily progressing, as necessarily having arrived at a higher and more elaborated condition than that which our ancestors reached, and as destined to progress still further. On the other hand, it is as well to remember that we are subject to the general laws of evolution, and are as likely to degenerate as to progress. As compared with the immediate forefathers of our civilisation — the ancient Greeks — we do not appear to have improved so far as our bodily structure is concerned, nor assuredly so far as some of our mental capacities are concerned. Our powers of perceiving and expressing beauty of form have certainly *not* increased since the days of the Parthenon and Aphrodite of Melos. In matters of the reason, in the development of intellect, we may seriously inquire how the case stands. Does the reason of the average man of civilised Europe stand out clearly as an evidence of progress when compared with that of the men of bygone ages? Are all the inventions and figments of human superstition and folly, the self-inflicted torturing of mind, the reiterated substitution of wrong for right, and of falsehood for truth, which disfigure our modern civilisation — are these evidences of progress? In such respects we have at least reason to fear that we may be degenerate. Possibly we are all drifting, tending to the condition of intellectual Barnacles or Ascidians. It is possible for us—just as the Ascidian throws away its tail and its eye and sinks into a quiescent state of inferiority—to reject the good gift of reason with which every child is born, and to degenerate into a contented life of material enjoyment accompanied by ignorance and superstition....

There is only one means of estimating our position, only one means of so shaping our conduct that we may with certainty avoid degeneration and keep an onward course.... To us has been given the power to *know the causes of things,* and by the use of this power it is possible for us to control our destinies. It is for us by ceaseless and ever hopeful labour to try to gain a knowledge of man's place in the order of nature. When we have gained this fully and minutely, we shall be able by the light of the past to guide ourselves in the future. In proportion as the whole of the past evolution of civilised man, of which we at present perceive the outlines, is assigned to its causes, we and our successors on the globe may expect to be able duly to estimate that which makes for, and that which makes against, the progress of the race. The full and earnest cultivation of Science—the Knowledge of Causes—is that to which we have to look for the protection of our race—even of this English branch of it—from relapse and degeneration. (58-62)

3. Thomas H. Huxley. From "The Struggle for Existence in Human Society." [*Nineteenth Century* 23 (February 1888): 61–80.] *Collected Essays. Vol. IX. Evolution and Ethics and Other Essays.* New York: D. Appleton, 1902. 195–236.

[No other single figure had a greater influence on the young Wells than Huxley (1825–95), the chief promoter of Darwinian ideas and the champion of science against the forces of superstition in the later Victorian age. A master of prose style, Huxley differed from Darwin in his refusal to associate evolution with inevitable social or moral progress, though he denied being a pessimist. Huxley's vision of evolution as a "materialized logical process" influenced *The Time Machine* in innumerable ways.]

... it is an error to imagine that evolution signifies a constant tendency to increased perfection. That process undoubtedly involves a constant remodelling of the organism in adaptation to new conditions; but it depends on the nature of those conditions whether the direction of the modifications effected shall be upward or downward. Retrogressive is as practicable as progressive metamorphosis. If what the physical philosophers tell us, that our globe has been in a state of fusion, and, like the sun, is gradually cooling down, is true; then the time must come when evolution will mean adaptation to a universal winter, and all forms of life will die out, except such low and simple organisms as the Diatom of the arctic and antarctic ice and the Protococcus[1] of the red snow. If our globe is proceeding from a condition in which it was too hot to support any but the lowest living thing to a condition in which it will be too cold to permit of the existence of any others, the course of life upon its surface must describe a trajectory like that of a ball fired from a mortar; and the sinking half of that course is as much a part of the general process of evolution as the rising. (199)

Pessimism is as little consonant with the facts of sentient existence as optimism. If we desire to represent the course of nature in terms of human thought, and assume that it was intended to be that which it is, we must say that its governing principle is intellectual and not moral; that it is a materialized logical process, accompanied by pleasures and pains, the incidence of which, in the majority of cases, has not the slightest reference to moral desert. (202)

4. H. G. Wells. From "Zoological Retrogression." *Gentleman's Magazine* **271 (September 1891): 246-53.**

[This essay, showing the strong influence of Huxley and Lankester, was Wells's most complete non-fictional discussion of the implications of biological degeneration. Intended for a non-specialist readership, it was the first work by Wells to have a transatlantic impact, for it was summarized under the title

---

1   A kind of microscopic algae.

"Degeneration and Evolution" in *Scientific American* (10 October 1891) and then reprinted in full in the Boston periodical *Living Age* in November 1891.]

Perhaps no scientific theories are more widely discussed or more generally misunderstood among cultivated people than the views held by biologists regarding the past history and future prospects of their province—life. Using their technical phrases and misquoting their authorities in an invincibly optimistic spirit, the educated public has arrived in its own way at a rendering of their results which it finds extremely satisfactory. It has decided that in the past the great scroll of nature has been steadily unfolding to reveal a constantly richer harmony of forms and successively higher grades of being, and it assumes that this "evolution" will continue with increasing velocity under the supervision of its extreme expression—man. This belief, as effective, progressive, and pleasing as transformation scenes at a pantomime, receives neither in the geological record nor in the studies of the phylogenetic[1] embryologist any entirely satisfactory confirmation.

On the contrary, there is almost always associated with the suggestion of advance in biological phenomena an opposite idea, which is its essential complement. The technicality expressing this would, if it obtained sufficient currency in the world of culture, do much to reconcile the naturalist and his traducers. The toneless glare of optimistic evolution would then be softened by a shadow; the monotonous reiteration of "Excelsior"[2] by people who did not climb would cease; the too sweet harmony of the spheres would be enhanced by a discord, this evolutionary antithesis—degradation.

Isolated cases of degeneration have long been known, and popular attention has been drawn to them in order to point well-meant moral lessons, the fallacious analogy of species to individual being employed. It is only recently, however, that the

---

1   Specializing in the evolution of a phylum or primary biological division of organisms.
2   "Excelsior" (Latin for "Higher!") alludes to the popular poem (1842) of that title by Longfellow.

enormous importance of degeneration as a plastic process in nature has been suspected and its entire parity with evolution recognised.

It is no libel to say that three-quarters of the people who use the phrase, "organic evolution," interpret it very much in this way:—Life began with the amoeba, and then came jelly-fish, shell-fish, and all those miscellaneous invertebrate things, and then *real* fishes and amphibia, reptiles, birds, mammals, and man, the last and first of creation. It has been pointed out that this is very like regarding a man as the offspring of his first cousins; these, of his second; these, of his relations at the next remove, and so forth—making the remotest living human being his primary ancestor. Or, to select another image, it is like elevating the modest poor relation at the family gathering to the unexpected altitude of fountain-head—a proceeding which would involve some cruel reflections on her age and character. The sounder view is, as scientific writers have frequently insisted, that living species have varied along divergent lines from intermediate forms, and, as it is the object of this paper to point out, not necessarily in an upward direction.

In fact, the path of life, so frequently compared to some steadily-rising mountain-slope, is far more like a footway worn by leisurely wanderers in an undulating country. Excelsior biology is a popular and poetic creation—the *real* form of a phylum, or line of descent, is far more like the course of a busy man moving about a great city. Sometimes it goes underground, sometimes it doubles and twists in tortuous streets, now it rises far overhead along some viaduct, and, again, the river is taken advantage of in these varied journeyings to and fro. Upward and downward these threads of pedigree interweave, slowly working out a pattern of accomplished things that is difficult to interpret, but in which scientific observers certainly fail to discover that inevitable tendency to higher and better things with which the word "evolution" is popularly associated.

The best known, and, perhaps, the most graphic and typical, illustration of the downward course is ... the fairly common Sea Squirts, or *Ascidians*, of our coasts. By an untrained observer a specimen of these would at first very probably be placed in the mineral or vegetable kingdoms. Externally they are simply shapeless lumps of a stiff, semi-transparent, cartilaginous substance, in which pebbles, twigs, and dirt are imbedded, and only the most careful examination of this unpromising exterior would discover any evidence of the living thing within. A penknife, however, serves to lay bare the animal inside this house, or "test," and the fleshy texture of the semi-transparent body must then convince the unscientific investigator of his error.

He would forthwith almost certainly make a fresh mistake in his classification of this new animal. Like most zoologists until a comparatively recent date, he would think of such impassive and, from the human point of view, lowly beings as the oyster and mussel as its brethren, and a superficial study of its anatomy might even strengthen this opinion. As a matter of fact, however, these singular creatures are far more closely related to the vertebrata — they lay claim to the quarterings, not of molluscs, but of imperial man! and, like novelette heroes with a birthmark, they carry their proofs about with them....

Like a tadpole, the [young ascidian] has a well-developed tail which propels its owner vigorously through the water. There is a conspicuous single eye, reminding the zoologist at once of the Polyphemus eye[1] that almost certainly existed in the central group of the vertebrata. There are also serviceable organs of taste and hearing, and the lively movements of the little creature justify the supposition that its being is fairly full of endurable sensations. But this flush of golden youth is sadly transient: it is barely attained before a remarkable and depressing change appears in the drift of the development.

The ascidian begins to take things seriously — a deliberate sobriety gradually succeeds its tremulous vivacity. L'Allegro dies away; the tones of Il Penseroso[2] become dominant.

On the head appear certain sucker-like structures.... The animal becomes dull, moves about more and more slowly, and

1 A single eye, like that of Polyphemus the Cyclops in Homer's *Odyssey*.
2 "L'Allegro" and "Il Penseroso" (both 1645) are companion poems by Milton, contrasting the cheerful and melancholy temperaments.

finally fixes itself by these suckers to a rock. It has settled down in life. The tail that waggled so merrily undergoes a rapid process of absorption; eye and ear, no longer needed, atrophy completely, and the skin secretes the coarse, inorganic-looking "test." It is very remarkable that this "test" should consist of a kind of cellulose—a compound otherwise almost exclusively confined to the vegetable kingdom. The transient glimpse of vivid animal life is forgotten, and the rest of this existence is a passive receptivity to what chance and the water bring along. The ascidian lives henceforth an idyll of contentment, glued, head downwards, to a stone,

The world forgetting, by the world forgot.[1]

Now here, to all who refer nature to one rigid table of precedence, is an altogether inexplicable thing. A creature on a level, at lowest, immediately next to vertebrated life, turns back from the upward path and becomes at last a merely vegetative excrescence on a rock.

It is lower even than the patriarchal amoeba of popular science if we take psychic life as the standard: for does not even the amoeba crawl after and choose its food and immediate environment? We have then, as I have read somewhere—I think it was in an ecclesiastical biography—a career not perhaps teemingly eventful, but full of the richest suggestion and edification.

And here one may note a curious comparison which can be made between this life-history and that of many a respectable pinnacle and gargoyle on the social fabric. Every respectable citizen of the professional classes passes through a period of activity and imagination, of "liveliness and eccentricity," of "*Sturm und Drang.*"[2] He shocks his aunts. Presently, however, he realizes the sober aspect of things. He becomes dull; he enters a profession; suckers appear on his head; and he studies. Finally, by virtue of these he settles down—he marries. All his wild ambitions and subtle aesthetic perceptions atrophy as needless

---

1   Pope, "Eloisa to Abelard" (1717), line 208.
2   Literally "storm and stress," a German expression referring to an artistic movement of the Romantic period specializing in the depiction of extreme emotions.

in the presence of calm domesticity. He secretes a house, or "establishment," round himself, of inorganic and servile material. His Bohemian tail is discarded. Henceforth his life is a passive receptivity to what chance and the drift of his profession bring along; he lives an almost entirely vegetative excrescence on the side of a street, and in the tranquillity of his calling finds that colourless contentment that replaces happiness.

But this comparison is possibly fallacious, and is certainly a digression. (246-50)

[Wells cites many more examples of degeneration in nature.]

These brief instances of degradation may perhaps suffice to show that there is a good deal to be found in the work of biologists quite inharmonious with such phrases as "the progress of the ages," and "the march of mind." The zoologist demonstrates that advance has been fitful and uncertain; rapid progress has often been followed by rapid extinction or degeneration, while, on the other hand, a form lowly and degraded has in its degradation often happened upon some fortunate discovery or valuable discipline and risen again, like a more fortunate Antæos,[1] to victory. There is, therefore, no guarantee in scientific knowledge of man's permanence or permanent ascendency. He has a remarkably variable organisation, and his own activities and increase cause the conditions of his existence to fluctuate far more widely than those of any animal have ever done. The presumption is that before him lies a long future of profound modification, but whether that will be, according to present ideals, upward or downward, no one can forecast. Still, so far as any scientist can tell us, it may be that, instead of this, Nature is, in unsuspected obscurity, equipping some now humble creature with wider possibilities of appetite, endurance, or destruction, to rise in the fulness of time and sweep *homo* away into the darkness from which his universe arose. The Coming Beast must certainly be reckoned in any anticipatory calculations regarding the Coming Man. (253)

---

1 In Greek mythology a giant who, when wrestling Heracles, would rise stronger each time he made contact with his mother, the Earth.

5. H. G. Wells. From *Text-Book of Biology* [University Correspondence College Tutorial Series]. 2 vols. Intro. G.B. Howes. London: W. B. Clive & Co., University Correspondence College P, 1893.

[As this short extract from the chapter entitled "The Theory of Evolution" from his first book suggests, Wells was aware of a huge untapped metaphoric potential in evolutionary biology and its connected sciences. Both *The Time Machine* and the yet unformed genre of science fiction are prefigured in such ruminations.]

In the place of disconnected species of animals, arbitrarily created, and a belief in the settled inexplicable, the student finds [in the theory of evolution] an enlightening realization of uniform and active causes beneath an apparent diversity. And the world is not made and dead like a cardboard model or a child's toy, but a living equilibrium; and every day and every hour, every living thing is being weighed in the balance and found sufficient or wanting.

Our little book is the merest beginning in zoology.... The great things of the science of Darwin, Huxley, Wallace, and Balfour[1] remain mainly untold. In the book of nature there are written, for instance, the triumphs of survival, the tragedy of death and extinction, the tragi-comedy of degradation and inheritance, the gruesome lesson of parasitism, and the political satire of colonial organisms. Zoology is, indeed, a philosophy and a literature to those who can read its symbols. (1:131)

---

1   Alfred Russel Wallace (1823-1913) was the naturalist who formulated a theory of natural selection independently from Darwin. "Balfour" refers probably to Francis Maitland Balfour (1851-82), the Scottish embryologist.

6. Thomas H. Huxley. From "Evolution and Ethics" [The Romanes Lecture, 1893]. *Collected Essays. Vol. IX. Evolution and Ethics and Other Essays*. New York: D. Appleton, 1902. 46–116.

[On 18 May 1893, Huxley gave the Romanes lecture at Oxford on "Evolution and Ethics," a subject that he had been struggling with ever since his reputation-making *Evidence as to Man's Place in Nature* (1863). A masterpiece of Victorian prose, "Evolution and Ethics" affirmed that natural cycles, such as that of the bean plant, involved growth followed by decay regardless of "moral desert." By analogy, this was also true of human civilizations—but Huxley appealed to man to apply his ethical sense to a morally indifferent universe, thereby starting the process of humanizing it. The influence of "Evolution and Ethics" on *The Time Machine* is very complex. It is particularly noticeable in the narrator's comments on the white flowers at the end of the novel, but there are also several ironic twists on some of Huxley's more earnest ideas. In this way Wells, launching his literary career, at once acknowledged his debt to and asserted his independence from his former professor.]

[Of the bean plant] By insensible steps, the plant builds itself up into a large and various fabric of root, stem, leaves, flowers, and fruit, every one moulded within and without in accordance with an extremely complex but, at the same time, minutely defined pattern.... But no sooner has the edifice, reared with such exact elaboration, attained completeness, than it begins to crumble. By degrees, the plant withers and disappears from view, leaving behind more or fewer apparently inert and simple bodies, just like the bean from which it sprang; and, like it, endowed with the potentiality of giving rise to a similar cycle of manifestations.

Neither the poetic nor the scientific imagination is put to much strain in the search after analogies with this process of going forth and, as it were, returning to the starting-point. It may be likened to the ascent and descent of a slung stone, or the course of an arrow along its trajectory. Or we may say that the living energy takes first an upward and then a downward road....

The value of a strong intellectual grasp of the nature of this process lies in the circumstance that what is true of the bean is true of living things in general. From very low forms up to the highest—in the animal no less than in the vegetable kingdom—the process of life presents the same appearance of cyclical evolution. Nay, we have but to cast our eyes over the rest of the world and cyclical change presents itself on all sides. It meets us in the water that flows to the sea and returns to the springs; in the heavenly bodies that wax and wane, go and return to their places; in the inexorable sequence of the ages of man's life; in that successive rise, apogee, and fall of dynasties and of states which is the most prominent topic of civil history. (47-49)

[Huxley's idea in these next two passages, that civilized man is no longer bound by the savage instincts necessitated by the struggle for existence, will be given a strongly ironic twist by Wells in his depiction of the Eloi, while Huxley's own ironic point about "fitness" in a cooling world will be dramatized strikingly by Wells in "The Further Vision."]

Man, the animal, in fact, has worked his way to the headship of the sentient world, and has become the superb animal which he is, in virtue of his success in the struggle for existence. The conditions having been of a certain order, man's organization has adjusted itself to them better than that of his competitors in the cosmic strife. In the case of mankind, the self-assertion, the unscrupulous seizing upon all that can be grasped, the tenacious holding of all that can be kept, which constitute the essence of the struggle for existence, have answered. For his successful progress, throughout the savage state, man has been largely indebted to those qualities which he shares with the ape and the tiger; his exceptional physical organization; his cunning; his sociability, his curiosity, and his imitativeness; his ruthless and ferocious destructiveness when his anger is roused by opposition.

But, in proportion as men have passed from anarchy to social organization, and in proportion as civilization has grown in worth, these deeply ingrained serviceable qualities have become defects. After the manner of successful persons, civilized man would gladly kick down the ladder by which he has climbed. He would be only too pleased to see "the ape and the tiger die."[1] (51–52)

There is another fallacy which appears to me to pervade the so-called "ethics of evolution." It is the notion that because, on the whole, animals and plants have advanced in perfection of organization by means of the struggle for existence and the consequent "survival of the fittest"; therefore men in society, men as ethical beings, must look to the same process to help them towards perfection. I suspect that this fallacy has arisen out of the unfortunate ambiguity of the phrase "survival of the fittest." "Fittest" has a connotation of "best"; and about "best" there hangs a moral flavour. In cosmic nature, however, what is "fittest" depends upon the conditions. Long since, I ventured to point out that if our hemisphere were to cool again, the survival of the fittest might bring about, in the vegetable kingdom, a population of more and more stunted and humbler and humbler organisms, until the "fittest" that survived might be nothing but lichens, diatoms, and such microscopic organisms as those which give red snow its colour; while, if it became hotter, the pleasant valleys of the Thames and Isis[2] might be uninhabitable by any animated beings save those that flourish in a tropical jungle. They, as the fittest, the best adapted to the changed conditions, would survive.

Men in society are undoubtedly subject to the cosmic process. As among other animals, multiplication goes on without cessation, and involves severe competition for the means of support. The struggle for existence tends to eliminate those less fitted to adapt themselves to the circumstances of their existence. The strongest, the most self-assertive, tend to tread down the weaker. But the influence of the cosmic process on the evolution of society is the greater the more rudimentary its

---

1   An allusion to Tennyson, *In Memoriam A.H.H.* (1850), 118, line 28.
2   The name by which the River Thames is known as it flows through Oxford.

civilization. Social progress means a checking of the cosmic process at every step and the substitution for it of another, which may be called the ethical process; the end of which is not the survival of those who may happen to be the fittest, in respect of the whole of the conditions which obtain, but of those who are ethically the best. (80-81)

[Huxley's concluding idea about the evolutionary importance of pain and sorrow is echoed strongly in the Time Traveller's naïve ruminations upon the "perfect comfort and security" of Eloi society in Chapter VII of *The Time Machine*.]

The theory of evolution encourages no millennial anticipations. If, for millions of years, our globe has taken the upward road, yet, some time, the summit will be reached and the downward route will be commenced. The most daring imagination will hardly venture upon the suggestion that the power and intelligence of man can ever arrest the procession of the great year....[1]

But if we may permit ourselves a larger hope of abatement of the essential evil of the world than was possible to those who, in the infancy of exact knowledge, faced the problem of existence more than a score of centuries ago, I deem it an essential condition of the realization of that hope that we should cast aside the notion that the escape from pain and sorrow is the proper object of life.

We have long since emerged from the heroic childhood of our race, when good and evil could be met with the same "frolic welcome";[2] the attempts to escape from evil, whether Indian or Greek, have ended in flight from the battle-field; it remains to us to throw aside the youthful over-confidence and the no less youthful discouragement of nonage. We are grown men, and must play the man

strong in will
To strive, to seek, to find, and not to yield.... (85-86)

---

1   For the significance of Huxley's "great year," see p. 123, n. 3.
2   This and the concluding quotation are both from Tennyson, "Ulysses" (1842), lines 47, 69-70.

7. [H. G. Wells.] "On Extinction." *Chambers's Journal of Popular Literature, Science, and Art* **10 (30 September 1893): 623-24.**

[From this short piece published anonymously, one may speculate that Wells conceived *The Time Machine* partly as a dramatization of the "tragedy of extinction" ending with "the most terrible thing that man can conceive as happening to man," as the Last Man is left alone to contemplate the annihilation of the human species.]

The passing away of ineffective things, the entire rejection by Nature of the plans of life, is the essence of tragedy. In the world of animals, that runs so curiously parallel with the world of men, we can see and trace only too often the analogies of our grimmer human experiences; we can find the equivalents to the sharp tragic force of Shakespeare, the majestic inevitableness of Sophocles, and the sordid dreary tale, the middle-class misery of Ibsen. The life that has schemed and struggled and committed itself, the life that has played and lost, comes at last to the pitiless judgment of time, and is slowly and remorselessly annihilated. This is the saddest chapter of biological science — the tragedy of Extinction.

In the long galleries of the geological museum are the records of judgments that have been passed graven upon the rocks. Here, for instance, are the huge bones of the "Atlantosaurus," one of the mightiest land animals that this planet has ever seen. A huge terrestrial reptile this, that crushed the forest trees as it browsed upon their foliage, and before which the pigmy ancestors of our present denizens of the land must have fled in abject terror of its mere might of weight. It had the length of four elephants, and its head towered thirty feet — higher, that is, than any giraffe — above the world it dominated. And yet this giant has passed away, and left no children to inherit the earth. No living thing can be traced back to these monsters; they are at an end among the branchings of the tree of life. Whether it was through some change of climate, some subtle disease, or some subtle enemy, these titanic reptiles dwindled in numbers, and faded at last altogether among things mundane. Save for the riddle of their scattered bones, it is as if they never had been.

Beside them are the pterodactyls, the first of vertebrated animals to spread a wing to the wind, and follow the hunted insects to their last refuge of the air. How triumphantly and gloriously these winged lizards, these original dragons, must have floated through their new empire of the atmosphere! If their narrow brains could have entertained the thought, they would have congratulated themselves upon having gained a great and inalienable heritage for themselves and their children for ever. And now we cleave a rock and find their bones, and speculate doubtfully what their outer shape may have been. No descendants are left to us. The birds are no offspring of theirs, but lighter children of some clumsy "deinosaurs."[1] The pterodactyls also have heard the judgment of extinction, and are gone altogether from the world.

The long roll of palæontology is half filled with the records of extermination; whole orders, families, groups, and classes have passed away and left no mark and no tradition upon the living fauna of the world. Many fossils of the older rocks are labelled in our museums, "of doubtful affinity." Nothing living has any part like them, and the baffled zoologist regretfully puts them aside. What they mean, he cannot tell. They hint merely at shadowy dead sub-kingdoms, of which the form eludes him. Index fingers are they, pointing into unfathomable darkness, and saying only one thing clearly, the word "Extinction."

In the living world of to-day the same forces are at work as in the past. One Fate still spins, and the gleaming scissors cut. In the last hundred years the swift change of condition throughout the world, due to the invention of new means of transit, geographical discovery, and the consequent "swarming" of the whole globe by civilised men, has pushed many an animal to the very verge of destruction. It is not only the dodo that has gone; for dozens of genera and hundreds of species, this century has witnessed the writing on the wall.

---

1   I.e., dinosaurs.

In the fate of the bison extinction has been exceptionally swift and striking. In the "forties" so vast were their multitudes that sometimes, "as far as the eye could reach," the plains would be covered by a galloping herd. Thousands of hunters, tribes of Indians, lived upon them. And now! It is improbable that one specimen in an altogether wild state survives. If it were not for the merciful curiosity of men, the few hundred that still live would also have passed into the darkness of non-existence. Following the same grim path are the seals, the Greenland whale, many Australian and New Zealand animals and birds ousted by more vigorous imported competitors, the black rat, endless wild birds. The list of destruction has yet to be made in its completeness. But the grand bison is the statuesque type and example of the doomed races.

Can any of these fated creatures count? Does any suspicion of their dwindling numbers dawn upon them? Do they, like the Red Indian, perceive the end to which they are coming? For most of them, unlike the Red Indian, there is no alternative of escape by interbreeding with their supplanters. Simply and unconditionally, there is written across their future, plainly for any reader, the one word "Death."

Surely a chill of solitude must strike to the heart of the last stragglers in the rout, the last survivors of the defeated and vanishing species. The last shaggy bison, looking with dull eyes from some western bluff across the broad prairies, must feel some dim sense that those wide rolling seas of grass were once the home of myriads of his race, and are now his no longer. The sunniest day must shine with a cold and desert light on the eyes of the condemned. For them the future is blotted out, and hope is vanity.

These days are the days of man's triumph. The awful solitude of such a position is almost beyond the imagination. The earth is warm with men. We think always with reference to men. The future is full of men to our preconceptions, whatever it may be in scientific truth. In the loneliest position in human possibility, humanity supports us. But Hood, who sometimes rose abruptly out of the most mechanical punning to sublime heights, wrote a travesty, grotesquely fearful, of Campbell's "The Last Man."[1] In this he probably hit upon the most terrible thing that man can conceive as happening to man: the earth desert through a pestilence, and two men, and then one man, looking extinction in the face. (623–24)

8. [H. G. Wells.] From "The Man of the Year Million: A Scientific Forecast." *Pall Mall Gazette* 57 (6 November 1893): 3.

[This essay was Wells's first major speculation about the "coming man." Its disconcerting vision of future humanity as the product of evolutionary forces acting over a very long period of time is a direct source for the depiction of the Martians in *The War of the Worlds* (1898). However, the essay's assault on Victorian complacency about mankind's inevitable progress towards perfection was continued first by *The Time Machine*, in which both Eloi and Morlocks are Men of the Year Million (give or take 200,000 years). "The Man of the Year Million" was reprinted as "Of a Book Unwritten" in *Certain Personal Matters* (1897).]

Accomplished literature is all very well in its way, no doubt, but much more fascinating to the contemplative man are the books that have not been written. ... primitive man, in the works of the descriptive anthropologist, is certainly a very entertaining and quaint person; but the man of the future, if we only had the facts, would appeal to us more strongly. Yet where are the books? As Ruskin has said somewhere, apropos of Darwin, it is not what man has been, but what he will be, that should interest us.

The contemplative man in his easy chair, pondering this saying, suddenly beholds in the fire, through the blue haze of his pipe, one of these great unwritten volumes. It is large in size, heavy in lettering, seemingly by one Professor Holzkopf, presumably Professor at Weissnichtwo.[2] "The Necessary Charac-

---

1   The allusion is to two poems: Thomas Campbell's "The Last Man" (1823) and Thomas Hood's "The Last Man" (1826).
2   Following Carlyle, the German names are fictitious and grotesque: Professor Wooden-Head at the University of Don't-Know-Where.

ters of the Man of the Remote Future deduced from the Existing Stream of Tendency," is the title....

"The theory of evolution," writes the Professor, "is now universally accepted by zoologists and botanists, and it is applied unreservedly to man. Some question, indeed, whether it fits his soul, but all agree it accounts for his body. Man, we are assured, is descended from ape-like ancestors, moulded by circumstances into men, and these apes again were derived from ancestral forms of a lower order, and so up from the primordial protoplasmic jelly. Clearly, then, man, unless the order of the universe has come to an end, will undergo further modification in the future, and at last cease to be man, giving rise to some other type of animated being. At once the fascinating question arises, What will this being be? Let us consider for a little the plastic influences at work upon our species.

"Just as the bird is the creature of the wing, and is all moulded and modified to flying, and just as the fish is the creature that swims, and has had to meet the inflexible conditions of a problem in hydrodynamics, so man is the creature of the brain: he will live by intelligence, and not by physical strength, if he live at all. So that much that is purely 'animal' about him is being, and must be, beyond all question, suppressed in his ultimate development. Evolution is no mechanical tendency making for perfection according to the ideas current in the year of grace 1892; it is simply the continual adaptation of plastic life, for good or evil, to the circumstances that surround it.... We notice this decay of the animal part around us now, in the loss of teeth and hair, in the dwindling hands and feet of men, in their smaller jaws, and slighter mouths and ears. Man now does by wit and machinery and verbal agreement what he once did by bodily toil; for once he had to catch his dinner, capture his wife, run away from his enemies, and continually exercise himself, for love of himself, to perform these duties well. But now all this is changed. Cabs, trains, trams, render speed unnecessary, the pursuit of food becomes easier; his wife is no longer hunted, but rather, in view of the crowded matrimonial market, seeks him out. One needs wits now to live, and physical activity is a drug, a snare even; it seeks artificial outlets and overflows in games. Athleticism takes up time and cripples a man in his competitive examinations, and in business. So is your fleshly man handicapped against his subtler brother. He is unsuccessful in life, does not marry. The better adapted survive."

The coming man, then, will clearly have a larger brain, and a slighter body than the present. But the Professor makes one exception to this. "The human hand, since it is the teacher and interpreter of the brain, will become constantly more powerful and subtle as the rest of the musculature dwindles."

Then in the physiology of these children of men, with their expanding brains, their great sensitive hands and diminishing bodies, great changes were necessarily worked. "We see now," says the Professor, "in the more intellectual sections of humanity an increasing sensitiveness to stimulants, a growing inability to grapple with such a matter as alcohol, for instance. No longer can men drink a bottle full of port; some cannot drink tea; it is too exciting for their highly-wrought nervous systems.... Fresh raw meat was once a dish for a king. Now refined persons scarcely touch meat unless it is cunningly disguised. Again, consider the case of turnips; the raw root is now a thing almost uneatable, but once upon a time a turnip must have been a rare and fortunate find, to be torn up in delirious eagerness and devoured in ecstasy. The time will come when the change will affect all the other fruits of the earth. Even now only the young of mankind eat apples raw—the young always preserving ancestral characteristics after their disappearance in the adult....

"Furthermore, fresh chemical discoveries came into action as modifying influences upon men. In the prehistoric period even, man's mouth had ceased to be an instrument for grasping food; it is still growing continually less prehensile, his front teeth are smaller, his lips thinner and less muscular; he has a new organ, a mandible not of irreparable tissue, but of bone and steel—a knife and fork. There is no reason why things should stop at partial artificial division thus afforded; there is every reason, on the contrary, to believe my statement that some cunning exterior mechanism will presently masticate and insalivate his dinner, relieve his diminishing salivary glands and teeth, and at last altogether abolish them."

Then what is not needed disappears. What use is there for external ears, nose, and brow ridges now? The two latter once protected the eye from injury in conflict and in falls, but in these days we keep on our legs, and at peace. Directing his thoughts in this way, the reader may presently conjure up a dim, strange vision of the latter-day face: "Eyes large, lustrous, beautiful, soulful; above them, no longer separated by rugged brow ridges, is the top of the head, a glistening, hairless dome, terete[1] and beautiful; no craggy nose rises to disturb by its unmeaning shadows the symmetry of that calm face, no vestigial ears project; the mouth is a small, perfectly round aperture, toothless and gumless, jawless, unanimal, no futile emotions disturbing its roundness as it lies, like the harvest moon or the evening star, in the wide firmament of face." Such is the face the Professor beholds in the future.

Of course parallel modifications will also affect the body and limbs. "Every day so many hours and so much energy are required for digestion; a gross torpidity, a carnal lethargy, seizes on mortal men after dinner. This may and can be avoided. Man's knowledge of organic chemistry widens daily. Already he can supplement the gastric glands by artificial devices. Every doctor who administers physic implies that the bodily functions may be artificially superseded.... A man who could not only leave his dinner to be cooked, but also leave it to be masticated and digested, would have vast social advantages over his food-digesting fellow.... Among some of these most highly modified crustaceans the whole of the alimentary canal—that is, all the food-digesting and food-absorbing parts—form a useless solid cord: the animal is nourished—it is a parasite—by absorption of the nutritive fluid in which it swims. Is there any absolute impossibility in supposing man to be destined for a similar change; to imagine him no longer dining, with unwieldy paraphernalia of servants and plates, upon food queerly dyed and distorted, but nourishing himself in elegant simplicity by immersion in a tub of nutritive fluid?

---

1 Smooth and round.

"There grows upon the impatient imagination a building, a dome of crystal, across the translucent surface of which flushes of the most glorious and pure prismatic colours pass and fade and change. In the centre of this transparent chameleon-tinted dome is a circular white marble basin filled with some clear, mobile, amber liquid, and in this plunge and float strange beings. Are they birds?

"They are the descendants of man — at dinner. Watch them as they hop on their hands — a method of progression advocated already by Bjornsen — about the pure white marble floor. Great hands they have, enormous brains, soft, liquid, soulful eyes. Their whole muscular system, their legs, their abdomens, are shrivelled to nothing, a dangling, degraded pendant to their minds.

The further visions of the professor are less alluring.

"The animals and plants die away before men, except such as he preserves for his food or delight, or such as maintain a precarious footing about him as commensals and parasites. These vermin and pests must succumb sooner or later to his untiring inventiveness and incessantly growing discipline. When he learns (the chemists are doubtless getting towards the secret now) to do the work of chlorophyll without the plant, then his necessity for other animals and plants upon the earth will disappear. Sooner or later, when there is no power of resistance and no necessity, there comes extinction. In the last days man will be alone on the earth, and his food will be won by the chemist from the dead rocks and the sunlight...."

Then the earth is ever radiating away heat into space, the Professor reminds us. And so at last comes a vision of earthly cherubim, hopping heads, great unemotional intelligences, and little hearts, fighting together perforce and fiercely against the cold that grips them tighter and tighter. For the world is cooling — slowly and inevitably it grows colder as the years roll by. "We must imagine these creatures," says the Professor, "in galleries and laboratories deep down in the bowels of the earth. The whole world will be snow-covered and piled with ice; all animals, all vegetation vanished, except this last branch of the tree of life. The last men have gone even deeper, following the diminishing heat of the planet, and vast steel shafts and ventilators make way for the air they need."

So with a glimpse of these human tadpoles, in their deep close gallery, with their boring machinery ringing away, and artificial lights glaring and casting black shadows, the professor's horoscope concludes. Humanity in ·dismal retreat before the cold, changed beyond recognition. Yet the Professor is reasonable enough, his facts are current science, his methods orderly. The contemplative man shivers at the prospect, starts up to poke the fire, and the whole of this remarkable book that is not written vanishes straightway in the smoke of his pipe. (3)

9. [H. G. Wells.] From "The Extinction of Man: Some Speculative Suggestions." *Pall Mall Gazette* 59 (25 September 1894): 3.

[Another attack on human complacency, showing how important the idea of inevitable human extinction was to Wells when he was composing *The Time Machine*. The giant land crabs mentioned here reappear in "The Further Vision."]

It is part of the excessive egotism of the human animal that the bare idea of its extinction seems incredible to it. "A world without *us!*" it says, as a heady young Cephalapsis might have said it in the old Silurian sea. But since the Cephalapsis and the Coccostens[1] many a fine animal has increased and multiplied upon the earth, lorded it over land or sea without a rival, and passed at last into the night. Surely it is not so unreasonable to ask why man should be an exception to the rule. From the scientific standpoint at least any reason for such exception is hard to find.

No doubt man is undisputed master at the present time — at least of most of the land surface; but so it has been before with other animals. Let us consider what light geology has to throw upon this. The great land and sea reptiles of the Mesozoic period, for instance, seem to have been as secure as humanity is

---

1 Cephalapsis and coccosteid are extinct fish from the very ancient Silurian geological period, approximately 450 million years ago.

now in their pre-eminence. But they passed away and left no descendants when the new orders of the mammals emerged from their obscurity. So, too, the huge Titanotheria of the American continent, and all the powerful mammals of Pleistocene South America, the sabre-toothed lion, for instance, and the Machrauchenia[1] suddenly came to a finish when they were still almost at the zenith of their rule. And in no case does the record of the fossils show a really dominant species succeeded by its own descendants. What has usually happened in the past appears to be the emergence of some type of animal hitherto rare and unimportant, and the extinction, not simply of the previous ruling species, but of most of the forms that are at all closely related to it. Sometimes, indeed, as in the case of the extinct giants of South America, they vanished without any considerable rivals, victims of pestilence, famine, or, it may be, of that cumulative inefficiency that comes of a too undisputed life. So that the analogy of geology, at any rate, is against this too acceptable view of man's certain tenure of the earth for the next few million years or so.

And after all even now man is by no means such a master of the kingdoms of life as he is apt to imagine. The sea, that mysterious nursery of living things, is for all practical purposes beyond his control. The low-water mark is his limit. Beyond that he may do a little with seine and dredge, murder a few million herrings a year as they come in to spawn, butcher his fellow air-breather, the whale, or haul now and then an unlucky king crab or strange sea urchin out of the deep water in the name of science; but the life of the sea as a whole knows him not, plays out its slow drama of change and development unheeding him, and may in the end, in mere idle sport, throw up some new terrestrial denizen, some new competitor for space to live in and food to live upon, that will sweep him and all his little contrivances out of existence, as certainly and inevitably as he has swept away auk, bison, and dodo during the last two hundred years.

For instance, there are the crustacea. As a group the crabs

---

[1]   Titanotheria were huge rhinoceri and macrauchenia were camel-like mammals, both of which became extinct during the Pleistocene period.

and lobsters are confined below the high-water mark. But experiments in air-breathing are no doubt in progress in this group — we already have tropical land-crabs — and as far as we know there is no reason why in the future these creatures should not increase in size and terrestrial capacity. In the past we have the evidence of the fossil *Paradoxides*[1] that creatures of this kind may at least attain a length of six feet, and, considering their intense pugnacity, a crab of such dimensions would be as formidable a creature as one could well imagine. And their amphibious capacity would give them an advantage against us such as at present is only to be found in the case of the alligator or crocodile. If we could imagine a shark that could raid out upon the land, or a tiger that could take refuge in the sea, we should have a fair suggestion of what a terrible monster a large predatory crab might prove. And so far as zoological science goes we must, at least, admit that such a creature is an evolutionary possibility.

[Wells goes on to propose that mutated forms of octopi, ants, or plague bacilli may also pose a threat to human dominance. Each possibility will form the basis of one of his speculative short stories of this period.]

No; man's complacent assumption of the future is too confident. We think, because things have been easy for mankind as a whole for a generation or so, we are going on to perfect comfort and security in the future. We think that we shall always go to work at ten and leave off at four and have dinner at seven for ever and ever. But these four suggestions out of a host of others must surely do a little against this complacency. Even now, for all we can tell, the coming terror may be crouching for its spring and the fall of humanity be at hand. In the case of every other predominant animal the world has ever seen, we repeat, the hour of its complete ascendancy has been the beginning of its decline. (3)

---

1 Huge trilobites of the Palaeozoic era.

Appendix B: The Evolutionary Context: Society

1. Thomas Carlyle. From *Past and Present*. 1843. London: Chapman & Hall, 1897.

[Thomas Carlyle (1795-1881), the Scottish historian and social prophet, whose work often attacked the Victorian *status quo*, was a major influence on the young Wells. *Past and Present* contrasts medieval and Victorian England at the expense of the latter. This extract from Chapter II is an obvious source for and one of the keys to the meaning of the central symbol of the White Sphinx in *The Time Machine*.]

How true ... is that other old Fable of the Sphinx, who sat by the wayside, propounding her riddle to the passengers, which if they could not answer she destroyed them! Such a Sphinx is this Life of ours, to all men and societies of men. Nature, like the Sphinx, is of womanly celestial loveliness and tenderness; the face and bosom of a goddess, but ending in claws and the body of a lioness. There is in her a celestial beauty,—which means celestial order, pliancy to wisdom; but there is also a darkness, a ferocity, fatality, which are infernal. She is a goddess, but one not yet disimprisoned; one still half-imprisoned,—the articulate, lovely, still encased in the inarticulate, chaotic. How true! And does she not propound her riddles to us? Of each man she asks daily, in mild voice, yet with a terrible significance, "Knowest thou the meaning of this Day? What thou canst do Today; wisely attempt to do?" Nature, Universe, Destiny, Existence, howsoever we name this grand unnamable Fact in the midst of which we live and struggle, is as a heavenly bride and conquest to the wise and brave, to them who can discern her behests and do them; a destroying fiend to them who cannot. Answer her riddle, it is well with thee. Answer it not, pass on regarding it not, it will answer itself; the solution for thee is a thing of teeth and claws; Nature is a dumb lioness, deaf to thy pleadings, fiercely devouring. Thou art not now her victorious bridegroom; thou art her mangled victim, scattered on the precipices, as a slave found treacherous, recreant, ought to be and must. (7)

2. Karl Marx. From various writings (1844-64).

[In *Experiment in Autobiography*, Wells notes that he first directly encountered Marxism in his second year at South Kensington, by which point he was able to evaluate and reject it as a plausible but dangerous creed based on resentment and malice. Though it is true that Wells was never in any sense a follower of Karl Marx (1818-83), as a socialist and a critic of Victorian society he could hardly help being indirectly influenced by such Marxian ideas as had permeated radical thinking about social class. In *The Time Machine* these ideas are evident particularly in the symbolic implications of the Eloi–Morlock relationship.]

i. From *Economic and Philosophic Manuscripts of 1844*. Ed. and intro. Dirk J. Struik. Trans. Martin Milligan. New York: International Publishers, 1964. 106-19.

[In "Estranged Labor" the young Marx deals with what he sees as the inevitable increasing estrangement between owners and workers in capitalist society. In *The Time Machine* Wells gives this split a biological dimension.]

On the basis of political economy itself ... we have shown that the worker sinks to the level of a commodity and becomes indeed the most wretched of commodities ... and that finally the distinction between capitalist and land rentier, like that between the tiller of the soil and the factory worker, disappears and that the whole of society must fall apart into the two classes—the property *owners* and the propertyless *workers*. (106)

It is true that labor produces for the rich wonderful things—but for the worker it produces privation. It produces palaces—but for the worker, hovels. It produces beauty—but for the worker, deformity. It replaces labor by machines, but it throws a section of the workers back to a barbarous type of labor, and it turns the other workers into machines. It produces intelligence—but for the worker stupidity, cretinism. (110)

[Marx's analysis of estrangement in "The Meaning of Human Requirements" in terms of the duality of light and darkness is clearly echoed in the world of A.D. 802,701.]

This estrangement ... produces sophistication of needs and of their means on the one hand, and a bestial barbarization, a complete, unrefined, abstract simplicity of need, on the other.... Even the need for fresh air ceases for the worker. Man returns to a cave dwelling, which is now, however, contaminated with the pestilential breath of civilization.... A dwelling in the *light*, which Prometheus in Aeschylus designated as one of the greatest boons, by means of which he made the savage into a human being,[1] ceases to exist for the worker. Light, air, etc.— the simplest *animal* cleanliness—ceases to be a need for man. *Filth*, this stagnation and putrefaction of man—the *sewage* of civilization (speaking quite literally)—comes to be the *element of life* for him. (148-49)

ii. From "The Holy Family (1844), or Critique of Critical Criticism against Bruno Bauer and Company." 1845. Karl Marx. *Writings of the Young Marx on Philosophy and Society*. Trans. and ed. Loyd D. Easton and Kurt H. Guddat. Garden City, NY: Anchor, 1967.[2] 361-98.

[In "Critical Comment No. II on Proudhon," Marx expands on the political dimension of the estrangement of classes, unwittingly casting some light on the Morlocks' eating habits.]

Proletariat and wealth are antitheses. As such they constitute a whole. They are both manifestations of the world of private property. The question at issue is the specific position they

---

1 See Aeschylus, *Prometheus Bound*, especially lines 448ff.

2 Copyright ©1967 by Doubleday & Company, Inc. All rights reserved. Reprinted by permission of Hackett Publishing Company, Inc.

occupy in the antithesis. It is not enough to describe them as two sides of a whole....

Within this antithesis the property owner is ... the *conservative* party, and the proletarian is the *destructive* party. From the *former* arises action to maintain the antithesis, from the *latter*, action to destroy it. (367)

iii. From Karl Marx and Frederick Engels. *Selected Correspondence*. Vol. I. Moscow: Foreign Languages Publishing House; and London: Lawrence & Wishart, 1955.

[Two comments from Marx's correspondence reveals that Darwin was an important common factor in Marx's and Wells's analysis of social estrangement in English society in particular.]

[From letter to F. Lassalle, 16 January 1861] ... Darwin's book [*The Origin of Species*] is very important and serves me as a natural-scientific basis for the class struggle in history. One has to put up with the crude English method of development, of course. (151)

[From letter to Friedrich Engels, 18 June 1862] It is remarkable how Darwin recognizes among beasts and plants his English society with its division of labour, competition, opening up of new markets, "inventions," and the Malthusian "struggle for existence."[1] It is Hobbes's *bellum omnium contra omnes*....[2] (156-57)

---

1   Thomas Malthus (1766-1834) was the English economist whose *Essay on the Principle of Population* (1798), inspired by the overcrowded conditions of the Industrial Revolution, was an important influence on Darwin's theory of natural selection.
2   "The war of every man against every man" as invoked by the English political philosopher Thomas Hobbes (1588-1679) in Chapter 13 of *Leviathan* (1651).

iv. From "Inaugural Address of the Working Men's International Association." 1864. Karl Marx and Frederick Engels. *Selected Works*. Vol. II. Moscow: Progress Publishers, 1969. 11–18.

[Perhaps one source for the name "Morlock" can be found in this well-known passage in which Marx refers to the dominant social class metaphorically feeding on the life of the workers.]

... the middle class had predicted, and to their heart's content proved, that any legal restriction of the hours of labour must sound the death knell of British industry, which, vampyre like, could but live by sucking blood, and children's blood, too. In olden times, child murder was a mysterious rite of the religion of Moloch,[1] but it was practised on some very solemn occasions only, once a year perhaps, and then Moloch had no exclusive bias for the children of the poor. (16)

3. Frederick Engels. From *The Condition of the Working-Class in England in 1844*. 1845. Trans. Florence Kelley Wischnewetzky. London: Allen & Unwin, 1892.

[Friedrich Engels (1820-95) was Marx's chief collaborator. German-born, but based in England for much of his working life, he observed at first hand the plight of the industrial classes in Manchester during the depression of the 1840s. His most important independent work, *The Condition of the Working Class* was not available in English translation until 1886. It is likely that Wells knew of Engels's work even if he had not actually read it before he wrote *The Time Machine*, for Engels's ideas, like Marx's, had permeated socialist and sociological thought by the early 1890s. The following selections, based on Engels's observation of class and economic divisions in nineteenth-century English society, strongly suggest themselves as a source for both the Eloi-Morlock relationship (in which an ironic reversal has occurred) and the physical appearance of the Morlocks.]

---

1 See II Kings 23:10.

[From "Competition."] The proletarian is helpless; left to himself, he cannot live a single day. The bourgeoisie has gained a monopoly of all means of existence in the broadest sense of the word. What the proletarian needs, he can obtain only from this bourgeoisie, which is protected in its monopoly by the power of the State. The proletarian is, therefore, in law and in fact, the slave of the bourgeoisie, which can decree his life or death. (76)

[From "Results"] ... the working class has gradually become a race wholly apart from the English bourgeoisie. The bourgeoisie has more in common with every other nation of the earth than with the workers in whose midst it lives. The workers speak other dialects, have other thoughts and ideals, other customs and moral principles, a different religion and other politics than those of the bourgeoisie. Thus they are two radically dissimilar nations, as unlike as difference of race could make them, of whom we on the Continent have known but one, the bourgeoisie. (124)

[From "Single Branches of Industry—Factory Hands." Engels quotes a Dr. Hawkins's testimony in a report on the condition of factory workers, then summarizes his conclusions.]

"I believe that most travellers are struck by the lowness of stature, the leanness and the paleness which present themselves so commonly to the eye at Manchester, and, above all, among the factory classes. I have never been in any town in Great Britain, nor in Europe, in which degeneracy of form and colour from the national standard has been so obvious.... I must confess that all the boys and girls brought before me from the Manchester mills had a depressed appearance, and were very pale...."

... That the growth of young operatives is stunted, by their work, hundreds of statements testify.... One of the largest manufacturers of Manchester, leader of the opposition against the working-men ... said, on one occasion, that if things went on as at present, the operatives of Lancashire would soon be a race of pigmies. (158-59)

4. Benjamin Disraeli, Earl of Beaconsfield. From *Sybil; or, The Two Nations*. Vol. I. 1845. [Earl's Edition, Vol. XIV.] New York and London: M. Walter Dunne, 1904.

[It was not only German socialists who observed an unprecedented class division developing in mid-nineteenth-century English society. Disraeli (1804-81), the leading Tory politician of the age and twice Prime Minister of England, was also a notable novelist. In the subtitle of *Sybil* he gave an enduring name—the Two Nations—to a phenomenon that Marx and Engels were analyzing simultaneously, and which Wells, from his later evolutionary perspective, would project forward into A.D. 802,701. This extract is from Chapter XI: "A Seraphic Appearance." A stranger, dressed in black, offers a disconcerting critique of early Victorian England to Lord Egremont. Notice how Disraeli uses the phrase "the struggle for existence" years before *The Origin of Species*.]

"It is a community of purpose that constitutes society," continued the younger stranger; "without that, men may be drawn into contiguity, but they still continue virtually isolated."

"And is that their condition in cities?"

"It is their condition everywhere; but in cities that condition is aggravated. A density of population implies a severer struggle for existence, and a consequent repulsion of elements brought into too close contact. In great cities men are brought together by the desire of gain. They are not in a state of co-operation, but of isolation, as to the making of fortunes; and for all the rest they are careless of neighbours. Christianity teaches us to love our neighbour as ourself; modern society acknowledges no neighbour."

"Well, we live in strange times," said Egremont....

"When the infant begins to walk, it also thinks that it lives in strange times," said his companion.

"Your inference?" asked Egremont.

"That society, still in its infancy, is beginning to feel its way."

"This is a new reign," said Egremont, "perhaps it is a new era."

"I think so," said the younger stranger.

"I hope so," said the elder one.

"Well, society may be in its infancy," said Egremont, slightly smiling; "but, say what you like, our Queen reigns over the greatest nation that ever existed."

"Which nation?" asked the younger stranger, "for she reigns over two."

The stranger paused; Egremont was silent, but looked inquiringly.

"Yes," resumed the younger stranger after a moment's interval. "Two nations; between whom there is no intercourse and no sympathy; who are as ignorant of each other's habits, thoughts, and feelings, as if they were dwellers in different zones, or inhabitants of different planets; who are formed by a different breeding, are fed by a different food, are ordered by different manners, and are not governed by the same laws."

"You speak of—" said Egremont, hesitatingly.

"The Rich and the Poor." (92-93)

5. Herbert Spencer. From *Social Statics; or, The Conditions Essential to Human Happiness Specified, and the First of Them Developed*. 1851. New York: D. Appleton, 1888.

[Spencer (1820-1903) was an English philosopher and sociologist whose attempt to provide a systematic account of all phenomena was very influential in the later Victorian age. (In 1894 Wells called him "a noble & wondrous thinker but lacking humour.") Spencer believed in the inevitability of progress, offering in *Social Statics* a "logical" proof of its necessity that is a classic expression of Victorian optimism, and that unquestionably influenced Darwin in such passages as his conclusion to *The Origin of Species* (see Appendix A1). It was the complacency arising from such optimism that was Wells's chief target in *The Time Machine*. The passage below is from Part I, Chapter II of *Social Statics*, "The Evanescence of Evil."]

All imperfection is unfitness to the conditions of existence.

This unfitness must consist either in having a faculty or faculties in excess; or in having a faculty or faculties deficient; or in both.

A faculty in excess, is one which the conditions of existence do not afford full exercise to; and a faculty that is deficient, is one from which the conditions of existence demand more than it can perform.

But it is an essential principle of life that a faculty to which circumstances do not allow full exercise diminishes; and that a faculty on which circumstances make excessive demands increases.

And so long as this excess and this deficiency continue, there must continue decrease on the one hand, and growth on the other.

Finally, all excess and all deficiency must disappear; that is, all unfitness must disappear; that is, all imperfection must disappear.

Thus the ultimate development of the ideal man is logically certain. ... humanity must in the end become completely adapted to its conditions....

Progress, therefore, is not an accident, but a necessity. Instead of civilization being artificial, it is a part of nature; all of a piece with the development of the embryo or the unfolding of a flower. ... so surely must the human faculties be moulded into complete fitness for the social state; so surely must the things we call evil and immorality disappear; so surely must man become perfect. (79-80)

6. Herbert Spencer. From *First Principles*. 1862. 4th. ed. 1880. New York: P. F. Collier, 1902.

[Spencer felt that evolutionary theory supported, rather than undermined, his optimism. Attempting to reconcile evolution and progress, he asserted that there was a law governing the development of all organisms, biological and social, that ensured that they would inevitably advance from homogeneous simplicity to heterogeneous complexity on their way to perfection. But ideas about biological degeneration as they came to the fore in the 1880s (see Appendix A2) provided evidence to those, like Wells, whose intuitions about existence differed from Spencer's, that such a law was based on wishful thinking, not science. The passage below is from Chapter XV of *First Principles*, "The Law of Evolution Continued."]

The advance from the simple to the complex, through a process of successive differentiations, is seen alike in the earliest changes of the Universe to which we can reason our way back, and in the earliest changes which we can inductively establish; it is seen in the geologic and climatic evolution of the Earth, and of every single organism on its surface; it is seen in the evolution of Humanity, whether contemplated in the civilized individual, or in the aggregations of races; it is seen in the evolution of Society, in respect alike of its political, its religious, and its economical organization; and it is seen in the evolution of all those endless concrete and abstract products of human activity, which constitute the environment of our daily life. From the remotest past which Science can fathom, up to the novelties of yesterday, an essential trait of Evolution has been the transformation of the homogeneous into the heterogeneous.

... As we now understand it, Evolution is definable as a change from an incoherent homogeneity to a coherent heterogeneity, accompanying the dissipation of motion and integration of matter. (358-59)

7. Jules Verne. From *The Child of the Cavern; or, Strange Doings Underground*]. Trans. W. H. G. Kingston. London: Sampson Low, Marston, Searle & Rivington, 1877. Trans. of *Les Indes-noires*. 1877.

[Jules Verne (1828-1905) was the French author of many adventure-romances with a scientific element, works that attained a global popularity. Verne and Wells felt they had little in common with one another (see Appendix G4), and most historians of science fiction have emphasized their very different roles in the evolution of the genre. However, the young Wells almost certainly read Verne's works, which became quickly available in English. The following passage from one of Verne's lesser-known romances suggests itself as a source for the subterranean habitat of the Morlocks.]

If, by some superhuman power, engineers could have raised in a block, a thousand feet thick, all that part of the terrestrial crust which supports the lakes, rivers, gulfs, and territories of the counties of Stirling, Dumbarton, and Renfrew,[1] they would have found, under that enormous lid, an immense excavation, to which but one other in the world can be compared—the celebrated Mammoth caves of Kentucky.

This excavation was composed of several hundred divisions of all sizes and shapes. It might be called a hive with numberless ranges of cells, capriciously arranged, but a hive on a vast scale, and which, instead of bees, might have lodged all the ichthyosaurii, megatheriums, and pterodactyles of the geological epoch....

Although unfit for any vegetable product, the place could be inhabited by a whole population. And who knows but that in this steady temperature, in the depths of the mines of Aberfoyle, as well as in those of Newcastle, Alloa or Cardiff[2]—when their contents shall have been exhausted—who knows but that the poorer classes of Great Britain will some day find a refuge? (88-91)

8. Henry George. From *Progress and Poverty*. 1880. London and Toronto: Dent, 1911.

[Henry George (1839-97), the American economist and social reformer, was known for his advocacy of a single tax and the nationalization of land, ideas promoted in his popular and highly influential critique of capitalism, *Progress and Poverty*. Wells read the book at Midhurst, and later credited it with awakening his interest in socialism. The following passages reveal the compatibility of George on social evolution with Huxley on biological evolution, and suggest that *The Time Machine* was also

---

1   Counties in Scotland.
2   Coal-mining areas of Great Britain.

influenced by George's rhetorical power and apocalyptic imagination.]

[From Book X Chapter I, "The Current Theory of Human Progress—Its Insufficiency"] ... if progress operated to fix an improvement in man's nature, and thus to produce further progress, though there might be occasional interruption, yet the general rule would be that progress would be continuous—that advance would lead to advance, and civilisation develop into higher civilisation.

Not merely the general rule, but *the universal rule*, is the reverse of this. The earth is the tomb of dead empires, no less than of dead men. Instead of progress fitting men for greater progress, every civilisation that was in its own time as vigorous and advancing as ours is now, has of itself come to a stop. Over and over again, art has declined, learning sunk, power waned, population become sparse, until the people who had built great temples and mighty cities, turned rivers and pierced mountains, cultivated the earth like a garden and introduced the utmost refinement into the minute affairs of life, remained but in a remnant of squalid barbarians, who had lost even the memory of what their ancestors had done, and regarded the surviving fragments of their grandeur as the work of genii, or of the mighty race before the flood. (342-43)

... an analogy may be drawn between the life of a society and the life of a solar system upon the nebular hypothesis. As the heat and light of the sun are produced by the aggregation of atoms evolving motion, which finally ceases when the atoms at length come to a state of equilibrium or rest, and a state of immobility succeeds, which can be only broken in again by the impact of external forces, which reverse the process of evolution, integrating motion and dissipating matter in the form of gas, again to evolve motion by its condensation; so, it may be said, does the aggregation of individuals in a community evolve a force which produces the light and warmth of civilisation, but when this process ceases and the individual components are brought into a state of equilibrium, assuming their fixed places, petrification ensues, and the breaking up and diffusion caused

by an incursion of barbarians is necessary to the recommence-
ment of the process and a new growth of civilisation. (344-45)

[From Book X Chapter III, "How Modern Civilisation May
Decline"] ... there are many things about which there can be
no dispute, which go to show that our civilisation has reached a
critical period, and that unless a new start is made in the direction of social equality, the nineteenth century may to the future
mark its climax.... Everywhere is it evident that the tendency
to inequality, which is the necessary result of material progress
where land is monopolised, cannot go much further without
carrying our civilisation into that downward path which is so
easy to enter and so hard to abandon. Everywhere the increasing intensity of the struggle to live, the increasing necessity for
straining every nerve to prevent being thrown down and trod-
den underfoot in the scramble for wealth, is draining the forces
which gain and maintain improvements. In every civilised
country pauperism, crime, insanity, and suicides are increasing.
In every civilised country the diseases are increasing which
come from overstrained nerves, from insufficient nourishment,
from squalid lodgings, from unwholesome and monotonous
occupations, from premature labour of children, from the tasks
and crimes which poverty imposes upon women. In every
highly civilised country the expectation of life, which gradually
rose for several centuries, and which seems to have culminated
about the first quarter of this century, appears to be now
diminishing.

It is not an advancing civilisation that such figures show. It is
a civilisation which in its under currents has already begun to
recede.... When the sun passes the meridian, it can only be
told by the way the short shadows fall; for the heat of the day
yet increases. But as sure as the turning tide must soon run full
ebb; as sure as the declining sun must bring darkness, so sure is
it, that though knowledge yet increases and invention marches
on, and new states are being settled, and cities still expand, yet
civilisation has begun to wane.... (383-84)

[From "Conclusion"] ... if human life does not continue beyond what we see of it here, then we are confronted with regard to the race with the same difficulty as with the individual. For it is as certain that the race must die as it is that the individual must die. We know that there have been geologic conditions under which human life was impossible on this earth. We know that they must return again. Even now, as the earth circles on her appointed orbit, the northern ice cap slowly thickens, and the time gradually approaches when its glaciers will flow again, and austral seas, sweeping northward, bury the seats of present civilisation under ocean wastes, as it may be they now bury what was once as high a civilisation as our own. And beyond these periods, science discerns a dead earth, an exhausted sun — a time when, clashing together, the solar system shall resolve itself into a gaseous form, again to begin immeasurable mutations. (398-99)

9. Edward Bellamy. From *Looking Backward 2000–1887*. Boston: Ticknor and Company, 1888.

[As the nineteenth century drew to a close, there was a widespread assumption that a social cataclysm was inevitable. The narrator, Julian West, of this famous and influential American utopian novel by Bellamy (1850–98), summarizes such gloomy assumptions as they were expressed in 1887 — a gloom which his narrative will attempt to dispel.]

Humanity ... having climbed to the top round of the ladder of civilization, was about to take a header into chaos, after which it would doubtless pick itself up, turn round, and begin to climb again.... Human history, like all great movements, was cyclical, and returned to the point of beginning. The idea of indefinite progress in a right line was a chimera of the imagination, with no analogue in nature. The parabola of a comet was perhaps a yet better illustration of the career of humanity. Tending upward and sunward from the aphelion of barbarism, the race attained the perihelion of civilization only to plunge downward once more to its nether goal in the regions of chaos. (23-24)

[A first glimpse of the city of the socialist utopia, by the sleeper, West, who awakens in A.D. 2,000 in Boston. This is the kind of future London that the Time Traveller expects to see, but which has been long in ruins by A.D. 802,701. In *The Time Machine* Wells positions himself as much against the utopianist Bellamy as against the Excelsior biologists.]

At my feet lay a great city. Miles of broad streets, shaded by trees and lined with fine buildings, for the most part not in continuous blocks but set in larger or smaller enclosures, stretched in every direction. Every quarter contained large open squares filled with trees, among which statues glistened and fountains flashed in the late afternoon sun. Public buildings of a colossal size and an architectural grandeur unparalleled in my day, raised their stately piles on every side. Surely I had never seen this city nor one comparable to it before. Raising my eyes at last towards the horizon, I looked westward. That blue ribbon winding away to the sunset, was it not the sinuous Charles? (52)

[West asks Dr. Leete, his guide in A.D. 2,000, about how the people of the future had solved the burning social issue of the late nineteenth century. West's use of metaphor casts further light on the significance of the White Sphinx in *The Time Machine*.]

"You told me when we were upon the housetop that though a century only had elapsed since I fell asleep, it had been marked by greater changes in the conditions of humanity than many a previous millennium.... To make a beginning somewhere, for the subject is doubtless a large one, what solution, if any, have you found for the labor question? It was the Sphinx's riddle of the nineteenth century, and when I dropped out the Sphinx was threatening to devour society, because the answer was not forthcoming. It is well worth sleeping a hundred years to learn

what the right answer was, if, indeed, you have found it yet."
(65-66)

10. Thomas H. Huxley. From "The Struggle for Existence in Human Society." [*Nineteenth Century* 23 (February 1888): 61-80.] *Collected Essays. Vol. IX. Evolution and Ethics and Other Essays*. New York: D. Appleton, 1902. 195-236.

[For Huxley, the Babylonian goddess Istar, who combined in herself the attributes of the Greek Aphrodite (love, sex) and Ares (war, violence), was an appropriate embodiment of Nature. This passage provides yet another gloss on the Sphinx-motif in *The Time Machine*.]

Let us be under no illusions then. So long as unlimited multi-plication goes on, no social organization which has ever been devised, or is likely to be devised, no fiddle-faddling with the distribution of wealth, will deliver society from the tendency to be destroyed by the reproduction within itself, in its intensest form, of that struggle for existence the limitation of which is the object of society. And however shocking to the moral sense this eternal competition of man against man and of nation against nation may be; however revolting may be the accumu-lation of misery at the negative pole of society, in contrast with that of monstrous wealth at the positive pole; this state of things must abide, and grow continually worse, so long as Istar holds her way unchecked. It is the true riddle of the Sphinx; and every nation which does not solve it will sooner or later be devoured by the monster itself has generated. (211-12)

11. William Morris. From *News from Nowhere; or, An Epoch of Rest. Being Some Chapters from a Utopian Romance*. Boston: Roberts Brothers, 1890.

[Morris (1834-96) was a poet, romancer, artist, designer, and the leading figure in the late-nineteenth-century revival of handi-crafts. A visionary socialist, he reacted strongly against Bel-lamy's industrial utopia, producing *News from Nowhere* as a counterblast to *Looking Backward*. Morris envisions a completely deindustrialized future England (based on an idealized later Middle Ages) in which society is organized on pure communist lines. Wells envisioned *The Time Machine*, especially those scenes set in A.D. 802,701, as an astringent corrective to *both* Bellamy and Morris. In this first passage, Morris's first-person protagonist, having fallen asleep in 1890 and awoken in the twenty-first century, views the Thames-side at Hammersmith. To underline his differences with Morris, Wells would set *The Time Machine* only a few miles upstream, in Richmond.]

I was going to say, "But is this the Thames?" but held my peace in my wonder, and turned my bewildered eyes eastward to look at the bridge again, and thence to the shores of the London river; and surely there was enough to astonish me. For though there was a bridge across the stream and houses on its banks, how all was changed from last night! The soap-works with their smoke-vomiting chimneys were gone; the engineer's works gone; the lead-works gone; and no sound of riveting and hammering came down the west wind....

Both shores had a line of very pretty houses, low and not large, standing back a little way from the river; they were mostly built of red brick and roofed with tiles, and looked, above all, comfortable and as if they were, so to say, alive, and sympathetic with the life of the dwellers in them. There was a continuous garden in front of them, going down to the water's edge, in which the flowers were now blooming luxuriantly, and sending delicious waves of summer scent over the eddying stream. Behind the houses I could see great trees rising, mostly planes, and looking down the water there were the reaches towards Putney almost as if they were a lake with a forest shore, so thick were the big trees.... (14-16)

[Meeting the women of the communist future for the first time, the protagonist is struck by their contrast with those of his own time. Compare the scene in which the Time Traveller first meets the Eloi.]

In this pleasant place, which of course I knew to be the hall of the Guest House, three young women were flitting to and fro. As they were the first of the sex I had seen on this eventful morning, I naturally looked at them very attentively, and found them at least as good as the gardens, the architecture, and the male men. As to their dress, which of course I took note of, I should say that they were decently veiled with drapery, and not bundled up with millinery; that they were clothed like women, not upholstered like arm-chairs, as most women of our time are. In short, their dress was somewhat between that of the ancient classical costume and the simpler forms of the four-teenth-century garments, though it was clearly not an imita-tion of either: the materials were light and gay to suit the sea-son. As to the women themselves, it was pleasant indeed to see them, they were so kind and happy-looking in expression of face, so shapely and well-knit of body, and thoroughly healthy-looking and strong. All were at·least comely, and one of them very handsome and regular of feature. They came up to us at once merrily and without the least affectation of shyness, and all three shook hands with me as if I were a friend newly come back from a long journey…. (23)

[The historian Old Hammond sums up past history, unwitting-ly offering a kind of prequel to The Time Traveller's voyage into futurity.]

"This is how we stand. England was once a country of clear-ings among the woods and wastes, with a few towns inter-spersed, which were fortresses for the feudal army, markets for the folk, gathering-places for the craftsmen. It then became a country of huge and foul workshops and fouler gambling-dens, surrounded by an ill-kept, poverty-stricken farm, pillaged by the masters of the workshops. It is now a garden, where noth-ing is wasted and nothing is spoiled…." (100)

[Wells was able to see rather further than Morris into the ironies emerging from this dialogue between Old Hammond and the protagonist.]

"... it is the childlike part of us that produces works of imagination. When we are children time passes so slow with us that we seem to have time for everything."

He sighed, and then smiled and said: "At least let us rejoice that we have got back our childhood again. I drink to the days that are!"

"Second childhood," said I in a low voice, and then blushed at my double rudeness, and hoped that he had n't heard. But he had, and turned to me smiling, and said: "Yes, why not? And for my part I hope it may last long...." (141–42)

12. Benjamin Kidd. *Social Evolution*. 1894. New ed. New York and London: Macmillan, 1895.

[Today, knowing so much more about genetics, we might hesitate to draw a close analogy between biological evolution and social development. But in the 1890s, before the mechanisms of heredity had begun to be understood, so high was the prestige of Darwinian biology that the embryonic social sciences were very much in its shadow. This can be seen in the following passages from an influential work by the English sociologist Benjamin Kidd (1858–1916), revealing the some of the ideas in the field circulating as Wells was composing the final versions of *The Time Machine*.]

[From Chapter I: "The Outlook."] By those sciences which deal with human society it seems to have been for long ignored or forgotten that in that society we are merely regarding the highest phenomena in the history of life, and that consequently all departments of knowledge which deal with social phenomena have their true foundation in the biological sciences.
... Yet the social phenomena which are treated of under the heads of politics, history, ethics, economics, and religion must all be regarded as but the intimately related phenomena of the science of life under its most complex aspect. The biologist whose crowning work in the century has been the establishment of order and law in the lower branches of his subject has carried us up to human society and there left us without a

guide.... The time has come ... for a better understanding and for a more radical method; for the social sciences to strengthen themselves by sending their roots deep into the soil underneath from which they spring; and for the biologist to advance over the frontier and carry the methods of his science boldly into human society.... (28–30)

[From Chapter II: "Conditions of Human Progress."] It is now coming to be recognised as a necessarily inherent part of the doctrine of evolution, that if the continual selection which is always going on amongst the higher forms of life were to be suspended, these forms would not only possess no tendency to make progress forwards, but must actually go backwards. *That is to say, if all the individuals of every generation in any species were allowed to equally propagate their kind, the average of each generation would continually tend to fall below the average of the generation which preceded it, and a process of slow but steady degeneration would ensue.* It is, therefore, an inevitable law amongst the higher forms, that competition and selection must not only always accompany progress, but that they must prevail amongst every form of life which is not actually retrograding. ... the wider the limits of selection, the keener the rivalry, and the more rigid the selection, the greater will be the progress. (39–40)

Appendix C: The Evolutionary Context: Culture

1. Winwood Reade. From *The Martyrdom of Man*. 1872. 2nd ed. London: Trübner & Co., 1875.

[*The Martyrdom of Man* by (William) Winwood Reade (1838-75) was an early and influential example of sweeping cultural history written from an agnostic-Darwinian point of view — Wells's own *The Outline of History* (1920) is a notable later example. Wells read *The Martyrdom of Man* at Up Park, and frequently cited it as important in shaping his early thinking. There are several important foreshadowings of the world of A.D. 802,701 in the passage below on the debt of the future to the past, including yet another possible source for the White Sphinx.]

[From Chapter IV: "Intellect."] This great and glorious city in which we dwell, this mighty London, the metropolis of the earth; these streets flowing with eager-minded life, and gleaming with prodigious wealth; these forests of masts, these dark buildings, turning refuse into gold, and giving bread to many thousand mouths; these harnessed elements which whirl us along beneath the ground, and which soon will convey us through the air; these spacious halls, adorned with all that can exalt the imagination or fascinate the sense; these temples of melody; these galleries, exhibiting excavated worlds; these walls covered with books in which dwell the souls of the immortal dead, which, when they are opened, transport us by a magic spell to lands which are vanished and passed away, or to spheres created by the poet's art; which make us walk with Plato beneath the plane trees, or descend with Dante into the dolorous abyss; — to whom do we owe all these? First, to the poor savages, forgotten and despised, who, by rubbing sticks together, discovered fire, who first tamed the timid fawn, and first made the experiment of putting seeds into the ground. And, secondly, we owe them to those enterprising warriors who established Nationality, and to those priests who devoted their life-time to the culture of their minds. There is a land where the air is always tranquil, where nature wears always the same bright yet lifeless smile; and there, as in a vast museum, are preserved the colossal achievements of the past. Let us enter the sad and silent river; let us wander on its dusky shores. Buried cities are beneath our feet; the ground on which we tread is the pavement of a tomb. See the Pyramids towering to the sky, with men, like insects, crawling round their base; and the Sphinx, couched in vast repose, with a ruined temple between its paws. Since those great monuments were raised, the very heavens have been changed. When the architects of Egypt began their work, there was another polar star in the northern sky, and the Southern Cross shone upon the Baltic shores. How glorious are the memories of those ancient men, whose names are forgotten, for they lived and laboured in the distant and unwritten past. (494-96)

2. Friedrich Nietzsche. From *The Complete Works of Friedrich Nietzsche*. Ed. Oscar Levy. *Vol. X. The Joyful Wisdom ("La Gaya Scienza")*. Trans. Thomas Common, with Poetry Rendered by Paul V. Cohn and Maud D. Petre. 2nd. ed. Edinburgh and London: J.N. Foulis, 1910. Trans. *Fröhliche Wissenschaft*. 1882, 1886.

[Though there is little likelihood that Wells had read any Nietzsche (1844-1900) when composing *The Time Machine*, it is also clear that the German philosopher's work by the mid-1890s had already started to strike indirectly many already receptive chords among his contemporaries. It is interesting to juxtapose Nietzsche's attempt at a transvaluation of human values from a nihilistic perspective in these now famous passages from *Joyful Wisdom*, with Wells's vision of nature by implication "entirely undeified" and of providentially-unsupervised cosmic evolution in "The Further Vision."]

[From Book III, section 109] *Let us be on our Guard.* — Let us be on our guard against thinking that the world is a living being. Where could it extend itself? What could it nourish itself with? How could it grow and increase? We know tolerably well what the organic is; and we are to reinterpret the emphatically derivative, tardy, rare and accidental, which we only perceive on the crust of the earth, into the essential, universal and eternal, as those do who call the universe an organism? That disgusts me. Let us now be on our guard against believing that the universe is a machine; it is assuredly not constructed with a view to *one* end; we invest it with far too high an honour with the word "machine." Let us be on our guard against supposing that anything so methodical as the cyclic motions of our neighbouring stars obtains generally and throughout the universe; indeed a glance at the Milky Way induces doubt as to whether there are not many cruder and more contradictory motions there, and even stars with continuous, rectilinearly gravitating orbits, and the like. The astral arrangement in which we live is an exception; this arrangement, and the relatively long durability which is determined by it, has again made possible the exception of exceptions, the formation of organic life. The general character of the world, on the other hand, is to all eternity chaos; not by the absence of necessity, but in the sense of the absence of order, structure, form, beauty, wisdom, and whatever else our aesthetic humanities are called. Judged by our reason, the unlucky casts are far oftenest the rule, the exceptions are not the secret purpose; and the whole musical box repeats eternally its air, which can never be called a melody, — and finally the very expression, "unlucky cast" is already an anthropomorphising which involves blame. But how could we presume to blame or praise the universe! Let us be on our guard against ascribing to it heartlessness and unreason, or their opposites; it is neither perfect, nor beautiful, nor noble; nor does it seek to be anything of the kind, it does not at all attempt to imitate man! It is altogether unaffected by our æsthetic and moral judgments! Neither has it any self-preservative instinct, nor instinct at all; it also knows no law. Let us be on our guard against saying that there are laws in nature. There are only necessities: there is no one who commands, no one who obeys, no one who transgresses. When you know that there is no design, you know also that there is no chance: for it is only where there is a world of design that "chance" has a meaning. Let us be on our guard against saying that death is contrary to life. The living being is only a species of dead being, and a very rare species. — Let us be on our guard against thinking that the world eternally creates the new. There are no eternally enduring substances; matter is just another such error as the God of the Eleatics.[1] But when shall we be at an end with our foresight and precaution! When will all these shadows of God cease to obscure us? When shall we have nature entirely undeified! When shall we be permitted to *naturalise* ourselves by means of the pure, newly discovered, newly redeemed nature? (151–53)

[From Book III, section 125.] *The Madman.* — Have you ever heard of the madman who on a bright morning lighted a lantern and ran to the market-place calling out unceasingly: "I seek God! I seek God!" — As there were many people standing about who did not believe in God, he caused a great deal of amusement. Why! is he lost? said one. Has he strayed away like a child? said another. Or does he keep himself hidden? Is he afraid of us? Has he taken a sea-voyage? Has he emigrated? — the people cried out laughingly, all in a hubbub. The insane man jumped into their midst and transfixed them with his glances. "Where is God gone?" he called out. "I mean to tell you! *We have killed him,* — you and I! We are all his murderers! But how have we done it? How were we able to drink up the sea? Who gave us the sponge to wipe away the whole horizon? What did we do when we loosened this earth from its sun? Whither does it now move? Whither do we move? Away from all suns? Do we not dash on unceasingly? Backwards, sideways, forewards, in all directions? Is there still an above and below? Do we not stray, as through infinite nothingness? Does not empty space breathe upon us? Has it not become colder? Does not night come on continually, darker and darker? Shall we not have to light lanterns in the morning? Do we not hear the noise of the grave-diggers who are burying God? Do we not

---

1   Idealist school of philosophers founded by Parmenides of Elea (5th century B.C.)

smell the divine putrefaction?—for even Gods putrefy! God is dead! God remains dead! And we have killed him! How shall we console ourselves, the most murderous of all murderers? The holiest and the mightiest that the world has hitherto possessed, has bled to death under our knife,—who will wipe the blood from us? With what water could we cleanse ourselves? What lustrums,[1] what sacred games shall we have to devise? Is not the magnitude of this deed too great for us? Shall we not ourselves have to become Gods, merely to seem worthy of it? There never was a greater event,—and on account of it, all who are born after us belong to a higher history than any history hitherto!" (167-68)

3. H. G. Wells. From "The Rediscovery of the Unique." *Fortnightly Review* 56 (July 1891): 106-11.

[This extract from the conclusion of Wells's first major published essay, while revealing several interesting Wellsian parallels with Nietzsche (see Appendix C2), concludes with a striking metaphor that sheds an interesting light on the significance of all the Time Traveller's references to matches.]

The work of Darwin and Wallace was the clear assertion of the uniqueness of living things; and physicists and chemists are now trying the next step forward in a hesitating way—they must take it sooner or later. We are on the eve of man's final emancipation from rigid reasonableness, from the last trace of the trim clockwork thought of the seventeenth and eighteenth centuries....

The neat little picture of a universe of souls made up of passions and principles in bodies made of atoms, all put together so neatly and wound up at the creation, fades in the series of dissolving views that we call the march of human thought. We no longer believe, whatever creed we may affect, in a Deity whose design is so foolish and little that even a theological bishop can trace it and detect a kindred soul. Some of the most pious can

---

1   Ritual purifications.

hardly keep from scoffing at Milton's world—balanced just in the middle of those crystalline spheres that hung by a golden chain from the battlements of heaven.[1] We no longer speculate

"What varied being peoples ev'ry star,"[2]

because we have no reason at all to expect life beyond this planet. We are a century in front of that Nuremberg[3] cosmos, and in the place of it there looms a dim suggestion of the fathomlessness of the unique mystery of life. The figure of a roaring loom with unique threads flying and interweaving beyond all human following, working out a pattern beyond all human interpretation, we owe to Goethe,[4] the intellectual father of the nineteenth century. Number—Order, seems now the least law in the universe; in the days of our great-grandfathers it was heaven's first law.

So spins the squirrel's cage of human philosophy.

Science is a match that man has just got alight. He thought he was in a room—in moments of devotion, a temple—and that his light would be reflected from and display walls inscribed with wonderful secrets and pillars carved with philosophical systems wrought into harmony. It is a curious sensation, now that the preliminary splutter is over and the flame burns up clear, to see his hands lit and just a glimpse of himself and the patch he stands on visible, and around him, in place of all that human comfort and beauty he anticipated—darkness still. (111)

---

1   See *Paradise Lost* (1667), II, lines 1051-52.

2   Pope, *An Essay on Man* (1733), I, line 27.

3   City that was the centre of the German Renaissance, perhaps here associated with the precise calculations of one of its notable residents, the astronomer Regiomontanus (1436-76).

4   See *Faust*, I ("Night") (1808), lines 151-59.

4. Max Nordau. *Degeneration.* [Trans. W. F. Barry.] New York: D. Appleton, 1895. Trans. *Entartung.* 1892.

[Nordau (1849-1923), an Austro-Hungarian journalist with a medical training, wrote in *Degeneration* one of the best-sellers of the 1890s, a apocalyptic polemic which widely popularized the supposed connection between biological degeneration and cultural expression, in particular by "proving" that unconventional or pessimistic modern works (e.g., by Ibsen, Zola, and Wagner) were symptoms of their authors' pathology. Though Nordau's work did not appear in English until the month before *The Time Machine* was published, and there is very little likelihood that Wells had read it before then, *Degeneration* is an articulation of very general fin-de-siècle cultural anxieties that are visible in innumerable ways in *The Time Machine*. These passages are both from Book 1: "Fin-de-Siècle," Chapter 1: "The Dusk of the Nations."]

[H]owever silly a term *fin-de-siècle* may be, the mental constitution which it indicates is actually present in influential circles. The disposition of the times is curiously confused, a compound of feverish restlessness and blunted discouragement, of fearful presage and hang-dog renunciation. The prevalent feeling is that of imminent perdition and extinction. *Fin-de-siècle* is at once a confession and a complaint. The old Northern faith contained the fearsome doctrine of the Dusk of the Gods. In our days there have arisen in more highly-developed minds vague qualms of a Dusk of the Nations, in which all suns and all stars are gradually waning, and mankind with all its institutions and creations is perishing in the midst of a dying world. (2)

[*Fin-de-siècle*] means a practical emancipation from traditional discipline, which theoretically is still in force. To the voluptuary this means unbridled lewdness, the unchaining of the beast in man; to the withered heart of the egoist, disdain of all consideration for his fellow-men, the trampling under foot of all barriers which enclose brutal greed of lucre and lust of pleasure; to the contemner of the world it means the shameless ascendancy of base impulses and motives, which were, if not virtuously suppressed, at least hypocritically hidden; to the believer it means the repudiation of dogma, the negation of a super-sensuous world, the descent into flat phenomenalism; to the sensitive nature yearning for æsthetic thrills, it means the vanishing of ideals in art, and no more power in its accepted forms to arouse emotion. And to all, it means the end of an established order, which for thousands of years has satisfied logic, fettered depravity, and in every art matured something of beauty.

One epoch of history is unmistakably in its decline, and another is announcing its approach. There is a sound of rending in every tradition, and it is as though the morrow would not link itself with to-day. Things as they are totter and plunge, and they are suffered to reel and fall, because man is weary, and there is no faith that it is worth an effort to uphold them. Views that have hitherto governed minds are dead or driven hence like disenthroned kings, and for their inheritance they that hold the titles and they that would usurp are locked in struggle. Meanwhile interregnum in all its terrors prevails; there is confusion among the powers that be; the million, robbed of its leaders, knows not where to turn; the strong work their will; false prophets arise, and dominion is divided amongst those whose rod is the heavier because their time is short....

Such is the spectacle presented by the doings of men in the reddened light of the Dusk of the Nations. Massed in the sky the clouds are aflame in the weirdly beautiful glow which was observed for the space of years after the eruption of Krakatoa.[1] Over the earth the shadows creep with deepening gloom, wrapping all objects in a mysterious dimness, in which all certainty is destroyed and any guess seems plausible. Forms lose their outlines, and are dissolved in floating mist. The day is over, and the night draws on. (5-6)

---

1 A volcano in Indonesia, producing in 1883 one of the greatest eruptions in history.

Appendix D: The Spatiotemporal Context: The Fourth Dimension

1. Edwin A. Abbott [as "A Square"]. From *Flatland: A Romance of Many Dimensions*. 1884. New and rev. ed. London: Seeley & Co., 1884.

[Abbott (1838-1926) was an English clergyman and mathematician, now chiefly remembered for his ingenious and amusing scientific romance about how the inhabitants of a two-dimensional world might perceive reality, and their probable difficulty in conceiving of our own three-dimensional universe. *Flatland* was published just as Wells was starting at South Kensington, where the novel clearly stimulated ideas among the students about the possibility of a fourth dimension. In 1937 Wells would cite *Flatland* as a primary origin of *The Time Machine*: see Appendix F17.]

[From Chapter 18, *"How I came to Spaceland, and what I saw there."* Square, the two-dimensional narrator, describes the feeling of entering a three-dimensional world. Compare the Time Traveller's sensations when first travelling through time.] An unspeakable horror seized me. There was a darkness; then a dizzy, sickening sensation of sight that was not like seeing: I saw a Line that was no Line; Space that was not Space: I was myself, and not myself. When I could find voice, I shrieked aloud in agony, "Either this is madness or it is Hell." "It is neither," calmly replied the voice of the Sphere, "it is Knowledge; it is Three Dimensions: open your eye once again and try to look steadily." (78-79)

[From Chapter 19, *"How, though the Sphere showed me other mysteries of Spaceland, I still desired more; and what came of it."* Two-dimensional Square argues with three-dimensional Sphere about the existence of a Fourth Dimension.] ... just as there *was* close at hand, and touching my frame, the land of Three Dimensions, though I, blind senseless wretch, had no power to touch it, no eye in my interior to discern it, so of a surety there is a Fourth Dimension, which my Lord perceives with the inner eye of thought. And that it must exist my Lord himself has taught me. Or can he have forgotten what he himself imparted to his servant?

In One Dimension, did not a moving Point produce a Line with *two* terminal points?

In Two Dimensions, did not a moving Line produce a Square with *four* terminal points?

In Three Dimensions, did not a moving Square produce — did not this eye of mine behold it — that blessed Being, a Cube, with *eight* terminal points?

And in Four Dimensions shall not a moving Cube — alas, for Analogy, and alas for the Progress of Truth, if it be not so — shall not, I say, the motion of a divine Cube result in a still more divine Organization with *sixteen* terminal points?

Behold the infallible confirmation of the Series, 2, 4, 8, 16: is not this a Geometrical Progression? Is not this — if I might quote my Lord's own words — "strictly according to Analogy"?

Again, was I not taught by my Lord that as in a Line there are *two* bounding Points, and in a Square there are *four* bounding Lines, so in a Cube there must be *six* bounding Squares? Behold once more the confirming Series, 2, 4, 6: is not this an Arithmetical Progression? And consequently does it not of necessity follow that the more divine offspring of the divine Cube in the Land of Four Dimensions, must have 8 bounding Cubes: and is not this also, as my Lord has taught me to believe, "strictly according to Analogy"? (88–89)

[From Chapter 22, *"How I then tried to diffuse the Theory of Three Dimensions by other means, and of the result."* Square, jailed for seven years for his belief in the world of three dimensions, despairs of ever converting the Flatlanders. In this passage is yet another source for the White Sphinx.] Yet I exist in the hope that these memoirs, in some manner, I know not how, may find their way to the minds of humanity in Some Dimension, and may stir up a race of rebels who shall refuse to be confined to limited Dimensionality.

That is the hope of my brighter moments. Alas, it is not

always so. Heavily weighs on me at times the burdensome reflection that I cannot honestly say I am confident as to the exact shape of the once-seen, oft-regretted Cube; and in my nightly visions the mysterious precept, "Upward, not Northward," haunts me like a soul-devouring Sphinx. (101-02)

2. C.H. Hinton. From "What Is the Fourth Dimension?" 1884. *Scientific Romances: First Series.* London: Swan Sonnenschein, 1886. 3-32.

[Charles Howard Hinton (1853-1907) was a British mathematician and supernaturalist chiefly remembered for his speculative essays on the possibility of a fourth dimension of space, as well as for his first use of the phrase "scientific romance," which Wells would later borrow as a label for his own fiction. "What Is the Fourth Dimension?" was first published as a pamphlet in 1884, then collected with other speculative pieces (chiefly non-fictional) as a book, *Scientific Romances: First Series*, in 1886. After the machine itself, the oldest element in *The Time Machine* is the Time Traveller's argument for the existence of the fourth dimension, and in dramatizing it Wells was unquestionably influenced by the following passages from Hinton.]

"Why should there be three and only three directions?" Space, as we know it, is subject to a limitation....

Suppose a being confined to a plane superficies,[1] and throughout all the range of its experience never to have moved up or down, but simply to have kept to this one plane. Suppose, that is, some figure, such as a circle or rectangle, to be endowed with the power of perception; such a being if it moves in the plane superficies in which it is drawn, will move in a multitude of directions; but, however varied they may seem to be, these directions will all be compounded of two, at right angles to each other. By no movement so long as the plane superficies remains perfectly horizontal, will this being move in the direction we call up and down. And it is important to

---

1   I.e., a plane having only length and breadth.

notice that the plane would be different, to a creature confined to it, from what it is to us. We think of a plane habitually as having an upper and a lower side, because it is only by the contact of solids that we realize a plane. But a creature which had been confined to a plane during its whole existence would have no idea of there being two sides to the plane he lived in. In a plane there is simply length and breadth. If a creature in it be supposed to know of an up or down he must already have gone out of the plane.

Is it possible, then, that a creature so circumstanced would arrive at the notion of there being an up and down, a direction different from those to which he had been accustomed, and having nothing in common with them? Obviously nothing in the creature's circumstances would tell him of it. It could only be by a process of reasoning on his part that he could arrive at such a conception. If he were to imagine a being confined to a single straight line, he might realise that he himself could move in two directions, while the creature in a straight line could only move in one. Having made this reflection he might ask, "But why is the number of directions limited to two? Why should there not be three?" (5-7)

For the sake of convenience, let us call the figure we are investigating—the simplest figure in four dimensions—a four-square.

First of all we must notice, that if a cube be formed from a square by the movement of the square in a new direction, each point of the interior of the square traces out part of the cube. It is not only the bounding lines that by their motion form the cube, but each portion of the interior of the square generates a portion of the cube. So if a cube were to move in the fourth dimension so as to generate a four-square, every point in the interior of the cube would start *de novo*,[1] and trace out a portion of the new figure uninterfered with by the other points.

Or, to look at the matter in another light, a being in three dimensions, looking down on a square, sees each part of it

---

1   Anew.

extended before him, and can touch each part without having to pass through the surrounding parts, for he can go from above, while the surrounding parts surround the part he touches only in one plane.

So a being in four dimensions could look at and touch every point of a solid figure. No one part would hide another, for he would look at each part from a direction which is perfectly different from any in which it is possible to pass from one part of the body to another. To pass from one part of the body to another it is necessary to move in three directions, but a creature in four dimensions would look at the solid from a direction which is none of these three. (13)

Let us investigate the conception of a four-dimensional existence in a simpler and more natural manner—in the same way that a two-dimensional being should think about us, not as infinite in the third dimension, but limited in three dimensions as he is in two. A being existing in four dimensions must then be thought to be as completely bounded in all four directions as we are in three. All that we can say in regard to the possibility of such beings is, that we have no experience of motion in four directions. The powers of such beings and their experience would be ampler, but there would be no fundamental difference in the laws of force and motion.

Such a being would be able to make but a part of himself visible to us, for a cube would be apprehended by a two-dimensional being as the square in which it stood. Thus a four-dimensional being would suddenly appear as a complete and finite body, and as suddenly disappear, leaving no trace of himself, in space, in the same way that anything lying on a flat surface, would, on being lifted, suddenly vanish out of the cognisance of beings, whose consciousness was confined to the plane. The object would not vanish by moving in any direction, but disappear instantly as a whole. There would be no barrier no confinement of our devising that would not be perfectly open to him. He would come and go at pleasure; he would be able to perform feats of the most surprising kind. (25)

3. "S." "Four-Dimensional Space." [Letter to the Editor, dated March 16, 1885.] *Nature* 31 (26 March 1885): 481.

[This letter to the editor of *Nature* has been cited as the first serious mention of the idea of time as the fourth dimension in an English-language scientific journal. That it should have appeared in a periodical founded by T. H. Huxley at a time when Wells was in his first year at the Normal School suggests that its author, identified only as "S," was possibly one of Wells's circle of students—or even Wells himself. Whoever "S" was, it is clear that time as fourth dimension was one of the ideas circulating in South Kensington while Wells was there, as he himself later recalled: see Appendix G3.]

Possibly the question, What is the fourth dimension? may admit of an indefinite number of answers. I prefer, therefore, in proposing to consider Time as a fourth dimension of our existence, to speak of it as *a* fourth dimension rather than *the* fourth dimension. Since this fourth dimension cannot be introduced into space, as commonly understood, we require a new kind of space for its existence, which we may call time-space. There is then no difficulty in conceiving the analogues in this new kind of space, of the things in ordinary space which are known as lines, areas, and solids. A straight line, by moving in any direction not in its own length, generates an area; if this area moves in any direction not in its own plane it generates a solid; but if this solid moves in any direction, it still generates a solid, and nothing more. The reason of this is that we have not supposed it to move in the fourth dimension. If the straight line moves in its own direction, it describes only a straight line; if the area moves in its own plane, it describes only an area; in each case, motion in the dimensions in which the thing exists, gives us only a thing of the same dimensions; and, in order to get a thing of higher dimensions, we must have motion in a new dimension. But, as the idea of motion is only applicable in space of three dimensions, we must replace it by another which is applicable in our fourth dimension of time. Such an idea is that of successive existence. We must, therefore, conceive that there is a new three-dimensional space for each successive instant of time; and, by picturing to ourselves the aggregate formed by the successive positions in time-space of a given solid during a given time, we shall get the idea of a four-dimensional solid, which may be called a sur-solid. It will assist us to get a clearer idea, if we consider a solid which is in a constant state of change, both of magnitude and position; and an example of a solid which satisfies this condition sufficiently well, is afforded by the body of each of us. Let any man picture to himself the aggregate of his own bodily forms from birth to the present time, and he will have a clear idea of a sur-solid in time-space.

Let us now consider the sur-solid formed by the movement, or rather, the successive existence, of a cube in time-space. We are to conceive of the cube, and the whole of the three-dimensional space in which it is situated, as floating away in time-space for a given time; the cube will then have an initial and a final position, and these will be the end boundaries of the sur-solid. It will therefore have sixteen points, namely, the eight points belonging to the initial cube, and the eight belonging to the final cube. The successive positions (in time-space) of each of the twelve edges of the cube, will form what may be called a time area; and, adding these to the twelve faces of the initial and final cubes, we see that the sur-solid has twenty-four areas. Lastly, the successive positions (in time-space) of each of the six faces of the cube, will form what may be called a time-solid; and, adding these to the initial and final cubes, we see that the sur-solid is bounded by eight solids. These results agree with the statements in your article.[1] But it is not permissible to speak of the sur-solid as resting in "space," we must rather say that the section of it by any time is a cube resting (or moving) in "space."

---

1   The "article" was an anonymous review of C.H. Hinton's *Scientific Romances*. No. 1. "What is the Fourth Dimension?" (1884) in *Nature* 31 (12 March 1885): 431.

4. E. A. Hamilton Gordon. From "The Fourth Dimension." Science Schools Journal 5 (April 1887): 145-51.

[Hamilton Gordon, Wells's fellow-student at the Normal School, read this paper to the Debating Society on 14 January 1887. In the penultimate paragraph, he ruefully notes the similarity of his ideas to Hinton's, but claims that he did not become aware of Hinton's work (see Appendix D2) until the paper was finished. The paper is more evidence of the importance of the idea of the fourth dimension at South Kensington, while Hamilton Gordon's dismissal of the idea of time as the fourth dimension suggests that even in 1887 Wells was a relatively original thinker whose mind was moving in the subversive direction pioneered by Abbott, rather than in the supernatural one suggested by Hinton.]

The question has been put to me with monotonous frequency, "What is the fourth dimension?" and it would be difficult to answer, were it not for the fact that the questioner usually answers it for himself, by suggesting some impossible thing. One thought it was "Time," another, "Life," a third "Heaven," while a fourth suggested "Velocity".... The most reasonable suggestion was that it was the "Soul," but with this I cannot agree at all. The soul is from its very nature immaterial, whilst the fourth dimension must necessarily be as material as the other three; the soul has none of the properties of a solid, namely size, inertia, &c.

What, then, is the fourth dimension?

Let us think out some of the phenomena we should observe if a body of the fourth power were to enter, or pass through, a plane of the third. Then let us see whether our experience furnishes us with any such phenomena, and draw our conclusions accordingly....

We must first of all imagine a plane figure in a plane to be endowed with senses of sight, touch, and hearing. Now let a solid body approach the plane; so long as it remains outside the plane it will be absolutely invisible, but as soon as it enters it, there will become visible that section of the solid which is made by the plane; and if the solid continued moving, different sections would be continually presented to view; finally, when the solid had passed through the plane, it would suddenly and mysteriously vanish, and the thought-endowed plane figure would be unable to conceive whence it came or whither it went.

Moreover, if there were some impenetrable object in the plane, such as an impassable line, so that figures in the plane could not pass it, it would form no obstacle whatever to a solid body, which would pass through, or rather, round it, quite unconsciously; so that it could enter enclosed places which would be quite unattainable to bodies moving in the plane alone.

Again, if a voice spoke out of the third dimension so as to be heard by our imaginary person in the second, the sound would appear to come from everywhere at once, or rather from no definite direction; in fact we should describe it as sepulchral....

Although, possibly, none of us here to-night may have seen a ghost, yet we have all heard plenty of well-authenticated ghost stories, and we at once perceive the similarity between the two sets of phenomena. (149-50)

5. Oscar Wilde. From "The Canterville Ghost: A Hylo-Idealistic Romance." 1887. *The Works of Oscar Wilde*. [Sunflower Ed.] Vol. IV. New York: Lamb Publishing Co., 1909. 87-152.

[Hinton's interest in the fourth dimension of space was to try to account scientifically for the phenomenon of ghosts; Hamilton Gordon's argument moves in a similar direction. This passage from an early ghost story by Oscar Wilde (1854-1900) shows how rapidly speculative ideas about the fourth dimension were being assimilated into popular culture at the time when Wells was first beginning to mull over ideas about a time machine.]

For a moment the Canterville ghost stood quite motionless in natural indignation; then, dashing the bottle violently upon the polished floor, he fled down the corridor, uttering hollow groans, and emitting a ghastly green light. Just, however, as he reached the top of the great oak staircase, a door was flung open, two little white-robed figures appeared, and a large pillow whizzed past his head! There was evidently no time to be lost, so, hastily adopting the Fourth Dimension of Space as a means of escape, he vanished through the wainscoting, and the house became quite quiet. (100)

6. William James. From *The Principles of Psychology*. **New York: Henry Holt, 1890.**

[William James (1842-1910), the American philosopher and older brother of Henry James, first came to prominence as the author of a vast overview of all that was known in 1890 of the science of mind, *The Principles of Psychology*. It is not known if Wells read James at this time, but it is clear from *The Time Machine* that he was familiar with some of the contemporary thought about how the mind perceives reality, space, and time, that is summarized so effectively by James in Chapter XV: "The Perception of Time."]

In short, the practically cognized present is no knife-edge, but a saddle-back, with a certain breadth of its own on which we sit perched, and from which we look in two directions into time. The unit of composition of our perception of time is a *duration*, with a bow and a stern, as it were—a rearward—and a forward-looking end....

When we come to study the perception of Space, we shall find it quite analogous to time in this regard. Date in time corresponds to position in space; and although we now mentally construct large spaces by mentally imagining remoter and remoter positions, just as we now construct great durations by mentally prolonging a series of successive dates, yet the original experience of both space and time is always of something already given as a unit, inside of which attention afterward discriminates parts in relation to each other. (1:609-10)

Suppose we were able, within the length of a second, to note 10,000 events distinctly, instead of barely 10, as now.... The motions of organic beings would be so slow to our senses as to be inferred, not seen. The sun would stand still in the sky, the moon be almost free from change, and so on. But now reverse the hypothesis and suppose a being to get only one 1000th part of the sensations that we get in a given time, and consequently to live 1000 times as long. Winters and summers will be to him like quarters of an hour. Mushrooms and the swifter-growing plants will shoot into being so rapidly as to appear instantaneous creations; annual shrubs will rise and fall from the earth like restlessly-boiling water springs; the motions of animals will be as invisible as are to us the movements of bullets and cannon-balls; the sun will scour through the sky like a meteor, leaving a fiery trail behind him.... (1:639)

7. Professor Simon Newcomb. From "Modern Mathematical Thought." [Address delivered before the New York Mathematical Society at the annual meeting, December 28, 1893.] *Nature* 49 (February 1, 1894): 325–29.

[The Nova Scotia-born mathematician, astronomer, and naval officer Simon Newcomb (1835-1909) was one of the most prominent American scientists of his generation. This is a passage from the actual address mentioned by the Time Traveller in Chapter 1 of *The Time Machine*, which allows us to date the opening dinner party at Richmond to early 1894.[1] Wells had clearly kept up with the evolving scientific debate on the fourth dimension, though it should be noted that Newcomb deals only with four dimensions of space. In early 1894 Newcomb was Professor of Mathematics and Astronomy at Johns Hopkins University.]

---

1   The Time Traveller notes in Chapter I that Newcomb's 28 December, 1893 lecture was "only a month or so ago." If he had attended it, then his dinner party would be in early February 1894. If he had like his creator merely read the text of the lecture in the 1 February 1894 issue of *Nature*, then the dinner party would be in March 1894, significantly the same month that the first instalment of the *National Observer* version of *The Time Machine* was published.

Now, it is a fundamental principle of pure science that the liberty of making hypotheses is unlimited. It is not necessary that we shall prove the hypothesis to be a reality before we are allowed to make it. It is legitimate to anticipate all the possibilities. It is, therefore, a perfectly legitimate exercise of thought to imagine what would result if we should not stop at three dimensions in geometry, but construct one for space having four. As the boy, at a certain stage in his studies, passes from two to three dimensions, so may the mathematician pass from three to four dimensions with equal facility. He does indeed meet with the obstacle that he cannot draw figures in four dimensions, and his faculties are so limited that he cannot construct in his own mind an image of things as they would look in space of four dimensions. But this need not prevent his reasoning on the subject, and one of the most obvious conclusions he would reach is this: As in space of two dimensions one line can be drawn perpendicular to another at a given point, and by adding another dimension to space a third line can be drawn perpendicular to these two; so in a fourth dimension we can draw a line which shall be perpendicular to all three. True, we cannot imagine how the line would look, or where it would be placed, but this is merely because of the limitations of our faculties. As a surface describes a solid by continually leaving the space in which it lies at the moment, so a four-dimensional solid will be generated by a three-dimensional one by a continuous motion which shall constantly be directed outside of this three-dimensional space in which our universe appears to exist. As the man confined in a circle can evade it by stepping over it, so the mathematician, if placed inside a sphere in four-dimensional space, would simply step over it as easily as we should over a circle drawn on the floor. Add a fourth dimension to space, and there is room for an indefinite number of universes, all alongside of each other, as there is for an indefinite number of sheets of paper when we pile them upon each other. (328)

Appendix E: The Spatiotemporal Context: Solar Death and the End of the World

1. Jonathan Swift [as "Lemuel Gulliver"]. From *Travels into Several Remote Nations of the World....* London: Benjamin Motte, 1726.

[In his preface to the Atlantic edition of *The Time Machine* (see Appendix G2), Wells noted that he had undergone a "cleansing course" of Swift between "The Chronic Argonauts" and the *National Observer* version of *The Time Machine*. As a scientific romance with a satirical edge, *The Time Machine* has a generic affiliation with Part III of *Gulliver's Travels*, "A Voyage to Laputa," while the apocalyptic ending of Wells's novel may well owe something to this passage on the anxieties generated by science from Part III of the famous satire by Swift (1667-1745).]

THESE People are under continual Disquietudes, never enjoying a Minute's Peace of Mind; and their Disturbances proceed from Causes which very little affect the rest of Mortals. Their Apprehensions arise from several Changes they dread in the Celestial Bodies. For instance; that the Earth by the continual Approaches of the Sun towards it, must in Course of Time be absorbed or swallowed up. That the Face of the Sun will by Degrees be encrusted with its own Effluvia, and give no more Light to the World.... That the Sun daily spending its Rays without any Nutriment to supply them, will at last be wholly consumed and annihilated; which must be attended with the Destruction of this Earth, and of all the Planets that receive their Light from it. (164-65)

2. **Professor W[illiam] Thomson [later Lord Kelvin]. From "On the Age of the Sun's Heat." *Macmillan's Magazine* 5 (March 1862): 388-93. [Rep. as "On the Age of the Sun's Heat." In Sir William Thomson and Peter Guthrie Tait. *Treatise on Natural Philosophy*. New ed. Vol. I Part 2. Cambridge: Cambridge UP, 1879. 485-94.]**

[William Thomson, 1st Baron Kelvin (1824-1907) was one of the most distinguished British mathematicians and physicists of the nineteenth century. He was one of the chief proponents of the doctrine of the irreversible cosmic dissipation of energy—the heat-death of the universe—according to the second law of thermodynamics. One of his most widely read papers contained an estimate of the *total* lifespan of the sun at possibly as little as ten million years, perhaps at most a hundred million years. (Nuclear energy, and the solar fusion reaction that liberates it, was not yet then understood.) Kelvin's paper caused alarm in the scientific community and cast a pall over the fin de siècle because it suggested such a comparatively brief future for life on earth. For the sun was assumed to be well into its lifespan, as millions—preferably hundreds of millions—of years were required by biologists to account for evolution. Indeed, evolution according to Kelvin's scenario would have to have taken place rather more quickly than Darwinists had assumed. It is the result of Kelvin's influence that Wells in *The Time Machine* proposes that divergence of the human species could have taken place in so short a time as 800,000 years, and that life on earth would certainly be ending thirty million years hence.]

The second great law of Thermodynamics involves a certain principle of *irreversible action in nature*. It is thus shown that, although mechanical energy is *indestructible*, there is a universal tendency to its dissipation, which produces gradual augmentation and diffusion of heat, cessation of motion, and exhaustion of potential energy through the material universe. The result would inevitably be a state of universal rest and death, if the universe were finite and left to obey existing laws. (388)

There is no difficulty in accounting for [the sun providing] 20,000,000 years' heat by the meteoric theory.[1]

It would extend this article to too great a length, and would require something of mathematical calculation, to explain fully the principles on which this last estimate is founded. It is enough to say that bodies, all much smaller than the sun, falling together from a state of relative rest, at mutual distances all large in comparison with their diameters, and forming a globe of uniform density equal in mass and diameter to the sun, would generate an amount of heat which, accurately calculated according to Joule's[2] principles and experimental results, is found to be just 20,000,000 times Pouillet's[3] estimate of the annual amount of solar radiation....

... there is reason to believe that even the most rapid conglomeration [of the bodies that supposedly originally coalesced to form the sun] that we can conceive to have probably taken place could only leave the finished globe with about half the entire heat due to the amount of potential energy of mutual gravitation exhausted. We may, therefore, accept, as a lowest estimate for the sun's initial heat, 10,000,000 times a year's supply at present rate, but 50,000,000 or 100,000,000 as possible, in consequence of the sun's greater density in his central parts.

The considerations adduced above, in this paper, regarding the sun's possible specific heat, rate of cooling, and superficial temperature, render it probable that he must have been very sensibly warmer one million years ago than now; and, consequently, that if he has existed as a luminary for ten or twenty million years, he must have radiated away considerably more than the corresponding number of times the present yearly amount of loss.

It seems, therefore, on the whole most probable that the sun has not illuminated the earth for 100,000,000 years, and almost certain that he has not done so for 500,000,000 years. As for the

---

1 Namely, that the loss of some of the sun's heat has been compensated for by meteors or other cosmic debris which, drawn into the sun by its gravitational force, would add to its pool of fuel and thus lengthen its lifespan.
2 James Prescott Joule (1818–89), the English physicist.
3 Claude Pouillet (1791–1868), the French physicist.

future, we may say, with equal certainty, that inhabitants of the earth cannot continue to enjoy the light and heat essential to their life, for many million years longer, unless sources now unknown to us are prepared in the great storehouse of creation. (393)

3. Balfour Stewart. From *The Conservation of Energy. Being an Elementary Treatise on Energy and Its Laws.* **2nd ed. London: Henry S. King, 1874.**

[Balfour Stewart (1828–87) the Scottish-born physicist, latterly Professor of Natural Philosophy at Owens College, Manchester, had an ability to explain clearly, sometimes through striking metaphors, the implications of the second law of thermodynamics for the future of humanity in books that were widely read as Wells was growing up. He noted, for example, that the sun expends its energy like a man "whose expenditure exceeds his income. He is living upon his capital, and is destined to share the fate of all who act in a similar manner" (152).]

Probable Fate of the Universe

209. ... We have spoken already about a medium pervading space, the office of which appears to be to degrade and ultimately extinguish all differential motion, just as it tends to reduce and ultimately equalize all difference of temperature. Thus the universe would ultimately become an equally heated mass, utterly worthless as far as the production of work is concerned, since such production depends upon difference of temperature.

Although, therefore, in a strictly mechanical sense, there is a conservation of energy, yet, as regards usefulness or fitness for living beings, the energy of the universe is in process of deterioration. Universally diffused heat forms what we may call the great waste-heap of the universe, and this is growing larger year by year. At present it does not sensibly obtrude itself, but who knows that the time may not arrive when we shall be practically conscious of its growing bigness?

210. It will be seen that ... we have regarded the universe,

not as a collection of matter, but rather as an energetic agent—in fact, as a lamp. Now, it has been well pointed out by Thomson,[1] that looked at in this light, the universe is a system that had a beginning and must have an end; for a process of degradation cannot be eternal. If we could view the universe as a candle not lit, then it is perhaps conceivable to regard it as having been always in existence; but if we regard it rather as a candle that has been lit, we become absolutely certain that it cannot have been burning from eternity, and that a time will come when it will cease to burn. We are led to look to a beginning in which the particles of matter were in a diffuse chaotic state, but endowed with the power of gravitation, and we are led to look to an end in which the whole universe will be one equally heated inert mass, and from which everything like life or motion or beauty will have utterly gone away. (152-53)

4. [Balfour Stewart and Peter Guthrie Tait.] From *The Unseen Universe; or, Physical Speculations on a Future State*. 3rd. ed. London: Macmillan, 1875.

[In *The Unseen Universe*, Stewart and Peter Guthrie Tait (1831-1901), Professor of Natural Philosophy at the University of Edinburgh and collaborator with Lord Kelvin, prepared the nineteenth-century reading public for the apocalyptic scenario in "The Further Vision."]

[From Article 114: "Degradation of Energy"; following a historical sketch of the Second Law of Thermodynamics.] It ... appears that at each transformation of heat-energy into work a large portion is degraded, while only a small portion is transformed into work. So that while it is very easy to change all of our mechanical or useful energy into heat, it is only possible to transform a portion of this heat-energy back again into work. After each change too the heat becomes more and more dissi-

---

1   See Appendix E2.

pated or degraded, and less and less available for any future transformation.

In other words, the tendency of heat is towards equalisation; heat is *par excellence* the communist of our universe, and it will no doubt ultimately bring the system to an end. This universe may in truth be compared to a vast heat engine, and this is the reason why we have brought such engines so prominently before our readers. The sun is the furnace or source of high-temperature heat of our system, just as the stars are for other systems, and the energy which is essential to our existence is derived from the heat which the sun radiates, and represents only a very small portion of that heat. But while the sun thus supplies us with energy he is himself getting colder, and must ultimately, by means of radiation into space, part with the life-sustaining power which he at present possesses. Besides the cooling of the sun we must also suppose that owing to something analogous to ethereal friction the earth and the other planets of our system will be drawn spirally nearer and nearer to the sun, and will at length be engulfed in his mass. In each such case there will be, as the result of the collision, the conversion of visible energy into heat, and a partial and temporary restoration of the power of the sun. At length, however, this process will have come to an end, and he will be extinguished until, after long but not immeasurable ages, by means of the same ethereal friction his black mass is brought into contact with that of his nearest neighbour.

115. Not much further need we dilate on this. It is absolutely certain that life, so far as it is physical, depends essentially on transformations of energy; it is also absolutely certain that age after age the possibility of such transformations is becoming less and less; and, so far as we yet know, the final state of the present universe must be an aggregation (into one mass) of all the matter it contains, *i.e.* the potential energy gone, and a practically useless state of kinetic energy, *i.e.* uniform temperature throughout that mass. (90–92)

5. **George Howard Darwin. From "The Determination of the Secular Effects of Tidal Friction by a Graphical Method."** *Proceedings of the Royal Society of London*, **XXIX** (1879), pp. 168–81. In *Scientific Papers. Volume II: Tidal Friction and Cosmogony*. Cambridge: Cambridge UP, 1908. 195–207.

[The "younger Darwin" mentioned by the Time Traveller in Chapter VIII was Charles Darwin's second son Sir George Howard Darwin (1845–1912), an astronomer recognized in his time as the leading authority on tidal effects. Below is Darwin's clearest explanation of how the frictional effect of gravity retards the motion of a planet like the earth—the equations underlying Wells's fin-de-siècle vision of a universe running down.]

Suppose an attractive particle or satellite of mass m to be moving in a circular orbit, with an angular velocity Ω, round a planet of mass M, and suppose the planet to be rotating about an axis perpendicular to the plane of the orbit, with an angular velocity n; suppose, also, the mass of the planet to be partially or wholly imperfectly elastic or viscous, or that there are oceans on the surface of the planet; then the attraction of the satellite must produce a relative motion in the parts of the planet, and that motion must be subject to friction, or, in other words, there must be frictional tides of some sort or other. The system must accordingly be losing energy by friction, and its configuration must change in such a way that its whole energy diminishes.

Such a system does not differ much from those of actual planets and satellites, and, therefore, the results deduced in this hypothetical case must agree pretty closely with the actual course of evolution, provided that time enough has been and will be given for such changes. (195)

6. George Howard Darwin. From "On the Precession of a Viscous Spheroid, and on the Remote History of the Earth." *Philosophical Transactions of the Royal Society*, **Part II. Vol. 170 (1879), pp. 447-530. In** *Scientific Papers. Volume II: Tidal Friction and Cosmogony*. **Cambridge: Cambridge UP, 1908. 36-139.**

[In *The Time Machine* Wells took into account G. H. Darwin's speculations on the specific orbital fate of the earth and moon in constructing the worlds of the far future. Just before the extract below, G. H. Darwin has established that in the distant future tidal friction will lengthen the earth day to almost 56 present days, while the moon will at first move away from the earth.]

... the sun's tidal friction will go on lengthening the day even beyond this point, but then the lunar tides will again come into existence, and the lunar tidal friction will tend in part to counteract the solar. The tidal reaction will also be reversed, so that the moon will again approach the earth. Thus the effect of the sun is to make this a state of dynamical instability. (102)

[Darwin argues that in the remote past both the day and month were about 5 hours 36 minutes in length.] First consider the case where the sun does not exist. Suppose the earth to be rotating in about 5½ hours, and the moon moving orbitally around it in a little less than that time. Then the motion of the moon relatively to the earth is consentaneous with[1] the earth's rotation, and therefore the tidal friction, small though it be, tends to accelerate the earth's rotation; the tidal reaction is such as to tend to retard the moon's linear velocity, and therefore increase her orbital angular velocity, and reduce her distance from the earth. The end will be that the moon falls into the earth....

Secondly, take the case where the sun also exists, and suppose the system started in the same way as before. Now the

1 Accords with.

motion of the earth relatively to the sun is rapid, and such that the solar tidal friction retards the earth's rotation; whilst the lunar tidal friction is, as before, such as to accelerate the rotation.

Hence, if the viscosity be very large the earth's rotation may be accelerated, but if it be not very large it will be retarded. The tidal reaction, which depends on the lunar tides alone, continues negative, and the moon approaches the earth as before. Thus after a short time the motion of the moon relatively to the earth is more rapid than in the previous case, whatever be the ratio between solar and lunar tidal friction. Hence in this case the moon will fall into the earth more rapidly than if the sun did not exist, and the dynamical instability is more marked.

If, however, the day were shorter than the month, the moon must continually recede from the earth, until it reaches the outer limit of a day of 56 m[ean] s[olar] days. (103)

7. [H. G. Wells.] From "The 'Cyclic' Delusion." *Saturday Review* 78 (10 November 1894): 505-06.

[Wells's perhaps simplistic interpretation of G. H. Darwin's speculations on tidal drag is clearly evident in this passage from one of his *Saturday Review* articles, preaching against constancy in nature.]

... we discover that ... apparent cycles seem cyclic only through the limitation of our observation. The tidal drag upon the planets slowly retards their rotation, so that every day is— though by an imperceptible amount—longer. "As certain as that the sun will rise" is a proverb for certainty, but one day the sun will rise for the last time, will become as motionless in the sky as the earth is now in the sky of the moon. According to Professor G. H. Darwin, the actual motion of a satellite is spiral; it recedes from its source and primary until a maximum distance is attained, and thence it draws nearer again, until it reunites at last with the central body. (506)

8. Camille Flammarion. From *Omega: The Last Days of the World*. New York: Cosmopolitan Publishing Co., 1894. Trans. *La Fin du monde*. 1893–94.

[The distinguished French astronomer Flammarion (1842–1925) popularized his discipline through both non-fictional works and scientific romances. *Omega* is the most ambitious of his fictions, revealing that in the early 1890s Wells had good scientific company for his apocalyptic fantasy in "The Further Vision." It is not known if *Omega* directly influenced *The Time Machine* (which was published a year after the English translation of *Omega*), but the similarities are striking. The extract is from Chapter IV: an astronomer from Colombia offers his theory of how the world will end.]

"One thing is certain, that the sun will finally lose its heat; it is condensing and contracting, and its fluidity is decreasing. The time will come when the circulation, which now supplies the photosphere,[1] and makes the central mass a reservoir of radiant energy, will be obstructed and will slacken. The radiation of heat and light will then diminish, and vegetable and animal life will be more and more restricted to the earth's equatorial regions. When this circulation shall have ceased, the brilliant photosphere will be replaced by a dark opaque crust which will prevent all luminous radiation. The sun will become a dark red ball, then a black one, and night will be perpetual. The moon, which shines only by reflection, will no longer illumine the lonely nights. Our planet will receive no light but that of the stars. The solar heat having vanished, the atmosphere will remain undisturbed, and an absolute calm, unbroken by any breath of air, will reign.

"If the oceans still exist they will be frozen ones, no evaporation will form clouds, no rain will fall, no stream will flow. Perhaps, as has been observed in the case of stars on the eve of extinction, some last flare of the expiring torch, some accidental development of heat, due to the falling in of the sun's crust,

---

1 The luminous and heat-radiating envelope of the sun.

will give us back for a while the old-time sun, but this will only be the precursor of the end; and the earth, a dark ball, a frozen tomb, will continue to revolve about the black sun, travelling through an endless night and hurrying away with all the solar system into the abyss of space. *It is to the extinction of the sun that the earth will owe its death, twenty, perhaps forty million years hence.*" (109-10)

Appendix F: Extracts from Wells's Correspondence

[The following extracts offer insight into the composition, reception, and interpretation of *The Time Machine*. All are taken from *The Correspondence of H. G. Wells*. Ed. David C. Smith. 4 vols. London: Pickering & Chatto, 1998. The punctuation, dating (conjectural or otherwise), and numbering of letters are Smith's. Parenthetical volume and page references follow each extract.]

1. From Letter 90 to Elizabeth Healey, 19 June [1888].

[This postscript to a letter from Wells in Staffordshire to Elizabeth Healey, one of the few female students at the Normal School and a lifelong friend, implies that the just-completed serialization of "The Chronic Argonauts" in *Science Schools Journal* was not the end of the matter—its prophetic voice had not yet finished what it had to say.]

The Chronic Argonauts is no joke. There is a sequel—It is the latest Delphic voice but the Tripod[1] is not yet broken. (1:108)

2. From Letter 155 to the Editor, *Fortnightly Review*, 5 September 1891.

[This passage from a letter to Frank Harris indicates that even though Harris had just rejected "The Universe Rigid," Wells thought highly enough of "The Chronic Argonauts" to send him a copy. It is not known what Harris's response was.]

Dear Sir,

Some days ago I left a copy of "The Chronic Argonauts", a story you had very kindly promised to read, at Henrietta Street. I need scarcely say that whatever advice you can give me, for its disposal, will confer a great favour upon me. (1:174)

---

1   The allusion is to the oracle of Apollo at Delphi, near where a golden tripod stood.

3. From Letter 173 to Amy Catherine Robbins, c. 22 May 1893.

[From the first known letter by Wells to Jane, this extract refers to his recent serious lung haemorrhage and its effect on his career.]

... I was so disgusted, when I woke in the dismal time before dawn on Thursday morning, to find myself the butt of *His*[1] witticism, that I almost left this earthly joking ground in a huff. However by midday on Thursday, what with ice and opium pills ... my wife and the doctor calmed the internal eruption of the joker outjoked, and since that I have been lying on my back, moody but recovering....

I guess class teaching is over for me for good, and that whether I like it or not, I must write for a living now. (1:190-91)

4. From Letter 197 to A. M. Davies, [1894].

[Arthur Morley Davies was another of Wells's fellow-students at the Normal School who became a lifelong friend. This extract refers to the revised *Time Machine* material as it was about to appear in W. E. Henley's *National Observer*.]

... I have also responded to an invitation by the *National Observer* and that old corpse of the Chronic Argo is being cut up into articles, one last Saturday (Time Travelling) one next number & possibly others to follow. It is quite recast. (1:214)

5. From Letter 204 to Elizabeth Healey, September 1894.

Dear Miss Healey,

Thanks for your inquiries about the Great Man. His Chronic Argonauts are with a fact hound (& author of a slang dictionary) named Henley. (1:220)

---

1   I.e., God's.

6. From Letter 211 to Elizabeth Healey, 22 December 1894.

You may be interested to know that our ancient Chronic Argonauts of the Science Schools Journal has at last become a complete story and will appear as a serial in the *New Review* for January. There was a puff preliminary in the P.M.G.[1] last night (Friday). I'm praying it may go. It's my trump card and if it does not come off very much I shall know my place for the rest of my career. Still we live in hope. (1:226)

7. From Letter 213 to J. M. Dent, 2 January 1895.

[Joseph Malaby Dent was the head of the publishing house that would bring out Wells's novel *The Wonderful Visit* in September this year.]

The *Time Machine* is on offer to Heinemann & I have reason to think he will take it. (1:228)

8. From Letter 216 to John Lane, 2 February 1895.

[From a letter to another publisher, revealing Wells's sense of the potential readership for his scientific romances. Lane would publish *Select Conversations with an Uncle* in June 1895.]

A collection of scientific papers such as I have suggested would appeal to the same class of people as the "Time Machine" story I have running in the *New Review*. (1:231)

9. From Letter 218 to Elizabeth Healey, 26 February 1895.

[This extract bespeaks Wells's growing confidence and excitement early in his *annus mirabilis*.]

I shall look to you to quote my books to me so soon as they appear. "There's Select Conversations with An Uncle (now

---

1 The *Pall Mall Gazette*.

Extinct.)" a book of cheerful rambling which Lane has in press, The Time Machine, which will follow this in June, & The Stolen Bacillus in September. Don't miss these treats. (1:233)

10. From Letter 219 to A. T. Simmons, [Spring 1895].

[So hectic was Wells's life as his literary career suddenly burgeoned that it is perhaps not surprising that he should still be calling *The Time Machine* by an earlier title. Tommy Simmons was another close friend from Wells's South Kensington days.]

The Island of Doctor Moreau is on offer with Methuens & an American firm, & from what Henley says of it it's going to go. I've just been seeing about a little house in Woking & I shall go there I hope in the course of a month & put in some good work. Heinemann hesitating to put the *Time Traveller* on the bookstalls at 1/6—& go for a big sale, or make it a 6/- book. In the first case he will have it out by Whitsuntide. *The Referee*[1] gave it two columns of notice last Sunday. I feel just like we used to do before our exam list came out.... (1:233-34)

11. From Letter 223 to Elizabeth Healey, [Spring 1895].

Thanks for the cutting. I'm having rather a good time just now with the notices.—but some of this sweetness will certainly beget sourness soon. *The Weekly Times & Echo*, the *Referee*, the *Review of Reviews*, & several other papers have men cover the column—so has the *Realm*. Le Gallienne[2] in the *Star* remarks that a thousand years in my sight are but as yesterday & compares me cheerfully to the talented author of the Bible. But it really is very generous of these men. I don't intend to go on shouting in this way. Don't lend that copy of yours too widely, mind—the public has got to buy the thing. (1:237)

---

1 A London Sunday newspaper. The serialization of *The Time Machine* in the *New Review* had attracted favourable reviews, and the novel was eagerly awaited.

2 Richard Le Gallienne (1866-1947), one of the more notable younger men of letters of the period.

12. From Letter 224 to T. H. Huxley, May 1895.

[A note sent with a presentation copy of *The Time Machine*. Huxley, who had been seriously ill since early April, died on 29 June, almost certainly without ever reading the work that he more than anyone else had inspired.]

Dear Sir:

I am sending you a little book that I fancy may be of interest to you. The central idea—of degeneration following security—was the outcome of a certain amount of biological study. I daresay your position subjects you to a good many such displays of the range of authors but I have this much excuse, I was one of your pupils at the Royal College of Science and finally: the book is a very little one. (1:238)

13. From Letter 226 to William Heinemann, 14 May 1895.

[This letter to the publisher of *The Time Machine* a couple of weeks before the novel came out reveals that Wells was no naïve and overawed debutante but already an experienced and professional man of letters who knew exactly how to go about securing his niche in the literary marketplace.]

I have been expecting to hear from you about the *Time Traveller*. I'm afraid people will be forgetting *The Review of Reviews* and *Referee* notices if the book is not fired off at them soon. I'm quite prepared to place myself in your hands with regard to price, get up &c, only if the price is to be 1/6 or lower I think I ought to have say 20% after the first 5000. But I don't want to haggle about details of that sort—the important thing to me is to get the book published. There's one point I have been thinking over & that is, that an initial publication at a low price involves some risk of the book being scantily reviewed. We appeal I think to a public which reads reviews. Don't you think an immediate publication at a minimual [*sic*] price of 4/- say with the ordinary discount followed by a cheap paper covered issue for the Christmas bookstall time wd be possible.

By the bye has the book appeared in America? I have hopes for it over there.

Pardon my troubling you, but naturally I am in considerable suspense.

Yours faithfully
H. G. Wells

The following publications wd I think look at the book with friendly interest.

The *Saturday Review* (the editor was praising the thing to me the other day).

> *The National Observer*
> *Nature*
> *The Observatory*
> *The Journal of Education*
> *The University Correspondent*
> *The Educational Review*
> *The New Budget*
> *The P.M.G. & St. James's Gazette*

I've had numerous signed articles in all of these things & fancy that a certain proportion of their readers wd. go for the book. I have indeed a kind of small public of my own in this constituency.

P.S. The extensive changes I have made in the early part of the book should prevent *Mudie's* binding up the *New Review*.[1] If they did, we could make a fuss in all the newspapers & advertise the thing. (1:240-41)

14. From Letter 233 to Grant Allen, late Summer 1895?

[A letter revealing Wells's commendable honesty, debt to, and

---

1   Wells suggests that the revisions he has made to the *New Review* serialization of *The Time Machine* should make it more difficult for Mudie's Select Circulating Library, who dominated the market for new fiction, simply to bind up the instalments in book form so as to avoid having to lay out money on the Heinemann hardcover.

considerable divergence from, Grant Allen, who was an important precursor in the field of scientific romance and who is mentioned by name in Chapter VIII of *The Time Machine* (see p. 105, n. 2). Wells had slated Allen's best-selling novel *The Woman Who Did* (1895) anonymously in the *Saturday Review*, but after Allen's "very kind acknowledgement" of *The Time Machine*, Wells here reveals his authorship of the review so as not to mislead Allen about his real views. Allen had actually known the reviewer's identity but had not allowed that to prejudice him against *The Time Machine*.]

Your very kind acknowledgement of my book is more than I expected. I'm glad indeed that you like the work of it. But there is one little matter which I feel bound to mention to you in view of your good opinion. You allude to possible reviews. I think before you say anything in the book's favour that you should know that I wrote the review of The *W*oman Who *D*id in the *Saturday*. So far as essentials go I hold by that review now, & any apology I could make for the Bank-Holiday[1] flavour of its style, the window smashing midnight-concertina-playing tone of it, wd I am afraid be a little belated now. But I sent the book to you, not in your aspect of prominent critic & with any designs upon your criticism, but simply because I wanted you to read it. I have as sincere an envy for the almost instinctive way in which you get your effects in your short stories & for your scientific essays, as I have — shall I say dislike? for your vein of sexual sentiment. It's an unpleasant explanation this, but I have brought it on myself by my action in sending you a copy of my book. That was really not an appeal to you as a public appreciator. Apart from the difference in temperament that comes out when I read your fiction, I flatter myself that I have a certain affinity with you. I believe that this field of scientific romance with a philosophical element which I am trying to cultivate, belongs properly to you. Hence the book I sent. And you go writing "Keynotes"[2] that I cannot admire,

---

1   I.e., uncouth, loutish.
2   *The Woman Who Did* was published by John Lane in the Keynotes series, known for its controversial themes.

goading me into ill-mannered & even unfair reviews, when there is this fantastic wonderland unexplored.

I cannot imagine that you will do anything but dislike me after this incident, but I trust that at any rate you will give me credit for not aiming at your public support. (1:245–46)

15. From Letter 237 to Sarah Wells, 13 October [1895].

My dear Mother,

Just a line to tell you that I am back with my old landlady here for three weeks (getting married).... My last book seems a hit—everyone has heard of it—and all kinds of people seem disposed to make much of me. (1:248)

16. From Letter 541 to "Vernon Lee," 6 August 1904.

[Vernon Lee (1856–1935), whose real name was Violet Paget, was a novelist and historian, and one of the most important fin-de-siècle women of letters. Wells's emphasis on the rapid composition of the Heinemann version of *The Time Machine* discounts the slow evolution of the text from "The Chronic Argonauts."]

I'm glad of your letter & your excellent criticisms.... All that you say of *The Time Machine* is after my heart. But that book like all my earlier work was written against time, amidst a frantic output of "humorous" journalistic matter. It took perhaps three weeks. (2:40)

17. From Letter 2250 to J. B. Priestley, 27 February 1937.

[This late letter to the English novelist and playwright Priestley (1894–1984) is particularly revealing on the origin, and continuation, of Wells's interest in the fourth dimension.]

I like *Midnight in the Desert*[1] very much, more particularly the

---

1 I.e., Priestley's *Midnight on the Desert: A Chapter of Autobiography* (1937).

descriptive stuff about Arizona & America generally. The fourth dimension stuff isn't so good. I am rather an old hand with that stuff & I know most of the pitfalls of analogy into which people fall. Dunne[1] was started upon the trail of his *Time Machine*, but I'm not responsible for the series of Observer's which he has produced as a salted snail produces bubbles. I was started by A. Square & "Flatland."[2] It's too intricate a question to argue in a letter, but I think you can get at the catch in the business, if you think what again must have happened to a Square lifted out of his two dimensional universe. It must remain *flat*. He would not see his former plane as A. Square assumed. He would simply be in another plane. If the latter were inclined to the former, he would see the former only as a linear trace (without detail) on the latter. Similarly, but more interestingly, with the three dimensional *Time Traveller*. Every time you bring in a fresh dimension, the analogies complicate & veer off. You can deal with our universe as a 3 dimensional system flying along a fourth dimension (Time) at a uniform velocity through a fifth dimension which velocity is somehow connected with gravitation & the velocity of light. Or you can deal with it as a universe rigid, predestinate, in which free will is an illusion. But by that time, the rope of analogy by which you have come to this point is very nearly frayed through. There is nothing left to clamber to dimension 6. It is transcendental. Not all the Dunnes that ever were, splitting the poor little heads in thought, for a billion years, will ever get to that much of super-solidity. Dim^nV is a mental phantom, Dim^n6 is incomprehensible. (4:135-36)

18. From Letter 2380 to the Editor, *British Weekly*, 26 June 1939.

[Wells defends himself against an accusation that he is a believer in Excelsior biology, and in the process asserts that his liter-

---

1   John William Dunne (1875-1949), author of *An Experiment with Time* (1927), from whose theories Priestley borrowed in his works which explore the nature of time.
2   See Appendix D1.

ary career and his vision of the human future has been consistent from *The Time Machine* on.]

[Mr. D. R. Davies] may, as he says, have read me in the past, but he seems to have been taught to read very badly if he can accuse me of believing in Herbert Spencer's inevitable progress.[1] What have my books been from *The Time Machine* to *World Brain* (and my *Fate of Homo Sapiens* now in the press) but the clearest insistence on the insecurity of progress and the possibility of human degeneration and extinction?

I think the odds are against man but that it is still worthwhile in spite of the odds. I decline to stampede. (4:227)

19. From Letter 2513 to the Editor, *The Listener*, 30 March 1942.

[In the dark days of wartime London, Wells intemperately defends himself against the younger generation in the shape of George Orwell, and affirms that, ever since *The Time Machine*, he has shown himself to be no believer in the saving powers of science.]

Your contributor "George Orwell" has, I gather, been informing your readers that I belong to a despicable generation of parochially-minded writers who believed that the world would be saved from its gathering distresses by "science." (I don't know why you should consider it necessary to mislead your younger readers by printing this stuff of Orwell's. Either he is malicious or he is monstrously ignorant.) From my earliest book to the present time I have been reiterating that unless mankind adapted its social and political institutions to the changes invention and discovery were bringing about, mankind would be destroyed. Modesty prevents my giving you a list of titles, but I find it difficult to believe that anyone who has read *The Time Machine* (1895), *The Island of Dr. Moreau* (1896), *The Land Ironclads* (1903), *The War in the Air* (1908), *The Shape of*

---

1   See Appendices B5, B6.

Things to Come, (1933), *Science and the World Mind* (New Europe Publishing Company, 1942), to give only six examples of a multitude, can be guilty of these foolish, (untruthful) generalisations. (I submit that Orwell is a temperamental case rather than a critic and that you do me a grave injury in letting him loose at me.) (4:326)

Appendix G: *Wells on* The Time Machine

1. H. G. Wells. From "Popularising Science." *Nature* 50 (26 July 1894): 300-01.

[In this short essay from *Nature* published just as its author was writing *The Time Machine* in Sevenoaks, Wells offers many hints about the kind of scientifically-informed writing that would be likely to capture the interest and imagination of the reading public. Note his emphasis on the contemporary taste for "good inductive reading," which he indulges so effectively via the Time Traveller's account of A.D. 802,701]

Very few books and scientific papers appear to be constructed at all. The author simply wanders about his subject. He selects, let us say, "Badgers and Bats" as the title.... He writes first of all about Badger A. "We now come," he says, "to Badger B"; then "another interesting species is Badger C"; paragraphs on Badger D follow, and so the pavement is completed. "Let us now turn to the Bats," he says. It would not matter a bit if you cut any section of his book or paper out, or shuffled the sections, or destroyed most or all of them. This is not simply bad art; it is the trick of boredom. A scientific paper for popular reading may and should have an orderly progression and development. Intelligent common people come to scientific books neither for humour, subtlety of style, nor for vulgar wonders of the "millions and millions and millions" type, but for problems to exercise their minds upon. The taste for good inductive reading is very widely diffused: there is a keen pleasure in seeing a previously unexpected generalisation skilfully developed. The interest should begin at its opening words, and should rise steadily to its conclusion. The fundamental principles of construction that underlie such stories as Poe's "Murders in the Rue Morgue," or Conan Doyle's "Sherlock Holmes" series, are precisely those that should guide a scientific writer. These stories show that the public delights in the ingenious unravelling of evidence, and Conan Doyle need never stoop to jesting.

First the problem, then the gradual piecing together of the solution. They cannot get enough of such matter. (301)

2. H. G. Wells. From "Preface to Volume I." *The Works of H. G. Wells. Vol. I. The Time Machine, The Wonderful Visit, and Other Stories.* **[Atlantic Edition.] New York: Charles Scribner's Sons, 1924. xxi–xxiii.**

[In his preface to the Atlantic edition, the world-famous man of letters reconsiders the book that launched his literary reputation almost thirty years earlier, and finds it "a little unsympathetic." The older Wells would be modest, even dismissive, about his achievement in *The Time Machine* and the other great early scientific romances.]

In this first volume are some of the author's earliest imaginative writings. The idea of "The Time Machine" itself, a rather forced development of the idea that time is a direction in space, came when he was still a student at the Royal College of Science. He tried to make a story of it in the students' magazine. If the old numbers of that publication for the years 1889 and 1890, or thereabouts, still exist, the curious may read there that first essay, written obviously under the influence of Hawthorne and smeared with that miscellaneous allusiveness that Carlyle and many other of the great Victorians had made the fashion. "Time Travellers" were not to be written of in those days of the twopence coloured style;[1] the story was called, rather deliciously, "The Chronic Argonauts" and the Time Traveller was "Mr. Nebo-gipfel." Similar pigments prevailed throughout. A cleansing course of Swift and Sterne[2] intervened before the idea was written again for Henley's *National Observer* in 1894, and his later *New Review* in 1895, and published as a book in the spring of the latter year. That version stands here unaltered. There was a slight struggle between the writer and W. E. Henley who wanted, he said, to put a little "writing" into the tale.

---

1   I.e., in an age that valued cheap showiness: the allusion is to the phrase "penny plain, twopence coloured."
2   For Swift see Appendix E1; Laurence Sterne (1713-68), the Irish comic novelist.

But the writer was in reaction from that sort of thing, the Henley interpolations were cut out again, and he had his own way with his text.

And now the writer reads this book, "The Time Machine," and can no more touch it or change it than if it were the work of an entirely different person. He reads it again after a long interval, he does not believe he has opened its pages for twenty years, and finds it hard and "clever" and youthful. And—what is rather odd, he thinks—a little unsympathetic. He is left doubting—rather irrelevantly to the general business of this Preface—whether if the Time Machine were a sufficiently practicable method of transport for such a meeting, the H. G. Wells of 1894 and the H. G. Wells of 1922 would get on very well together. But he has found a copy of the book in which, somewhen about 1898 or 1899, he marked out a few modifications in arrangement and improvements in expression. Almost all these suggested changes he has accepted, so that what the reader gets here is a revised definitive version a quarter of a century old. (xxi-xxii)

3. H. G. Wells. From "Preface." *The Time Machine: An Invention.* With a Preface by the Author Written for This Edition; and Designs by W.A. Dwiggins. New York: Random House, 1931. vii-x.

[A preface, interesting for its post-Einsteinian perspective on the context of the novel's composition, to an illustrated deluxe edition of *The Time Machine*.]

The *Time Machine* was published in 1895. It is obviously the work of an inexperienced writer, but certain originalities in it saved it from extinction and there are still publishers and perhaps even readers to be found for it after the lapse of a third of a century. In its final form, except for certain minor amendments, it was written in a lodging at Sevenoaks in Kent. The writer was then living from hand to mouth as a journalist. There came a lean month when scarcely an article of his was published or paid for in any of the papers to which he was accustomed to contribute and since all the offices in London that would tolerate him were already amply supplied with still unused articles, it seemed hopeless to write more until the block moved. Accordingly, rather than fret at this dismaying change in his outlook, he wrote this story in the chance of finding a market for it in some new quarter. He remembers writing at it late one summer night by an open window, while a disagreeable landlady grumbled at him in the darkness out-side because of the excessive use of her lamp, expanding to a dreaming world her unwillingness to go to bed while that lamp was still alight; he wrote on to that accompaniment; and he remembers, too, discussing it and the underlying notions of it, while he walked in Knole Park with that dear companion who sustained him so stoutly through those adventurous years of short commons and hopeful uncertainty.

The idea of it seemed in those days to be his "one idea." He had saved it up so far in the hope that he would one day make a much longer book of it than the *Time Machine*, but the urgent need for something marketable obliged him to exploit it forth-with. As the discerning reader will perceive, it is a very unequal book: the early discussion is much more carefully planned and written than the later chapters. A slender story springs from a very profound root. The early part, the explanation of the idea had already seen the light in 1893 in Henley's *National Observer*. It was the latter half that was written so urgently at Sevenoaks in 1894.

That one idea is now everybody's idea. It was never the writer's own peculiar idea. Other people were coming to it. It was begotten in the writer's mind by students' discussions in the laboratories and debating society of the Royal College of Science in the eighties and already it had been tried over in various forms by him before he made this particular application of it. It is the idea that Time is a fourth dimension and that the normal present is a three-dimensional section of a four-dimensional universe. The only difference between the time dimension and the others, from this point of view, lay in the movement of consciousness along it, whereby the progress of the present was constituted. Obviously there might be various "presents" according to the direction in which the advancing section was cut, a method of stating the conception of relativity that did not come into scientific use until a considerable time later, and as obviously, since the section called the "present" was real and not "mathematical," it would possess a certain depth that might vary. The "now" therefore is not instantaneous, it is a shorter or longer measure of time, a point that has still to find its proper appreciation in contemporary thought.

But my story does not go on to explore either of these possibilities; I did not in the least know how to go on to such an exploration. I was not sufficiently educated in that field, and certainly a story was not the way to investigate further. So my opening exposition escapes along the line of paradox to an imaginative romance stamped with many characteristics of the Stevenson and early-Kipling period in which it was written. Already the writer had made an earlier experiment in the pseudo-Teutonic, Nathaniel Hawthorne style, an experiment printed in the *Science Schools Journal* (1888-89) and now happily unattainable. All the gold of Mr. Gabriel Wells[1] cannot recover that version. And there was also an account of the idea, set up to be printed for the *Fortnightly Review* in 1891 and never used. It was there called "The Universe Rigid." That too is lost beyond recovery, though a less unorthodox predecessor "*The Rediscovery of the Unique*," insisting upon the individuality of atoms, saw the light in the July issue of that year. Then the editor Mr. Frank Harris woke up to the fact that he was printing matter twenty years too soon, reproached the writer terrifyingly, and broke type again. If any impression survives it must be in the archives of the *Fortnightly Review* but I doubt if any impression survives. For years I thought I had a copy but when I looked for it, it had gone.

The story of the *Time Machine* as distinguished from the idea, "dates" not only in its treatment but in its conception. It seems a very undergraduate performance to its now mature writer, as he looks it over once more. But it goes as far as his philosophy about human evolution went in those days. The idea of a social differentiation of mankind into Eloi and

---

1   A wealthy American rare-book dealer.

Morlocks, strikes him now as more than a little crude. In his adolescence Swift had exercised a tremendous fascination upon him and the naive pessimism of this picture of the human future is, like the kindred *Island of Doctor Moreau*, a clumsy tribute to a master to whom he owes an enormous debt. Moreover, the geologists and astronomers of that time told us dreadful lies about the "inevitable" freezing up of the world—and of life and mankind with it. There was no escape it seemed. The whole game of life would be over in a million years or less.[1] They impressed this upon us with the full weight of their authority, while now Sir James Jeans[2] in his smiling *Universe Around Us* waves us on to millions of millions of years. Given as much law as that man will be able to do anything and go anywhere, and the only trace of pessimism left in the human prospect today is a faint flavour of regret that one was born so soon. And even from that distress modern psychological and biological philosophy offers ways of escape.

One must err to grow and the writer feels no remorse for this youthful effort. Indeed he hugs his vanity very pleasantly at times when his dear old *Time Machine* crops up once more in essays and speeches, still a practical and convenient way to retrospect or prophecy. *The Time Journey of Doctor Barton*,[3] dated 1929, is upon his desk as he writes—with all sorts of things in it we never dreamt of six and thirty years ago. So the *Time Machine* has lasted as long as the diamond-framed safety bicycle, which came in at about the date of its first publication. And now it is going to be printed and published so admirably that its author is assured it will outlive him. He has long since given up the practise of writing prefaces for books, but this is an exceptional occasion and he is very proud and happy to say a word or so of reminiscence and friendly commendation for that needy and cheerful namesake of his, who lived back along the time dimension, six and thirty years ago. (vii–x)

---

1 See Appendices E2-E8.

2 English physicist and astronomer (1877-1946), author of popular works on astronomy in the 1920s and 1930s.

3 Subtitled *An Engineering and Sociological Forecast Based on Present Possibilities*, ed. John Hodgson (1929).

4. H. G. Wells. From "Preface." *Seven Famous Novels.* **New York: Knopf, 1934. [vii]-x.**

[This preface to an omnibus edition of Wells's science-fiction novels is particularly revealing on the question of the genre to which *The Time Machine* and related fiction belong—its tradition, how best to write it, and what to call it.]

Mr. Knopf[1] has asked me to write a preface to this collection of my fantastic stories. They are put in chronological order, but let me say here right at the beginning of the book, that for anyone who does not as yet know anything of my work it will probably be more agreeable to begin with *The Invisible Man* or *The War of the Worlds. The Time Machine* is a little stiff about the fourth dimension and *The Island of Dr. Moreau* rather painful.

These tales have been compared with the work of Jules Verne and there was a disposition on the part of literary journalists at one time to call me the English Jules Verne.[2] As a matter of fact there is no literary resemblance whatever between the anticipatory inventions of the great Frenchman and these fantasies. His work dealt almost always with actual possibilities of invention and discovery, and he made some remarkable forecasts. The interest he invoked was a practical one; he wrote and believed and told that this or that thing could be done, which was not at that time done. He helped his reader to imagine it done and to realise what fun, excitement or mischief would ensue. Many of his inventions have "come true." But these stories of mine collected here do not pretend to deal with possible things; they are exercises of the imagination in a quite different field. They belong to a class of writing which includes *The Golden Ass of Apuleius*, the *True Histories of Lucian, Peter Schlemil* and the story of *Frankenstein*. It includes too some admirable inventions by Mr. David Garnett, *Lady into Fox* for instance.[3]

---

1   The American publisher Alfred A. Knopf.
2   See Appendix B7.
3   The fantastic romances, ancient and modern, mentioned by Wells are: *Metamorphoses, or The Golden Ass* by Lucius Apuleius (fl. A.D. 155); *The True History* by Lucian of Samosata (c. A.D. 115-200); *Peter Schlemihl's Remarkable Story* (1814) by

They are all fantasies; they do not aim to project a serious possibility; they aim indeed only at the same amount of conviction as one gets in a good gripping dream. They have to hold the reader to the end by art and illusion and not by proof and argument, and the moment he closes the cover and reflects he wakes up to their impossibility.

In all this type of story the living interest lies in their non-fantastic elements and not in the invention itself. They are appeals for human sympathy quite as much as any "sympathetic" novel, and the fantastic element, the strange property or the strange world, is used only to throw up and intensify our natural reactions of wonder, fear or perplexity. The invention is nothing in itself and when this kind of thing is attempted by clumsy writers who do not understand this elementary principle nothing could be conceived more silly and extravagant,. Anyone can invent human beings inside out or worlds like dumb-bells or a gravitation that repels. The thing that makes such imaginations interesting is their translation into commonplace terms and a rigid exclusion of other marvels from the story. Then it becomes human. "How would you feel and what might not happen to you," is the typical question, if for instance pigs could fly and one came rocketing over a hedge at you. How would you feel and what might not happen to you if suddenly you were changed into an ass and couldn't tell anyone about it? Or if you became invisible? But no one would think twice about the answer if hedges and houses also began to fly, or if people changed into lions, tigers, cats and dogs left and right, of if everyone could vanish anyhow. Nothing remains interesting where anything may happen.

For the writer of fantastic stories to help the reader to play the game properly, he must help him in every possible unobtrusive way to *domesticate* the impossible hypothesis. He must trick him into an unwary concession to some plausible assumption and get on with his story while the illusion holds. And that is where there was a certain slight novelty in my sto-

---

Adalbert von Chamisso (1781-1838); *Frankenstein, or The Modern Prometheus* (1818) by Mary Shelley (1797-1851); and *Lady Into Fox* (1922) by David Garnett (1892-1981).

ries when first they appeared. Hitherto, except in exploration fantasies, the fantastic element was brought in by magic. Frankenstein even, used some jiggery-pokery magic to animate his artificial monster. There was trouble about the thing's soul. But by the end of last century it had become difficult to squeeze even a momentary belief out of magic any longer. It occurred to me that instead of the usual interview with the devil or a magician, an ingenious use of scientific patter might with advantage be substituted. That was no great discovery. I simply brought the fetish stuff up to date, and made it as near actual theory as possible.

As soon as the magic trick has been done the whole business of the fantasy writer is to keep everything else human and real. Touches of prosaic detail are imperative and a rigorous adherence to the hypothesis. Any *extra* fantasy outside the cardinal assumption immediately gives a touch of irresponsible silliness to the invention. So soon as the hypothesis is launched the whole interest becomes the interest of looking at human feelings and human ways, from the new angle that has been acquired. One can keep the story within the bounds of a few individual experiences as Chamisso does in *Peter Schlemil*, or one can expand it to a broad criticism of human institutions and limitations as in *Gulliver's Travels*. My early, profound and lifelong admiration for Swift, appears again and again in this collection, and it is particularly evident in a predisposition to make the stories reflect upon contemporary political and social discussions. It is an incurable habit with literary critics to lament some lost artistry and innocence in my early work and to accuse me of having become polemical in my later years. That habit is of such old standing that the late Mr. Zangwill in a review in 1895 complained that my first book, *The Time Machine*, concerned itself with "our present discontents."[1] *The Time Machine* is indeed quite as philosophical and polemical and critical of life and so forth, as *Men Like Gods* written twenty-eight years later. No more and no less. I have never been able to get away from life in the mass and life in general as

---

[1] See Appendix H9.

distinguished from life in the individual experience, in any book I have ever written. I differ from contemporary criticism in finding them inseparable.

For some years I produced one or more of these "scientific fantasies," as they were called, every year. In my student days we were much exercised by talk about a possible fourth dimension of space; the fairly obvious idea that events could be presented in a rigid four dimensional space time framework had occurred to me, and this used as the magic trick for a glimpse of the future that ran counter to the placid assumption of that time that Evolution was a pro-human force making things better and better for mankind. *The Island of Dr. Moreau* is an exercise in youthful blasphemy. Now and then, though I rarely admit it, the universe projects itself towards me in a hideous grimace. It grimaced that time, and I did my best to express my vision of the aimless torture in creation. *The War of the Worlds* like *The Time Machine* was another assault on human self-satisfaction.

All these three books are consciously grim, under the influence of Swift's tradition. But I am neither a pessimist nor an optimist at bottom. This is an entirely indifferent world in which wilful wisdom seems to have a perfectly fair chance. It is after all rather cheap to get force of presentation by loading the scales on the sinister side. Horror stories are easier to write than gay and exalting stories. ([vii]–ix)

5. H. G. Wells. From *Experiment in Autobiography: Discoveries and Conclusions of a Very Ordinary Brain (Since 1866)*. 1934. Philadelphia and New York: Lippincott, 1967.

[These passages from Wells's great autobiographical work offer many insights into the context of *The Time Machine*'s composition.]

In the students' Debating Society ... I heard about and laid hold of the idea of a four dimensional frame for a fresh apprehension of physical phenomena, which afterwards led me to send a paper, "The Universe Rigid," to the *Fortnightly Review* (a paper which was rejected by Frank Harris as incomprehensible), and gave me a frame for my first scientific fantasia, the *Time Machine*, and there was moreover a rather elaborate joke going on ... about a certain "Universal Diagram" I proposed to make, from which all phenomena would be derived by a process of deduction. (One began with a uniformly distributed ether in the infinite space of those days and then displaced a particle. If there was a Universe rigid, and hitherto uniform, the character of the consequent world would depend entirely, I argued along strictly materialist lines, upon the velocity of this initial displacement. The disturbance would spread outward with ever increasing complication.) But I discovered no way, and there was no one to show me a way to get on from such elementary struggles with primary concepts, to a sound understanding of contemporary experimental physics. (172)

... I began a romance, very much under the influence of Hawthorne, which was printed in the *Science Schools Journal*, the *Chronic Argonauts*. I broke this off after three instalments because I could not go on with it. That I realized I could not go on with it marks a stage in my education in the art of fiction. It was the original draft of what later became the *Time Machine*, which first won me recognition as an imaginative writer. But the prose was over-elaborate and with that same flavour of the Babu, to which I have called attention in my letter to Dr. Collins.[1] And the story is clumsily invented, and loaded with irrelevant sham significance. The time traveller, for example, is called Nebo-gipfel, though manifestly Mount Nebo had no business whatever in that history. There was no Promised Land ahead. And there is a lot of fuss about the hostility of a superstitious Welsh village to this Dr. Nebo-gipfel which was obviously just lifted into the tale from Hawthorne's *Scarlet Letter*. And think of "Chronic" and "Argonauts" in the title! The ineptitude of this rococo title for a hard mathematical invention! I was over twenty-one and I still had my business to learn. I still jumbled both my prose and my story in an entirely incompetent fashion. If a young man of twenty-one were to

---

1   Babu was a prose style associated with Indian clerks with a poor command of English. For the letter alluded to, see *Experiment in Autobiography* 6:2.

bring me a story like the *Chronic Argonauts* for my advice to-day I do not think I should encourage him to go on writing.

But it was a sign of growing intelligence that I was realizing my exceptional ignorance of the contemporary world and exploring the possibilities of fantasy. That is the proper game for the young man, particularly for young men without a natural social setting of their own. (253-54)

At about the same time that Hind[1] set me writing short stories, I had a request from the mighty William Ernest Henley himself for a contribution to the *National Observer*…. I resolved to do my very best for him and I dug up my peculiar treasure, my old idea of "time-travelling," from the *Science Schools Journal* and sent him in a couple of papers. He liked them and asked me to carry on the idea so as to give glimpses of the world of the future. This I was only too pleased to do, and altogether I developed the notion into seven papers between March and June. This was the second launching of the story that had begun in the *Science Schools Journal* as the *Chronic Argonauts*, but now nearly all the traces of Hawthorne and English Babu classicism had disappeared. I had realized that the more impossible the story I had to tell, the more ordinary must be the setting, and the circumstances in which I now set the Time Traveller were all that I could imagine of solid upper-middle-class comfort.

With these *Time Traveller* papers running, with quite a number of stories for Hind germinating in my head, with a supply of books to review and what seemed a steady market for my occasional, my frequent occasional, articles in the *Gazette*, it seemed no sort of risk to leave London for a lodging at Sevenoaks…. Abruptly the *National Observer* changed hands. This was quite a sudden transaction; the paper had never paid its expenses and its chief supporter decided to sell it to a Mr. Vincent who also took over the editorial control from Henley. Mr. Vincent thought my articles queer wild ramblings and wound them up at once. At the same time the *Pall Mall Gazette* stopped using my articles. (433-35)

---

1   C. Lewis Hind, editor of the *Pall Mall Budget*.

It seemed rather useless to go on writing articles. All the periodicals to which I contributed were holding stuff of mine in proof and it might be indiscreet to pour in fresh matter to such a point that the tanks overflowed and returned it. But I had one thing in the back of my mind. Henley had told me that it was just possible he would presently find backing for a monthly. If so, he thought I might rewrite the *Time Traveller* articles as a serial story. Anyhow that was something to do and I set to work on the *Time Machine* and rewrote it from end to end.

I still remember writing that part of the story in which the *Time Traveller* returns to find his machine removed and his retreat cut off. I sat alone at the round table downstairs writing steadily in the luminous circle cast by a shaded paraffin lamp. Jane had gone to bed and her mother had been ill in bed all day. It was a very warm blue August night and the window was wide open. The best part of my mind fled through the story in a state of concentration before the Morlocks but some outlying regions of my brain were recording other things. Moths were fluttering in ever and again and though I was unconscious of them at the time, one must have flopped near me and left some trace in my marginal consciousness that became a short story I presently wrote, *A Moth, Genus Novo*.[1] And outside in the summer night a voice went on and on, a feminine voice that rose and fell. It was Mrs. — I forget her name — our landlady in open rebellion at last, talking to a sympathetic neighbour in the next garden and talking through the window at me. I was aware of her and heeded her not, and she lacked the courage to beard me in my parlour. "Would I *never* go to bed? How could she lock up with that window staring open? Never had she had such people in her house before, — never....

It went on and on. I wrote on grimly to that accompaniment. I wrote her out and she made her last comment with the front door well and truly slammed. I finished my chapter before I shut the window and turned down and blew out the lamp. And somehow amidst the gathering disturbance of those days the *Time Machine* got itself finished. Jane kept up a valiant front and fended off from me as much as she could of the

---

1 A story first published in the *Pall Mall Gazette* in March, 1895.

trouble that was assailing her on both sides. But a certain gay elasticity disappeared. It was a disagreeable time for her. She went and looked at other apartments and was asked unusual questions.

It was a retreat rather than a return we made to London, with the tart reproaches of the social system echoing in our ears. But before our ultimate flight I had had a letter from Henley telling me it was all right about that monthly of his. He was to start *The New Review* in January and he would pay me £100 for the *Time Machine* as his first serial story. One hundred pounds! And at the same time the mills of the *Pall Mall Gazette* began to go round and consume my work again. (436-37)

I was now in a very hopeful and enterprising mood. Henley had accepted the *Time Machine*, agreed to pay £100 for it, and had recommended it to Heinemann, the publisher. This would bring in at least another £50. I should have a book out in the spring and I should pass from the status of journalist—"occasional journalist" at that, and anonymous—to authorship under my own name. And there was talk of a book of short stories with Methuen. Furthermore John Lane was proposing to make a book out of some of my articles, though for that I was to get only £10 down. The point was that my chance was plainly coming fast. I should get a press—and I felt I might get a good press—for the *Time Machine* anyhow. If I could get another book out before that amount of publicity died away I should be fairly launched as an author and then I might be able to go on writing books. This incessant hunt for "ideas" for anonymous articles might be relaxed and the grind of book-reviewing abated. (446-47)

6. H. G. Wells. From "Fiction About the Future."
H. G. Wells's Literary Criticism. Eds. Patrick Parrinder and Robert M. Philmus. Brighton: Harvester, and Totowa, NJ: Barnes & Noble, 1980. 246-51.

[This extract from a transcript of a broadcast on Australian radio on 29 December, 1938, less than a year before the outbreak of World War II, contains one of the last comments Wells had to make on *The Time Machine*.]

I have been asked to give a talk on the Australian air on some subject connected with literature. It has occurred to me that you might be interested in a few things I have thought and observed about one peculiar sort of book-writing in which I have had some experience. This is *Fiction about the Future*. Almost my first published book was *The Time Machine*, which went millions of years ahead, and since then I have made repeated excursions into the unknown....

I doubt whether one can call anything of this sort literature in the sense that it aims to be something perfect and enduring. Maybe no literature is perfect and enduring, but there is something specially and incurably topical about all these prophetic books; the more you go ahead, the more you seem to get entangled with the burning questions of your own time. And all the while events are overtaking you.... You might even think there was something malicious about the future, as though it didn't like to be prophesied and dodged me about. I thought that anyhow I was pretty safe to take my *Time Machine* some millions of years ahead and show the sun cooled down to a red ball and the earth dried up and frozen. That was what science made of the outlook in 1893. But since then all sorts of mitigating considerations have arisen, and there is no reason, they tell us now, to suppose there will not be humanity, or the descendants of humanity, living in comfort and sunshine on this planet, for millions of years yet—provided always they do not blow it to pieces in some great war-climax. (246-47)

Appendix H: Reviews of The Time Machine

1. From "The New Review." *Review of Reviews* [London] 11 (March 1895): 263.

[This short notice reveals that *The Time Machine* attracted favourable attention as a serial several months before it appeared in book form. The reviewer has been identified as either W. T. Stead (1849-1912), the editor of the English edition of *Review of Reviews*, or his assistant Grant Richards (1872-1948).]

H. G. Wells, who is writing the serial in the *New Review*, is a man of genius. His invention of the Time Machine was good, but his description of the ultimate evolution of society into the aristocrats and the capitalists who live on the surface of the earth in the sunshine, and the toilers who are doomed to live in the bowels of the earth in black darkness, in which they learn to see by the evolution of huge owl-like eyes, is gruesome and horrible to the last point. The story is not yet finished, but he has written enough to show that he has an imagination as gruesome as that of Poe. (263)

2. From "The World Several Millions of Years Hence. A Vision of the Fate of Man." *Review of Reviews* [New York] 11 (June 1895): 701-02.

The powerful imaginative romance which Mr. H. G. Wells has contributed to the *New Review* under the title of "The Time Machine" is brought to a close in the May number. There is no falling off in the thrilling and ghastly interest of the story. The idea is that a man invented a machine by which he could travel backward and forward in time, and the inventor in this story describes what he sees and hears when he projects himself several millions of years into the future, and sees the fate of our planet in its last days. In April the story broke off when mankind had developed backward on two lines — the well-to-do and aristocratic section becoming weak, helpless, amiable and refined creatures, who lived in the light of day on flowers and fruits, while the working-class, relegated to underground caverns, had grown into loathsome vampire fiends, who at nightfall came to the surface of the earth and killed the delicate civilized race that lived in the sunlight, and carried them below to stock their larder. In the new number he projects himself many more millions of years ahead. All trace of civilization has disappeared, and the world is given over, so far as he can see, to degenerate men and monstrous insects. [A summary follows of the final instalment of the *New Review Time Machine*, ending with the Time Traveller's return to his own time.] Such, with the exception of the epilogue, is the end of a very powerful story, which impresses the imagination more than anything of the kind since Richard Jefferies' marvelously powerful tale, "After London."[1] (701-02)

3. "Speculative and Pessimistic." *New York Times* (23 June 1895): 27.

"You see," said the philosophical inventor to his audience, the psychologist, the medical man, the rector, and the Filby, (and Filby was a mere nobody,) "you see, a real body must have length, breadth, thickness, and duration. Then there are four dimensions, three of which we call the three planes of space, and a fourth we call time. Now, granting that much, you will understand how I have invented a machine which will run backward or forward on time. I will show you a working model."

The inventor places on a table something like an alarm clock. He touches a spring, there is a buzz, and the whole thing disappears. The inventor explains how it has slid into space. Then he exhibits his working apparatus. A-straddle of that he launches himself forward into A.D. 802701. What he sees is horrible. There are two races, each degraded. The underground ones devour the upper ones. His escape depends on a

---

1   *After London, or Wild England* (1885) by Richard Jefferies (1848-87) is a notable fantasy about a return to barbarism after a mysterious astronomical catastrophe.

lump of camphor and a box of safety matches. Speculations of all kinds are numerous and ingenious. With the commonplace Filby, who was brain weary at the beginning of the story, we were afraid that that tired feeling would be cumulative when the conclusion of "The Time Machine" was reached. It is a pessimistic business. (27)

4. "In A.D. 802,701." *Spectator* 75 (13 July 1895): 41-43.

[The reviewer has been identified as Richard Holt Hutton (1826-97), the *Spectator*'s literary editor.]

Mr. H. G. Wells has written a very clever story as to the condition of this planet in the year 802,701 A.D., though the two letters A.D. appear to have lost their meaning in that distant date, as indeed they have lost their meaning for not a few even in the comparatively early date at which we all live. The story is based on that rather favourite speculation of modern metaphysicians which supposes *time* to be at once the most important of the conditions of organic evolution, and the most misleading of subjective illusions. It is, we are told, by the efflux of time that all the modifications of species arise on the one hand, and yet Time is so purely subjective a mode of thought, that a man of searching intellect is supposed to be able to devise the means of travelling in time as well as space, and visiting, so as to be contemporary with, any age of the world, past or future, so as to become as it were a true "pilgrim of eternity."[1] This is the dream on which Mr. H. G. Wells has built up his amusing story of "The Time Machine" (of which Mr. William Heinemann is the publisher). A speculative mechanician is supposed to have discovered that the "fourth dimension," concerning which mathematicians have speculated, is Time, and that with a little ingenuity a man may travel in Time as well as in Space. The Time-traveller of this story invents some hocus-pocus of a machine by the help of which all that belongs or is affixed to that machine may pass into the Future by pressing down one

---

1 See P. B. Shelley, "Adonais" (1821), xxx, line 264.

lever, and into the Past by pressing down another. In other words, he can make himself at home with the society of hundreds of thousands of centuries hence, or with the chaos of hundreds of thousands of centuries past, at his pleasure. As a matter of choice, the novelist very judiciously chooses the Future only in which to disport himself. And as we have no means of testing his conceptions of the Future, he is of course at liberty to imagine what he pleases. And he is rather ingenious in his choice of what to imagine. Mr. Wells supposes his Time-traveller to travel forward from A.D. 1895 to A.D. 802,701, and to make acquaintance with the people inhabiting the valley of the Thames (which has, of course, somewhat changed its channel) at that date. He finds a race of pretty and gentle creatures of silken organisations, as it were, and no particular interests or aims, except the love of amusement, inhabiting the surface of the earth, almost all evil passions dead, almost all natural or physical evils overcome, with a serener atmosphere, a brighter sun, lovelier flowers and fruits, no dangerous animals or poisonous vegetables, no angry passions or tumultuous and grasping selfishness, and only one object of fear. While the race of the surface of the earth has improved away all its dangers and embarrassments (including, apparently, every trace of a religion), the race of the underworld, — the race which has originally sprung from the mining population, — has developed a great dread of light, and a power of vision which can work and carry on all its great engineering operations with a minimum of light. At the same time, by inheriting a state of servitude it has also inherited a cruel contempt for its former masters, who can now resist its attacks only by congregating in crowds during the hours of darkness, for in the daylight, or even in the bright moonlight, they are safe from the attacks of their former serfs. This beautiful superior race of faint and delicate beauty is wholly vegetarian. But the inferior world of industrious dwellers in darkness has retained its desire for flesh, and in the absence of all other animal life has returned to cannibalism; and is eager to catch unwary members of the soft surface race in order to feed on their flesh. Moreover, this is the one source of fear which disturbs the gentle pastimes of the otherwise successful subduers of natural evils. Here is Mr. Wells's dream of the two branches into which the race of men, under the laws of evolution, had diverged:— [Quotes passage from Chapter XIII, "I grieved to think how brief the dream" to "and as that I give it to you."] The central idea of this dream is, then, the unnerving effect of a too great success in conquering the natural resistance which the physical constitution of the world presents to our love of ease and pleasure. Let a race which has learned to serve, and to serve efficiently, and has lost its physical equality with its masters by the conditions of its servitude, coexist with a race that has secured all the advantages of superior organisation, and the former will gradually recover, by its energetic habits, at least some of the advantages which it has lost, and will unite with them the cruel and selfish spirit which servitude breeds. This is, we take it, the warning which Mr. Wells intends to give:— "Above all things avoid sinking into a condition of satisfied ease; avoid a soft and languid serenity; even evil passions which involve continuous effort, are not so absolutely deadly as the temperament of languid and harmless playfulness." We have no doubt that, so far as Mr. Wells goes, his warning is wise. But we have little fear that the languid, ease-loving and serene temperament will ever paralyse the human race after the manner he supposes, even though there may be at present some temporary signs of the growth of the appetite for mere amusement.

In the first place, Mr. Wells assumes, what is well-nigh impossible, that the growth of the pleasure-loving temperament would not itself prevent that victory over physical obstacles to enjoyment on which he founds his dream. The pleasure-loving temperament soon becomes both selfish and fretful. And selfishness no less than fretfulness poisons all enjoyment. Before our race had reached anything like the languid grace and frivolity of the Eloi (the surface population), it would have fallen a prey to the many competing and conflicting energies of Nature which are always on the watch to crush out weak and languid organisations, to say nothing of the uncanny Morlocks (the envious subterranean population), who would soon have invented spectacles shutting out from their sensitive eyes the glare of either moon or sun. If the doctrines as to evolution have any truth in them at all, nothing is more certain than that the superiority of man to Nature will never endure beyond the endurance of his fighting strength. The physical condition of the Eloi is supposed, for instance, so to have accommodated itself to external circumstances as to extinguish that continual growth of population which renders the mere competition for food so serious a factor in the history of the globe. But even supposing such a change to have taken place, of which we see no trace at all in history or civilisation, what is there in the nature of frivolity and love of ease, to diminish, and not rather to increase, that craving to accumulate sources of enjoyment at the expense of others, which seems to be most visible in the nations whose populations are of the slowest growth, and which so reintroduces rivalries and war. Let any race find the pressure of population on its energies diminishing, and the mutual jealousy amongst those who are thus placed in a position of advantage for securing wealth and ease, will advance with giant strides. The hardest-pressed populations are not the most, but on the whole the least, selfish.

In the next place Mr. Wells's fancy ignores the conspicuous fact that man's nature needs a great deal of hard work to keep it in order at all, and that no class of men or women are so dissatisfied with their own internal condition as those who are least disciplined by the necessity for industry. Find the idlest class of a nation and you certainly find the most miserable class. There would be no tranquillity or serenity at all in any population for which there were not hard tasks and great duties. The Eloi of this fanciful story would have become even more eager for the satisfaction of selfish desires than the Morlocks themselves. The nature of man must have altered not merely accidentally, but essentially, if the devotion to ease and amusement had left it sweet and serene. Matthew Arnold wrote in his unreal mood of agnosticism:—

> "We, in some unknown Power's employ,
> Move on a rigorous line;

Can neither, when we will, enjoy,
Nor when we will, resign."[1]

But it is not in some "unknown Power's employ" that we move
on this "rigorous line." On the contrary, it is in the employ of a
Power which has revealed itself in the Incarnation and the
Cross. And we may expect with the utmost confidence that if
the earth is still in existence in the year 802,701 A.D., either the
A.D. will mean a great deal more than it means now, or else its
inhabitants will be neither Eloi nor Morlocks. For in that case
evil passions will by that time have led to the extinction of
races spurred and pricked on by conscience and yet so frivolous
or so malignant. Yet Mr. Wells's fanciful and lively dream is
well worth reading, if only because it will draw attention to the
great moral and religious factors in human nature which he
appears to ignore. (41-43)

5. "Fiction. *The Time Machine.*" *Literary World* [Boston] 26 (13 July 1895): 217.

This is the latest edition to the handy Buckram series. The
author, Mr. H. S. Wells,[2] calls it "an invention," and an uncom-
monly ingenious and interesting invention it is. The "Philosophical Inventor," believing in the "Fourth Dimension," makes
a machine that shall travel through time in any direction that
the driver determines. Upon it he explores time; and on a certain day when he has appointed a dinner party for a few friends
he appears among them in an amazing plight, dusty, pale, haggard, ghastly, and bewildered. Later, his guests listen to his narrative of a journey through time on into the future for thousands of years. What was the result as he found it to civilization
and humanity one cannot conjecture without following his
absorbing story. In the year 802,701 the human race had
become like the figures on Dresden ware, in consequence of
the new conditions, where there was no longer need for physi-

---

1 Matthew Arnold, "Stanzas in Memory of the Author of 'Obermann'" (1849), lines 77-80.
2 The first printing of the Holt U.S. edition misspelled the author's initials.

cal courage, but all was comfort and security. — Henry Holt &
Co. 75c. (217)

6. "*The Time Machine*. By H. G. Wells. (London: Wm. Heinemann, 1895.)" *Nature* 52 (18 July 1895): 268.

Ingeniously arguing that time may be regarded as the fourth
dimension of which our faculties fail to give us any distinct
impression, the author of this admirably-told story has conceived the idea of a machine which shall convey the traveller
either backwards or forwards in time. Apart from its merits as a
clever piece of imagination, the story is well worth the attention of the scientific reader, for the reason that it is based so far
as possible on scientific data, and while not taking it too seriously, it helps one to get a connected idea of the possible results
of the ever-continuing processes of evolution. Cosmical evolution, it may be remarked, is in some degree subject to mathematical investigations, and the author appears to be well
acquainted with the results which have been obtained in this
direction. It is naturally in the domain of social and organic
evolution that the imagination finds its greatest scope.

Mounted on a "time-machine" the "time-traveller" does not
come to a halt until the year eight hundred and two thousand,
and we are then favoured with his personal observations in that
distant period. In that "golden age," the constellations had put
on new forms, and the sun's heat was greater, perhaps in consequence of the fall of a planet into the sun, in accordance with
the theory of tidal evolution. "Horses, cattle, sheep, and dogs
had followed the ichthyosaurus into extinction"; but, most
remarkable of all, "man had not remained one species, but had
differentiated into two distinct animals," an upper-world people
of "feeble prettiness," and a most repulsive subterranean race
reduced to mere mechanical industry. It is with the time-traveller's adventures among these people, and their relations to
each other, that the chief interest of the story, as such, belongs.

Continuing his journey to an age millions of years hence,
nearly all traces of life had vanished, the sun glowed only with a
dull red heat, tidal evolution had brought the earth to present a

constant face to the sun, and the sun itself covered a tenth part of the heavens. These and other phenomena are very graphically described, and from first to last the narrative never lapses into dulness. (268)

7. From "Fiction." [Combined review of] *Select Conversations with an Uncle.* **By H. G. Wells. London: John Lane, 1895.** *The Time Machine.* **By H. G. Wells. London: William Heinemann, 1895.** *Saturday Review* **80 (20 July 1895): 86–87.**

... in "The Time Machine" Mr. Wells obliges us to take him very seriously. It is a story which may not attain a popularity — one can prophesy nothing in these days of shoddy successes — but it is certainly a story of remarkable ability. Mr. Wells has been brave enough to essay a species of literature in which many others have failed, and his effort is a conspicuous success. Lord Lytton's "Coming Race" was a poor sort of invention, and nothing very much can be said in favour of "Erewhon."[1] "The Time Machine" is not in their category. To be sure, the basis of the story is scientific — an ingenious notion at that. We do not profess to follow the Time Traveller's reasoning, any more than his friend the editor did, but he very nearly convinces us that Time is only a fourth dimension of space, and that, with a little cunning, we can move about in it freely. The Time Traveller constructs a machine for the purpose, and hence flows the tale. As a mere narrative it is excellently told, and the plot is distressingly interesting. But higher qualities mark the book.... [Quotes passage from Chapter IV, "I pressed the lever over" to "the moon a fainter fluctuating band."] Could anything be more finely imagined or more admirably expressed? Indeed, the imagination in Mr. Wells's book is as amazing as the invention. The drama of the world's tragedy unfolds itself before the Time Traveller. We conceive that man should grow from more to more and civilize the world. That is the stock theory of our latter-day optimism. If Mr. Wells's heresy be false, it is still

---

1 The allusions are to the utopian fantasies *The Coming Race* (1871) by Edward Bulwer Lytton (1803–73) and *Erewhon; or, Over the Range* (1872) by Samuel Butler (1835–1902).

finely conjectured; and we are not so sure about its being false. He supposes that the division of society into two distinct classes, the workers and the leisured, may end in so rigid a system of caste that far away down the ages the two orders have become distinct and separate. Evolution has worked its will upon both, and the one lives underground, a horrible kind of vermin, while the other, its victim, in the irony of rolling centuries, has developed into a pretty feeble creature that dabbles with flowers and gambols all the day. We will not unfold the awful experiences of the Traveller among these beings, his own descendants, so to speak, in the year 802,000. We will confine ourselves to one more quotation from which our readers may estimate Mr. Wells's powers of description.... [Quotes passage from Chapter XIV, "The crawling multitude of crabs" to "I felt I was fainting."] The picture of this horrible desolation in the twilight of the world is magnificent, and barely represented by these detached fragments. We have quoted the extracts at some length as the only means of calling attention to a book of remarkable power and imagination, and to a writer of distinct and individual talent. (87)

8. "A Pilgrim Through Time." *Daily Chronicle* [London] (27 July 1895): 3.

No two books could well be more unlike than "The Time Machine" and "The Strange Case of Dr. Jekyll and Mr. Hyde," but since the appearance of Stevenson's creepy romance[1] we have had nothing in the domain of pure fantasy so bizarre as this "invention" by Mr. H. G. Wells. For his central idea Mr. Wells may be indebted to some previously published narrative suggestion, but if so we must confess ourselves entirely unacquainted with it, and so far as our knowledge goes he has produced in fiction that rarity which Solomon declared to be not merely rare but non-existent—a "new thing under the sun."[2]

The narrative opens in the dining-room of the man who is known to us throughout simply as the Time Traveller, and who

---

1   *The Strange Case of Dr Jekyll and Mr Hyde* (1886) by R. L. Stevenson (1850–94).
2   See Ecclesiastes 1:8.

is expounding to his guests a somewhat remarkable theory in esoteric mathematics. He says:——

[Quotes passage from Chapter I, "'You know, of course, that a mathematical line'" to "'from the beginning to the end of our lives.'"]

By this Poe-like ingenuity of whimsical reasoning the Time Traveller leads up to his great invention—nothing less than a machine which shall convey him through time, that fourth dimension of space, with even greater facility than men are conveyed through the other three dimensions by bicycle or balloon. He can go back either to the days of his grandsires or to the days of creation; he can go forward to the days of his grandsons, or still further, to that last *fin de siècle*, when earth is moribund and man has ceased to be. The one journey of which we have a record is a voyage into far futurity, and when after a wild flight through the centuries the Time Traveller stops the machine the dial register tells him that he is in or about the year 802,000 A.D. Man is still existent, but a remarkable change has passed upon him. The fissure of cleavage between the classes and the masses instead of being bridged over or filled up has become a great gulf. In centuries of centuries the environment of the more favoured has become so exquisitely adapted to all their needs, and indeed to all their desires, that the necessity for physical or mental activity is so many generations behind them that it does not survive even as a memory; the powers of body and mind which are distinctively manly have perished in ages of disuse, and they have become frail, listless, pleasure-loving children. The workers, on the other hand, have become brutalised, bleached, ape-like creatures, who live underground and toil for their effeminate lords, taking their pay, when they can, by living upon them literally in a horrible cannibalistic fashion. The adventures of the Time Traveller among the Eloi and the Marlocks [*sic*] are conceived in the true spirit of fantasy—the effect of remoteness being achieved much more successfully than in such a book, for example, as Lord Lytton's "The Coming Race." Still more weird are the further wanderings in a future when man has gone, and even nature is not what it was, because sun, moon, stars, and earth are tottering to their doom. The description of the sea-coast of the dying ocean, still embracing a dying world, and of the huge, hideous, creeping things which are the last remains of life on a worn-out planet has real impressiveness — it grips the imagination as it is only gripped by genuinely imaginative work. It is in what may be described literally as the "machinery" of the story that Mr. Wells's imagination plays least freely and convincingly. He constantly forgets — or seems to forget — that his Traveller is journeying simply through *time*, and records effects which inevitably suggest travel through *space*. Why, for example, should the model of the machine vanish from sight when in the second chapter it is set in motion? Why, in the last chapter, should the machine itself disappear when the Traveller has set out on his final journey; why on his progress through the centuries should it jar and sway as if it were moving though the air; why should he write of "slipping like a vapour through the interstices of intervening substance," or anticipate sudden contact with some physical obstacle? To these questions Mr. Wells will probably reply that it is unfair to blame an artist for not surmounting difficulties which are practically insurmountable; but the obvious rejoinder is that it is unwise to choose a scheme from which such difficulties are inseparable. Still, when all deductions are made "The Time Machine" remains a strikingly original performance. (3)

9. Israel Zangwill. From "Without Prejudice." *Pall Mall Magazine* 7 (September 1895): 151-60.

[Zangwill (1864-1926), only a couple of years older than Wells, had come to prominence in 1892 with his novel *Children of the Ghetto*, about the experience of Jewish immigrants in the East End of London.]

Countless are the romances that deal with other times, other manners; endless have been the attempts to picture the time to come. Sometimes the future is grey with evolutionary perspectives, with previsions of a post-historic man, bald, toothless and fallen into his second infancy; sometimes it is gay with ingenuous fore-glimpses of a renewed golden age of socialism and sentimentality. In his brilliant little romance *The Time Machine* Mr. Wells has inclined to the severer and more scientific form of prophecy—to the notion of a humanity degenerating inevitably from sheer pressure of physical comfort; but this not very novel conception, which was the theme of Mr. Besant's *Inner House*, and even partly of Pearson's *National Life and Character*,[1] Mr. Wells has enriched by the invention of the Morlocks, a differentiated type of humanity which lives underground and preys upon the softer, prettier species that lives luxuriously in the sun, a fine imaginative creation worthy of Swift, and possibly not devoid of satirical reference to "the present discontents." There is a good deal of what Tyndall[2] would have called "scientific imagination" in Mr. Wells' further vision of the latter end of all things, a vision far more sombre and impressive than the ancient imaginings of the Biblical seers. The only criticism I have to offer is that his Time Traveller, a cool scientific thinker, behaves exactly like the hero of a commonplace sensational novel, with his frenzies of despair and his appeals to fate, when he finds himself in danger of having to remain in the year eight hundred and two thousand seven hundred and one, into which he has recklessly travelled; nor does it ever occur to him that in the aforesaid year he will have to repeat these painful experiences of his, else his vision of the future will have falsified itself—though how the long dispersed dust is to be vivified again does not appear. Moreover, had he travelled backwards, he would have reproduced a Past which, in so far as his own appearance in it with his newly invented machine was concerned, would have been *ex hypothesi*[3] unveracious. Had he recurred to his own earlier life, he would have had to exist in two forms simultaneously, of varying ages—a

---

1 The allusions are to the dystopian romance *The Inner House* (1888) by Walter Besant (1836-1901) and to *National Life and Character: A Forecast* (1894) by Charles Henry Pearson (1830-94).

2 John Tyndall (1820-93), the distinguished physicist.

3 According to the supposition upon which the argument is based.

feat which even Sir Boyle Roche[1] would have found difficult. These absurdities illustrate the absurdity of any attempt to grapple with the notion of Time; and, despite some ingenious metaphysics, worthy of the inventor of the Eleatic paradoxes,[2] Mr. Wells' *Time Machine*, which traverses time (viewed as the Fourth Dimension of Space) backwards or forwards, much as the magic carpet of *The Arabian Nights* traversed space, remains an amusing fantasy. That Time is an illusion is one of the earliest lessons of metaphysics; but, even if we could realise Time as self-complete and immovable, a vast *continuum* holding all that has happened and all that will happen, an eternal Present, even so to introduce a man travelling through this sleeping ocean is to re-introduce the notion of Time which has just been expelled. There is really more difficulty in understanding the Present than the Past or the Future into which it is always slipping; and those old Oriental languages which omitted the Present altogether displayed the keen metaphysical instinct of the East. And yet there is a sense in which the continued and continuous existence of all past time, at least, can be grasped by the human intellect without the intervention of metaphysics. The star whose light reaches us to-night may have perished and become extinct a thousand years ago, the rays of light from it having so many millions of miles to travel that they have only just impinged upon our planet. Could we perceive clearly the incidents on its surface, we should be beholding the Past in the Present, and we could travel to any given year by travelling actually through space to the point at which the rays of that year would first strike upon our consciousness. In like manner the whole Past of the earth is still playing itself out — to an eye conceived as stationed to-day in space, and moving now forwards to catch the Middle Ages, now backwards to watch Nero fiddling over the burning of Rome…. In verity, there is no Time Traveller, Mr. Wells, save Old Father Time himself. Instead of being a Fourth Dimension of Space, Time is perpet-

---

1 Irish politician (1743-1807) known for his unintentionally comic sayings, e.g., "it is impossible I could have been in two places at once, unless I were a bird."
2 I.e., Zeno of Elea (fl. c. 460 B.C.), inventor of such famous paradoxes as "Achilles and the Tortoise."

ually travelling through Space, repeating itself in vibrations farther and farther from the original point of incidence; a vocal panorama moving through the universe across the infinities, a succession of sounds and visions that, having once been, can never pass away, but only on and on from point to point, permanently enregistered in the sum of things, preserved from annihilation by the endlessness of Space, and ever visible and audible to eye or ear that should travel in a parallel movement. It is true the scientists allege that only light can thus travel through the infinities, sound-waves being confined to a material medium and being quickly dissipated into heat. But light alone is sufficient to sustain my fantasy, and in any case the sounds would be æons behind the sights. Terrible, solemn thought that the Past can never die, and that for each of us Heaven or Hell may consist in our being placed at the point of vantage in Space where we may witness the spectacle of our past lives, and find bliss or bale in the panorama. How much ghastlier than the pains of the pit, for the wicked to be perpetually "moved on" by some Satanic policeman to the mathematical point at which their autobiography becomes visible, a point that moves backwards in the infinite universe each time the green curtain of the grave falls over the final episode, so that the sordid show may commence all over again, and so *ad infinitum*. Pascal[1] defined Space as a sphere whose centre is everywhere and whose circumference is nowhere. This brilliant figure helps us to conceive God as always at the centre of vision, receiving all vibrations simultaneously, and thus beholding all Past time simultaneously with the Present. We can also conceive of Future incidents being visible to a spectator, who should be moved forward to receive the impressions of them æons earlier than they would otherwise have reached him. But these "futures" would only be relative; in reality they would already have happened, and the absolute Future, the universe of things that have *not* happened, would still elude our vision, though we can very faintly imagine the Future, interwoven inevitably with the Past, visible to an omniscient Being some-

---

1 Blaise Pascal (1623-62), the French mathematician and philosopher.

what as the evolution of a story is to the man of genius upon whom past and future flash in one conception. Mr. Wells might have been plausibly scientific in engineering his Time Machine through Space and stopping at the points where particular periods of the world's past history became visible: he would then have avoided the fallacy of mingling personally in the panorama. But this would not have suited his design of "dealing in futures." For there is no getting into the Future, except by waiting. You can only sit down and see it come by, as the drunken man thought he might wait for his house to come round in the circulation of the earth; and if you lived for an eternity, the show would only be "just about to begin." (153-55)

10. From "The New Books. 1. Notes from Our London Correspondent." *Review of Reviews* [New York] 12 (October 1895): 496–98.

"The Time Machine" deserves its place [as the best-selling new book of September 1895]. It is an "invention" in every sense of the word: its motive is thoroughly original and its treatment shows imagination of no common order. Mr. Wells' rise into popularity has been by leaps and bounds. It is not many months since the *Pall Mall Budget* published his first short stories (stories of so fresh and absorbing a character that I am glad to see that Messrs. Methuen announce their collection in book form), and now "The Time Machine" is the talk of the town.... (496)

Appendix I: Contemporary Portraits of Wells

1. "New Writers: Mr. H. G. Wells." *Bookman* 8 (August 1895): 134–35.

[This anonymous biographical sketch of Wells, presumably the result of an interview, offers a vivid picture of a new writer—and a new kind of writer—who has just shot to public attention.]

Mr. H. G. Wells is a comparatively new addition to the ranks of those who live by imaginative writing. Until two years ago he had published nothing except a few contributions to the educational papers, one short article in the *Fortnightly Review*, some scientific essays, and a concise cram-book in Biology for the London University science examinations. At that time he had abandoned any literary ambitions he may have entertained, and was almost wholly engaged in educational work, and, but for the accident of a violent hæmorrhage from the lungs, might still be so engaged. But his lung collapse rendered a more sedentary employment imperative, and he turned to journalism. What he regarded as an overwhelming misfortune proved in the end to be a really very good thing for him. Mr. J. M. Barrie was—all unconsciously—his mentor, for it was by following the suggestions contained in "When a Man's Single"[1] that Mr. Wells secured a footing as a writer of "middle articles," contributing first to the *Globe*, and then chiefly to the *Pall Mall Gazette* and the *St. James's Gazette*. His work attracted the marked attention of Mr. H. B. Marriott Watson, of the *Pall Mall Gazette*, and through him he came under the influence of that vigorous stimulant of seedling authors, Mr. W. E. Henley, to whom the "Time Machine" is dedicated, and to whose buoyant good opinion its completion is largely due. Prior to the writing of the "Time Machine," Mr. Wells had tried his hand at short sensational stories involving scientific ideas, at the invitation of

---

1 *When a Man's Single: A Tale of Literary Life* (1892) by J.M. Barrie (1860–1937).

Mr. Lewis Hind, the editor of the now departed *Pall Mall Budget*. Mr. Wells is still a frequent contributor to the *Pall Mall Gazette*, and was until about two months ago upon the regular staff of that paper; in addition he is now upon the staff of the *Saturday Review*, and upon the reviewing staff of *Nature*. But the friendly reception accorded to the "Time Machine" has not been lost upon him, and already two other imaginative works by him are approaching completion. One of these, which is to be called "The Island of Doctor Moreau," deals grotesquely with some of the possibilities of vivisection, and will present certain novel and exceedingly unpleasant monsters to the reader's imagination. In the other,[1] the "horrible" element will be discarded for humorous satire, and the vicar, doctor, and other typical characters in a little South-country village will be excited by a wonderful visitor from an unknown world.... Both of these works, as well as "The Stolen Bacillus," a bookful of short stories originally contributed to the *Pall Mall Budget* (which Messrs. Methuen and Co. are to publish) will probably appear before the end of the year. Mr. Wells is twenty-eight years of age. His uncertain health forces him to avoid social occasions, and to live in retirement out of London. He was born at Bromley, in Kent, and educated partly in a private school there, and partly at the Midhurst Grammar School. He studied science (chiefly Zoology and Geology) at the Royal College of Science, and took the degree of B.Sc. in the University of London, with honours in both those subjects. He organised and for several years conducted the biological teaching for the London science and medical degrees in the University Tutorial College, a successful private coaching establishment in Red Lion Square. (134–35)

2. "Picaroon." From "Mr. H. G. Wells." *Chap-Book* [Chicago] 5.8 (1896): 366–74.

[A biographical sketch, revealing as a highly sympathetic American view of Wells at the start of his literary career.]

---

1   I.e., *The Wonderful Visit*.

When I say that Mr. Wells is the most notable of the younger English writers, and more notable than a good many of the older ones, I am ready to make good my words. There is no man in whom I have greater literary faith; no man from whom better work may be expected. To him more than to anyone else do I look for the cleansing of the English novel, for the effective damming of that stream of crude philosophy and cheap sentiment which has deluged English literature and drama for the last five years. It seems to me that Mr. Wells has it in him to write a really great novel; and I would not willingly risk my critical reputation by saying as much for any other writer. (366)

Mr. Wells is only twenty-eight years old, short, well-built, a finely developed head with a striking forehead, bluish eyes that show traces of hard work, and a straggling moustache. He has had a remarkable career. His father was a tradesman in a small and unprofitable way of business. Mr. Wells, I believe, was apprenticed to the business himself in his early years. He told me once that he had received no education up to the time he was eighteen. Then he educated himself; he studied in his off hours and took a science scholarship at South Kensington. He became a coach and interested himself generally in education. He was for a time the editor of the *Educational Times*, and still keeps a stern and watchful eye on the authorities at the London University. The incessant strain of these two professions broke down his health, never too robust; and after a severe illness he took to literature. There may not be much in all this to astonish an American. You have to know England well, you have to have felt its class restrictions and the iron hand of custom yourself to quite appreciate the pluck and endurance of a man—especially a man of the lower middle class—who educates himself out of the groove he was born in. I admire any man who performs the feat; and if he takes to writing books, I buy them at once and with confidence. Mr. Wells began his literary life by writing articles on chance subjects—fanciful, descriptive, humorous, according to the mood of the moment. The *Pall Mall Gazette*, under the brilliant editorship of Mr. Cust, was by far the most striking paper in London. Mr. Cust accepted the first article Mr. Wells sent in and refused no others. They soon became—at any rate to me—the most welcome feature in the paper. (367-68)

While these articles were running through the *Pall Mall Gazette*, Mr. Wells was contributing a series of short tales to the *Pall Mall Budget*, afterwards republished by Methuen & Co. under the title of *The Stolen Bacillus*. They have, most of them, a semi-scientific foundation. Two of them, *Æpyornis Island* and *The Lord of the Dynamo*, are among the very best short stories written in recent years…. We should have to go to the land of Guy de Maupassant[1] to find an adequate comparison.

Mr. Wells' first great bid for fame was made a little over a year ago when Messrs. Heinemann published *The Time Machine*, which attracted a good deal of notice, as it appeared serially in the *New Review*. The book was a decided success, something like 12,000 copies being rapidly sold. People began to wake up to the fact that Mr. Wells was a new force in English literature. The book surprised even those of us who had closely followed Mr. Wells' work. That it would show extraordinary cleverness and be admirably written we all knew. But we did not expect to find in it an imagination of the very first order, evenly sustained, never out of control, and shot through with gleams of a poetic fancy. The story is briefly this: A mathematician, conceiving time as a fourth dimension of space, invented a machine that will travel into the future. He arrived at the year 802,701 A.D. In the sunset of mankind he finds two distinct races—the Eloi, beautiful little beings, childlike, innocent, happy, idle, living still on the surface of the earth; and the Morlocks, the underground toilers, savage, brutal, hideous, working that the Eloi may do nothing. Their wages are the flesh of their masters. Once every month, before the birth of the new moon, they come up to earth and attack the Eloi. Such as they capture they drag down to their subterranean caves and eat. The adventures of the Time Traveller among these people—the theft of his machine by the Morlocks, his visit to their haunts in search of it, and his fight with them in

---

1   The great French short-story writer (1850-93).

the burning forest—are full of breathless interest and incomparably told. And further on, when he has left the era of the Eloi and their slayers millions of years behind, there is a wonderful picture of the slow decay of the world in the twilight and night of time. It is free from any blemish of rhetoric; but it has all the eloquence and force which are born of the union of deep thought and imagination with simple expression and luminous diction. The book is not a polemic, nor is Mr. Wells a propagandist. He is simply a writer who happens also to be a student of science. But running through the man and his books is a vein of scientific socialism. It gives to *The Time Machine* an added worth and dignity. The book is brilliant merely as a story; but Mr. Wells has sown his pages—as does every really great writer, no matter what his subject may be—with those significant images and far-reaching suggestions which suddenly light up a whole range of distant thoughts and sympathies within us; which, in an instant, affect the sensibilities of men with a something new and unforeseen; which take them out of themselves and awaken the faculty and response of intellect and speculation. (369-71)

In himself, Mr. Wells is very much like his books—flashing in and out of many moods, and all of them delightful. In casual conversation you note the oddly humorous twist of his ideas, the faculty of standing apart from the ordinary line of observation and looking at everything, at himself even, from a new point of view. That, I take it, is what he aims at in literature— to establish a new proportion, to show the world under a new aspect. The peculiar union in him of the scientific and literary temperaments gives him a rare advantage. He has what very few writers have, a stock of knowledge—hard, dry knowledge—to draw from. His ambition is to become the novelist of the lower middle class in England, to be a George Gissing[1] with humour. He has every qualification for the task. He knows the ropes, he is intensely democratic in sentiment, and he has an eye for externals as quick as Dickens. He is a man to keep your eye on. (373-74)

---

1   The English novelist (1857-1903), later a friend of Wells.

Selected Bibliography

[This bibliography offers suggestions for further reading to those interested in H.G. Wells, *The Time Machine*, and time travel. It does not attempt to be inclusive.]

Wells Bibliographies

Hammond, J.R. *Herbert George Wells: An Annotated Bibliography of His Works*. New York and London: Garland, 1977.

H.G. Wells Society. *H.G. Wells: A Comprehensive Bibliography*. 4th ed. (revised). London: H.G. Wells Society, 1986.

Hughes, David Y. "Criticism in English of H.G. Wells's Science Fiction: A Select Annotated Bibliography." *Science Fiction Studies* 6.3 (November 1979): 309-19.

Scheick, William J. and J. Randolph Cox. *H.G. Wells: A Reference Guide*. Boston: G.K. Hall, 1988.

Wells Autobiography and Biography

Foot, Michael. *H.G.: The History of Mr. Wells*. London: Doubleday, 1995.

Hammond, J.R. *H.G. Wells and Rebecca West*. New York: St Martin's P, 1991.

———, ed. *H.G. Wells: Interviews and Recollections*. London and Basingstoke: Macmillan, 1980.

Mackenzie, Norman and Jeanne. *H.G. Wells: A Biography*. New York: Simon and Schuster, 1973.

Smith, David C. *H.G. Wells: Desperately Mortal: A Biography*. New Haven and London: Yale UP, 1986.

Wells, G.P., ed. *H.G. Wells in Love: Postscript to* An Experiment in Autobiography. Boston and Toronto: Little, Brown, 1984.

Wells, H.G. *Experiment in Autobiography: Discoveries and Conclusions of a Very Ordinary Brain (Since 1866)*. 1934. Philadelphia and New York: J.B. Lippincott, 1967.

West, Anthony. "H.G. Wells." In Anthony West, ed. *Principles and Persuasions*. New York: Harcourt, 1957. Reprinted in *H.G. Wells: A Collection of Critical Essays*. [Twentieth-Century Views] Ed. Bernard Bergonzi. Englewood Cliffs, NJ: Prentice-Hall, 1976. 8-24.

West, Geoffrey [Geoffrey H. Wells.]. *H.G. Wells*. Intro. H.G. Wells. New York: Norton, 1930.

Wells Correspondence

Crossley, Robert, ed. "The Correspondence of Olaf Stapledon and H.G. Wells, 1931-42." *Science Fiction Dialogues*. Ed. Gary Wolfe. Chicago: Academy Chicago, 1982. 27-57.

Edel, Leon and Gordon N. Ray, eds. *Henry James and H.G. Wells: A Record of Their Friendship, Their Debate on the Art of Fiction, and Their Quarrel*. London: Hart-Davis, 1959.

Gettmann, Royal A., ed. *George Gissing and H.G. Wells: Their Friendship and Correspondence*. Urbana: U of Illinois P, 1961.

Ray, Gordon N. *H.G. Wells and Rebecca West*. London: Macmillan, 1974.

Smith, David C., ed. *The Correspondence of H.G. Wells*. 4 vols. London: Pickering & Chatto, 1998.

Smith, J. Percy, ed. *Bernard Shaw and H.G. Wells*. [Selected Correspondence of Bernard Shaw.] Toronto, Buffalo and London: U of Toronto P, 1995.

Wilson, Harris, ed. *Arnold Bennett and H.G. Wells: A Record of a Personal and Literary Friendship*. London: Hart-Davis, 1960.

Annotated Editions of *The Time Machine*

Geduld, Harry M, ed. *The Definitive Time Machine: A Critical Edition of H.G. Wells's Scientific Romance*. Bloomington and Indianapolis: Indiana UP, 1987.

McConnell, Frank D., ed. *The Time Machine. The War of the Worlds. A Critical Edition*. New York: Oxford UP, 1977.

Parrinder, Patrick, ed. and intro. *The Time Machine* and *The Island of Doctor Moreau*. By H.G. Wells. [The World's Classics.] New York: Oxford UP, 1996.

Stover, Leon, ed. *The Time Machine: An Invention: A Critical Text of the 1895 London First Edition, with an Introduction and Appendices*. Jefferson, NC and London: McFarland, 1996.

Criticism I: On Wells's Fiction in General

Aldiss, Brian W., with David Wingrove. "The Great General in Dreamland: H.G. Wells." *Trillion Year Spree: The History of Science Fiction*. London: Gollancz, 1986. 117-33.

Batchelor, John. *H.G. Wells*. [Introductory Critical Studies]. Cambridge: Cambridge UP, 1985.

Bellamy, William. *The Novels of Wells, Bennett and Galsworthy 1890-1910*. London: Routledge & Kegan Paul, 1971.

Beresford, J.D. *H.G. Wells*. London: Nisbet, 1915.

Bergonzi, Bernard. *The Early H.G. Wells: A Study of the Scientific Romances*. Manchester: Manchester UP, 1961.

Borges, Jorge Luis. "The First Wells." *Other Inquisitions, 1937-1952*. Trans. Ruth L.C. Simms. Intro. James E. Irby. Austin and London: U of Texas P, 1975. Trans. of *Otras inquisiciones*. 1952. 86-88.

Caldwell, Larry W. "Time at the End of Its Tether: H.G. Wells and the Subversion of Master Narrative." *Cahiers Victoriens et Edouardiens de l'Université Paul Valéry, Montpellier* 46 (October 1997): 127-43.

Carey, John. *The Intellectuals and the Masses: Pride and Prejudice Among the Literary Intelligentsia, 1880-1939*. London: Faber, 1992. 118-51.

Caudwell, Christopher. "H.G. Wells: A Study in Utopianism." *Studies in a Dying Culture*. London: John Lane The Bodley Head, 1938. 73-95.

Costa, Richard Hauer. *H.G. Wells*. [TEAS 43.] 1967. 2nd. ed. New York: Twayne, 1985.

Crossley, Robert. *H.G. Wells*. [Starmont Reader's Guide 19.] Mercer Island, WA: Starmont House, 1986.

Draper, Michael. *H.G. Wells*. [Macmillan Modern Novelists]. Basingstoke and London: Macmillan, 1987.

Hammond, J.R. *An H.G. Wells Companion: A Guide to the Novels, Romances and Short Stories*. London and Basingstoke: Macmillan, 1979.

Haynes, Roslynn D. *H.G. Wells: Discoverer of the Future: The Influence of Science on His Thought*. New York and London: New York UP, 1980.

Hillegas, Mark R. "Cosmic Pessimism in H.G. Wells's Scientific Romances." *Papers of the Michigan Academy of Science, Arts, and Letters* 46 (1961): 655-63.

———. *The Future as Nightmare: H.G. Wells and the Anti-Utopians*. New York: Oxford UP, 1967.

Hughes, David Y. "Bergonzi and After in the Criticism of Wells's SF." *Science Fiction Studies* 3 (1976): 165-74.

———. "The Garden in Wells's Early Science Fiction." In *H.G. Wells and Modern Science Fiction*. Eds. Darko Suvin and Robert M. Philmus. Lewisburg: Bucknell UP and London: Associated UP, 1977. 48-69.

Huntington, John. *The Logic of Fantasy: H.G. Wells and Science Fiction*. New York: Columbia UP, 1982.

———. "The Science Fiction of H.G. Wells." *Science Fiction: A Critical Guide*. Ed. Patrick Parrinder. London: Longman, 1979. 34-50.

Kagarlitski, J. *The Life and Thought of H.G. Wells*. London: Sidgwick and Jackson, 1966. Trans. of *Herbert Wells: ocherk zhizni i tvorchestva*.

Lake, David. "The Current Texts of Wells's Early SF Novels: Situation Unsatisfactory." *Wellsian* 11 (Summer 1988): 3-12.

McCarthy, Patrick A. "*Heart of Darkness* and the Early Novels of H.G. Wells: Evolution, Anarchy, Entropy." *Journal of Modern Literature* 13.1 (March 1986): 37-60.

McConnell, Frank D. *The Science Fiction of H.G. Wells*. Oxford: Oxford UP, 1981.

Morton, Peter R. "Biological Degeneration: A Motif in H.B. [sic] Wells and Other Late Victorian Utopianists." *Southern Review* [Australia] 9 (1976): 93-112.

———. *The Vital Science: Biology and the Literary Imagination, 1860-1900*. London, Boston and Sydney: George Allen & Unwin, 1984.

Murray, Brian. *H.G. Wells*. [Literature and Life: British Writers.] New York: Continuum, 1990.

Nicholson, Norman. *H.G. Wells*. [The English Novelists.] Denver: Alan Swallow, 1950.

Parrinder, Patrick. *H.G. Wells*. 1970; New York: Capricorn, 1977.

———. "H.G. Wells and the Fall of Empires." *Foundation* 57 (Spring 1993): 48-58.

———, ed. *H.G. Wells: The Critical Heritage*. London and Boston: Routledge & Kegan Paul, 1972.

———. "Science Fiction as Truncated Epic." *Bridges to Science Fiction*. Ed. George E. Slusser, George R. Guffey and Mark Rose. Carbondale and Edwardsville: Southern Illinois UP, 1980. 91-106.

———. *Shadows of the Future: H.G. Wells, Science Fiction and Prophecy*. Liverpool: Liverpool UP, 1995.

——— and Robert M. Philmus, eds. *H.G. Wells's Literary Criticism*. Brighton: Harvester P, and Totowa, NJ: Barnes & Noble, 1980.

Philmus, Robert M. and David Y. Hughes, eds. *H.G. Wells: Early Writings in Science and Science Fiction*. Berkeley, Los Angeles and London: U of California P, 1975.

———. "Wells and Borges and the Labyrinths of Time." *Science Fiction Studies* 1.4 (Fall 1974): 237-48. [As "Borges and Wells and the Labyrinths of Time." In *H.G. Wells and Modern Science Fiction*. Eds. Darko Suvin and Robert M. Philmus. Lewisburg: Bucknell UP and London: Associated UP, 1977. 159-78.]

Pritchett, V.S. "The Scientific Romances." [from *The Living Novel*, 1946]. In *H.G. Wells: A Collection of Critical Essays*. [Twentieth-Century Views.] Ed. Bernard Bergonzi. Englewood Cliffs, NJ: Prentice-Hall, 1976. 32-38.

Raknem, Ingvald. *H.G. Wells and His Critics*. Trondheim: Universitetsforlaget, 1962.

Ruddick, Nicholas. "The Wellsian Island." *Ultimate Island: On the Nature of British Science Fiction*. Westport and London: Greenwood P, 1993. 62-71.

Showalter, Elaine. "The Apocalyptic Fables of H.G. Wells." *Fin de Siècle/Fin du Globe: Fears and Fantasies of the Late Nineteenth Century*. Ed. John Stokes. Basingstoke and London: Macmillan, 1992. 69-84.

Sommerville, Bruce and Michael Shortland. "Thomas Henry Huxley, H.G. Wells, and the Method of Zadig." *Thomas Henry Huxley's Place in Science and Letters: Centenary Essays*. Ed. Alan P. Barr. Athens and London: U of Georgia P, 1997. 296-322.

Stableford, Brian. "H.G. Wells." *Scientific Romance in Britain 1890-1950*. New York: St. Martin's P, 1985. 55-74.

Stover, Leon. "H.G. Wells, T.H. Huxley and Darwinism." *H.G. Wells: Reality and Beyond: A Collection of Critical Essays Prepared in Conjunction with the Exhibition and Symposium on H.G. Wells*. Ed. Michael Mullin. Champaign, IL: Champaign Public Library, 1986. 43-59.

Suvin, Darko. "Wells as the Turning Point of the SF Tradition" and "*The Time Machine* Versus *Utopia* as Structural Models for SF." *Metamorphoses of Science Fiction: On the Poetics and History of a Literary Genre*. New Haven and London: Yale UP, 1979. 208-42.

Weeks, Robert P. "Disentanglement as a Theme in H.G. Wells's Fiction." *Papers of the Michigan Academy of Science, Arts, and Letters* 39 (1954): 439-44. Reprinted in *H.G. Wells: A Collection of Critical Essays*. [Twentieth-Century Views.] Ed. Bernard Bergonzi. Englewood Cliffs, NJ: Prentice-Hall, 1976. 25-31.

Williamson, Jack. *H.G. Wells: Critic of Progress*. Baltimore: Mirage P, 1973.

Zamyatin, Evgenii. "Wells's Revolutionary Fairy Tales." [Abridged from *Herbert Wells*, 1922)]. In *H.G. Wells: The Critical Heritage*. Ed. Patrick Parrinder. London and Boston: Routledge & Kegan Paul, 1972. 258-74.

Criticism II: On *The Time Machine* in Particular

Abrash, Merritt. "The Hubris of Science: Wells' Time Traveller." *Patterns of the Fantastic II*.[Starmont Studies in Literary Criticism No. 3.] Ed. Donald M. Hassler. Mercer Island, WA: Starmont, 1985. 5–11.

Begiebing, Robert J. "The Mythic Hero in H.G. Wells's *The Time Machine.*" *Essays in Literature* 11.2 (Fall 1984): 201–10.

Bergonzi, Bernard. "The Publication of *The Time Machine* 1894–5." *Review of English Studies*, n.s 11.41 (1960): 42–51. Reprinted in *SF: The Other Side of Realism*. Ed. Thomas D. Clareson. Bowling Green: Bowling Green U Popular P, 1971. 204–15.

Chamberlain, Gordon B. "Decoding *Across the Zodiac*; or, H.G. Wells Unburdened." *Foundation* 37 (Autumn 1986): 36–47.

Connel[l]y, Wayne C. "H.G. Well's [*sic*] *The Time Machine*: It's [*sic*] Neglected Mythos." *Riverside Quarterly* 5.3 (1972): 178–91.

Crossley, Robert. "In the Palace of Green Porcelain: Artefacts from the Museums of Science Fiction." *Fictional Space: Essays on Contemporary Science Fiction*. Ed. Tom Shippey. Oxford: Blackwell, and Atlantic Highlands, NJ: Humanities P, 1991. 76–103.

Derry, Stephen. "The Time Traveller's Utopian Books and His Reading of the Future." *Foundation* 65 (Autumn 1995): 16–24.

Eisenstein, Alex. "*The Time Machine* and the End of Man." *Science Fiction Studies* 3 (July 1976): 161–65.

———. "Very Early Wells: Origins of Some Major Physical Motifs in *The Time Machine* and *The War of the Worlds.*" *Extrapolation* 13.2 (1972): 119–26.

Farrell, Kirby. "H.G. Wells and Neoteny." *Cahiers Victoriens et Edouardiens de l'Université Paul Valéry, Montpellier* 46 (October 1997): 145–58.

Gustafsson, Lars. "The Present as the Museum of the Future." *Utopian Vision, Technological Innovation and Poetic Imagination*. Eds. Klaus L. Berghahn and Reinhold Grimm. Heidelberg: Carl Winter Universitätsverlag, 1990. 105–10.

Hammond. J.R. "The Significance of Weena." *Wellsian* 18 (Winter 1995): 19-22.

———. "*The Time Machine*: The Riddle of the Sphinx." *H.G. Wells and the Modern Novel.* New York: St. Martin's P, 1988. 73-84.

Hennelly, Mark M., Jr. "*The Time Machine*: A Romance of 'The Human Heart.'" *Extrapolation* 20.2 (Summer 1979): 154-67.

Hughes, David Y. "A Queer Notion of Grant Allen's." *Science Fiction Studies* 25.2 (July 1998): 271-84.

Hume, Kathryn. "Eat or Be Eaten: H.G. Wells's *The Time Machine.*" *Philological Quarterly* 69.2 (Spring 1990): 233-51.

Huntington, John. "*The Time Machine* and Wells's Social Trajectory." *Foundation* 65 (Autumn 1995): 6-15.

Ketterer, David. "Oedipus as Time Traveller." *Science Fiction Studies* 9 (November 1982): 340-41.

Lake, David J. "The Drafts of *The Time Machine*, 1894." *Wellsian* 3 (Spring, 1980): 6-13.

———. "Wells's Time Traveller: An Unreliable Narrator?" *Extrapolation* 22.2 (Summer 1981): 117-26.

———. "The White Sphinx and the Whitened Lemur: Images of Death in *The Time Machine.*" *Science Fiction Studies* 6.1 (March 1979): 77-84.

Loing, Bernard. *H.G. Wells à l'oeuvre: Les débuts d'un écrivain.* Paris: Didier Erudition, 1984.

———. "H.G. Wells at Work (1894-1900): A Writer's Beginnings." *Wellsian* 8 (Summer 1985): 30-37.

Mackerness, E.D. "Zola, Wells, and 'The Coming Beast.'" *Science Fiction Studies* 8.2 (July 1981): 143-48.

Manlove, Colin. "Dualism in Wells's *The Time Machine* and *The War of the Worlds.*" *Riverside Quarterly* 8.3 (July 1990): 173-81.

Mullen, R.D. "Scholarship and the Riddle of the Sphinx." *Science Fiction Studies* 23.3 (November 1996): 363-70.

Niederland, William G. "The Birth of H.G. Wells's *Time Machine.*" *American Imago* 35.1-2 (1978): 106-12.

Parrinder, Patrick. "*News from Nowhere, The Time Machine*, and the Break-Up of Classical Realism." *Science Fiction Studies* 3 (November 1976): 265-74.

——. "*The Time Machine*: H.G. Wells's Journey Through Death." *Wellsian* 4 (Summer 1981): 15-23.

Philmus, Robert M. "The Logic of 'Prophecy' in *The Time Machine*." [Revision of the section "*The Time Machine*; or, The Fourth Dimension as Prophecy," in *Into the Unknown: The Evolution of Science Fiction from Francis Godwin to H.G. Wells* (Berkeley, Los Angeles and London: U of California P, 1970, 69-78), itself a revision of an article in *PMLA* 84 (1969): 530-35.] In *H.G. Wells: A Collection of Critical Essays*. [Twentieth-Century Views.] Ed. Bernard Bergonzi. Englewood Cliffs, NJ: Prentice-Hall, 1976. 56-68.

——. "Revisions of the Future: *The Time Machine*." *Journal of General Education* 28.1 (Spring 1976): 23-30.

Porta, Fernando. "One Text, Many Utopias: Some Examples of Intertextuality in *The Time Machine*." *Wellsian* 20 (Winter 1997): 10-20.

Sargent, Lyman Tower. "*The Time Machine* in the Development of Wells's Social and Political Thought." *Wellsian* 19 (Winter 1996): 3-11.

Scafella, Frank. "The White Sphinx and *The Time Machine*." *Science Fiction Studies* 8.3 (November 1981): 255-65.

——. "From Reason to Intelligence: Wells's White Sphinx as Chronotrope of Nineteenth Century Science." *Cahiers Victoriens et Edouardiens de l'Université Paul Valéry, Montpellier* 46 (October 1997): 181-89.

Scholes, Robert and Eric S. Rabkin. "*The Time Machine* (1895)". In *Science Fiction: History. Science. Vision*. London: Oxford UP, 1977. 200-04.

Sommerville, Bruce David. "*The Time Machine*: A Chronological and Scientific Revision." *Wellsian* 17 (Winter 1994): 11-29.

Tucker, Kenneth. "*The Time Machine*: H.G. Wells's Early Fable of Human Identity." *Journal of Evolutionary Psychology* 9.3-4 (1988): 352-63.

Wasson, Richard. "Myth and the Ex-Nomination of Class in *The Time Machine*." *Minnesota Review* 15 (Fall 1980): 112-22.

———. "Myths of the Future: *The Time Machine.*" *The English Novel and the Movies.* Ed. Michael Klein and Gillian Parker. New York: Ungar, 1981. 187-96.

Willis, Martin T. "Edison as Time Traveler: H.G. Wells's Inspiration for His First Scientific Character." *Science Fiction Studies* 26.2 (July 1999): 284-94.

Time Travel Studies in Physics and Science Fiction

Bork, Alfred M. "The Fourth Dimension in Nineteenth-Century Physics." *Isis* 55.3 (1964): 326-38.

Campbell, Joseph Keim, ed. *Time Travel: A Philosophical Reader.* Peterborough, ON: Broadview, 2001.

Carter, Paul A. "The Fate Changer: Human Destiny and the Time Machine." *The Creation of Tomorrow: Fifty Years of Magazine Science Fiction.* New York: Columbia UP, 1977. 89-113.

Deutsch, David, and Michael Lockwood. "The Quantum Physics of Time Travel." *Scientific American* 270.4 (March 1994): 68-74.

Edwards, Malcolm J. and Brian Stableford. "Time Travel." *The Encyclopedia of Science Fiction.* Ed. John Clute and Peter Nicholls. New York: St. Martin's P, 1993. 1227-29.

Gardner, Martin. "Time Travel." *Time Travel and Other Mathematical Bewilderments.* New York: W.H. Freeman, 1988. 1-14.

Goswami, Amit, with Maggie Goswami. "Time for the Stars." *The Cosmic Dancers: Exploring the Science of Science Fiction.* New York: McGraw-Hill, 1983. 90-113.

Hollinger, Veronica. "Deconstructing the Time Machine." *Science Fiction Studies* 14.2 (July 1987): 201-21.

Lem, Stanislaw. "The Time-Travel Story and Related Matters of Science-Fiction Structuring." 1970. Trans. Thomas H. Hoisington and Darko Suvin. *Microworlds: Writings on Science Fiction and Fantasy.* Ed. Franz Rottensteiner. San Diego: Harvest/HBJ, 1984. 136-60.

Nahin, Paul J. *Time Machines: Time Travel in Physics, Metaphysics, and Science Fiction.* New York: American Institute of Physics, 1993.

Nicholls, Peter. "Time Travel and Other Universes." *The Science in Science Fiction.* Ed. Peter Nicholls. New York: Knopf, 1983. 88-101.

Russell, W.M.S. "Time Before and After *The Time Machine.*" *Foundation* 65 (Autumn 1995): 24-40.

Slusser, George and Danièle Chatelain. "Re-Writing *The Time Machine* around Mrs. Watchett." *Cahiers Victoriens et Edouardiens de l'Université Paul Valéry, Montpellier* 46 (October 1997): 191-211.

"Time and Nth Dimensions." *The Visual Encyclopedia of Science Fiction.* Ed. Brian Ash. New York: Harmony, 1977. 144-54.

Works Cited

Aldiss, Brian W. and David Wingrove. *Trillion Year Spree: The History of Science Fiction*. London: Gollancz, 1986.

Bergonzi, Bernard. *The Early H.G. Wells: A Study of the Scientific Romances*. Manchester: Manchester UP, 1961.

——. "The Publication of *The Time Machine*, 1894-1895." 1960. In *The Other Side of Realism: Essays on Modern Fantasy and Science Fiction*. Ed. Thomas D. Clareson. Bowling Green: Bowling Green U Popular P, 1971. 201-15.

Bork, Alfred M. "The Fourth Dimension in Nineteenth-Century Physics." *Isis* 55.3 (1964): 326-38.

"Bouts of Spontaneity, H.G. Wells' Secret of Writing." *New York Herald* (15 April 1906): 3:5.

Desmond, Adrian. *Huxley: From Devil's Disciple to Evolution's High Priest*. 1994, 1997. Harmondsworth: Penguin, 1998.

Gardner, Martin. "Time Travel." *Time Travel and Other Mathematical Bewilderments*. New York: W.H. Freeman, 1988. 1-14.

Geduld, Harry M, ed. *The Definitive Time Machine: A Critical Edition of H.G. Wells's Scientific Romance*. Bloomington and Indianapolis: Indiana UP, 1987.

Mackenzie, Norman and Jeanne. *H.G. Wells: A Biography*. New York: Simon & Schuster, 1973.

Nahin, Paul J. *Time Machines: Time Travel in Physics, Metaphysics, and Science Fiction*. New York: American Institute of Physics, 1993.

Orwell, George. "Wells, Hitler and the World State." 1941. *The Penguin Essays of George Orwell*. Harmondsworth: Penguin, 1984. 194-99.

Philmus, Robert M. and David Y. Hughes, eds. *H.G. Wells: Early Writings in Science and Science Fiction*. Berkeley. Los Angeles and London: U of California P, 1975.

Raknem, Ingvald. *H.G. Wells and His Critics*. Trondheim: Universitetsforlaget, 1962.

S. [pseud.] "Four-Dimensional Space." [Letter to the Editor, dated March 16, 1885.] *Nature* 31 (26 March 1885): 481.

Smith, David C., ed. *The Correspondence of H.G. Wells.* 4 vols. London: Pickering & Chatto, 1998.

Stableford, Brian. *Scientific Romance in Britain 1890-1950.* New York: St. Martin's P, 1985.

Stover, Leon, ed. *The Time Machine: An Invention: A Critical Text of the 1895 London First Edition, with an Introduction and Appendices.* Jefferson, NC and London: McFarland, 1996.

Wells, H.G. *Experiment in Autobiography: Discoveries and Conclusions of a Very Ordinary Brain (Since 1866).* 1934. Philadelphia and New York: Lippincott, 1967.

——. "Preface" [1931]. *The Time Machine: An Invention.* With a Preface by the Author Written for This Edition; and Designs by W.A. Dwiggins. New York: Random House, 1931. vii-x.

——. "Preface" [1934]. *Seven Famous Novels.* New York: Knopf, 1934. [vii]-x.

West, Geoffrey [Geoffrey H. Wells]. *H.G. Wells.* Intro. H.G. Wells. New York: Norton, 1930.

Using 2 137 lb. of Rolland Enviro100 instead
of virgin fibres paper reduces your ecological footprint of:

Trees: 26 ; 0.5 American football field
Solid waste: 2,236lb
Water: 17,679gal ; a shower of 3.7 day
Air emissions: 5,809lb ; emissions of 0.5 car per year